FOR LIFE AND LOVE

FOR LIFE AND LOVE

THE MARAUDER CHRONICLES: FORGOTTEN NAMES SERIES

JOHN-MICHAEL P. PHILLIPS

PRIMIX PUBLISHING
THE WRITE CHOICE

Primix Publishing
East Brunswick Office Evolution
1 Tower Center Boulevard, Ste 1510
East Brunswick, NJ 08816
www.primixpublishing.com
Phone: 1-800-538-5788

This book is a work of fiction. Names, characters, places and incidents either are a product of the author's imagination or is fictitious. Any resemblance to actual persons, living or dead, events or locales is entirely coincidental.

Published by Primix Publishing: 12/05/2024

ISBN: 979-8-89194-358-2(sc)
ISBN: 979-8-89194-359-9(e)

Library of Congress Control Number: 2024924991

CONTENTS

**THE
MARAUDER CHRONICLES**
John-Michael P. Phillips

PART one

FORGOTTEN NAMES

Section 1

FOR LIFE AND LOVE

PROLOG: NEW AND OLD

Memories and History

To say the day was one of sorrow was like saying the universe was big. It didn't describe the breadth of loss felt by the ones allowed to watch, or even by the limited number of those allowed to know about the execution. If Wolf Pack knew, in general, there would be riots to free the two heroes. Their four armies might even turn on the council. Other Packs might turn against their societies to save them. Whether for nefarious reasons or honorable may not be able to be distinguished.

And that I am allowed to know and choose to do nothing just adds to the blood on my hands, the older gentleman thought.

He allowed his mind to wonder as he was the only person in the room. It was secured against monitoring so there were no chairs to sit on, nor any decorations on the walls. The room was not one for enjoyment but meant to watch executions. The walls were metal, plan and slick, with a glass view facing into the pit that was two kilometers in diameter (1.2 miles). In the center, the prisoners could be clearly seen within their Advanced Battle Armor Suits, or Abas for short.

The Zhayedan was as tall as the Elite, but the Elite had the advantage of higher number of weapons, speed and ability. Elites, the rarest of the Abas, hardly found pilots capable of linking with the stronger robotic components. If the pilots were not perfect with the programming, then the linking would fail. More often than not, the pilot was ripped to pieces or their insides turned liquid. That was true for all Abas though. The smaller ones more accepting, the larger ones less.

Zhayedan were the second largest designs and the superior when it came to the trinity ranked designs. Light, Medium Heavy styles of Scout, Sentinel and Zhayedan. Then the Elites were a class of their own. There was no reason to distinguish them. There weren't enough across any single pack to need to.

Most of the warrior cast were in Sentinel styles. Most the Dragons, Abas pilots that were converted to cyborgs, were more of a police force in the Lerikatia planetary system stayed in Scout designs. The fighting Dragons were more Sentinel and Zhayedans. Scouts did better in policing situations within the smaller confines of the peaceful planets.

They were not the ones he needed to save. He just had to keep his focus on the long game, no matter how much it hurt. His time for punishment would come. So would the time for punishing his enemies.

The older gentleman stared out into the barren

red-sand desert. Ramstar, the moon of Daritock it all started on, had a foreboding sky covering the crimson surface. It was said to be that color for all the human blood which had been spilt on it. It was the site of hundreds of thousands of recorded honor battles between the Packs of War throughout the almost seven centuries of history they shared in System Duce.

The battles and color of the moon was not the only reason it was the most cherished of the moons of Daritock. It was also the moon the Crusader Olympia was held on. A great honor for the Pack that maintained control of it. The last being the reason these two would have been hard sought if their execution were known of.

Wolf Pack held the honor of the moon currently. It was the only moon in the Sasaria side of the bi-star system which held the same time as Standard Military Time (SMT). When armies were spread across different planetary systems, and moons, it was important to have a single time and measurement in which all records could be matched. They matched the records to this crimson colored moon, but it was not the original setting. This was System Duce after all. The second system.

The SMT was measured in three hundred sixty-five days for the standard cycle, or year, which was currently 668.7.12 or the twelfth day of the seventh month of the 668th year of the Packs or Duce Standard Time. Twenty-four-hour rotation marked a standard day. Every seven years, they had to add a day to calculate for the slight overrun of the time to continue to align to the planet's rotation.

The red surface was important to them, but the older gentleman doubted there were many left who knew the significances of its rotation pattern and surface color. Most thought time was standardized to match Ramstar's rotation. The moon named as a pseudonym for their ancient god Aries, the father of man and war. Due to the blessing of allowing the Packs to be born, every seventh year, the leap year of the planet, was celebrated with reducing fighting, higher honor awards for non-warriors and periods of serving those that served. As a reminder of the time Ramstar honorably served Zeus before Zeus left to create more universe and monitor the other galaxies. Aries proved his honor and took rule of this galaxy, becoming Mars as Zeus expanded his power to become Jupitar.

Most believed Ramstar's importance came to honor it as the first moon to be settled by the Pack after the Great Leap. Technically, it was settled before the Packs of War were created and the First Agreement of Tribute set. The real reason it was chosen as the first moon was not something that was taught within the schools or history of the Packs.

To help the *people* remember where and why they were here, Ramstar was named and celebrated. Aries, who commissioned the creation of the Trinity of Races or Triad-Mars, was the basis for the creation of the Packs. It was why the Packs controlled the Daritock system and fought across Venginus planetary system. The Lerikatia Tri-Planetary System was were the non-warrior trinity existed in peace with the Grameracks. The Keiso planets were the closest to the sun and were controlled by circuits and Iron Lung Cyborgs since they were the only ones able to live on the planets. Each planetary system was broken up by an asteroid belt, as although all but Keiso had a mix of every race within it.

If the ancient stories were to be believed, the gods separated their two basic components to better understand their own creation. They hoped to stop the fighting amongst themselves, since it was limiting their ability to continue to create, as they were directed by their predecessors, the titans and the ancient gods before them.

Continuing the cycle of creating lessor beings, Aries suggested separating their two parts into mortal existences, which had not been done before them. All conscious being were immortal. Afterall, why be conscious if it was going to end? What purpose did it serve?

Yet, immortality meant conflicts couldn't be resolved through force, and the gods were not great at talking without a physical altercation also being needed to bring about a balanced understanding. Having that much time meant arguments were extremely heated, and sometimes childish. Aries was credited for the solution, giving birth to something more than just fighting . . . war!

The creation of humans and circuits from the polar existence in which the gods themselves existed. Those creations in turn reached to the stars and created a semblance of the gods in their own creation, the cyborgs. And from that creation, the trinity was born.

Hogwash! The history of the gods was before the Packs, yet, the circuits held to this as if it were important, but nothing else was. Maybe the circuits weren't as interested in exploring the meaning. Supposedly, they lost the data of the original starting point of mankind, or the Triad really. Circuits, cyborgs, and humans. Who really came first since there is no real record or recordings?

Of course, the circuits no longer have memory of the period before the great leap. They don't have memories of why we came here as if they just recorded over the data by accident or something. Who does that? It's like losing proof of landing on your first external moon or planet.

Of course, we lost that with the loss of all the other memories. Are we now doomed to repeat the mistakes that led us here? Or maybe not, since some still remember. Some were smart enough to write things down where circuits could not corrupt, manipulate, modify or destroy it. But is it enough?

The older gentleman smiled at the thought. Unfortunately, looking at the surface brought back memories of the many times he himself spilt blood here. He could be believed the sadistic reasoning for is color. But it was red long before man ever stepped foot on it after coming to an agreement with the Grameracks. They were a lizard like people who previously held the honor of protecting this side of the binary star system. A system christened Duce after the arrival of the humans.

And called Arthantha before the arrival of humans by the Kalictithians. I am glad they proved to be a better fighting race than the Grameracks or we might have had to face these new problems before we were ready. I am not sure we will be as it is.

The Grameracks were almost never seen this far out from Sasaria, the star the Packs planets mostly circled. Venginus was the name of the other star, and home to the Desitians and Kalictithians, the ultimate enemies of the Packs. Or that was the way it had been before.

Even with a completed atmosphere for several hundred years, nothing grew on the planet outside of the special houses. The ground was tainted with too much blood, both of circuits and humans, for anything to grow on it. In his opinion, two more were to join the soiled ground, yet their life essence wouldn't exist long enough to reach the ground and drowned out future life.

Wolf Pack won a fifty-year peace agreement with the other packs for the moon because of the two who were now facing execution for treason. Treason not against Wolf, or not directly, since they did leave without permission. No, it was against Kavanac Darcouv, the Black Wing, one of the seven wings of the Dragons. They were the only ones aligned against

Più Alto Drago, the leader of the Cyborgs, and the highest amongst them.

Kavanac Darcouv was not a widely known name. It was not something they advertised, but of the three families of the cyborgs, every Kavanac Darcouv was linked back to Serpico in some way. Ironically, very few cyborgs could trace their genealogy back to a cyborg parent, unless they became cyborgs after the birth of their child. Yet, everyone joined a family, and not always based on the genealogy.

The same could be said for the families of the Packs though. Families pick the members, and the members accept the family. No one is born into a family in the Pack. Even those that are have to prove their worth to them.

Kavanac Darcouv suffered a devastating blow from the two Abas pilots over the last five years. Of course, this information was privileged to very few trusted mouths that would not repeat the information to anyone. At least not on purpose.

Più Alto Dragon, the Bat Phone and a limited number of council members that were at the trial all know as well. I am sure the Serpico family is not happy about that many knowing how much control they have lost. How much the Watchers can no longer monitor or control.

The question remains even in their weakened state. Is Serpico the head or the hand? I will have to save these thoughts for another time. It is dangerous to consider now. Afterall, my son is one of their many agents, the man thought as he looked at the gentleman who just entered the room.

A younger man and two very small children, in the middle of their toddler years but didn't resembled either man, joined him in the high tower of Nagara. The older man stole a glance at the children, who seemed to be quietly sucking down the liquid-nutrition shakes. If he were honest with himself, they looked nothing alike while looking exactly the same to him. His well-trained eyes could see them for what they were . . . true twins.

The younger man came in full dress, but it had not been as a show of respect to those dying. It was to show his father the accolades he earned during his father's long absence at the frontlines. Both knew the father was scheduled to be home at this time. The trial had taken most of his time prior to this engagement. The execution would see his time ending, if he was returning back to Venginus, where Zankatia was currently circling.

The older gentleman also wore his best dress, but he wore it for the dead. Several layers of ribbons and medals decorated both sides of his chest as the old man was in every major action in the last thirty-plus years. Yet one stood out as the most distinguished. The medal given for victory in the Crusaders Olympia. Not the one that everyone who participated in for victory, or those that lost would receive. But the one that said he led the victorious army.

Every person who attended the brief was wearing their uniforms, but only a few went to Best Dress formal. It was to cherish those who were about to die. Those that didn't were trying to say they deserved the sentence. Like many divisions in the Pack, it was down the lines of Cyborgs and Humans.

He turned his eyes from the people entering and back to the surrounding area. This time, he looked at the circular building that surrounded the execution point. Seven towers were built with a visible sight of the execution the Cyborgs were about to perform. Only the highest tower was in perfect perpendicular alignment with it. Currently it was assigned to Wolf, ironically, due to the two that were being executed.

And since the cyborgs were not given a tower, they built the space station in which they would watch as well as provide the execution from.

The younger man looked down at his watch before adjusting his stance and looking back out the window.

"Seven more minutes," he provided as if asked how much time the couple had remaining.

The older man didn't respond to the first words spoken by his son. Instead he looked back out, considering the impact of what this tragic moment truly meant. The reason behind the need to execute them.

For Wolf Pack to destroy one of their own Elite pilots, honorable or not, was a mark of the power of the Watchers. The Watchers was the assigned duties of the Serpico family. Duties that seemed to be where they divided against Più Alto Drago, who was about maintaining the reasons for the Pack.

The Cyborgs were supposed to be the peacekeepers

amongst the warrior cast known as the Packs. They were also tasked with monitoring the circuits, the other human groups that were not warriors, or not Pack members, and any other races under the Trinity's protection. Currently it was the Grameracks and Tutevibians.

Unlike the Grameracks, who were happy in peace, the Tutevibians stayed with the Packs and were happy in war. Their entire race, like the Packs, were designed around being ready to fight. Prior to the Packs, that didn't include the purpose of honor, but they readily accepted the understanding and practice after being defeated by Murchadh, a great human general of the Warrior's Pack. Also like the Packs, they seemed to be irked by the Watchers, although a few of their numbers had been converted to cyborgs. Everyone that did joined the Serpico family.

The Watchers didn't like to be reminded of those times though. Prior to these two, it was the first and last time they suffered their greatest loss. It was just after the loss of the first Più Alto Drago, near 63 DST.

Yet, without that loss, it was not likely the Packs would have met their true destiny or fulfilled their purpose. The older man just hoped one of these children were finally that hope, born to bring back what had long ago been lost and yet to be created. The Rebirth of the true purpose of the Packs.

Awaiting Death

The older man let out a long sigh while never taking his eyes off the couple. He wanted a miracle from the sleeping gods he knew did not exist. Yet, he wanted the stories of them being sired by the gods to be true, or even the one God long forgotten by society as a whole. If anything would save them, he would openly worship them and do anything they asked.

In the end, the old man accepted what he had known had been true. The gods were not asleep—they were dead or man was dead to them. Humanity just needed something to believe in. Something had to kindle hope and be perfect for human creations never were.

The Bat Phone Council, a council that did not exist on any official listing, was created by the highest-ranking generals of the Packs. They knew the truth due to the proof on an ancient data journal left to them by Murchadh, the first Commander and Chief. The Commander and Chief was the elected leader of the hidden council that would ensure the honorable actions of all the armies, the council, and the Triscifield. If the Commander called, all the armies of the Pack would answer.

And I do not call. I will not call. I will let them die.

Circuits were left out of the agreements of war. It was that way to ensure that they would not suspect the humans' ultimate betrayal and attack first. Their logic would lead them to the path. It had before. Circuits were allowed to keep a small force of warbots for their planets only, but the manufacturing was maintained by the Triscifield, the scientist of the Packs.

That didn't stop the human warriors who were joined by circuits and cyborgs from allowing them to be turned to pieces during battle. The cyborgs had a better chance at living, but the circuits that felt the need to test their mantel against an uncheck enemy often found themselves maneuvered just right into being destroyed. Yet, their data packs always came back showing no betrayal on their side. Desitians were extremely aggressive against the circuits.

Androids were the one exception to circuits, other than the half breed cyborgs that were allowed to go to war with the Packs. They did not try their hands in human affairs but kept to the back lines on support and medical staff mostly. Operators were the most common area to find Androids, although their attempts to act human often left them acting emotional at the worst of times.

Like their cyborg counter parts, they seemed to be reaching from the circuit side to become human. The Cyborgs were seen as humans trying to become circuits. Both found their ways into the warriors' side. Androids didn't want to go to the front lines directly. They appreciated their lives. The cyborgs, aside from Dragons, often operated with teams of other cyborgs, only mixing in at the platoon and higher levels.

Lodestar shook his head, bringing him back to the observation room. Thinking of the formations of the groups was just his way of trying not to think of the two that were out there, waiting to die. His son must have picked up on his angst, and tried to interrupt his thoughts with a question.

"So, the Abas have been completely gutted?" the younger man asked, knowing the answer.

He had been trying to stretch his stature past the older man's but was still a few centimeters short. Even in his older years, he wanted to pass his father at something, and height was probably the easiest to accomplish, yet his father would not give him even this. He had to earn every centimeter.

"Yes, they were only able to move out into position of execution. Their Abas should have run out of power by now," he answered with a cold voice that said he didn't wish to continue talking about anything else along the current lines.

"Well, at least you got the children into school," the younger man tried a different topic, hoping for a better result.

It didn't appear that he was willing to just allow the moment to move on in silence. The old man would have to reply.

Silence wasn't working for me either. Just the questions seems the wrong ones at the wrong time.

Falstar caught a shift on the slightly wrinkled face of the man next to him. It was a face of mixed emotions, although no normal person would have been able to read the slight flinch in the eyes. He had spent most his life studying the face and knew the slight movements' meanings.

Lodestar long turned grey and had only a few thin strands of hair atop his head. Most of those were lost over the last five years. The thick grey sides were cut short around the ears and all the way around the back of the skull. Even in his elder years, he kept a sharp mind.

"The children should not be punished for the acts of their parents," he replied finally after what seemed to be a long pause.

It followed the shift in his face by only seconds.

"Is that what the council said when you agreed to pay the price?" he asked suddenly.

Falstar's real intentions for starting the conversation was to ask about the other rumor he heard, and this was the only way for him to build up to it without being so direct.

"They paid the price for their children to get into the schools. I just offered a little more to ensure they would be given the opportunity to get into Abas School," Lodestar provided the answer with a sigh, trying to tell his son this could wait. "And it wasn't a high price. I will never go to war again, but I will be able to teach the next generation. I guess my actions will be monitored a little closer. See if I'm getting to the point of losing my intelligence and needing to pass the torch before retiring to Lerikatia or facing a suicide mission."

Lodestar knew they would be more than

monitored. He made threats toward the council, and two of his team members gutted the power against Più Alto Drago, which was a strategic weapon that was often left in power to keep the cyborgs a little divided.

It brought a dangerous question to the council. Were they, the human warriors, working to bring their own war within the Sasarian Empire prior to the entry of war into the next enemies war? Would giving him his own school prove it more or lead to it faster? Afterall, having that much influence over a generation would give him access to thousands of young moldable minds.

Knowing the way, the circuits would consider it, it would be the most logical step to either prove it before it was too late or to stop it completely. There would be no other side to the move. The council cyborgs could see a few other paths, including ones that did not involve a war from the human side at all.

Più Alto Drago ensured her select group carried the memories of those forgotten well worked within their circuits. Less than a millennium wasn't long enough to remove the memories of what humans were capable of becoming. Especially, not with the original agreement handing over them.

"I guess, after so many campaigns, you would like to return to Varanasi, or would you go so deep as Lerikatia to teach the children of peace keeping forces?" the younger man asked with a little jest in his voice.

No true Abas warrior ever settle in Lerikatia,

unlike other veterans. It was not that they could not find peace with themselves there, but the people seemed to find less peace with their presents, and the presents of their war machine. It was a reminder their precious working machines could easily be converted into battle ready fighters if the need arose.

It was also a reminder to the Abas warriors that there were leagues of pilots that were not warriors, but farmers, minors, builders and other ancillary services necessary. Everyone was trained to fight and could access simple weapons. Everyone learned to fight over here. You never knew if you would be attacked or invaded by Silent Knights or some other force, known or unknown. Local or stranger. Learning to fight kept people comfortable in the ability to protect themselves and the ones they loved.

Capable of fighting for the freedom of others but choosing to instead enjoy it at the cost of someone else's life. Maybe that is why they are less comfortable with us. Or maybe we are uncomfortable with them, and they are reacting to our emotions.

"Listen to my son, Falstar, teasing the division commander Lieutenant General Lodestar as if he were a common soldier. It really has ended for me on the frontlines, hasn't it?" he laughed back. "No, I will be remaining here in the Daritock system at the new school they are building under this city. I am going to be the Headmaster of the fifth forward school, whose primary teachings will be based around the new missions." He smiled at his son, knowing what the information would mean to him.

Falstar was awarded a high distinction by having his last two years of school forfeited to be placed in the schools. He was tapped to be the headmaster of an Abas pipeline experimental school, the youngest and only one that wasn't drawn from the front line. They selected him for his rare talent of identifying members he could guide from great to exceptional. A talent he developed under his mother's early guidance but mastered on his own.

Four schools solely controlled by the Wolf Pack, which had never been allowed in Pack Schools before, were secretly placed throughout the outer region of Daritock. Their purpose was to train for the approaching enemy and send the graduating students into the outer boarders of their enemy and deeper to place a pre-evasion force and disrupters into the approaching empire.

Of the four schools already created, Falstar students won the only two graduating titles with ease. It didn't look like the titles would be taken from him anytime soon. His mother, General Illuminator, the senior general of Wolf Pack, had the same knack. Her team members had the highest promotion rate after graduation, including to the elite ranks.

The Five Year was a period after graduation when the War Council could promote warriors to their final ranks without the approval of the council. It was when most elites were selected. Illuminator's natural talents of selecting people and getting them promoted during those periods had never been seen. Wolf, with her has the General of their four armies, saw the most approvals across the board. As General, she was the one that selected the talents for the armies in the Varanasi schools.

"I am sure a great vanguard for the fifth and final school was looked at well. But let's face it. Your students need a challenge," Lodestar answered the look of thought on his son's face.

"I am not the only retired battle commander coming to the schools. Master Raven, Giga Plexus, Hero, and Gatling are all coming as instructors. Nox, Quick Hit, and Chameleon will be replacing the other Headmasters. I have three more years before my school will be filled with students from all over Sasaria. I am in the process of identifying them now.

"But why do we need all these war heroes off the lines of defense? Hell, with such an array of names, I am surprised Ultimate Munitions isn't being brought in to relieve me."

"Do you really think you are the replaceable one? It is because you are too good for your competition that they changed the ranking structures. We are not sure, even with this group being brought in, that it will be easy to defeat you. Besides, if they were going to bring in another Elite to a school, it would only be to train an uprising Elite pilot. If any of us were blessed with such an excellent student, it wouldn't matter in the End Games what we taught them.

"Our Abas-excluded schools are to teach the next generation to be as good, if not better than us. Nox was an instructor before, and she was pulled to the frontlines, upon request, with a group that she had spent several years cultivating.

"Her platoon made up twenty-five of the Abas on the battlefield during the Crusaders Olympia. But you would have already known that with your request."

"Yes, my request. How did you know? Never mind. Of course, they would have notified you. And you said . . ."

"I had to decline the request," Lodestar answered his son with true regret in his voice.

He didn't wait for the emotions to settle before he continued.

"Nox has already taken a mate and had her child. The message that she posted was confused in translation. She was not looking for a father but a sergeant to take care of her child while she was still on the frontlines.

"It is no longer required due to her being assigned here. Even being Red Born, we expect great things from the child. She'll enter school about a year after those two."

"She is to have a child, and it is Red Born? I would have thought such things at ranks so high would be shunned, if not outlawed. Blue Blood are superior in so many ways that the Red Borne should belong to only those of outsiders, Scouts and the lowest of the Sentinels."

"There is one thing you missed in never seeing battle. There are times when even the lightest Scout can be more important than the heaviest Zhayedan. When those born of natural birth and conception without genetic enhancements and improvements become stronger and more perfect than those of the Blue Blood," Lodestar tried to hint at something to his son, but he would never understand. "Besides, there must be a choice. It is the basis of our laws. And she *had* the child."

Falstar had not been introduced to such needs in battles. He did not known some sacrifices are what give you the advantage for the higher ranks to go in and win the day, but more times it is the heart that wins the wars. Information gathered, targets marked, suicide bombers had to give up so much to hit a lighter, insignificant target, those who had accepted death and stayed in battle to take out just one more enemy at the cost of their own lives. All of this was part of war, and very few who were willing to give all were found in the higher ranks.

More often, they were the first to give up and take the life of a Domestique over a single death that would allow their pack to win the battle, and possibly the war. The graciousness acts of the sacrificed, however, still left the dead . . . dead.

This was not the only need or contributions the Red Borne provided—far from it. They fought gallant battles, often worked harder to earn family names. They showed true loyalty, not loyalty to power. They accepted if someone was placed above them for the right reasons, and often tried to make the ones placed above them that didn't deserve it better. True loyalty was something they learned by not having it bred into them.

Why did they have to fall after receiving the highest Honors? What could have possessed them to abandon their positions, their pack, and their lives? Why does my father still admire them after they tainted his greatest victory?

If their crimes were ever known, it would rock the very foundations of scrupulousness within the Wolf Pack, if not the entire Pack Alliance. They proved to be the absolute best of all the Packs. In the end, they turned their backs to become part of the Silent Knights. It was the only true criminal group in the outer realm. Standing orders were to try to bring the members back in alive for admittance and rehabilitation. The true orders were to kill them all whenever found.

Even if they were brought back, they would not be rehabilitated by training but by being processed into Cyborgs. Most were of different warrior breeds, although there were a few civilians. It didn't matter. When a Silent Knight society was discovered, it was usually utterly destroyed.

Children were the one exception. Children were the most important thing in the Packs and the Sasarian Empire. When possible, children were spared. Although if a child raised a weapon against a warrior, the child was no longer a child.

Not to say the Silent Knights didn't get their own devastating attacks. Often killing some of the best warriors in cowardly ways, the society had been a constant thorn in the side of the packs, and even of the Lerikatians, who suffered the most from their attacks. Circuits and Robots seemed to be the least-targeted group, which changed from their beginnings.

It was a message in their methods. It said they wanted to take irreplaceable lives. Death was their goal, and they were good at reaching their goals.

"Death to some is just another beginning. Maybe the gods will allow them to begin again," Falstar offered to comfort his father.

Deep in his bones, he knew the pilots deserved the death they were getting even though this type of honorable death was saved for only the highest venerated veterans and had only been given if gravely sick, or already passed. It was a symbol of them dying in battle against such odds that no planet could even survive.

The Star Carrier should be firing its orbital bombardment lasers any second now. What are they waiting on?

Past Time

Lodestar let out a loud laugh, breaking the silence. The children were still in their stroller, but their bottles were empty. Falstar had left them behind him, but able to see out the window. He moved up next to his father, standing with his hands behind his back.

"It would have been a better death for them to die in battle. But alas, dying in battle wasn't their way. Gran Masetro Della Morte and Stealth Master proved to be absolutely horrible at it."

He gave a small laugh outside. He was thinking back on several reports received about the destruction of another Dragon Team that had attempted to apprehend them. Another set of Hunters destroyed. Another company of warbots decimated.

Five years, and they practically brought the hunters to nothing. But the last one, we need the last one still. Hope must never die. Especially for your enemy.

Anger flooded through Falstar. He couldn't understand why his father still held these two traitors in such high regard. He didn't understand why they were being honored now.

"They lost their names. They are lucky their children were accepted back into our ranks of prestigious schools even if they are starting at the bottom. Why do you care about them so much?"

Jealousy surged through the younger man faster than he could control it. Even his cyborg mind couldn't suppress it. He had lost his father's attention enough to the parents. He knew the old man did not possess a memory of the two of them able to bring a smile of admiration and pride to his face. Yet, several thoughts of those two traitors in battle did.

Lodestar did not acknowledge his son's outburst.

To do so may call him to dishonor, and potentially a challenge. Ignoring the burst and giving him a moment to collect himself was a way for Lodestar to allow him to act as if it never happened.

The time of firing had long passed. Falstar checked his watch. He took his eyes from the window and looked down at the children.

What game are the cyborgs playing. Are they trying to torcher them by making them wait longer? Or is there an engagement to stop this? Will they be saved in the end?

Lodestar finally spoke, giving enough time to pass for the comments not to be considered.

"Red Borne or not, they have an exceptional DNA pattern. There is no need to keep them from surpassing what their parents accomplished. Besides, they have no memories of the crimes their parents have committed.

"Infants are born without knowledge of what they are. It is the purest existence we will ever have. Then we discover we are individual . . . we become self. That is when we start our training of life and end our innocence."

Falstar jumped on the opportunity to argue with his father on this topic.

"Only the warrior caste of Sasaria takes the children into separate training so early. It is only now, with the council's infinite wisdom, we have accomplished so much through the Blue Blood Program. We have reached even further into the genetic coding to create Abas pilots and other warriors that will surpass all with the genetic coding. You'll see, based on the success, or lack of success, these forward schools will have when compared to the others.

"Wolf Blue Blood will rule the battlefields as the Red Borne blood turns soil to mud under our superior creations. We may have lost the original coding for the superior Humans given to us by the gods, but mark my words, Father, the Blue Bloods measurements we will develop in this experiment will be superior to anything we have ever seen. It is a good thing we are sending these students into the enemy's lines to prepare them for what is coming."

"I hope you are wrong, for then we would be nothing but biological Robots," his father answered him under his breath.

He took his eyes from the twin children and looked back at what brought them into this world.

He added aloud to cover his original breathed answer, "No matter where you come from, or what you were born to do, you are only innocent until you realize you are an individual. From then on, you are seeking power and placement in the world. I have good reason to believe you might have been born that way."

Lodestar took his eyes from both generations of the family and looked deeply into his son's eyes. A smile might have crossed his face, but it was gone as soon as their eyes met, and he gave his son a blank stare to answer his question of truth or jest.

The younger man was not sure how to respond to the old man.

"May I quote you on that one day, if I see fit?"

"You may." The answer was cold.

Lodestar returned to a full posture and looked to be stone. Something drove him into a defensive posture, but Falstar was not sure what it could have been. His father was one of the few humans Falstar knew that could do this statue thing. It didn't even seem to breath until he came back to life. Cyborgs that were advanced enough could do it, but then it wasn't really a talent or trick.

Falstar thought back to the last time he'd seen the two facing death now. It was four years ago, during the last of the Placements of Honor for the Crusader Olympia. Falstar was with his father, watching him select the talents that he would take into the battles. It was the first time since the first Crusader Olympia that Wolf participated.

Falstar remembered the day because it was the day of his Ceremony of Acceptance. He was finally accepted and allowed to take his father's surname, the honored House of Stidolph. It was not only one of the highest three houses in Wolf. Fenrir, the original General of Wolf and Aiolfi were the other two high honor houses of Wolf Pack. Sharing the surname meant he measured up to the family that genetically spawned him.

He could track his entire line up to the beginning of the house as one of the five original warrior members from either the paternal or maternal side of his family. Even with such a history, his DNA was scrubbed and modified to make him better.

Neither Aiolfi nor Fenrir families asked for his favor since his generation name petitioned him immediately after his acceptance into the Wolf Pack Abas Training Schools following the second General Echelon of training. In normal schools, that was when the Packs, through the Lead Generals, selected warriors. It was not often a powerful house would petition to such a young candidate. Especially one that was not likely to be a warrior. Second Echelon had been when he was marked as a likely talent for training.

Higher honor families typically liked to wait for them to earn an Honor Level high enough to prove the candidate to be worthy of the house's attention. And to ensure they were selected and accepted the Pack that called them up.

Giving Falstar the recognition at such an early age set him higher than most within his class. It empowered him with prestige, which he utilized to gather even more followers. Of those, he helped develop four selected to Elite status within Wolf. No one had seen a group produce so much in one set of years. Elites were typically ten-thousand warriors and over a thousand Abas pilots to one selection within the schools.

Amanda was the first ever to be selected for Elite at the end of the second Echelon.

His own talents were high enough for him to earn a rating of Zhayedan during first ranking, proving the genetic superiority of the house. But his talents were realized on the battlefield, as it was in selecting and directing talent. None of his selected ranked less than Heavy Sentinel, Abas Killer Design (AKD).

In a way, the upper houses were securing their superiority. It could backfire on them if the student proved lower than par even with the huge beginning advantage. Proving they continued to be worthy through their classes and testing was completely on the student.

Lodestar thought of when House Stidolph told him of their plans. Illuminator, his wife, was the one that suggested it, recognizing his true talents early. Lodestar looked at the toddlers beside him. They were the same age he and Illuminator first left Falstar.

I wonder if a family will choose you, not knowing your history or genetic code. If they did, they would be fighting to get you to accept them. They did for your mother. Maybe not knowing who your forefathers are will be better.

Lodestar looked out at the two who gave him everything he had now. They were under his command structure since they came out of school, over fifteen years ago. They won the most important battle Wolf Pack ever engaged in. Now they awaited death for a second time. They were counting down eternity for the second time under his command.

He looked at the timer. Ten minutes past the scheduled execution time.

"Where is Nox?" Falstar suddenly asked.

"Excuse me?" Lodestar asked confused as to where the question had come from.

His mind shifted to another of his special people as his eyes shifted back to the twins.

"Nox? Why is she not here? She trained them during her school instructor tour and then served with them later. Wasn't she also in the command center with you when you commanded the battle?"

"This room was set up for only the four of us for obvious reasons. She is watching from another room."

Lodestar waited for a second and then added, "She does not know about these two. Very few will ever know the truth.

"Nox was given a private room to watch with her daughter. With a package I have entrusted to her. By the way, she was on the battlefield that day, not in the command center as was previous. She replaced a member because he became severely sick."

Lodestar looked out at his men one last time before he turned his eyes to the heavens. A beam of light lit the entire horizon and blinded those watching as it engulfed the two dishonored war heroes. When their vision cleared, the windows were caked with the dirt that attempted to evade the heat of the blast.

There was no way to see the final result of the laser from the space station above; for the old man, there was no need. His subordinates of almost two decades were gone forever. He wished he knew some of the children, the Honor Levels those two had earned him. Because of them, he was able to get three more produced, or so he was told. He felt as if he owed them at least the story of the ones who earned his children's life. Illuminator was only allowed to carry one of them. The only girl.

She'll be the same year as those two. I wonder what school she will be going to. She's a beautiful girl. I wonder where she got the hair color from. It's similar to her aunts on my brother's side.

Falstar could see the old man's mind started to run back to the ruling. The council didn't want to leave the children under the old warrior's leadership. There was no doubt in his ability to lead, or even teach them. No, it was their belief he might develop favoritism for the children due to their DNA donors.

Falstar knew, no matter their parents' DNA, they were, after all, just Red Born. It was not likely they would be impressive. He did accept them in his school though. The council said the other Headmaster's might show favoritism.

He didn't understand the comment until now. The other *current* Headmaster's wouldn't have known who they were. Nox was the only new Headmaster not coming from the council.

Falstar would have preferred for the twins to go to Nox's school, but considering she was there when their parents had gone, the same fear of nepotism existed. Nox also knew the existence of the children. She was brilliant. It wouldn't take much attention and she could figure out where they came from. She might take it as a personal debt to raise them to the level their parents reached no matter what it took.

They had to earn their own honors. Neither could be accepted after what the parents did with a shadow over them. Blanking the past, and giving them a fresh, empty start was best.

"Headmaster," Falstar used the title for the first time with his father. "Do you wish for me to keep you informed of the Red Born?"

The open request was done for the love that his father had shown in tracking his own progress.

"You don't expect them to go very far, do you?" his father answered back with a sigh.

The sigh said he had expected and would have strived for more from them. The sigh caused the twins to be forced to dishonor Falstar's precious school instead of another's. His father might expect more from them because of who their parents were, but Falstar saw parents assume too much of the students that came out of their genes.

While Falstar believed Blue Bloods were superior, he had to admit the majority of this selected team in school were Red Borne. Three of four of his Elites were Red Borne. He didn't expect much from these two, but he would not limit them. Wolf deserved better. He would force them to the best level they could be. He just didn't expect it to be very high.

"I promise you, Headmaster, that they will be treated fairly. I won't treat them any differently than if I did not know their past, but I do doubt they will be able to compete with the genetically matched children, yes. Unfortunately, our schools will have few to none of them."

"I would like to have regular updates and unedited video. I want to compare them to the ones of their parents. I still have some in my private archives. You also know all of their history is to be removed. By large, no one is to be able to access their information.

"It is, of course, for the safety of the twins for their history to be erased, and their parents' history changed. You will have Master Raven. Be especially careful of what he learns, or he will have to be removed."

His voice cracked as he sounded more as if he was trying to convince himself.

"I will send you a copy of those I believe you will find interest in, in the normal fashion of such trade. Tell me if you need others."

Realizing that he was reaching the end of his time with his father, he had to ask the Headmaster directly. There was no time to wait to lead him to the question without asking. Falstar wanted the information, whether or not he had to ask for it.

"Yes, Headmaster. I would appreciate that," he first responded to the kind offer, although he doubted he would need it to develop challenges for the children.

"Sir, might I also ask about the other topic of that day? Did you really ask for a tech child to be allowed to enter your school?"

"Yes, I asked for a tech-born child to be able to join this year. Her mother was a five-year. They have accepted her if someone dies within a replacement year for her, or others are willing to move up to make room. I am trading favors with the devil, but in the end, I got two things I wanted. Well, as soon as one of the others dies, I will have the two deals I have worked.

"It is unfortunate no matter the talent she shows, she will be locked into Scout. At least her children will be free to decide their own path and prove worthy of something better."

"Sir, with all due respect, why would you try to ensure the advancement of inferior DNA? What did you give up?"

"I will never petition to be a member of the council. The recognition of these three Abas pilots fall on the head of the council now. No one will ever know that they are my prodigies, hand selected for success. If they fail, they fail; but if they succeed, then General Brazil gets all the acknowledgement of discovering them. Unless of course, they prove extremely superior, then the honor is theirs alone."

"They must know that you have a unique talent for picking out the best. I only wish I had an equal talent to yours. I understand you giving it up for your people, but why give that up for a . . . tech class? That seems to be the selling of a soul for a glass of water when there is a lake but around the next bend."

"That is the question, yes. Why help someone of a lower caste than me? Well, I can only say that it comes from so many years of battle."

Lodestar thought back to one of Falstar's favorite hobbies in school. Training hunting dogs.

"It is like giving your oldest and best dog a soft bed and special treatment before he finally dies. He is of no use to you anymore, but he has earned your love and respect just the same. My engineer has earned the pallet by the fireplace and soft meat for him every night.

"You do have talent like your father and especially your mother. You just have to let it mature away from the beliefs of others and allow your own experiences to lead you."

The last thing said was to assure his son that he had listened to all of what Falstar said, and to tell Falstar he took notice of his success. Falstar knowing that Brazil would be impacted by the honor the children earned was a double edge sword for him as well. But he would wield it like any other.

"Aye, sir."

The old man looked back at the dirt-covered windows as Falstar turned toward the children. One of the children started to cry behind them.

"You should be so lucky to make a noise, boy. Be quiet! Show respects for your dead with what honor they have left you. Let them go to the next world without your worthless tears and moaning. The time for that has passed. It is time for you to honor the dead through victorious actions, not loss."

His voice was barely audible to even himself, but his heart felt them loud and clear. The child must have felt them too. It stifled the sound to moans, although the tears still streamed down its chubby cheeks unchecked.

Schools of the Wolf Pack

The planetary system of Varanasi supported the warriors of Daritock and their armies. The Four-Echelon system was set up to divide students after their first four years of training. After the seventh year of life, they were given the tasking that they mentally, physically and intellectually qualified for.

For the warrior caste, they were not separated into what would be their Pack until their third Echelon, around their fourteenth year of life. Then at twenty-one, they either entered the Packs or went on to Mastery courses. Abas, Senior Medical Doctors, Engineers, Triscifieldist, and other specialty groups were all required Master training and required the fourth Echelon.

The promise of staying in the Pack your lineage started in was high, but to maintain equalization, there were times that better or lesser students were shifted around to ensure each pack maintained a certain level of qualifying warriors.

For Wolf, this changed with the five outer schools. While the majority were to be sent into an unknown space area, some would remain behind, but would not be counted toward their warrior's count for selection during this period. Wolf was the smallest of the

Packs, so it was not likely to give them a greater advantage unless a member remaining behind or who went forward was exceptional at gathering members.

If a student was born to the warrior caste, especially those of the Abas rank, and did not earn the right to become a warrior by their twelfth year of life, they were tested for warrior support caste.

Intelligence, mental development, resilience, and personality test were among all the warriors core measurements, as well as the others. Basic skills, learning styles and speed of learning were also tested. Methods of learning were determined but were not detractors from being selected.

Abas pilots had to be accepted by the core machine in addition to all the other testing and validations. They were the only warriors that required the machines to choose them as well. If they were not selected, they would be downgraded to a different warrior type.

The ones that were unable to qualify for any type of warriors were called "five years" for being passed over five years in a row to become a warrior. The five years were not considered a dishonor.

The student might have had anything to cause them to act irregularly in battle. Or there were enough warriors for the classes during their years. Their scores wouldn't qualify high enough. The test ensured those that were best to be trained were.

The children of a Five-Year were given access to enter the school of their family's previous rank. The children started being tested at seven years of age. If they failed, then that family line was stricken from the previous caste and moved to the other. If the child was able to pass, in all but certain Abas schools, they were given free rein to move throughout the ranks as any other student. Some Abas Schools, such as Wolf and Avion Proie locked them in the lowest levels to ensure the blood line was truly pure in the next generation.

These rules and the rules of Honor and Privilege had been modified for the five schools Wolf earned after winning the last Crusader Olympia. It was the first time they entered since the very first one. Wolf, the smallest of the Packs, took on the honor of Home Guard, ensuring the protection of the Daritock System from internal and external threats.

The Cyborgs, specifically the Watchers, run by the Serpico Family were the official peacekeepers and monitors of the Packs of War for the Lerikatia Empire. But the human packs didn't trust the Dragons, as cyborg warriors were referred. Especially the Abas pilots that converted to the joined existence of circuits and humans. Unlike the others who were cyborg warriors of whatever style of warrior they were, Abas pilots were human; cyborg pilots were dragons. There were no connections between them.

The five forward schools were unlike the rest of the Pack schools located in the Varanasi Planetary system. Varanasi was the sixth planet from the Sasaria Sun, with Daritock being the seventh and last planet that solely circled Sasaria.

Zankatia was the only planetary system, a gas giant, that circled both Venginus, the other star in the binary star system and Sasaria. Some Triscifieldist, the scientist of the Packs and Sasarian Empire, believed there were others that now appeared destroyed based on the three asteroid rings and belt within the binary system.

Students were allowed to leave the school on holiday three times a year for two weeks, although most students declined the chance. Often feeling the need to catch up on studies or to just get ahead meant they didn't leave the schools. Trying to get in and out might cost them a few extra days of their holiday for travel.

For Wolf's new schools, the students were selected from certain breeding lines and all came from only Wolf's genetics. Every one of the 130 students selected for each year of the 21 years they would train there were Abas pilots only. Yet, the entire student body consisting of 2,730 students wouldn't have filled a single graduating class of any other Abas school in any other planetary system.

Lighter pilots often made up the greatest number of trained pilots for the Packs. Sentinels made up the highest number in Wolf's forward schools. The forward schools also trended to giving heavier armors away before the students were released to their *secret* mission.

High honored Scout and Low Sentinel pilots often put their privileges toward children. It was one of the only things members of the Pack could bank privileges toward, like retiring early or extended periods of no duties. It was also one of the most expensive, like retiring, unless you earned them through honorable actions.

Others used their privileges to be brought back to schools to be instructors to teach the tactics that kept them alive. It might not have seemed it to the forward school students, but the Packs wanted to keep their light Abas pilots as much as the heavy ones. It was time consuming training more. The actions they performed where highly needed.

Garrison duty and city guards were two of the highest needs for the lighter Abas Warriors in the Packs. Since they were smaller, they could fit into buildings easier to search or secure them if the need arose. The city also gave them greater attacking advantages and cut down on collateral damages.

The larger frames were better for open warfare and battle line fighting. Unfortunately, Silent Knights and Desitians did not always line up to fight, nor did they care about reducing the collateral damage of Lerikatia and Pack cities.

With over two-hundred-ten planetoids, and four hundred society space stations being fought over on just the Sasaria side of the system, including Venginus, there were a lot of cities to protect. The Silent Knights had at least fifty un-registered or stolen space stations as well.

The Packs only protected Daritock, Zankatia

and Varanasi though. Cyborgs and paramilitary peacekeepers took care of the Lerikatia and Keiso planetary systems. The Packs had stations on the Venginus side of System Duce in parts of the Dark Space.

They were maintained and supplied through Worm Heads since it would take years to travel to from the regular rotation of Zankatia. Launchers couldn't be used because they would give away the locations too easily. Many of those stations were destroyed or stolen if discovered by the Silent Knights, so secrecy was always a priority.

Lerikatia held twenty-two settled bodies and eighteen unsettled moons in their planetary systems. Zankatia's forty-four moons were all habitable, and in addition, the gas giant had 27 active, registered stations within its atmosphere. Less than half were Pack occupied. It hadn't been settled, since it was the location of all the fighting that had been taking place well before the Packs arrived.

Zankatia Planetary System was the last refuge of the Tutevibians before they joined the Packs. However, their joining did not provide Zankatia as an established planet system of Lerikatia Empire. It was the most contested area in System Duce, then and now. Yet, the forward schools were not being trained to face Desitians or Kalictithians.

A Three-Echelon System was emplaced for their unique training courses and styles instead of four. The First Echelon the students ranged between three to ten, spending the first years learning in a general environment before being brought to the outer schools. This included basic classes in history, math, reading, writing, technology usage, hand to hand combat, small arms combat, physical education, basic strategic planning, conflict resolution and basic team work and leadership. Although the first couple years was designed around play learning and the second part started to become structured to prepare them for the Second Echelon.

Basic first aid and other shorter courses were also taught after entering the second half of the first echelon, but not constantly like the main courses. They were shorter, skills development sessions, not learning sessions and basic skills mastery sessions. Students would go through them each year as a refresher and were expected to be able to implement the training.

The Second Echelon typically ran from eleven to twenty-one years of age. This period required them to complete additional specific fields of training to their schedules. They were still required to take the basic classes for the first half of the eight years. However, the hours were shorter and self-learning was encouraged. Once the course was completed, they no longer had to attend or continue to complete work for it. Then they would move to only their development courses that concentrated on what they would be doing for the Pack.

Instructors were not always present for every class,

except specialty classes. Students were provided the information they needed to learn and were left to move forward at their own pace. Those that did not complete the bare minimum requirements had to complete them before moving to the Third Echelon or be dropped from the courses. If they failed too many, they were dropped from the school. No student to date had failed to complete enough courses.

Those able to complete the minimum requirement in basic areas by the end of the midterm cycle could choose to continue with additional learning in those areas or drop the subjects completely. Any member able to complete full courses earlier than the midterm cycle were given additional honor ranks and privileges for the rest of the second and third echelon. A bonus that could mean advancement or prevention of being dropped. It was one of the few honor rewards that could not be removed during school.

The third echelon was set for five years. It was primarily for Mastery of skills, although very few qualified for the title "Master". For those not looking to get a Master Title, it was a time of improvement more than perfecting. No classes were required.

If an Abas pilot chose to do nothing but fight in the arenas to gain Honor and Opportunities, they were allowed. It was not a choice many made due to the risk. They could also choose to be deployed to the Armies early. However, the chances of getting promoted were less and demoted more, so it was also not a risk many chose.

By maintaining some classes, pilots could offset the loss of Opportunities for post battle repairs or other items and privileges. They could swing the pendulum on promotion as well based on performance in classes. Since classes were not mandatory for appearance and were self-paced it was a simple choice. However, if progress or mastery had not been made in them, then the Master Instructor could drop the student from the course.

The Opportunities System was also unique to the Forward Schools, as the students learned. Normally in the Packs, all warriors were provided repairs, system upgrades, weapon change outs, and equipment based on mission needs and performance alone. This stayed true in school and out of it. It was part of their Basic Honor Rank Privileges. Abas Pilots were no different, and often received many more privileges for their basic rank then other warriors within senior ranks. There was no Opportunity System.

In the Pack, everyone was provided basic items, even if they didn't actively provide to society as a positive member. Those who didn't provide to society would not get more than they absolutely needed, no matter the form of their existence: circuit, human, cyborg, Tutevibian, or Gramerack. No Tutevibian or Gramerack had ever received basic provisions.

Humans would be given the exact number of calories they needed to survive based on body type. It was served once to three times a day at dispensers and would either come out in a paste or as a loaf.

Humans were given loose fitting clothing designed to keep them covered and protected from the current weather but nothing else. The clothing was fabricated to be uncomfortable to help with motivation. The member could turn them in every third day when they took a shower in the public cleaning areas. New, clean cloths would be provided for them when they were done being scrubbed.

They were provided a hovel to protect them from the elements as well. But there were no additional comforts including bedding, cushioning or room. If they tried to use what they were provided as a means of trade, then they would be isolated, guarded and monitored. Food would be provided intravenously with pain inducing medications. If they continued to do so, they were sentenced to worse activities.

Medical was also bare minimum and rudimentary when provided. If they broke a bone, it would be set and casted, but allowed to heal slowly and scar. They might have to use maggots to clean the rotten flesh or wounds. They would be provided plants that they would have to mash or prepare themselves for pain relief. Yet, they were treated and helped to get healthy again.

The choice remained for them to make though. They could live at the bottom with no privileges in life or they could perform to help society be better; or they could choose to die. If they chose to become better and work with society, then they would slowly gain their privileges based on their provisions back to society. It would be restricted for up to a year depending on how long they remained un-involved.

But for every stick in society, there was the carrot as well. Humans who were the best performers in their areas and expertise were rewarded with additional ranks beyond their stations, longer holding of privileges, years reductions until their Age of Peace or retirement, additional children at no personal cost or better locations to live and perform. Low performers might not ever reach the Age of Peace, where they would no longer be required to perform for society and would be provided at the highest levels they earned. They could spend the entire 120 plus years of life after school working.

Circuits, and Cyborgs were subject to the same rules. Circuits didn't resist changing as long as humans. Sometimes for them, it was minutes to days at most. They ended up choosing to be recycled or destroyed or going back into their proper places. The power they were provided were dirty, their processes restricted, the repair parts downgraded or not provided if not essential and communications or access to networks lost.

Cyborgs never seemed to move against society. The few that tried were brought back to whichever of the three families that every cyborg belonged to. Within days, they could be seen performing stronger than ever or were dead. Whatever happened behind those walls was affective.

The Wolf Forward Schools were only for Abas

Warriors. After the students entered the Second Echelon, they were expected to fight and earn almost everything they would normally receive for being warriors. They had lower Privilege Levels than regular Abas Warriors, while in school and possibly after. They had to earned their upgrades and weapon switches. They were responsible for gaining access to better equipment.

Those that were higher ranked got many of these things as they progressed or by use of their additional privileges instead of trading opportunities. Still, every member was expected to negotiate and barter even if given the privileges without the use of opportunities. The final, additional stick was if they didn't get what they needed, they ended up doing without or being removed from the schools.

The carrot was simple. You had a better chance of surviving school and would be more comfortable the better you performed against everyone else. If you couldn't be the best, join a team or find protection. Develop survival skills because survival was the first requirement to graduate.

Students were issued their first Personal Arm Computers, aka PACs, as well when they entered the Second Echelon. This marked the beginning of them earning actual Honor Ranks, Privileges and Opportunities within the school. Honor Ranks were determined by the level of Abas, the missions and assignments completed, and any positive actions minus the missions failed, negative actions or failures to show progression within one quarter of the school time. Honor Rank set the number of privileges and opportunities each student earned from the previous quarterly payout.

Honor Ranks determined most of the aspects of student life, in and out of school. Things like the quality of uniforms the school provided, medical, and training within the classrooms were not impacted. However, if you wanted a special uniform or design, extra hot water, additional training material, or special equipment for you that was not shared with others, then it took Opportunities. When they were awarded their Abas, and entered the second echelon, they would have to trade Opportunities to get repairs, additional weapons, special weapons, and access to information and equipment. These were things that would normally be provided in the Pack just because you were a warrior, much less being an Abas Pilot.

Opportunities were used as a form of currency amongst the school students and the support staff, the school itself, and contact or access to outside entities. The idea and use of Opportunities did not exist in the Pack itself, therefore any transaction outside the school was closely monitored and brokered through operators.

It was only privileges and additional privileges when it came to the Packs. Everything that was needed and wanted for your position or mission was provided. The level or quality was based on your rank and purpose within society. Additional levels of privileges were used to get things that were considered above your station or common access of your rank. This was due to limited resources needing to be maintained for the highest return on investment.

In society, if you wanted a motorcycle, you would take a mission in which you would use a motorcycle of the class you wanted. If you completed the mission with the cycle, you could keep it or return it. However, if you maintained it, then you had to maintain the level of additional privileges needed to power it, provide maintenance support, or replace equipment, as necessary. The owner could get these things by taking on additional missions instead of utilizing Privilege Levels above their Honor Level.

Missions were often bid for by teams or individuals unless assigned or selected. Being assigned or selected generally meant being able to request any equipment you wanted within reason and restrictions. Bidding meant betting high enough to be successful, but low enough to get selected. If you weren't selected, either because you bid what the offeror believed was too low to be successful or higher than the accepted offer, then you would be without. If you didn't get enough missions your performance levels would start to drop, and you would risk being reduced in privileges and rank. This stayed true until retirement, where you were locked in for the remainder of your life.

Students in the new school didn't get additional privileges. Each rank came with a set amount. They received Opportunities and had to use those for services they would normally get for just being an Abas Pilot. Even negotiating and bartering would not be conducted once they were within the Packs. At least it was not done by the Warrior Caste.

In the Forward Schools, Opportunities were updated four times a year based on your average Honor Rank for the three months of the previous quarter under Duce Standard Time (DST). A student would gain Opportunities every first day of the month but could also be awarded them for special performances, betting against others or if they accomplished some great task or were successful in battle. These methods typically increased the ways Opportunities were gained as students progressed through the second and third echelons as the primary ways to earn Opportunities.

Bartering and negotiating within the schools was part of the curriculum. Negotiating was a skill that every student had to learn. It was expected to be part of every aspect of their lives, including conflict management, betting, and grading.

If a student wanted to use additional opportunities, they would have to negotiate with the members that were performing the work to the level of opportunities being offered. If it had to do with the school or equipment, then they had to go to the Headmaster or the designated leader of that part of the school. If it was for a certain class, then they had to go to the professor or the Master Professor of the subject or department.

General Opportunities were only able to be kept for a standard year if they were given by Honor Ranks. It became a use or lose, to prevent coasting. Those that were earned through other means could be kept until the end of school but were required to be used in proportion to the General Opportunities. This again was a foreign concept to the Packs but was introduced in these schools. There was an ungodly cap for every student based on the level of their Abas and Honor Rank, but no one had ever come close to reaching them.

Students of all ranks received the same basic hygienic materials, food, bedding, and PACs, as well as any other electronics or special devices used for their classes and general studies. Enhancements for all these were available, and there was more than one way to acquire them. Opportunities was the primary way to acquired them. They could be awarded for actions like completion of difficult missions or task. Students could bet against others who had them as part of a challenge agreement between students or later between students and instructors, professors, and even Pack Members.

Department Heads of Special Instructions could authorize the giving of some items to students they believed earned the right to have them, even if their Honor Levels would not normally approve it. Earning the right did not cost Opportunities, for it was part of the given for reaching the requirement to receive it. This was the closest the students came to being treated like real Pack Warriors.

The first two echelon shower bays were open rooms with nozzles pointed straight down from the ceiling. A student would stand in a square and the water would start. If they moved out of the square to wash or brush off, the water would stop.

The temperature of the water was based off the body temp and the level and type of contaminants on the skin. If the student was covered in mud or dirt or other toxins that would be hard for water to get off, they would go to the scrap room. However, there was a limited amount of adjusted water for each of the first echelon students, and then for the entire barracks when it came to second echelon. When it ran out, only cold would flow. As the shower times continued, the water continued to get colder. Rumors said some students had to brush the ice out of their hair after.

Soap was added to the water depending on what was needed as it came out. Soap, unlike the adjusted water, never ran out. This meant the students were only required to bring a scrub ball with them to the showers. The scrub balls were more of an octagonal-shaped scrubber with different levels of exfoliation brushes depending on how clean you needed to be.

Baths became limited after entry to Second Echelon for those in the barracks, after showers and with limited access. There was a low number of soaking / massaging baths in the Second Echelon

Area. They were restricted to the classes which had the hardest physical training phases that day. They had to be assigned by the Instructor and were limited on the time able to be spent in them.

Students who wanted to work out sore muscles in the heated waters shared baths. Large, groups would crawl into the bathtubs together. Up to four people could fit in one without touching. By Second Echelon, the students were expected to self-police, even while being monitored. This led to some students trying to force a greater number of the weaker performers into one bathing pool, while the few enjoyed more of the other pools with less than the recommended number.

The scrubs, undergarments, and uniforms were turned in twice a week for cleansing, unless otherwise required by mission or performance. Like soap, this was a privilege that was not reduced or taken away no matter the rank. However, privileges and opportunities would have the clothing returned with different levels of softener, pressed, polished, folded, hung, stored or just piled on top of your rack.

Many of the school facilities were shared amongst each echelon, but it was first-come first-serve on the materials. There were also two berthing areas: lights and heavies. This meant the best places and times were fought for with minor challenges.

The Wolf Pack, in these schools, acted in the belief of letting the lights learn to fight for every inch of their life. It was designed this way to help improve their killer instinct on the battlefield. Something the light-armored Abas would need to last through the first cycle of new battles they were to face.

Second Echelon performers could earn their own rooms or be joined to a team to get out of the general barracks, but it was harder since teams usually kept their rooms for Third Echelon members. Third Echelon members without teams stayed in the barracks of the Second Echelon but didn't suffer as many limitations.

Heavy Abas selectees received most study material of their classes directly to their devices. This allowed them to maintain their studies anywhere. Their PACs had upgrades provided as privileges. Lights could use opportunities to get the same, but it had to be maintained. Most found it difficult and better to compete or share, freeing up opportunities to maintain their equipment or get a few personal comforts. Life as a light was more team and compromise.

Life of the Heavies was not easy, but easier. While they were given better access and less need to compete for some of the personal comforts, they had to maintain higher levels of progress, scores and advancement. Failing at the higher levels often meant quicker reductions and losses of those personal comforts' week to week. Lights might see reductions monthly or quarterly.

To maintain the berthing areas required the expenditure of opportunities. The heavy classmen were expected to fight for the materials not assigned to them in their studies with others that were not taking the same classes. This taught them that all they needed was not always provided and you too had to fight to earn what might give you the edge over someone else. Fail and lose quality of life. Or learn to make do without it.

During the second half of the Second Echelon, it was common for the heavies to have their own resistant gyms, showers and individual studying area built attached to their berthing compartment. With two to room and eight to a set, fights within the rooms were common on the chores that had to be completed and for those that would be standing by for the inspections. Any activity that took time away from them advancing through knowledge gain was fought over in some type of low-level challenge. Fighting to enforce one or two to cover the duties while the others were free gave them something else to fight for.

The heavy classes and the light classes were often secluded separate from each other in training. It was to ensure the hungers of the two were fueled in ways that would bring the best results. Shared facilities, student gatherings, and social events such as dancing and formal meals allowed the sets of pilots to familiarize with each other.

Socialization and partnering was especially important when they reached the second half of the Second Echelon. Then students had to start participating in more team battles, understanding team strategy and developing long term sustainment practices. The greatest challenge of this was not being trained together. Another common factor they would face after school.

Betting was one of the most popular means of gaining advancements, parts, or better material without spending one's own opportunities. Trading opportunities was a common way for the light classes to help one person earn enough Honor Levels for all to be able to use the advanced items. Pooling, as it was called, was only authorized for the lighter Abas sets and teams.

There were safeguards in place to keep a student from betting more than they could cover. Such as, no student was allowed to bet more than two quarters forward. Even if they lost their Honor Rank and were reduced to less opportunities then they earned, then those that they saved would be used to cover the bet. If they didn't have additional in reserve, then they would have to perform extra work for the school to earn additional opportunities. They would have to execute this on top of their classes and would risk losing even more Honor Ranks if they didn't.

If their Honor rank dropped too low, then they were removed from school. No student ever chanced this more than twice. No student was yet removed for this reason.

While the forward schools were different, Headmaster Falstar was the primary designer of the program based on the need and battles they would be facing. As classes graduated and were tested in the new fields, the training program proved successful for the mission. Although, even with the training, as planned, the majority of the missions still failed to meet all requirements.

CHAPTER 1

ENTRY

The twin brothers remembered walking into barracks their first day after completing understudy classes. The date was 673.4.15 DST, or the fifteenth day of the fourth month of the six-hundred-seventy-third year Duce Standard Time. It was month after their seventh birthday, from what they were told. No parent had ever shown up for them or talked to them.

Operators would come and spend time with them though. The androids always spent time with students that didn't have parent to visit. While they enjoyed speaking with the androids, the androids could not provide them any history on who they were. No other student seemed to have this particular issue.

In the Packs, students not having parents come to visit them was common. They may be dead or on deployment, fighting Desitians in the Zankatia planetary system; the only planetary system that circled both stars of the system. Most with family names associated had someone from their family come to tell them about their history, but not all families sent connecting members to the children and not at every visit period either.

The Headmaster was outside the entry, watching each student come through. It was strange to them, because they had never been directly observed by him, but when he looked at them, his face seemed to change to one of disgust. As far as they knew, they had done nothing to earn his abhor. The few minor fractions they had been caught for didn't seem to align to this level of abominate. The look was fleeting, and his eyes continued to scan the rest of the students, never returning to them.

The Pack was a warrior society, designed for the defense of Lerikatia Empire. Daritock and Varanasi were the sixth and seventh planetary systems of the Sasaria Star, where the Packs maintained their warrior society. Zankatia was the most contested of the planetary systems, being fought and lost depending on which side of the system it was currently rotating around during its 150 standard year cycle.

Lerikatia was the middle three planets, where most the humans and Grameracks were free to live in peace. A peace maintained by the Cyborgs. Keiso, the closest two planets to Sasaria, was occupied by circuits and some iron lung cyborgs who maintained their policing but was the only planetary systems without any semblance of bio-sentient life.

The twins considered their grades. There was no

measurement of success of learning during their first four years. Still, basic reading, writing, and history and traditions had been pounded into the twins over the last four years. They performed well as far as they could tell, with little to no additional support or help needed.

It seemed they may have been wrong in their assumptions based on the look from the Headmaster and being the last group to be selected to advance forward in school. They started to worry they would not be given an official student number. Most considered this the period when training really began, and you started to earn the right to get into an Abas, Advanced Battle Armor Suits. The pilots of these were considered to be the best of the best when it came to the Warrior Caste.

Most the infractions the twins were caught for had to do with going into the Abas bays and trying to *play* with them. A couple times they had blown up some equipment when they fired the weapons off, but that wasn't counted against them. Supposedly, they shouldn't have been able to fire the weapons, and was the responsibility of the engineers and security members to keep them out.

They were curious if it mattered they were the last selected. They were seven years old the day they were allowed to test for an Abas, everyone was excited and scared. If any of them failed, they would be removed from the schools' selection. Supposedly it was the last time you could be removed and allowed to go to the other schools.

From what the operators had told the twins, life was different in those schools. They didn't care about them. They had two goals they could remember setting since they could . . . well, remember. Become an Abas pilot. Then become the best Abas pilot.

As all the newly arriving students entered their assigned barracks block an older child stood in front of them. His stance said he was assuming he would be able to command by just presents. They felt he came a short and ignored him.

"For those of you who are new here, you will want to pay close attention to these rankings. They will tell you where you will fall as you progress. For now, all of you should consider yourselves Scout Class Light Armors."

"Aren't we all Scout Class Light Armors right now?" a shorter than average dark-haired, dark-skinned child asked.

"We have been here longer and have earned higher Honors. You don't have any and are starting at the bottom. Besides, it is easy to tell where you are going to fall after your first few months. Especially by the end of the first year. We will have to see where you are then," he gave a wicked smile before continuing.

"Unfortunately, I will have to wait for you to reach your second echelon before I will get to challenge you. Some of us are about to be promoted out, but don't think I will forget this disrespect though. I never do!

"I will name you Slain like those on the bottom of this list," the tall, red-skinned boney boy laughed cynically.

Several other students behind him were snickering, including a few females that looked barely older than the twins. Most of the students gathered around the paper to look at the ranks that had been established. They wanted to fall into what they assumed were norms for the barracks. Five of them, including the dark-skinned boy, the twins and two girls walked away to put the few items they still had into their racks.

The display showed:

ARMOR CLASS	NAMED	RANK
Scout Class Light	Slain	0
Scout Class Medium	Smacks	1
Sentinel Class Light	Light Scales	2
Scout Class Heavy	Shaved	3
Sentinel Class Medium	Balancers	05-Apr
Zhayedan Class Light	Slayers	6
Sentinel Class Heavy	Shadows	7
Zhayedan Class Medium	Superiors	8
Zhayedan Class Heavy	Masters	9
Elite	You Wish!	Ha! Ha!

The twins understood the need to build a ranking structure, but they also felt as if they were not really part of it. They didn't care about anyone else. Only their goals. They hadn't felt a challenge in anything asked of them yet. They were only nervous when it came to test for their Abas. Otherwise, they were indifferent to anyone and everyone else.

Let them be what they wish to be. We have our own goals. As long as they don't interfere in them, then we can co-exist.

Still, some semblance of structure was needed for the 390 students who had to share 30 showers and 10 baths. Operators were present to ensure basic safety, but the students were entering the self-policing stages. It was better for them to start learning to exist within these tight confines together.

There had to be a ranking or there would be chaos. It also started the beginning of their training of competition. While it wasn't official until second echelon, it started here. They had to fight for what they wanted or lie down and accept they were not worthy.

When the twins got to their racks, they found data pad they would use until issued their PACs. It gave the requirements for naming, class schedules, and the additional or changed rules that came with this barracks. The twins didn't see the ranking structure in it.

Naming wouldn't start until the Second Echelon, but they were still expected to follow and understand at their current level. The Rules of Naming were posted at the display panels next to every entrance and exit of every class, room, eating and gathering area as well as in front of the toilets and on the sides and doors of the stalls.

General information was always flashing through the panels. It was based on who was supposed to be using the areas at the time, or the majority that were expected there. Once you received your PAC, it would provide specific information. The pads they had now were able to provide some specifics, but it was based on the class, not the individual.

The pads also provided their current opportunity level. Only enough opportunities were given to challenge one person per month in anything but an Abas Battle. Naming challenges were not authorized with such a low-bid challenging. Betting on battles and challenges was opened for the students now, but it wouldn't count. The betting total was maintained separately from their actual accounts so they could monitor their successes.

The moment they received their PACs their bets would be registered. Then someone had to be willing to take the bet offered for it to be finalized. If a bet didn't get finalized, then it was like it was never offered. Some bets could be taken by multiple people or parties and the winnings divided based on the percentage that was taken. If the percentages accepted were less than the total bet, then the winnings were limited to only what was accepted.

Boards throughout the school were posted with the bids for bets. Even the instructors were allowed to post bets since the system was anonymous for open bets. People were allowed to post and accept closed bets as well. If two people wanted to make a bet, it was not required for them to go through the betting system, just have a witness or recording of it.

Called bets, which were a verbal calling of any bet on anything, could be accepted by anyone within earshot. Pools were gathered by the circuits that recorded them. These bets were not limited to one-on-one acceptance and were the most popular amongst the students who tried to earn fortunes of opportunities on the bets alone. Plethora of opportunities could be exchanged within minutes.

Those that called out for one of the sides or multiple sides and won would get back what they called, plus the equal percentage of the winnings to the amount of the winning pool. The more that bet on the obvious winners, the less the winnings. The higher the risk, the higher the rewards. If someone called for more than one side, each call was considered its own bet.

The biggest disadvantage with accepting a called bet was that the winnings were divided by those that had bought into it. The total pot was divided by percentage of input opportunities, so while the betters didn't lose opportunities, the gains might be as high.

The twins quickly absorbed this new information as they settled into their racks. They brought up the new class information and began working on absorbing it. The look from the Headmaster seemed to make them more driven to prove themselves.

"They say that it is supposed to make us better by separating us," a female voice interrupted the twin's solo readings.

She was part of the sheep that stayed to listen to the air bag that was blowing gas. Or at least that's what the dark-haired twin thought. He was glad for his brother that she was in their cube.

Everyone believed she would be deemed placed on the light side due to her parents both being Medium Scout pilots. She was like the twins, where no one came to visit her, even the family that they belonged to. Unlike the twins, she had a letter from her parents, talking about her history and family lines.

About thirty or forty percent of the students in their class fell into this rank. Even though the twins had no idea what their genealogy was, they were often treated like her and the others that had no visitors. They were considered to be amongst the lower or lesser groups. Since it had most leaving them alone, they were happy with it.

Each rack area had six people in it. Three on each side with about a meter between the racks. When they came to the barracks, the cube, or group of six was assigned, but the individual racks were divided by the individuals assigned to the cube.

"It does for most of them," another female, taller than the first answered.

Her parents had been killed as well, but she had visitors. They were still friends and were often seen with three or four others, mostly girls. They were average at best in performance for the group, but again that was assuming by the twins since there had been no grading structure.

"It does because the instructors whore over them. Look at those that are practically given carte blanche. They have the ability to improve because they have the means, they have the time and they have the necessity."

"You might be a little Zevra now, but you'll see. This system has proven to be effective before. Remember, Wolf won the Crusader Olympia to earn these schools. They had to have done something right to beat the rest of the Packs.

"The council had to have approved this treatment. If the council approved it, it must be right. It's been this way always, and most likely always will be."

"Just because we have always done it that way, does not mean it is the best way to continue to do it."

"Then what would you suggest, council woman?" her friend added with a slight laugh.

It was playful, not demeaning. This was not the first time they had discussed these topics, but they still didn't come to common ground.

Life is not meant to be fair. It is meant to be lived, the dark-haired twin thought.

The smaller girl, with long, dirty blond hair and small body frame, looked at the two lower racks. It didn't appear the twins were in there. She almost wished they were to *accidently* overhear hear.

"There are some that do not get any attention

from the instructors and yet, still surpass even the best of the class."

"I would rather tell Crimson she could eat a rotten egg then ask them for anything. They are so strange the instructors don't go near them. But you are right, they seem to best everyone when we competed.

"They even call each other brothers, although they look nothing alike. Must be desperate to have family. Or the way the one with dark-hair speaks for the one with white-hair. Just looks at him like he spoke. Having a conversation that only he can hear. But the other one does give the impression that he is speaking, in some way. It's creepy."

"I heard the android tell them they were twins. It was the only thing the operators knew about their lineage. They were not even sure if they were born in a carrier or by their natural mother. Just that they were natural twins.

"It was right after that incident when the power generator blew up in Bay Seven. You were with your family."

"Did you see what the white-haired one did in class to the cyborg that came in to assist us?" the taller one tisked. "I bet they did something to that power supply. I heard it was hit by a laser or something though. From someone misfiring their Abas weapon.

"Still, students 1321456 and 6541231 can stay right where they are, alone and on top together. Come on. We need to get to the showers while the water's hot."

"The quiet one is cute. I like him," the smaller girl blushed as she leaned in and whispered in carrying voice. "He could teach me to be better than any instructor or professor in this school."

"He might if he ever said a word," her friend responded loudly, shaking her head in disbelief at her friend. "Come on, I want to take a shower before all the hot water runs out and everyone else is in there. Maybe we will see him, and you can ask him for private lessons in being quiet."

She paused at the end of the cubical and turned back to her shorter friend.

"Come to think of it, I don't think I have ever seen them in there. Have you?"

"They seem to go in there either before everyone gets back from extra studies or early in the morning," she defended unnecessarily as she finished gathering her things and walked off.

After the two girls were gone from the cubical, one of the curtains where the twins slept flipped back.

"You could teach her to be better. It wouldn't be that hard. She has a lot of potential."

A hand came out from the other one and gave a signal that wasn't as polite as his brother's voice.

"Hey, don't shoot me for agreeing with her. Besides, you have watched her enough to know exactly where she needs help. A few corrections and she would be close to the top performers. And, I don't think that you can take your eyes off her most the time."

Another rude hand signal came out, although the brother on the right didn't bother looking.

"Didn't you blow the cyborg's arm off for being rude to her? It shouldn't have made the mistake of exposing its joint, but still, you were a little excessive taking its last human appendage," the one on the right added with a little laugh, before the curtain switched again and quietness settled.

The twins knew the one on the left would love to teach the little pilot. He just didn't want to deal with the rest of the click. He decided it might be better to wait until he could get her alone or join a team with her on it. Then he could find a way to lure her off.

The dark-haired one thought it was a childish plan, but they were children. At least that's what everyone kept telling them. They didn't act like the other children. They didn't act like anyone else, which was why the instructors seemed to leave them to their own devises. They didn't need their assistance.

Teams were the easiest way for lights to advance. The duties were spread based more on rank and honors earned for the team. If a Scout or Sentinel was about to go into a battle that was important to the team, they wouldn't be expected to take part in the duties as often the week prior, so they could prepare for the challenge. The more battles you entered, the less duty you preformed, the more recognition you earned, the better chances of advancement.

Teams could also take over areas of the school to secure a zone of private operations and advantages for the heavier Abas to join them. Although certain things could not be taken over to ensure that every student still had a chance to advance themselves. Teams were allowed to take over all the blacked-out regions of the school map.

For this reason, each school maintained at least seven named teams and two unnamed or underground teams. The named teams had a minimum area that had to remain theirs, but that would only be four rooms with shared facilities. If a named team was completely wiped out, a new name and base team had to be selected by the Headmaster.

The unnamed teams were also allowed to fight for the secret rooms of the schools but couldn't officially hold any spaces. Due to training in areas that required unmapped and hidden areas, these regions were built into every school. They were not on the map and not officially held by anyone. It was up to those that found them to hold them. If they failed, they lost the areas.

The known areas were treated like territory when facing Pack. They had to formally request to battle for the areas within Honor Rules. The unknown areas were treated like fighting the Desitians, free for all. Take by any means except really killing fellow students.

The dark-haired twin suggested taking a team barracks for the two of them and selecting at least two other members, maybe three to round out the team. Then just keep them for the rest of school. The white-haired, taller twin thought taking the underground areas was a better choice. Then they didn't have to have known members and could work better secretly.

The twins knew as they progressed through the first four years of the second echelon, the students were moved into different type of barracks. They still shared the common rooms, but those deemed lights stayed in a six-man cubical while the heavies moved into four-man cubicles closer to the common areas and showers.

The common areas were open to anyone that did not have extra study. It was up to the students to manage their time between training and the ability to relax. For some, it was mandatory for them to take a break and go into those rooms for at least an hour. Access was never restricted from anyone though.

The common rooms consisted of a viewing lounge, game room, a billiard room, a library and an exercise rooms. These were surrounded by five dorms and one Facility Room where the showers, baths, sinks, laundry drops, cleaning supplies and other systems were kept.

The game room held different strategic games to challenge the children's minds against each other. Several would play for hours, honing their abilities of finding weakness and strength in their opponents and themselves. Most games were either modified or created to teach sacrifice and battle movements on the simplest levels. Since being advanced to student numbers, these were monitored now. In the second

Echelon they would be graded and used to identify where the student would be best placed and how to get the best results from them.

The viewing lounge had four view screens showing different battles of the packs in the past. They showed both the reasons for the wins and the losses, as well as the results of the battle. They would go back over the battle and show where actions could have changed the outcomes or would have proved more efficient. The most critically reviewed were those won by Wolf. After all, not every win was a perfect battle. It set the message of constant improvement.

Wolf had fewer frontline battles and more strategic gain series of battles. These were shown in clusters of different types of battles, outlining how Generals made calculated moves to lose something to gain something better. The students were taught not every loss was a true loss, nor did all wins lead to the greater good.

Bear Sleuth also showed more cluster battle styles. It usually took many different battles, including some Bear Sleuth were not involved in to find the true purpose of the first fights that started the series. Some took years of back tracking to discover the starting point. Although they seemed to attack when opponents were weaker. They had a knack for identifying the greatest weaknesses, even if the ones they were going after believed it was a strength.

The Warriors were also strategic but in a very direct way. Horse was similar to them but seemed to be more proper and showier in their battle styles. Horse always seemed to try to win, even if winning would be bad for them. It was a tactic that cost them often.

Lion was the same as Horse, but angrily aggressive in their tactics. They fought to win, but instead of taking on any challenge, they seemed to target weaker prey like Bear Sleuth. Only it wasn't as calculated and designed for the longer games like Bear.

Jegermuri, like the name implied, stayed more in the watery and gaseous regions. They also seemed to be the ones that fought the most in open space. They had the largest Navies and occupied the most stations as well. Planetary battles for land mass was not outside their wheelhouse, but they didn't seem to engage for them unless they were protecting their lands.

As far as the Packs went, they seemed to have the most original maps of their territories when it came to land mass within the Daritock region. Yet their space expansion and stations spread across the asteroid belts and on Zankatia was the greatest of all the Packs as well.

Avian Proie was the strangest to watch. The majority of their battles were against Dragons and circuits. Even when they were fighting in Desitian controlled areas, they would go out of their way to destroy Dragons and circuits. They were the only Pack to take a circuit-controlled moon on Daritock, cutting them from having any single isolated region in the planetary system.

They would weaken areas and lose them, often to Lion or Bear Sleuth, in order to take other areas from the Cyborgs and circuits. There was a deep-seated hatred there, but the twins had not been able to discover why. It seemed the only sentient circuits they allowed in their ranks were androids, from what the operators were able to tell them.

The reviews were usually interesting but designed to teach the students that even if you were capable of always winning, you could still improve. When they got to Second and Third Echelon, it would be part of their general studies to go through battles they participated in and review them in front of others.

"Don't settle for winning when you can win perfectly," was the constant saying of the instructors on the reviews.

A few battles were shown as perfect wins with minimal damage and losses. Wolf never had one. Warriors had the most, and the ones that performed them were Blue Blood line tied back to Murchadh or one of the other big names that started the Packs. Even though few were shown, the schools wanted the students to know it was possible to accomplish.

The exercise room and library were usually frequented by those that didn't spend too much time in visual study of battles. Very few of the viewing room regulars went to the weight room and library for extra personal training regularly. Cardio and physical conditioning was held first thing in the morning for all the students, and again with several other classes depending on what was to be covered that day.

All aspects of life were graded by the school. It was all evaluated and considered what would be best for the students before the students even knew the actions were being taken to guide them to where they would fulfill their natural talents best. With so much depending on placement for both the Pack and the Abas pilot, the decisions had to be perfect. It was the reason no pilot was locked in until after the End Games.

The End Game of Varanasi was the final test for all the graduating warriors. Packs would face off in a month-long, seven-sided engagement to see how the students performed. It ranked each pilot in with the rest of the schools of the pack. The more warriors demonstrated effectively from their specific training, the higher Honor Rating they earned. If pilots earned high enough rating points, they could shift an entire class. If an Abas pilot didn't perform up to par, then they too could be shifted down into a different style of warrior based on their specialty.

The Masters of each school rated on their areas of specialty and ranked all the members that had taken their classes in the third echelons. It was only based on students that had entered the class in the third echelon, which also inspired students to take specific classes of talents and interest.

The End Game of Daritock was to be the real

battle test where the students faced off in a two-week battle scenario. It was supposed to be a purification of battle to rule out any weeds that might have slipped through. It was the level of the final step to true acceptance as a member of the Pack.

Some rumors said it was too much to end your training on. It took too much to see so many die around you just to prove one school was the best. They said the end product might be one of the best warriors, but they lacked parts of life. They also said it was likely they wouldn't play well with others.

The dark-haired twins didn't believe them anyway, since it wasn't on the tablet, but was very curious about the End Games. So far the brothers hadn't been able to crack the code to get into the plans for one. Still, being only seven years old, they figured they had time.

Some said the End Games of Daritock did not make warriors but barbarians. Perfectly trained barbarians that had no other life then to fight and win. If they left a village destroyed behind them, they wouldn't turn around to look at the smoke rising; just look forward to the next battle like some kind of Tutevibian. Of course, those who were willing to say it aloud never made the mistake of saying it in front of one of the alumni, from what the operators told the twins.

CHAPTER 2

NEW TOOLS

The twins started to stand out to their instructors before the end of their first year of the second step of the First Echelon. Normally, senior staff members did not come down to look at those that hadn't even been given access to an Abas. They felt the real judgment didn't come until they were completed by the larger battle armors. Yet, these two seemed to draw them in like flies to honey.

If they could be taken to start their masters now, half the staff would have been in battles over who would be their instructors. The other half seemed to be planning on how to take the twins out before the twins had proven the instructors insufficient by comparison. It wasn't that they didn't want them, but there was other recognition given when defeating students who showed extreme talents like they had. In some circles, those were seen has higher distinctions then training them to be the best before they were defeated.

Every student was required to take Military History, Basic Abas Strategy and Operations, Basic Weapon Handling, Basic Blade Handling, Basic Survival Techniques, Language, Reading and Comprehension, Mathematics, History of the Packs, Life Science and Anatomy with First Aid Applications, Basic Security Engaging and Disengaging, as well as Battle Honors and Ceremonies. They tied in top position in every class. They were already three years ahead of their training requirements as well. In some of the advanced classes, they outscored everyone, including all their predecessors of the Warrior Schools of Varanasi in classes that were comparable to these without input or help from the instructors.

"Sir, they seem unnatural. Are we sure they were Red Born? Are we even sure they are not some type of child Cyborg? No one has ever been able to reach such levels in every subject before," Falstar asked the three-dimensional image of his father's head.

"Do you believe they are Cyborgs, Falstar? Wouldn't you know better than most? You, after all, have several contacts within their ranks.

"No one knows what they are. All we are sure of is their linage and performances in the Pack School now. The parents openly admitted that they were Red Born at the trial. It was accepted there. They would not have had access to Triscifield of any Pack to allow them to perform a cleansing. And you know we checked every child coming into the school to ensure they were pure human.

"The DNA screening was obviously erased to hide the genetic links, but some parties know the truth. They are twins, as much as they do not resemble each other. Blue Blood Abas pilots who develop as twins are forced to absorb the other as soon as it is detected by the breeders during cell development. There are those that are not detected or refuse to absorb one another of course. The parents can also choose not to go along with the merger. It is on this that I would say they are not Blue Blood," Headmaster Lodestar answered his son.

"They are human, red borne children of natural genealogy. Consider what their parents were capable of. Consider especially the mother. Then consider what you have done to push them already. They are driven to succeed. That was your plan, right?"

It was a well-known fact, but having it pointed out was a way of showing Falstar he must take the time to consider everything. What made these two different?

What makes them different is their parents blood lines and the fact the parents were traitors. If they weren't and the children were known about, they would be doted on. I still believe the children need to be monitored closer, but my father is right. The DNA of those blood lines are superior. Their ability to learn quickly has been seen in other children. It's rare, but the genes have been seen across multiple caste. Is any of this special or is it that I am being blinded by what I know of them?

"When you decided to send them to my school, you told me they were not special and not to treat them any different than any of the other students here. But now they—"

The Headmaster cut his son off before he put more on the table than Lodestar wanted to talk about.

"No, they are special, if for no more reason then where they came from. You were asked not to treat them any more special than a normal student and to prepare them for war. You are more than capable of testing them to the best of their abilities.

"Let them continue on the path their talent sets for them. Treat them as you would any that had come to your school where you did not find anything special in their past, but they show a great talent. Please keep me informed."

"Have you seen what they have requested for expertise? It was in my last package about them. And they have not reached a level of being selected yet. Their scores have reached the level for them to be selected, way beyond any before. I would like to know what your opinion on this is."

The statement was made in a voice that could have almost been seen as disrespectful, but Lodestar recognized the emotions his son had failed to keep out. The twins were surpassing every previous student to walk through these schools. Most this capable would have been sent through the other schools to keep them in the Packs.

It was unnatural at best. If he had not known their

past, he would have been looking into it deeper. He wanted to know why they had been selected to come here. Instead he was questioning his father, but not expecting satisfying answers.

If it were any other set of students, I would have requested them to be sent back to the other schools. That was the plan, but we have never had to do it. It would throw off the experiments anyway.

Lodestar expected as much from his son. It was his nature to question those who were not of the proper birthright, as it was for all those born Blue. Lodestar also knew that his son was capable of training the boys to reach their full potential. If his son had not been Blue Blood Born, his father would not have been able to ask him to take the mission that he so willingly accepted at an age that he couldn't fully understand it.

The mission that drove us apart for me to accomplish one more thing before my time ended. Was the price worth it? Will I find out? So many games. So much time spent to bring about the rebirth? Did we do it right? Was it the right time? There is no more time, Lodestar thought through it all, yet again.

"Yes, a remarkable schedule of talents, if I do say so," Lodestar finally answered as his eyes rose from the message at the bottom of his head. "They are taking more than the norm, and even beyond those who are desperately trying to prove themselves worthy of higher Abas status than their parents. I must say that it is up to you to decide if they can handle it. If they can't, then it would show their Red Borne failures."

"They are Red Born," Falstar added in a defeated voice, having to admit that the best students he had ever seen went against the ideals he had held onto for so long.

There was a census among the Triscifield that spoke of the need to keep Red Borne Children within all lines of the Pack for growth and renewal. Was this the final product of uncontrolled gene manipulation?

Falstar knew of secrets that were not discussed as well. Plans of the cyborgs to end agreements that dated back to the beginning of the Packs. Most believed it completed before the death of the parents. If the cybernetic and circuit minds of the council had not been modified, more would know the truth. But Falstar did not risk discussing that with anyone.

"Of course, they can't handle it. I doubt even the best Blue Blood Abas Pilots could handle the load and still be competitive. Maybe an Elite, but the couple that I have been able to rear through the school didn't even take this type of training load.

"Let's say for argument sake, I authorize the workload and they collapse under the strain of it. What could have been two of the best warriors to leave these schools end up dead because they couldn't handle the overloaded stress I authorized."

"You did not say, Red Borne this time. Do you think of them as more than just their birth right?"

"Do not change the subject. We can discuss this later if you wish. I have heard the speeches often enough, but I want to know your honest opinion on this."

"I would take the blame of the authorization if I thought you would let me, but you would no more allow this then to allow me to just win in the End Games. With this said, and meant with all honor to your name, I would create a way for you to protect them while you authorize it and let them be challenged.

"Even you want to know if they can do it. You want to push them even harder than this because deep inside you have faith in them. Follow your human heart and mind.

"Watch them, as you already are. You know the signs. They can't hide them from you.

"What it comes to after that," Lodestar continued not giving Falstar a chance to defend his position on the subject, "is the authorization with stipulations. The stipulations can be put into place to protect you and them. They give you a free hand in driving their training to levels to whatever you think will make them reach their full potential. Nothing more than you did with Ayandra, and she became an Elite."

Falstar knew that his father was trying to challenge him to test the twins and push them as hard as he could. To accept would be to take his father's mission again. In his mind, he put his head in his hands to hold it together while it pounded with the weight of the decision. On the outside he calmed himself to give no more away then was humanly possible to defend.

"I'd also like to ask you why they feel they would have to prove themselves if they don't know where they came from. They were raised in the birthing cells until they came to awareness. Being surrounded by Blue Bloods might have motivated them to the point of self-destruction. Even with the stipulations, I do not wish to have their failures over my head."

"There are Red Borns who stay there too. When both parents are dead or in battle ranks or deployed. They, the twins and the orphaned Red Borns, did not have the stories or the visitors like most Blue Bloods. What stories could a scout really tell?"

Lodestar looked deep into his son's eyes as he asked the question. It wasn't often that he referred to the lighter ranks being less than the heavy ranks. It was against his nature, but if Falstar had been willing to accept cracks in his theory then his father was returning the favor and showing his own weakened foundation.

"It is more common a battle buddy from some skirmish will tell of them being sacrificed for the greater good. Saying the Scout born Blue Blood will be created due to the great remembrance, so your life means even less due to a better replacement being created in the aftermath of their death. Not something you want to tell a child that may one day out rank you and will remember your words as if they were the gospel of the sleeping gods.

"Would you want to lie to someone who could order your death at any time after they realized the truth? No, they probably don't know where they came from. Because they do not know, they are going to push themselves until they find their limits, collapse or kill themselves, as you indicated.

"They are going to push the limits as far as they can. It is how they hope to find the secrets of their parents and their blood lines. This you can tell, because they are taking all the potential histories to study. They are trying to find the connection to the past.

"I say this is not the time to ere on the side of caution. I would suggest you just let them find their limits and stop them before it becomes too much. When the day ends, I have faith that you will be able to forge them into the greatest warriors they could be. After all, no one else seems to have the talent that you do in bring the best of those you choose to concentrate on out better."

"We don't even know their true story. All we know is they were born after the Crusader Olympia. We start preparing by gathering information. Now these *children* are in our schools, learning our battle tactics, trying to learn everything they possibly can. Why? For Wolf Pack?

"The speed at which they learn would make them more likely to be Cyborgs. What if their parents were converted and then brought these *children* to spy on our kind? It is all unknown! They are too perfect to be Red Born, and they are not Blue Blood. Explain what they really are! You have the answers!"

"I have none that I can give you," Lodestar answered with a great sorrow in his voice.

Falstar didn't know what to say to his reaction or that his father had told him a direct truth that gave him more answers then Falstar could have ever hoped for. It appeared the twins were not the only ones that might crack under the pressure of getting them to reach their highest potential. Falstar tucked the thought away for a second.

"I heard you got your tech child Abas pilot entered last year. Who died?" Falstar questioned his father.

He was not ready to answer what side he was leaning toward in front of his father. The truth was, even if he wasn't willing to admit it, the challenge of pushing them was enough for him to agree to the call.

Others had to be notified before he could decide the best action. These twins had more attention than any other student in any of the schools. That was saying something, considering what was going on in Varanasi currently.

"It was a starting Third Echelon Heavy Sentinel who tried to modify some of his own systems. He crossed his life support lines, and they shorted out. There was no chance of saving him in the poison swamp atmosphere of sermonic quarter. The stupid are born to die."

Falstar added, "Isn't everyone?" as Lodestar continued with "I am glad that we eliminated this one before he took others with him."

"A member in Second-Echelon took a promotion

for moving up, which caused a domino down the line. It seemed several had been waiting for him to kill himself so they could take an advancement in graduating time. There's a group of students I'll have to watch that seem to be up to something. Might involve Giga Plexus."

Falstar shook his head. He didn't agree with his father's plan on this, but it was important to figure out how deep the rot went.

The coldness in Lodestar's voice said the student was probably more than just stupid, as well. Falstar saw the reports. He knew the son belonged to one of the council members. He was pushed into a Heavy Sentinel level because of his genes, and the council would not let him go down to a level where he would be able to truly hold a good advantage for the pack.

It could have been as much suicide from the pressure of not really living up to expectations or ability as it was stupidity. Such is earned when a family does not wait to put the name on a child. The stupidity did not rest with just the student.

And it is possible he was not as stupid, but someone wanted him to look that way. It wouldn't be the first time Pack members did what was necessary.

"As for the tech Abas, she performs quite well. Her scoring is high enough to start her second term at the same time as those of her age group. We were able to get her in at the beginning of this cycle when the Abas pilot went into medical watch. We didn't expect him to make it, so we went ahead and let her get in.

"Fortunately for us, our predictions were correct in assumption. He attempted to fight for survival, but unfortunately, he wasn't strong enough to hold on. Shame. If he was allowed to struggle at the lower levels instead of being given advantages, he may have learned how to fight to survive," Lodestar added, again, not sounding sincere. "The irony of it is quite fascinating. I will have to write about it."

"I see. Congratulations, by the way. I thought I would have you this year in the End Games, but you always seem to know how I am going to play my students. I should try something different next year."

"I hope that you are not disappointed. Your students did improve best overall. We just came out on top in the end."

Lodestar wanted to tell his son where he was making his mistakes, but he himself made plenty this year to still learn from.

Remove the board from your eye before you attempt to pull the splinter from your brother's. In my case, I would want to put the board up side my brother's head, but that is a different issue, Lodestar thought internally.

"Yes, your people seem to be able to dig deep in the end and really make it count. It was impressive to watch them pull it out. When will the new protocols come into effect? I look forward to seeing what will come about from them, when it is less head-to-head and truer to life, as they say."

"I don't mind talking about this, but I wouldn't mind talking about something besides work. What do you say?"

"Sure. Your latest speech acceptable?" Falstar asked, knowing that it was skimming the work area.

"Yes, that is. I am a little surprised to hear you address it now."

"Now is the perfect time to address it with the possible proof of the pudding in my school. I don't know if it will come about the way you think, but I believe you might be right about the loss of some talents in the manipulation of DNA. It should be limited and allowed to develop freely in the Blue Blood's next generation.

"The more you see the manipulation, the greater the loss of personality. It is like a fresh android that hasn't learned to act human," Falstar started with the points that he agreed with his father.

It was polite to start with what he agreed with. Falstar and Lodestar continued to chat for an hour before they finally said their friendly good-byes and promised to continue the argument at a later time. Falstar made many arguable points that were not brought up yet. He did agree with his father on other points though. More with the twins acting as proof.

The first conversation kept coming back to Falstar. He continued to think it out in his head. He couldn't understand how two Red Borne had done so well. There were students who scores were close in Canine

Prime and Gray Wolf Prime. Certainly not in every class, though.

The students often showed a unique talent, or a few unique talents isolated in one area. It was developing those talents with complimenting talents based on the way they honed their skills that made Falstar so good. Reading the way they trained and producing a schedule that made their mind work to perfection.

How do you train students to use their minds around specific talents when they don't have specific talents? They are surpassing in every area. Books, physical, mental challenges, specialties. This would not only be a great challenge for them, but for me to develop a way to train them to be their best.

There is a way. I haven't ever used it, but it might work. What would be the result though? You don't make elite warriors with soft hands and easy lives.

Falstar cut a small smile at the thought. One master instructed him not to allow them to advance. The other side was trying to push them to the edge. It was time to test his newest theory.

I wonder what it would take to make the perfect warrior. The pain would be . . . excruciating for both of us. The risk tremendous, especially if I fail. I'm willing. Are one of you able?

All Falstar knew about the parents had impressed him, but neither of them was listed Red Borne. They came from families who set the precedence in Wolf Pack. When they disappeared, their families removed them from the genealogical graphs. Their names removed from the books. No record of their existence would ever be found again. The DNA removed from the records, never to be used. A complete purge of the stain.

No record, but the blood line continues. Did I fail in not seeing where they came from originally? Could he be right in that Blue Bloods alternating into Red Borne would create a cleaner transition of talent?

I forgot to look at where the parents had come from and marking the DNA because they were traitors. But I can follow the line to find the mixes. I know where I am going, and I know where to start. The beginning.

That is where my father and I differ. He remembers them as where the lines originally came from as much as where these children came from. I blinded myself at the traitorous parents and the failures they came to be and forgot the blood lines they did carry before.

How do you make the best better? How do you make the best better than they themselves can accomplish on their own when they accomplish more than any alone? What tools do you use when the normal tools aren't good enough?

Yes. That will be the best way. It's time to make new tools!

CHAPTER 3

ACCEPTANCE

For the twins the first tiers of their education skipped by in an isolated existence. No man may be an island amongst themselves, but they continued to be an island of only two. Their scores kept them out of the required extra training. Unlike many others who were not required to go, they chose to continue their extra training on their own.

Their instructors didn't mind them out of class. At times they were disruptive if not left alone. If left alone, then other students seemed to wonder why they were allowed to ignore the instructions and not participate directly in class activities. Class leaders had also given up on trying to direct them. It was less painful.

Rumors of them being Cyborgs who were testing against the Humans helped to isolate them more. At some points in time, they almost thought it might be a secret they didn't know either but having emotions and lacking a few of the other basic features told them they were in no way machine.

Nite, the dark-haired twin, felt a little disappointed, thinking he could become more with his Abas that way. Mike felt as if they didn't need it to become more. They just needed their Abas to start training with them.

When asked a question, the twins answered exactly what was asked. If an instructor tried to grill them, they could take the instructors to levels the instructors themselves didn't understand. Then they would ask questions the instructors were unable to answer. It took a few of the instructors by surprise and requested the twins to be moved to advanced classes. The Headmaster grudgingly approved them, but only to save face of the instructor with the other students.

During their physical training, when paired against other students, they would attack with perfect movements. It was a one-sided dance of perfection ending with the other student being carried out. One instructor through they would take it easy on females or smaller class members they had defended before. They were mistaken.

No instructor would challenge them either. Especially after they cleaned up what was left from the cyborg. The taller twin, with white hair used a small explosive triggered by the cyborgs circuits to blow its human arm clean off. The cyborg had hurt a smaller female student just before issuing the challenge, but it wasn't permanent. More embarrassing.

When the cyborg asked for a volunteer, expecting to see no one step up, Mike did. The cyborg told him to bring anything he wanted to the fight. As usual, he said nothing. No one knew he collected the weapon or why he had it. The instructors didn't ask either.

When the instructors put them against each other, every punch between them was thrown, blocked, countered, reversed, countered again, and reversed again until there was no clear winner. The twins would just stop and bow to each other. Sometimes they would just shift through stances, never making a move forward. Then stop and bow and walk away.

Watching the videos in slow progression didn't help them find a weakness to exploit either. They would change styles to counter the other to have the twin counter again with a different style. Some styles the instructors couldn't even recognize. Others were not taught in Wolf.

Some students didn't believe the twins were even brothers. Friendships like these were often developed in the first years and continued into the Pack. Wolf Pack encouraged such unity and tried to place groups who were very productive together within the Pack. At the same time, they separated groups who got into trouble.

The twins seem to be the latter, yet nothing was done to separate them either. No one seemed to want to have them apart anyway. Then there was no alternative, but to face them against someone.

Students were already refusing, making instructors the last option.

Nite, who was thought to be the oldest, had black hair, normally slicked back and parted down the middle with the look of two crashing waves meeting at the center of his forehead. He kept it between 4" and 6" long on top and tapered on the sides to a short and neat style. His eyebrows sat low and shadowed his deep-set hazel eyes. The rare occasion when he smiled looked more malicious than happy. For some, his mere presence drove spikes of ice into their hearts.

His eight-year-old body was already showing signs of his wide shoulders and a lower balance position. He kept a lean, flexible look of perfection while being of shorter and stockier build, like an inverted triangle. His eyes burned with a fire, not of passion but of pure war and death. Those willing to meet them remembered one thing when they looked away. Never again, look into those eyes if he was your opponent.

Mike, was like a mirror of his brother. His eyes were stone in both color and feelings instead of colorful feeling. Mike slim but athletic to his brother's wider build. Nite seemed to be just short of average for their age group. Mike was on the taller side. Some believed he also had less personality than Nite.

Mike never smiled or showed any expression. It was the same face always. He barely spoke in front of anyone. When he did, it sent tingles down the students' backs as if they heard death calling their name from across the room in nothing but a whisper.

Some of the instructors were infected by it as well. They would either try to call on him more often until they realized they could not build an immunity to it, or they never called on him again where he had to vocalize his answer.

More often he sent answers to the instructors by messaging them. Recently, it seemed, the twins learned to change the display screen controlled by the instructors. The first instructor to have this happen to them tried to figure out what they had done wrong and change it back before they realized it wasn't them.

Mike looked down at his brother and realized that today they had reached their eighth cycle after birth. It was 674.3.14. He wondered if his brother had realized this, or even cared that it was today. The operators who watched over them would have something special for them in their racks toward the end of the night. They always got them things they normally couldn't get access to.

They had the barracks to themselves while everyone else attended extra studies to prepare for getting selected for Abas sizing. Mike looked at the time and became disappointed. The peace they were enjoying was about to end.

With the students came the noise. There would be no more relaxing until the others went to sleep. Mike never thought to why people bothered him, but most did by mere presents. It was one of the reasons for feeling the need of seclusion against Nite's thoughts of reaching out and manipulating situations.

Where Mike mastered moving through the shadows, Nite mastered moving in the open and appearing invisible. Some students said he could hide while standing directly in front of you. When Mike hid, it was as if he bent shadows lights around him. You would not be able to see where he was when you looked at him, but then your eyes would move away, and he would appear when you looked back.

Nite and Mike slept across from each other on the bottom of a six-person cubical. Two girls of no particular interest slept above Nite. A third female shifted back into their cubicle a few months earlier. She had been forced to move out by a guy that thought they were higher ranking. He hoped living near the twins would help him get closer to them.

Mike seemed to disagree. It took very little to convince them. She slept directly above Mike again. Even after the one left, Mike did not allow anyone to move in long, although many tried. Not that the occupants knew it was Mike.

They would find their rack had a sudden short, destroying their personal equipment. Or bugs crawling throughout it, or it was drenched in some liquid or worse, covered in itching powder. Pranks were common, and that rack seemed to be cursed. None of the plagues bothered the others in the cubical.

Mike also didn't take ask the female directly to move back in. Instead, he just attacked whoever thought it was a good idea. Her other rack was near other friends, catty corner to their cubical to the left.

It was almost never pranked. She had a reputation for paying people back way worse than she received. Like the rest of them, she claimed she didn't do it.

Once she moved back, the curse seemed to be broken. Whether it was the berthing operators that provided the hints, or that the last person that was told to move in there doubled up with someone else, Nite wasn't sure. It might have been one of the students that figured it out, since her number wasn't there when they left, and when they returned it had been. The one that refused to move was in her old rack.

Then it appeared Mike wasn't happy with that either. He no longer seemed to be pranking the rack. Just complaining about the noise. He believed the three females were attempting to master the art of driving people insane with obscene noises. Noises ordinarily referred to as vocal conversation or talking.

He did not work to remove the females from around them. And their cubical area, other than the cursed rack, had been off limits from pranks. It said something must be worth keeping the cacophony around. The other two females were part of the group the girl spent time together with.

The one above him was the one he complained the most about. Especially after she returned. Nite felt the way he complained about her talking wasn't that she was talking, but that she was not talking to him.

Anytime she seemed to be at his rack, Mike would look up from his reading and his attempts to look like he was hiding but still allowing her to see him.

Nite had seen his brother's attention change when she spoke as well, and it was not a face of annoyance.

Nite admitted her insight was beyond the other two when she allowed it to slip out, but she never ventured far from the cubicle without at least two friends in tow. They even traveled in packs to the facilities together. It was as if there was a conspiracy to never allow Mike the opportunity to talk to her alone. A master of hiding and luring, yet he couldn't get this single female alone for a moment.

Nite used this as a teasing point for his brother of how Mike would start talking, giggling, and caring about what others thought. Then he would get carried off in the crowds and lost as an individual. By the time he finally made it back to Nite, he too would be one of "them".

As often as Nite teased his brother, he never directly attached Mike's attention for the one girl. Nite tried to do the opposite but was often warned against interference from Mike. He was not fearful of what his brother would do, but more just respected his wishes.

The male slept in the sixth spot was almost as quiet as Mike. When he did choose to speak to one of the girls, he would ridicule them in a direct, corrective way. Destined to be a scout because he was a fifth year, he tried to prove he was above his locked in station. He acted as if he was born of some higher gene, like a Blue Blood. It was such a strong cleansing, he was promoted back up to Abas. Although he never said directly he was Blue Blood.

Nite assumed he liked the girl as well. She was small, amber skinned with monolid eyes and flat black hair. He was usually right in his corrections of her, but he made as many mistakes.

Nite could have removed him, but that just meant someone else would be moved in. The females chewed him out one evening, when the other girl cried. At least that seemed to have some effect on him.

Nite considered providing small hints to start turning him toward being as good as he claimed he was. For Nite, it would start off small with anonymous tips to see if he would listen and try to get better. If he did, training him from afar would be something to play with to help Nite pass the time. Might be an opening that Mike could use as well.

His name was Shawn Hati. Like his surname's origin, he was a Moon Chaser. He slept his days away when not in class. Instead, he spent the long hours of night training. His flexibility and quiet movements ensured he would rate counter assassin. He was extremely talented with small arms, knives, and locks. During the room sweeps, fort seizure, head-to-head team drills, and security movements, Shawn continued to exceed past most of the other students.

This was expected from a name like Hati. The Moon Chasers were an Elite Soldier Team for decades and were all Superlative Nano-Suit Warriors. The name *Moon Chasers* was given to the special units of Wolf due to the Hati bloodline showing such a talent, but Shawn knew that it was better to be a low-level Abas pilot than a top-level Moon Chaser.

After all, the Moon Chasers never won a Full Battle Set against the Abas pilots. No other army regiment had. The Moon Chasers and those like them, were supposed to be the best of the best for their field, but the best of all was the Abas.

He was scrawny and tall for his age. Even with spaghetti-like appendages, he was extremely strong, quick, and resilient. Inside the virtual Abas, he seemed to lock up and lose the funny confidence that had made him so perfect in all the other trainings. In his mind, he was a light scout, and a light scout he would always be.

The females returned to their racks to gather what Nite thought numbered close to a hundred hygiene items that they carried to the showers. Afraid to ask what the stuff was for he kept his eyes locked on *World Battle Tactics*. The book was describing battle patterns for space engagements to planetary tactics used by Pack Navies. The videos in the book were extremely helpful to understand the actual tactics being used. It also helped him determine how to counter them.

Mike just finished making his rack by pinning and tying the sheets to the mattress. He had decided it was tight enough to keep them smooth, but he needed to check if it would hold after he was in it and the isles were clear.

He disappeared into his cubbyhole of a bed and rolled frantically as if he was having a seizure. Once satisfied he had caused equal destruction to four Tutevibians trying to jump him in the middle of the night, he rolled back out to check the tightness.

His girl was suddenly standing in the aisle between the racks and was looking at him, almost nervously. Nite gave her a couple pointers on moving in the open. She must have taken them for Mike not to notice her approaching.

"Do you think that we could go over those . . . uhm . . . things that we discussed in blade training this morning?"

Nite's eyes wondered around. He couldn't detect the other two girls. He assumed they vanished toward the showers, but she seemed to be waiting for Mike to stop his horizontal rack jig. Once the sound of destruction had stopped, she came back into the isle, hoping to surprise him, Nite was sure.

Mike's attention was drawn to her voice. He didn't seem to be able to react to the question she was asking out of complete shock of her being there and talking to him. He couldn't even hold the look of confusion off his face until Nite gave the sound of clearing his throat to stir his brother back into the moment.

With the swiftness of the wind, Mike pulled his knife; the point was in the side of her neck but had not broken the skin. She took a deep breath and held her spot, not sure of why he had suddenly attacked and what had stopped the killing move.

"Put your hand over his thumb. Roll it away from your neck. At the same time, move your head to the opposite direction. Once your head is clear to turn back, look at your attacker. Then take the palm of your other hand and jam it toward his nose. As long as the strike hits the face, you should be able to get the separation. That is when you snap the arm using the straggle technique. Do it now."

Nite answered for Mike as he slid his rack curtains a little more open. He acted as if he was still reading his book. Mike would stop her if she did something wrong. Since he had been paying particular interest in her performance earlier, he knew she had the move down pat.

The girl looked at Mike, and then dropped her eyes down toward Nite's voice. Nite hadn't taken his eyes from his book and yet knew exactly what was happening between her and his brother.

Student 9824651, the girl, had not really thought of the other boy being in there.

This is the first chance I have really had to get him alone and see if he would speak to me. I can't stop now, just because I didn't notice you were still here. I will have my rock, even if I must go through you!

She thought of him like granite, due to the color of his eyes. They were as inviting as a rough rock that was warmed by the sun, or still cool on a hot day. A rock could be very comfortable place to sit and enjoy a day of study or rest if you knew the edges.

She started through the motions like the gruff

voice commanded. When she went for the final strike, she had forgotten to hold back and make it look like she had made a mistake. He easily dodged her best palm punch, leaving her pressed close against his body facing away from him. Instead of tensing, she suddenly felt relaxed and safe.

She took a deep breath, as if she would absorb every moment of this memory forever. A little giggle was followed by a look up at the guy she had loved from a distance for so long.

He has the most beautiful eyes I have ever seen! Sparkling like diamonds, but only for me.

The thought was quiet, but her heart raced even more when he finally allowed his eyes to meet hers full on.

Nite looked up at Mike in surprise. The role he had dawned had offered her several attack points from this position and limited his. It was a bad move, but it was the only one that would put her this close to him. He was quite interested in the reaction that his brother would give the girl once she went for a move. He had not expected him to give her so many openings.

Instead she giggled at him. That was a strike neither of the had a defense for. Nite had never read a counter for the giggles move.

Maybe it's an advanced tactic. It took both of us out of our game. Huh. How did that work? Would it only work for a female? Do women use it often when they are older? How would you counter it?

Mike looked down at her, not him. A new look of confusion shadowed Mike's face as he wondered what he should do next. Nite, of course, was no help. He rolled his back to them and went back to his book. Privacy was the best he could or would offer for his brother.

"My name is Mike."

His voice was strained, but he spoke with his normal air of confidence and superiority.

The same way Nite did whenever he was talking to someone for him. Nite always used that voice when talking for his brother, and for the first time, Mike was using it to talk for himself. It was not the normal death rattle that he gave others when they forced an answer from his lungs. That he did out of pure pleasure for the reaction. Yet, this seemed right, like it would be his natural voice if he ever used it with others.

"I . . . Selina," she said as her young body seemed to be finding it hard to think or speak.

The shared moment seemed to last hours, but Nite couldn't have counted the seconds between. He did consider the shock of hearing both give their real names. It wasn't student names.

Some passed their given names out like candy to those they considered friends, very few used them openly. Most either used family names or some version of their student number. No one gave it on the first real conversation you had with someone. And

Mike, never. They barely referred to each other by the names the Androids said came from their parents.

If the parents were dead before you were born, then it fell to the family. If the family didn't want to claim you, then it fell to a circuit. Depending on the honors you earned in school, people being allowed to refer to you by your given name was a great honor or disrespect.

Nite couldn't help but interrupt the little privacy he had given them. The realization of what they had done was just too much for him to consider without visual aid. Yet, even looking out, he couldn't believe the level of comfort both seemed to have for each other.

Still in his arms, she and he were carrying on a conversation. A full-blown conversation Nite chose to block from his ears, yet he was talking to someone else. The voice was still the one that Nite had used for him, but he figured that was because the girl had not given him enough to give her his own voice.

Selina's long dirty blond hair danced around the center of her back in a braid. Her eyes were very clear, but dark copper brown. Selina had long eyelashes that seemed to tickle her eyebrows. She had a softness in her round face and warm ivory skin, although Nite could tell that when she was older, it would look more triangle and beautiful in an innocent, elfish sort of way.

Nite was more interested in his brother's reaction, who was now blushing and acting nervous. Something

Nite considered a little unbecoming of someone who trained so hard to hide emotions. He hoped he would never meet a female that made him act as stupid as his twin looked now.

It was not that he didn't like looking at females like some of the boys. It was he didn't want to act like that when one came up to him. He wanted to continue to be confident, blocking out the true emotions and thoughts from his face and showing only a mirror of what was being given, or a proper response. There was no need to give someone so much information about his thoughts as his brother was giving the room now. Nite knew when his day came, he just might be as goofy as his younger brother was now.

Mike and Selina had stayed up for hours talking. The conversation was more Selina talking and Mike nodding and writing things down for her or showing her with hand gestures the twins designed for simple conversations.

He had stopped the ludicrous expressions and went back to blank after meeting Nite's angry eyes when they broke apart. The angry eyes were because Mike was acting the idiot while people were in the barracks with them. Embarrassed more by his brother catching him than by the actions themselves, he stopped immediately.

Nite kept rolling over and looking up to find the two still conversating. He was surprised people who were raised together only shortly after birth would have so much to talk about. She was still doing most of the talking.

Nite didn't understand why they had so much to talk about. Yet, he respected his brother's privacy. He let the bits of conversation drift in one ear and out the next until he found sleep again. Mike was not going to be happy when he was tired during their training session later that night.

CHAPTER 4

GAINS

Nite finally awoke to silence with the two talkers in their respected beds. It was 0230, and time for the twins' morning workout. Neither of them had to set a wake up to get up. They just did.

Nite looked at his brother's rack and decided to leave his brother until he returned. It was a big step for Mike. If Mike didn't wake up automatically, Nite would not interrupt him. The events of last night seemed more important than a morning workout. One practice would hardly mean anything in the long run anyway.

Nite snuck into the simulation room and hooked himself up. They were allowed to practice anytime they wanted, but they had to record their sessions. It wasn't that they had a choice; you had to log into the profile provided. It did all the tracking and grading.

The first echelon was limited to what they could train in. None were allowed to move out of Scout designs. They were told it was too early and too dangerous for them to be experimenting. Failures at this stage could cause mental blocks. Mental blocks would hold them back from reaching their full potential.

Nite hated having to record every move he made. The brothers created two new profiles and backdated their entry date to give them full access. The data of the profiles were kept on private data server they built from parts they took from the advanced training sections and hidden in the unmarked areas.

They were now given the freedom to fight and practice any way they wanted. The names were never given room for saving information attached to them on the actual server. No one would be able to access the save crystal, so the data wouldn't be retrievable. Instead, it reported being saved to a different crystal, where the light information would be lost.

Nite and Mike would normally go through advanced training scenarios on third day mornings. Most of the time, they took a Canis Lupus out; or when they really wanted to test themselves against the undefeatable, they went with the Canis Lycaon designs. This time, since Nite was alone, he selected the Canis Dirus for the first time. He wasn't sure if they would ever let him pilot one of these beasts. Almost no one earned an Elite within the schools. In this hacked simulation, he could do what he wanted, though. It didn't matter what the school thought about it.

Nite loaded up the system for two team battles and went to work. He reached his fifth scenario; his team was supposed to tag the enemy drop ship for the Star Fighters before the drop ship could lift off.

They did not have solar support so if it was able to break atmosphere, it would escape with the stolen data. The scenario was set up for an eight to ten Abas section, but Nite faced them with one light scout he was using to spotting and tagging and the Dire Wolf.

Just before he reached his first radar contact; an Abas, the alarm sounded, signaling someone else joining in on his team. He couldn't tell who had come in, but he was sure it wasn't Mike. It just didn't feel like a Mike entry.

The pilot paused the scenario, so he could come to Nite's wing position. Nite still hadn't turned on his radar, a tactic he used to cover his movements, so he had to visually spot the Abas coming up on his side.

The closest the Abas looked to be a Canis Lycaon configuration with an odd coloring in the cover design. Instead of a fur look, or ghillie suit style, it looked like black feathers and yellow eyes. It even seemed to have a beak instead of a muzzle, but everything else, body frame, weapon style, leg placement all spoke of Wolf. It seemed so wrong and so right at the same time.

"Who's trying for the grand prize?" the pilot suddenly called over the com lines.

"Grand prize? Oh, the Canis Dirus. I am just trying to see how I fit in an Elite. I didn't think it would even accept me."

Honestly, Nite had no doubt in his mind. Even if this hadn't been a scenario, the Abas felt like home to him. Nothing had the same feeling of home as this one.

"Dire Wolf! It is called a Dire Wolf. Mine is called a Timber Wolf, although its design is modified to meet my naming. The Raven Wolf. Unfortunately, it died a long time ago. About eleven years now."

That was around the Crusader Olympia, Six-Sixty-three. Before I was born.

"That is the way you refer to them on the battlefield, by the way. They like those names better than the proper names the cyborgs and circuits try to give them. Most people in the Third Echelon have learned that."

He read the profile. He thinks I'm older than I am. Why is he in here?

"You sound young, a little too young to be in this scenario. Who are you?"

"I'm Student 1321456, First Echelon."

Nite responded as he would in any class. It was habit. Nite might have hacked the system, but he wouldn't lie about what he was doing. Besides, if they hacked it once, they could do it again.

"FIRST TERM! You shouldn't even be able to handle a Dire Wolf, much less live through a level 12 scenario alone without more supplies than your three trucks can give you. Which programmed Abas are you using for your team? No one else is registered other than the one light scout for this mission. Is there a second pilot in the cockpit with you? Are you using the virtual training aid?"

"I didn't program any group Abas to fight with me, just a scout. I wanted to face the scenario alone. My scout was maintaining the mark, so I could fight the ground forces. This is the first time I have done the scenario alone," Nite again slipped, but he figured he would cover it by keeping talking.

"And with all due respect, I think that the VTA is worthless and stupid. You are not going to be able to pause in the middle of live battle, and there isn't going to be someone there telling you how to fight every step of the way either."

Nite changed to a mockingly childish female voice.

"'Fire your large lasers on the marked target. See how it has successfully removed the armor covering the rear of the engine. Now you have a better shot at the critical components in the center torso areas while you remain to the rear of the Abas.' That is just worthless. You should battle for battle training.

"Besides, who is going to take a critical shot in the rear and not turn to face the one that was capable of getting close to them? You would turn around and eliminate the target before the finished the job.

"Second if you just hit with rapid fire and reduce your power to seventy-three percent, then you will be able to target three hard shots that will give you at least two full streams into the critical zone, even if you hit higher armor. This should be enough to shut down most missiles on a Zhayedan, and completely destroy anything lighter."

"I must be talking to an expert in battle, first echelon," the gruff voice seemed to answer mockingly. "Let's see how well you do then, youngling."

The gruff voice gave a heckled laugh. The screen blackened, then opened to a new territory. It was a lightly wooded area with a small pond off to the north side. The Canis Lycaon vanished from Nite's visual sightings. Turning on his radar wouldn't give him much information but would allow the other pilot to spot him.

Nite looked over the train map. He had about four good points at which the Zhayedan could hide. He also knew that the instructor was not expecting him to do much against him. He could use this to his advantage. He moved forward slowly and awkwardly.

"This should draw him out," Nite said aloud to himself, but felt as if he were talking to someone with him.

The awkward movements and lighting the radar as if to try to find him was a reverse trap method. It would likely work on the instructor, since he was expecting simple mistakes. Even if the student was in a Dire Wolf, the instructor assumed he knew everything since he was First Echelon.

It did. The Canis Lycaon immediately popped up from the water, only revealing half his body. Nite maneuvered the Dire Wolf like a vet to face his enemy. The Raven Wolf unleashed a set of missiles out of its bay. The streamlines zipped in on Nite's right before the anti-missile system of the Abas lit off. The missiles countered by spitting out its multiple mini-missiles.

Nite's Abas responded to the danger without a scratch on the paint as he rolled with the incoming damage. His anti-missile system was perfect in taking out the dangerous minis while the others seemed to fly around or bounce off from his movement. The little missiles failed in their job to weaken his armor for the second set, which went wide from his movements.

Nite unleashed an overpowered, full melee into the upper torso of the Raven Wolf with four high-powered lasers, four medium-powered lasers, and two tungsten slugs from each of the twin shoulder-mounted coil guns. He followed that up with his own salvo of missiles before dropping into the high grass and rolling for the light covering trees for cover.

The torso's polished look was blackened with damage as the last two slug shots allowed the light from the other side to break through. The Abas fell back into the water, marking its decent with bubbles and blood. The missiles followed it into the water, throwing water high into the air.

The rainbow colors from the breaking light and the mix of internal system's fluids swirled in the air. Nite thought it might make a beautiful picture when he replayed the moment later. Like the color wheel of an artist painting a masterpiece. Only the masterpiece he was painting was death.

OH MERDE! That was probably an advanced instructor. They'll know what we've been up to. Why wasn't he in his own Abas training or accessing the system? That would have kept him out of this room where he could access our program.

Nite realized he might have painted his own masterpiece of disaster as he watched the last of the bubbles pop on the surface. That day, he knew he would never stop trying to improve himself until he was granted his true home, a Dire Wolf Abas.

He knew this instructor was going to be pissed. Nite had to get out of there before the instructor could be retaliated, like so many before. If he wasn't found in the room, he could always deny ever being there.

CHAPTER 5

CAUGHT

Nite reluctantly released himself from the VR cockpit and leapt from the simulator, barely taking the time to release his suit. The instructor lunged out of his simulator without releasing his gear; it slammed him back against the fake cockpit before he could reach Nite. Nite turned at the unexpected sound to discover its source. He cursed his young instincts and curiosity for they had cost him precious escape time.

Nite expected the instructor to yell at him for breaking the rules or report him so he would be punished. He had seen him clearly now. He had to do something. Lower Nite's Honor Levels in some way, anyway to get Nite back for playing him for the fool he obviously assumed Nite was.

Just looking at his uniform, he could tell he was a master instructor. He might have lost his home before he ever had the chance to be allowed in it.

I won't give up that easily. I won't!

"You purposely acted like you couldn't pilot the Abas to draw me out of my hiding spot," he half yelled while he was taking deep breaths and yanking the attaching lines from his gear.

His dark face was flushed with blood from the strain of the pain that the simulator causes when you died.

"Good job. I shouldn't have underestimated you like that. The tactic probably worked because you figured I would. Lighting your radar was an obvious mistake. I shouldn't have responded like an idiot," he added as he got the last line off.

He took a deep breath after detaching the last cords off his VR suit. Nite realized the instructor was still being shocked while he had them attached because his voice settled. His face seemed to go back slowly to what Nite assumed was a normal, dark chocolate color.

"Thank you, sir," Nite bowed slightly before turning to leave.

He wanted to head out before the instructor started asking too many more questions or started to change his mind on how he felt about the situation. He could have claimed that was a way to dismiss him from the instructor's presence if he was ever asked why he had left.

"Who are your parents? They must be at least heavy Zhayedan for you to be so good so young. Hell, they might have been Elite, but I didn't think we were getting any of those children here," the man had reached out to stop Nite as he asked the question.

Nite had not even heard him move from his leaning point on the simulator; he turned and looked at the instructor with a little confusion. He had felt his hands approach but had not heard anything to tell him it was moving. If he had, Nite would have been ready with more than just an intense look meant to stop before he continued the instructors beating in other ways.

What did the instructor just said? No elite's children were allowed to come to these schools. Why are they not allowed? And obviously that eliminates us being from the great winners of the Crusader Olympia. I was hoping we had some small chance, however unlikely.

He has information I can use though. It might be worth trying to get on his good side, if only temporarily. I'll have to ask the operators about him the next chance I get.

The instructor's eyes were as black as his hair. The curls were neatly braided back in rows away from his face and hung free down his back. Nite could tell that the man kept his hair in that style for a long time because it looked so natural on him.

Nite expected the man to be angry, but he looked at Nite with soft eyes. His eyes seemed to urge him not to run and allow the man to give him a second to catch his breath. It made Nite want to run that much faster.

But how did he get so close to me without me hearing

him? Nite's thought kept playing over and over in his head as he watched the man with steady eyes.

"I don't know. My brother and I were never told," he finally answered.

Nite waited too long. He had to show the proper respects to the instructor. There was no way to leave now. He would have to stay until he was dismissed.

"You have a brother here? What year?"

"Same year." He kept the answer brief, like they did in class.

Nite started to look a little more nervous than he wanted, but he wasn't sure how not to with so many things on his mind. He was making too many mistakes. Giving away too much information. But he had already given his ID. The instructor had seen him. He was better off with the truth at this point. Maybe lead him into a false sense of trust with more slips.

"We completed our first cycle of warrior training yesterday."

"Oh, so you are one of *those* brothers. From the look of your scores, I would have figured you could hide your emotions better. What classes are you thinking of taking when you are moved up? I have been waiting for them to send the approval. I already wrote one up for the two of you."

Nite's first instinct was to ask how the man knew they were signing up for his class, but that would be giving away them not having as much information on him as he obviously had on them. Nite would not allow the mistake to continue long. Before the day ended, Nite swore he would know every facet of this man's history as written by the Pack.

"All the advanced courses in blades, small arms, Abas operations, Abas battle techniques, field medic, torture tactics, security systems and breaching, espionage, psychological warfare, hand-to-hand combat, chemical warfare, and warfare history. We have to continue taking all the base courses as well, but I don't consider them hard enough to mention."

"Do you plan on sleeping? Or is that not worthy of mentioning either?"

"I have read half of the books already, and most the classes so far have seemed pretty elementary from what we could find of them on the system computers. My brother and I shouldn't have a problem completing any of them ahead of time. We have already started. We have been through a good part of all the non-Abas simulations, and we are in our third echelon of Abas simulation battles for this school. We don't sleep more than five hours a night to get extra training in.

"When we are not training, we read and study by ourselves. I have a few bad marks from instructors who didn't appreciate me ignoring them. I don't believe that will limit me from getting selected though. You would know better than me."

Nite wasn't sure why he was telling the instructor so much more than he would normally mention, but something was telling him the instructor would help him more than hinder him. A part of him just seemed to trust the man, if for no other reason than he had already proven to be a superior to the twins. Something that only one other had proven so far in all the school.

There was also something about the way the man was moving that told Nite they met before. It was not like this one where they were talking, but both the brothers had found help before when they couldn't figure something out, even at this young of an age.

A data pad left in a secret passage, or a mark or score that led them to a room full of equipment. The equipment was never complete. It always needed work, but what they needed to get it going was there.

There had to be someone willing to give them the help. This man moved in a way neither of them knew about . . . yet. It was logical this man was the one that offered them help, and he was telling him nothing. After all, everything he said was documented. The instructor could just pull it up on his PAC if he wanted. If he wrote acceptance letters, he had already done it.

Mike had made a friend earlier in the day, and the balance of the world might have just given Nite an alley as well. The two were not in the same boat as far as what they could do for the twins, but Mike was not interested in using his friend. Nite was only interested in using his ally.

And the mirror continues brother. Strange as it is. Helpful this time.

"You are going to use your arm personal computer to hide that you are not paying attention in class," the instructor laughed. "Most people try to find things they have an interest in then attempt to master those. That way, they can earn the title of master. You and your brother don't think this will be wiser?"

The man was not asking the question his words had brought forth. Nite picked up the changing tones in his voice.

"We didn't pick anything that we couldn't handle. If we did, then after a cycle, we can change our schedule. We have no choice if we are ever going to earn the reputation required to be true warriors.

"We have no families willing to pick us up and help us out. We have ourselves. With only ourselves, we will prove we are the best." Nite looked defiantly into the eyes of the man.

The instructor stood up to full height, showing how tall he really was. Nite had expected the man had a natural look of well-defined muscles under his uniform, but he couldn't tell with the pilot cover suit over the nano pilot suit.

The lean body, smooth movement and extreme height marked him as the Espionage Master. The height had little to do with it other than they knew the profile. The way he moved with the rest of his body framing reminded him of Shawn. Their training may have been similar, but his was beyond well practiced.

"What Abas do you plan on applying for?"

"They won't let us apply for any specific Abas yet. Since they didn't ask, we haven't answered. We would like to prove ourselves worthy of the heavy classes at the end of our first echelon. From there, we will work as hard as we can to prove ourselves worthy of the highest recognitions."

Nite felt the last answer showed his age more than any he had given so far. It was a surprise how upset he was by allowing that to happen. Yet it was again a feeling of trust and unity that came with telling this man exactly what he felt and wanted. After tonight, he wanted the Dire Wolf.

"Well, you handled that Elite pretty well. I am Professor Master Raven. My family name is Dracon. You earned the right to know it destroying me so efficiently back there. I prefer you keep that yourself. Destroying me, that is. The family name as well. I would like to give you the respect of one for the agreement on the other."

"Raven, as in a bird of death. That is an unusual name for someone in Wolf."

Nite tried to gain his own feelings of lost honor by giving away a childish reason for wanting to advance. It also explained the funky design on his machine.

Raven Wolf. I didn't see that one in the bays.

"I won my End Games battle with flying deaths. My named changed that day to Master Raven, with honors from Raven Utimus herself. She was the head of Avian Proie when I graduated. I guess it was to show respect after turning me down.

"I requested Avion Proie as my primary since they were my bloodline. Wolf was my third choice.

Sometimes the ignorance you have as a child is better understood by your elders.

"You will not be formally named until you leave school and your name is engraved in the Wall of Honor of Timber Wolf Academy. Then you are a real part of Wolf," he stressed with the pure love of the Pack. "For me, the Wall of Honor of Wolf was less of a birthright then an actual earning. Many of Avian Proie expected me to join them with my blood lines. I thought it as well, although I was close to a Wolf Pilot in our younger years. It's different in those schools then it is here.

"For better or worse, you'll all be Wolf. I would have liked to see what would have happened with a few of you if you were not only Wolf."

The fire was still in his eyes, which showed he had once been a great fighter. Once, but something had happened to diminish those fires. Nite could tell they didn't burn like they once had.

Eleven years. Did he never have his Abas replaced? Did he never take another mission? Why would any pilot choose that?

"If you were in the great battle, why did you lose the luster within your eyes? Were you forced back to the schools?"

"Oh, you figured it out that fast. I requested to come back here. Yet, in a way, I was forced. No one would select me to have my Abas built. I haven't been able to get a mission to cover it.

"I was in the Crusader Olympia. I . . . I was . . .

was the one that was hit by the Bertha round. I went nuclear, but my cockpit's auto-eject worked perfectly.

"A second later, while I sat in the ejection seat, I watched five other pilots get caught in the fires. They flew into the air like little blazing excursions from a star, only to be pulled back into the all assuming body. They were pulled back into the hells of the battlefield; we were never able to recover any of their cybernetic parts.

"Some call me lucky. I am not sure how lucky I am. I'm here, teaching, because I never want to be the one that causes that kind of loss again. After all, if it wasn't for . . . if it wasn't for some great Wolf pilots, we would have never won it."

"There is little information on those pilots. The Honored Unnamed, as they are referred. I researched them, but they have had their records scrubbed. Supposedly, they were removed so that no other packs could kill them. But that is hardly an acceptable reason. Why not be allowed to fight any longer or be allowed to retire if peace is what you wanted?

"They do not have any children listed either. It would seem with the respect they had earned in that fight alone, they would be allowed to have enough to fill an entire year full of their children for one school. To prevent DNA mixing, obviously not at the same time."

Raven laughed a little, as he seemed to want to cry more than laugh. There was something sad that Nite couldn't pick up on.

"They couldn't have that many for fear of mixing DNA, even spread out. But why do you say that, young one?"

"That is not the way of the pack. To hide because you fear death, after you have earned so much facing Death and beating it back. To scrub your names from history so anyone can feel as if they can reach that potential.

"It doesn't carry the separation that the Pack seems to prefer. Fighting amongst families within each Pack, internal fighting within individual Packs between their armies, tension among the different fractions all trying to prove they are the best. Even the unity of the Trinity is built on separation and continued aggression.

"Conflict is growth. Growth is progression. Without progression there is only stagnation. Stagnation is death.

"In all of our history, it is the names of powerful, successful people. The accomplishments of their acknowledged children and genetic lines tie us to our own histories. It tells us we should honor and hold the honors of our past. It tells us to accomplish what our namesake is capable of, or to strive beyond because you might prove honorable enough for another name to be added to the histories.

"With all these honorable names, especially without Wolf having many, would we choose to erase the ones who earned us this," Nite waved his hands around indicating the schools that were earned in the last Crusader Olympia. "Why do we not have the most honored named and the families brought to the front. These schools should be carrying their names instead of the generic circuit created ones. Why choose to ignore what is obvious? Something about them has to be hidden, and that means they have to be. Why?"

"What brought these thoughts about?" Dracon asked, truly interested.

Even those who studied the Crusader Olympia never came to the same conclusions, much less come to them at eight.

"It was the viewing screen's lack of information on the story that drove us to find the missing answers. It is almost as important to us as finding our history."

Nite paused in a thought Mike and he had agreed on.

"Neither my brother nor I think we are the offspring of those two. It would not be logical or fit into the Pack's plan. Like you said, these schools are not filled with the most promising of students. It is interesting the way the Pack removes what information it feels is not worthy of keeping for public access. They are such simple things, but to hide what?"

"I can say seeing that battle has changed my mind of Red Born. The two pilots that won were Red Borne from a Sentinel and a Zhayedan and two Zhayedan's. It is said that they were Blue Blood, but they told stories to their closest friends about truly being red born."

"Were you one of their close friends?"

"I am a spy master. I am what I am. The one that came from two Zhayedan's was the Dire Wolf pilot. Man, was she beautiful. Not that I ever had thoughts of being with her or anything like that. She was too crazy in all the right ways for being an elite pilot.

"Just the way she moved and handled herself. It was an amazing thing to watch. The two of them together on the battlefield that day was the only thing better. Although they fought each other as much as they came together that day.

"Intimacy comes from conflict as well. Did you know? Without conflict, there is no intimacy. Intimacy is the respected difference between the two people. Afterall, if two people are the exact same in a relationship, then are they not repetitive and unnecessary?

"As for the way you see the pack, it is not just tensions and fractions. It is hard to unite people and easier to keep them looking at different areas to blame for difficulties in their lives, so they don't blame those that rule them. It is the easiest way to rule humans. Kinda like absolute logic is the best way to rule circuits.

"Humans must have separation and choice. Yet they must have the ability to make the choice as well, even if on a lower level. Only the greatest leaders can unite people.

"Those that aren't leaders try to keep them torn apart and misconstrue words. They lead by fear and highlighting failures of others without creating solutions.

"It's a reason for our council to have limited terms. They must live in the lives they create for others. It's harder to rule by fear when you have a limited time to complete your agendas.

"The rule is pushed down. Results are measured. Those successful are used to build a system. The system is installed and measured and corrected as necessary until someone finds a new system that is better."

Nite nodded as he spoke. It was the way of the Pack. Not just Wolf. Wolf had their own ways, but the Pack and the Council as a whole did operate that way. And each Pack had their own systems. Each trying to prove and improve.

Different systems for different people. People allowed to move to where they were most comfortable. Where they were willing to put in for the benefit for society.

"As for your parents, you could have some powerful genes and not even know it. Many great pilots were killed that day. Many children were left without parents after it as well. You wouldn't have been born long after, and your mother might have died giving birth to the two of you.

"Its common amongst twins. One of the reasons why it is normally stopped as soon as they discover the development. She dies, giving birth to the two of you and you would know nothing of your parents.

"Pack members don't always practice controlled

pregnancy. She may have been unable to list your father or determine the DNA before her death. The Pack couldn't tell you who she was at that age. And until your accepted, you can't enter your DNA into the system to find its matching genealogy.

"Only she could have registered you genetically, as the biological parent. Only after you were born. If she did, she couldn't do it. It's not uncommon for Red Borne. The one truth you can get from this is you are Red Born. Blue Blood children are registered as soon as they are scrubbed for implantation."

"More important than where you come from is where you allow yourself to go. Oh and don't mention that I told you about those pilots. Nothing of them or that day has been cleared for common knowledge yet. Not even all the battle actions of the Crusader Olympia are freed for viewing.

"The ones you see are all edited and have been changed from the actual battle. It's funny, such a great victory being hidden in its true actions. Like you asked, why hide the heart of two perfect pilots keeping the hopes of Wolf Pack alive."

"What would you do if you did see them?" Nite couldn't help but ask the question.

He had relaxed now more than ever. The camera scrambler still had over two hours of cover time. No one would be able to tell what they were really doing. The scrambler would keep the cameras repeating what they had seen a few seconds before the actual item had crossed its view path. This was one of the devices they had to fix.

"What would I do? I don't know. I think I would be breathless for a long time. After all, they are the ones who prevailed when I had caused the absolute destruction for Wolf Pack. I bet they don't want their identities released because of saps like me that would do anything for the opportunity just to say, 'Thank you'."

"I see. Thank you, sir," Nite sighed.

He knew the professor wanted to answer his earlier question. He wanted to give Nite a reason to trust the Pack, if not Wolf. After listening to Master Raven so long, he realized it just didn't seem right.

No, there was something else there. It might cost him his life to find out, and after he discovered his parents, he would dedicate his time to finding the truth of the battle, even if he had to become a Domestique of Pack Avian Proie, the other Pack competing in the finals of the Crusader Olympia.

"No, thank you. And I can't wait to have you in class," the professor held his hand out to Nite for him to take.

Nite sat down on the side of the wall, but the instructor had beaten him to his feet.

"Which one are you over?" Nite asked.

He knew that as professor, he was the master teacher of one of the classes and most likely espionage since he already admitted to being a spy master. Since he had taken all the classes offered, Nite was sure he would have him. Low level instructors were not master qualified and held no real position in the school's hierarchy.

"Espionage, as I am sure you already assumed, but good asking anyway! I believe that you will be very good in that class. In fact, I know that you have already been practicing the fundamentals of it. I have seen you and your brother quite often wondered which of my future students were practicing so well.

"You made a lot of mistakes that only someone like me would see. I will be watching," he smiled. "In fact, I always am."

The instructor laughed as he disappeared right in front of Nite's eyes. Nite didn't waste time waiting for answers or trying to find him. There were too many other questions for him to work out now, and information to share with his brother.

CHAPTER 6

LOSSES

Almost four cycles passed since the morning Nite went to training alone, the day after their birthday. Birthdays were only important in the Pack when it came to being rejected for training courses. After that, age only said how many years you were smart enough to live through. They had one more major milestone to make it too . . . true Abas Selection, which would be happening soon.

Mike had not missed a day since the morning after meeting her; neither had Selina. She was as good as Mike at espionage and hardware development. Recently she proved she could take Nite out from a distance in an Abas with advantages. Those advantages usually involved Mike helping her, her in a larger frame and Nite in a much smaller one. She could also hold her own in fighting after a few months of polishing against both the brothers when they were in a three-way fight.

She changed several of her classes at the last minute before schedules were finalized for their two tiers of First Echelon. She wanted to be with them. With what they discovered she was finding talents that weren't known before now. Talents they discovered through their less than honorable practices.

Selina impressed Nite in several different manners, but most of all was the way she fought in the Abas. Even though she was from a lineage of scouts, she would go head-to-head with anything. She often used her size and speed to lure them into traps. When she would get hurt, Nite and Mike would order her to disappear from the battle or would swoop down and destroy the target.

When they practiced late at night, Selina would only spend half the time in the larger Abas. She was a natural with them as well. The mobility of the scout helped her pilot the larger frames, forcing them to move with her and not be limited by the extra armor and weight. As time passed in the simulations, the Abas, no matter the size, moved liked her in her own body.

Yet she never stopped completely training in a scout. She felt her destiny was locked in with her Red Borne birth to two light Scouts. Mike said even if the schools limited her, the Five Year would see her in a Zhayedan. They worked more on merit and ability, not genetic history, and politics, like these schools seemed to be more imbedded in.

Master Raven stopped them in their attempts to

sneak around the school together. He immediately made note of the growth and discourage them using such a high number all the time in real events. Although, every time they made a mistake in their movements, he seemed to step out from nowhere and correct them.

Master Raven did this even when they were not where they were supposed to be. He wouldn't ever yell at them or attempt to take Honor from them for them being where they were restricted from. Instead, he felt it necessary to ensure they did what they were attempting with the most useful tactics. He would just politely correct their technique and then disappear as fast as he appeared.

Selina scored high enough to move into the heavy class, if on the light side, and like the twins, awaited, to be selected. It was a nice surprise to be able to surpass her parents under the twins' influence, yet part of her waited for the other shoe to drop.

The trio became inseparable. Her old friends still talked to her, but as they used to. A wall seemed to have developed between them. Not because of what the twins expected, but that she dedicated herself to training the way they did. It built walls because they turned their backs on the normal paths.

The day she broke her friend's nose using a technique they had not been taught in general studies was the end. Her failed block seemed to be the last brick in their walls. While they remained cordial toward each other, they were guarded.

There were no differences between the way the two boys and the girl treated each other when around others. Selina would speak for Mike sometimes instead of Nite. She embarrassed a couple of the instructors the way they did. But she would sit between them, with her friends on the other side of the table and talk. Hold them both when they were walking or lean on the one that was not participating if the other was called up.

Although Selina didn't show Mike any direct favor when they were with others, the other females seemed to stay away from him. It was like she put a female repellent on him. Maybe it was something Nite couldn't detect, but he knew it wasn't on him.

Nite was happy for his brother having it, being that he only wanted to be with Selina. He was happy for the mirror experience as well. Plenty of females seemed to be taking notice and chasing after his attentions over the last year. None were the ones that were with Selina and most were already in Second Echelon.

Moon Chaser and the Small Girl were growing closer as well. That was the way Nite referred to them, although they were not allowed to start naming yet. The moon chaser may have expected Nite was the one providing the anonymous hints to help him improve, but he didn't let on. Nite liked the way it was going and decided he didn't want to be directly involved in the training. This was more fun.

He never felt the pang of jealousy for his brother

in his happiness. It was the same for Mike, who had been happy not to be chased like his brother and could enjoy the presence of Selina. Selina loved both the brothers very deeply; for both she would give her life, but only one was given her heart. One had her living her life.

Selina's story was similar to several other Red Borne Abas pilots in the school, where her parents gained permission to conceive her. She often held to the fact that her parents wanted her and didn't just earn her. They fought well in the Crusader Olympia against Pack Avian Proie. It was a simulation she fought with Mike sometimes, only when her parents died, Selina and Mike were often still able to continue through the rest of the fighting, even as scouts.

They were stationed on one of the outer rim moons when they died. The Traverse Fleet was attacked while they were coming in for a landing by Silent Knights. All the people on board were killed.

The story said her parents, or anyone else, never had a chance to get to their Abas. The Silent Knights were blamed for the dishonorable attack. It was one of the few successful battles they never took credit for.

Selina was delivered to the child center around the age of two, about a year before selection. Her parents left her there before they went to the outer rim. There were seven other children whose parents died during the same raid. All of them were brought to the same home, and that was part of the click she always hung out with. All the children were Red

Born, and after the deaths of their parents, they lost contact with their higher-ruling families.

Without the influence of their parents, the respect of their family names entering school, and with the fact that they were Red Born, they were marked as expected light Abas pilots before they even got into the Abas Schools. Most of the children turned toward hate for their parents as time passed, cursing them for not allowing their birth through the breeders and giving them the rights of the Blue Bloods of the society.

They did not understand that even if the children had been claimed as theirs, it might not have meant only their DNA went into the child. For a couple to have a true child of their own, the child had to be Red Born. To the society, Blue Blooded was more important, but to the ones in love or those who wanted to keep their true DNA lines going, their choice rested in having Red Borne children.

Zhayedan and Elite were almost never allowed free birth procedures. They had already proved to be of higher genetic quality, so studying and improving on what they could was more beneficial to the packs. They were guaranteed children, and quite often at least four to five for those were mixed with average breeding. With the greater number of offspring, they also had to worry about crossbreeding. This was another reason for the council to investigate the request and have the heavier two groups completely removed from the Red Birth process.

By producing more children from the heavies and assaults, their offspring would be forced into fighting each other for the higher seats and would force the lower bloodlines out of the Abas process completely. Over the years, the Packs had planned to work the lesser bloodlines out and flood them with what they considered higher genetic coding. The coding would stay with them for generations.

She remembered the first day she saw the twins. The memory was embedded in her as one of the first things she remembered. It was not really them that she remembered, but the reaction of the adults as they were brought in that made them rememberable.

They were only two and a half, but everything changed when those two came into the room. It was rumored this was the third move to a different holding house. The holding houses were where the orphans were sent when the families did not want to take them until the time of selection.

She wasn't sure why, but everyone said they were going to be selected for Abas. That was guaranteed. She thought they would be special, but the humans seemed to stay away from them. Only the androids would be with them. The androids seem to dote on them constantly though.

It was the same in the schools here. No one got the operators to give them the special attention those two got. But no one treated the operators as equals like they did either.

Maybe that's why the operators treat them so well. I'll have to remember that for the future.

When they came, the families came back. Almost every child in the holding houses was visited by someone. Selina didn't have such luxury. Her parents had earned Higher Honors in the great battle but hadn't been continually active since then. The lack of movements from them lowered their levels before they were sent to the outer realm.

Selina lost everything before it ever started. This didn't make her hate her parents. They had not been active because they had been trying to raise her.

These thoughts were often the ones carried with Selina when she was in her simulated Abas. That was until she noticed Mike. For some reason, she never associated the memory of the two children being led into the room with the two brothers she was going to school with until much later.

When she did, she was looking at Mike. He did something strange that reminded her of when he was younger. She smiled and from that point she knew she wanted to be with him forever. A childish thought at six years old but it was truer now then it was then.

The moment Mike started instructing her, everything began to change. The students the instructors felt were a waste of time, Selina gathered under her wing and began to instruct as the twins had taught her. She used her time during class, and often Mike or Nite would be standing nearby giving the instructors all the more reason to stay away. Those born under heavy Sentinels and Zhayedan parents were cherished by the instructors.

Mike believed they only improved because they were shown more attention. He would often comment on this as a failure of Wolf Pack. Like talking, he only did it when no one else was believed to be around. He would not try to change it; he just wanted to keep the note for future reference and plans.

The twins broke through the instructors barriers like a tank through a block wall. Like an enemy tank, they blew everything to hades, not taking in the collateral damage they may have been causing. With the help of Selina, they were able to teach others a day's lessons within a couple hours.

Selina taught the others because the twins did not want to bring more into their circle, especially Mike. He seemed to find most people a waste of material, but like his brother he liked to see how they improved when provided proper instructions. She gave them the outlet to help while keeping their self-required distance.

******

Dracon reviewed his plans for the trio once they reached the Second Echelon in another couple weeks. Like the twins, he did not include them taking on more direct followers. They would not be spending as much time training the trainer, but doctoring the instruction books to save them time.

Fix one book and disseminate it with the different styles of learning all covered. The books would act as instructors freeing them to master what they wanted to improve. As they learned and figured out for others, they would improve themselves and learn to self-correct. It was part of the plan, anyway.

He was sitting in the teacher's lounge debating the best way to go about the mass movement of the school when four of the first-term instructors came in. He remained quietly in the dark back corner, where he kept his chair and listened to what they had to say.

"So, they are removing her from the school," a kind old voice started after they were sure they were alone. "I wonder why?"

"Yes, but she will be going to another forward school. They said it's because we have too many lower pilots." This was the voice of a middle-aged woman.

"But she has scored high enough for her to reach the higher level. Why not let her advance and earn her way into heavies?" This was a younger woman's pleading voice asked.

There was an obvious knowledge no one in this room had any real authority on the matter. It was more a declaration of the obvious solution those in charge did not want to implement because they were not trying to solve the problem.

"Her average scores are not that high. Somehow the other two are helping her when we are not paying attention," the middle-aged woman spoke again.

Not that you would pay much attention to them

anyway Dracon though as he settled in with a fear of knowing exactly what was about to happen.

"What are you talking about? Her average scores have her above all the Scout class and well over half the Sentinel Classes. She deserves to be moved. They all do."

"I think they all should be separated. It is unnatural for any one Red Borne to be that good, much less three. They must be cheating. That's why Falstar has the other two remaining in light Scouts after entering the Second Echelon.

"If only we could catch them. And now they are starting to help the others cheat. It has to be something. The Scout Classes scores are too high recently."

Yeah, it's like someone's paying attention to the individual, using the way they learn, not the generic training that only helps a few and providing helpful criticism they can understand. I think it's called . . . teaching*!*

This was a snooty male that Dracon new well. It was Rage Runner, the head of the lower-class professors. Rage Runner was a second echelon heavy instructor before Dracon came to the schools. He was moved down with the honorable mark to help the lower levels raise their standards. In truth, the second and third had had enough of his ravings and were going to kill him if he hadn't been moved. Amongst the first echelons, he was a god.

Maybe it's time to move him to another school. Nox

can handle him. Or she might motivate him to move back to open engagements instead of the school.

Dracon stayed back, wanting to hear more of what was going on and to ensure that they were talking about the three he suspected, although there was little hope it was anything different.

"We are right on with our scout pilots as well, especially if we let her move to sentinel classes. She won't even be our problem in four more weeks. They will be moving her at the beginning of the second term. She has scored high enough for that," the younger woman supplicated as if it would change the girl's fate. "Besides, if they were cheating, you figured we would have been able to prove it since they have been together for almost four years."

"Falstar has already made the preparations for the transfer. There is nothing that we can do. Can we please talk about something else?" the old medium pilot plainly stated.

The disgust in his voice was not well hidden. Dracon doubted it was meant to be. It was more of a warning against pushing the topic.

Dracon also knew him from the great battle. He had taken out a heavy. His Abas still had most of its armor, but his cockpit had been almost destroyed. The explosion severely injured a second Abas from Horse Harras. When his cockpit was crushed by the last Elite of Horse Harras, he lost his legs, one complete arm, and half of the other. They were now bionic attachments.

Unlike Cyborg attachments, these were very painful to move and never gave you the freedom and speed the cyborg parts did. They could only replace appendages with the machine attachments, and it took a lot of training to get them to perform the way you wanted. It was more common to see them on the older pilots that didn't want to be a cyborg and were being sent to pasture until they found their own ends.

"I for one am glad to see her leaving. I agree with Rage Runner that we should separate them all," the middle-aged woman injected as if the old man's request was never made.

"You would! I don't frankly care to discuss this anymore either. You can choose to ignore me as well, but I will make sure you won't talk long after!"

The young woman picked up the container she was drinking from and pointed the bottom at the middle-aged woman. Dracon's interest fell off, and he ducked out through his secret entrance. Their conversation drifted to a silence as he sped down the hidden halls.

******

The next morning, Dracon left his class to find Selina. He was unable to reach them the night before because she was in the common area the entire time, working with others. For him to appear there to talk to her could cause several problems for both of them.

This morning, his trip was short. He heard faint

sobs as he passed one of the secret exits from his classroom.

"Selina, I heard the bad news, but it is hardly something to cry over. Please calm down."

"Sorry . . . Professor . . . it's just . . ." Selina began to cry again.

Dracon pulled something out of his pocket and handed it to her as he held her close. He made sure no one who would see them in passing would realize what he was doing or saying.

"Don't answer aloud. Do you know what this is?" She nodded yes. "Do you know how to use it?" She nodded yes again. "Do you understand what I am telling you?" She whipped her eyes and nodded one last time. "You will not lose them."

Dracon gave her the item and left the halls for the sanctuary of his hidden passages. He had the object to give to the twins, so they could hold a private conversation. It was the most secured way to do it, but now the real purpose of his actions had sprung to life in front of him.

I wonder if they can impact other schools. I wonder if we can raise the curriculum higher here, with the Red Borne. This would be an interesting game. The council will not like it.

CHAPTER 7

CONNECTION

The weeks went quickly for Selina, Mike, and Nite. They continued training, but Mike and Selina were often counting the seconds they had left. Even Nite was distracted, but he tried to hide it.

One thing they agreed on, this was not forever. No matter how hard they had to work or what they had to do, they would be together. Nite was more distracted by how to communicate with Selina while she was gone. It was the lynch pin to is plan. She added too much to their training to let that vital piece go.

The lower instructors pulled her away a week before she was scheduled to leave to tell her she would be transferred to the new school. The middle-aged woman selected to deliver the message tried to give it the best spin she could. She spoke of her average scores not being high enough here, and her having a better chance at advancement in the new school. She told Selina she was more than capable of producing the same results alone, and she couldn't wait to see her in the End Games with a Zhayedan.

The fake sincerity of the other two, and the over playing of the middle-aged woman was almost enough to make Master Raven choke. Selina looked her dead in the eyes and showed no emotion to the conversation. The other two instructors tried for a few more digs to get something out of the girl. Mike taught her too well on how to be silent and unemotional.

Like a ton of bricks, the realization they already bugged the teacher's lounge hit him. It would make sense to know what the instructors had to say. If you were going to outdo them, you had to bug more than that. Master Raven might have been teaching them a little too much too early. It also meant when they split to do operations, he tracked one or two of them while the other group moved in to install the plants without him knowing.

Did they purposely fail to find out what group I was tracking? Or did they know the entire time?

******

Selina's trip would take a day through Pack space, then, at her new school, she would move right into the second echelon classes. As far as the schools were concerned, she would no longer have contact with anyone else from her original school until after Second Echelon Midterm when she could communicate more openly across Timber Wolf Network, aka TWN , pronounced twin.

Knowing they were down to a week, was like watching the executioners ax start sliding up for the final swing. Days left. Then hours. Time was the enemy, but an enemy they could not fight. Instead they went to the simulators until their last hour. Sometimes in battles. Sometimes just enjoying the peace.

The last hour and the final walk, the brothers were not allowed to go with her. Master Raven chose to walk her to the ramps where the ships would take her. As far as the school was concerned, they had never met. He was just the designated Master Instructor assigned to ensure she and her Abas were properly set up on the transport.

She kept the secret he asked, in not telling the twins there was a way to communicate once she left. In keeping it, she felt as if it didn't exist. At the end of their time, the secret the two shared brought her closer to trusting Master Raven. She understood the need.

It forced them to act as if this was their last days. No one would believe them if they didn't act as if something were wrong. And if they had to pretend, the twins had no basis for understanding how to.

From the hidden shadows where Mike awaited Selina's arrival from the public path, he considered ending Dracon's life. He was sure the spy master could have told them earlier than they discovered and helped in heading off the situation. Mike was not sure why he blamed Master Raven, especially when he had no proof.

Selina and Nite both agreed he didn't know of any other solution. Nor did he know any earlier than they did since they heard Falstar receive orders. If the Headmaster couldn't change it, then it wasn't likely Master Raven could have either. They overheard the Headmaster discussing it with Bird Eye.

Dracon never held back on information they asked or failed in helping them when asked to. He helped them become better as well. He may not include them in everything he was doing or monitoring, but who would expect him to. They were eleven.

They did not tell him everything they learned, discovered or created. Nor did they tell him everything they were working on. And it was he who taught them the skills they needed to discover what they had.

These memories steadied Mike's hand and kept him from killing Master Raven on the platform. A quiet look from Selina who seemed to know exactly where he was, even though she should have never seen him approach from her angle, told him this was not the last. He realized he was upset because Master Raven was going to get the last goodbye, the last embrace, the last moments with her.

Her look told him otherwise. Her look told him, as he often had to tell her in the beginning, wait . . . the right time is coming.

Master Raven got to his knees to hug her. But

at the angle Mike could see he was not holding her but covering talking so low Mike couldn't hear the conversation. He realized he never had a one-on-one conversation with Master Raven. Nite and Selina were both privy to them.

He could feel his anger and distrust rising again. He wouldn't let these feelings ruin the last moments with his best friend. It seemed like ages before Master Raven left her, but when he did, he walked quickly, not wasting another second of Mike's time. It was as if he knew Mike was there as well.

"What did he have to say?" Mike's anger shot out before he could contain it.

"Directions for something he gave me. I can't show you right now! It will help with my risky plan."

Mike looked at her, and all the anger that built up evaporated with the beating of his heart for her. "I . . . I am sorry, I can't right now."

"What do you think it will be like at your new school? Do you think they will try to hold you back? If they don't, you could make Zhayedan no problem. You have the skill."

Selina leaned into Mike and spoke right into his ear, with a voice that was hardly audible, the way Master Raven had spoken to her.

"I want to leave the Pack, Mike. I want the three of us to go. I want to go with you even if Nite won't give up on them. When the time comes, I want to leave."

"We shouldn't talk about this here."

Mike tried to keep his voice calm, but the excitement in his heart leapt and pounded more than it ever had. He knew she could feel it, for hers reacted the same way.

Selina finally agreed to leave with him, with them when the time came. He would live the rest of his life with his Totally Talented Girl. It was the nickname he had given her the first night, when he said she was more than she allowed herself to be.

It was the moment he knew he always wanted her with him. The Pack may separate them, but Mike would keep a part of her with him.

"I don't want to be here anymore. I know there must be more than just the Packs, but I am tired of the way we are treated. There must be a way to get to the something that has to be out there. Something has to be beyond the Packs, something beyond these wars. It is there, waiting for us. I know it is."

"If there is, we will find it, but let's not talk about it here. I wanted to give you something as well. It is the only thing I have from my parents. It tells me they were alive when I was born. That is how Nite and I know we were Red Borne. And those few scattered memories we told you about."

As Mike was talking, he was reaching behind him. Under his jacket he'd worn to hide the item with him. His eyes darted over everything to ensure no one was watching. He unceremoniously shoved it into her hands as fast as he could. Mike snatched his hands away quickly, so she would not be able to give it back to him.

"This is your birth cloth." Her voice was tight with the realization of what Mike was giving her.

"Yes. I want you to have it, so you will always remember me."

He wanted to reach out to hold her forever. They were very young, but he knew Selina and he were meant to be together. It was like his Abas and him. Yet, the Abas wasn't in the right form, and Selina would always be right.

"I'll no more forget you than forget myself. But I am going to give this back to you once we are together again. If a gift comes full circle when the two inamoratas are separated for a time, then the circle can never be broken. They will always be connected." She turned into his arms and breathed in the scent of the blanket. "Besides, you will be able to give it to our children if we live that long," she added to herself with barely an audible voice.

"Once we are together again!" Mike whispered into her ear.

The breath that came with the words sent chills up her spine. Selina's arms were trapped between Mike's and her body, with the cloth locked in her hands. Mike held her with such strength Selina couldn't feel where she stopped, and he began. This was the first time Mike ever gave her any sign of affection where they could be seen by others. It was the first time he said they *would* be together. In Mike's way, he just told her he loved her.

When Mike finally let her go, he turned and walked away without looking back. Selina lost his movements in the shadows as hot tears streamed down her face and clouded her eyes before she too turned away.

She only cried once since she had met him. Now she felt as if she would never stop, due to the pain in her chest. Hearing words she would not even allowed herself to dream of until now and her heart felt like it was being ripped out of her chest with each step he took away from her.

She held the blanket to her face, not wanting any memory kept in those tears to escape her.

"Here my heart will always remain until you are given back to the one you belong. To the one I love."

******

Nite waited and watched his brother pass through the passages as if a ghost floating and impossible to be seen by others, yet visible to the entire world. If someone wanted to end his brother's life, now would be the time. He became too involved in his grief to see anything else.

Nite moved quickly ahead to a secret passage they discovered a few days earlier. He pulled his brother through it, slamming him against the wall. Instead of a fight breaking out and them holding the battle until a victor could clearly be named, Mike slid down the wall and started to openly wail in an almost silent cry and wheezing breath.

Even Nite couldn't stop himself from settling down next to Mike. Dracon had been moving with him in the shadows protecting Mike as much as ensuring he didn't do anything stupid either. He held his brother as the sobs turned to retches, and finally settled with a calmness that only a long, grievous cry can give you.

"I expected you to at least cover your emotions long enough to get back to the barracks," Nite started critically.

His brother had not cried until they were completely immersed in darkness, but the sight of his face showed the pain and loss more than anything that had ever been displayed on their faces before.

"Please don't start. This is beyond what you can hide."

Mike took several short breaths while trying to speak before he breathed a long one out.

"There is nothing beyond hiding. Did we not decide this long ago? We don't have a choice. We must cover our actions as much as we would cover our faces in disgrace!"

Nite was harsh, but he had to be. He could not let his brother set into a deep level of depression, or Mike would lose sight of the goals. If they did not complete them, then Selina might be lost to them forever. If Mike failed, then he would no longer be the one that Selina had loved, and he wasn't sure what that would mean to them. Time was said to make the heart grow fonder, but it also changed people. Mike had to change for the better to keep Selina.

Nite took a moment to listen to the surrounding area to ensure they were still alone. Even Dracon had given them a wide birth. There were only a couple of people in the school that could have gotten close to them now. Nite was sure at this moment, he could have even sensed them, his internal alerts were so high due to his brother's weakness.

Mike leaned his head against the cold, damp stone wall. With a deep, long breath, he caught himself. He fixed his face so the emotions no controlled his actions.

The gods help whoever he targets next, Nite thought to himself as he watched his brother's rage become bottled to be released.

"Have you found anything out?" he finally asked.

"I can't find anything. I can't get past the security. If they didn't take Selina, we would have been through the first series sometime this week. It is going to take at least three of us all attacking at the same time to get close to getting by. Then there is still no guarantee we will find anything. No one here has detected us, at least. I still have access to all the information going across the nets."

"You think they found out?" Mike seemed to have locked in only on the first part of the update.

Nite felt he should have known the mention of

Selina's part first would monopolize Mike's mind. Even if they were special, they were still human. At least, Nite thought they were human.

Nite took a long moment to reflect on what he wanted to say to his brother.

"No. The only one who knew we were up to anything was Dracon. He wouldn't tell on us no matter where we were discovered. In fact, I think if he knew, he might try to teach us what we would need to know, or even be our third."

The suggestion was out before Nite realized he had even said it. It wasn't the right time, and he might have just ruined any chance of ever getting Dracon to be part of them.

The truth was someone might have discovered them. They made mistakes, but he didn't believe they would be able to trace it back to three eleven-year olds. They hid their training on these topics under their hidden accounts. If they discovered them, then the trio would be facing worse problems them having one taken before they could break the codes.

"Then why not run to him now? Why do you wait here for me when you finally have the opening to bring him into what we are doing? Then not only will he know about our training, he will know about what we are seeking. He, a part of the system, will know all of our secrets."

"Because if they did find out, and that is the reason Selina was removed from our group, then we can't risk any more losses. Dracon, whatever you think of him, is still a valuable asset, and one with many other uses than being a third. We will have to be careful of our selections for assets from now on and try to keep them secret."

"Friends," Mike corrected. "She was our friend. I do not think we should put anyone else through the punishment we have just set before her. How could we ask anyone to suffer as she is and will? No, we must develop high enough that only the two of us are required, or have Selina somehow brought back. There is no room for more."

Mike's cold emotions settled back over on his calm exterior, but Nite could still hear the heat from his voice. So much pain. The pain would drive him. Nite just had to lay the tracks in the right direction to ensure where he was driven was productive. He also needed to remind his brother to free himself of the weight of his feelings.

Feeding to the fires! Nite thought to himself, but his mind's voice sounded distant, almost different. Feminine.

It was a trick a child at the development center was taught by his superior family while Nite and Mike where scurrying through the ducts of the cooling units. The idea of that also came from someone else's family member, commenting on the size of the child and how they could make it through the vents easy enough if they ever wanted to hide. They went in great detail of the talents needed.

The operators helped them get in and figure out

how to navigate the ducks, even though they were just toddlers. Nite always thought the operators gave them too much freedom to figure things out when they were children, but they never allowed them to be alone either. The boys never stopped trying to learn more. The operators encouraged them to do it anyway they could.

The skill of feeding the fire came from a mother was standing next to her young son directly under the vent. She talked only loud enough for the three children to hear what she was saying while she held him and circled under the vent. He would not be selected to go to the school for a very long time and doubted that he would remember a word of it. He wasn't even moving yet.

She wore the uniform of a Heavy Zhayedan pilot; one that was highly decorated. Nite and Mike didn't know about the great battle then, but she must have been a surviving pilot. He wondered if their parents had been there.

She told her son about creating a fire inside your mind and feeding all emotions into it until there was a calm peace about you. When you reached the point, then you settled down to the warmth of the fire, but without ever feeling the enjoyment of it. It was known as battle trance, and it would not be taught to them until much farther in the schools, she said. She walked him through the steps until he had finally stopped crying and settled his body down.

She then told him that it was often best to consider

life from this point. It was the time to make the decision and consider people and their actions. They would act on emotion while others would act on logic. Mastering identifying types of people or learning to drive them to the way you wanted to react would allow you to direct and manipulate their actions. It would tell you what direction they would attack and defend from.

Nite and Mike looked at each other. Both walked through the steps the mother discribed, and the faces they were looking into were the same cold faces everyone would remember. Cold stone carved from the hardest rocks of cores of the planets, unshatterable, indestructible, adamant of no emotion. In their bodies, they would forever hold this trance, for to them they were always in battle.

It took time for Mike to finish feeding the emotions his brother could see and then could feel through their very special connection. Nite did the same, feeling the loss of Selina for the first time. In the burning, they did not lose the feelings, merely placed them where they could look upon them, study them from a distance, and keep their outer appearance calm, steady, ready, and balanced.

If you allow emotions to control your reactions, then you are guided by others to your own failure. If you use logic to control your actions, then you are guiding yourself to failure and allowing others to dictate logic to you. If you accept your emotions are not yours to control, but feel, while understanding them and choosing your reactions to your ultimate plan, then you are the master. A master of the only one you can control . . . yourself.

"Obviously, she was more than that for you," Nite bought himself back to think of Selina's departure. "For now, we can only deal with what is presented to us, not what is in the past. We will be together again. We will see her at the End Games.

After that, if we are successful, we will never be separated again. It is a short period of time, even though it will likely double our current lives and then some. There is much to do, too much for you to get in this state. It is time to reset the path and stay with it."

"Yes, I will see her then."

Mike locked his fist almost as if swearing to something deep inside, but then released all his emotions to the fires that raged in him. Nite got a flash of the blue flames stretching the apex of his mind's burning room. Mike walked out from the center of the fire like a being of ice and stone.

"Master Raven wanted to give you something, but he didn't want to risk someone seeing you together on the platform with Selina. He didn't want to make a connection to the three of you. Here," Nite handed Mike an item wrapped in black cloth.

The cloth was a concealment cloth used to keep the item from being detected from the scanners. It was something used by the third echelons to sneak items in which may not have been approved for their level of training, even though being able to do it was as much a graded part of their training as getting out of the school to get the items.

The Pack would never remove a personal possession, but the trick the older students had to do was get it to their rooms. It was one Nite and Mike already started. They were using many of the unexplored areas of the lower levels as their personal sanctuaries as well.

Mike quickly unwrapped what appeared to be secured transmitter/receiver used for planet-to-ship communications. Top-level spies were the only ones given solar communication equipment, or even allowed to use this particular model. It was used by those capable of infiltrating a group and who needed to communicate with a central until that could be across the galaxy.

The item was set to a specific DNA. When not in use, it was designed to take the form of certain items usually found in rooms. This one was an alarm system for a rack, footlocker, or closet. If it was reset for a new DNA, all the data and the connection to the others would be removed. It could then be reprogrammed for up to two other connections.

Mike looked at Nite and then back to the device.

"This is set up for three-way communication. Where are the other two?"

"I can only tell you I got this one from Dracon as a second. The question isn't where the other two are but where is the first one?"

Mike looked at his brother for a brief moment.

"Selina!"

It appears we won't be as separated as they thought, Mike thought has he went back to Selina's worlds.

I can't show you right now! It will help with my risky plan.

CHAPTER 8

THE PUDDING

The week following Selina's transfer, the twins were selected for the full advancement into the Second Echelon with fifteen others. They were the last of the selected for their age group. It was the final set of Abas pilots to make up this cycle's class. This was the first real step into becoming an Abas pilot. It was a great gift to receive on the twelfth anniversary of their birth, 678.3.14.

They were excited but already looked in on this room to pick out a place to sleep once they read the report identifying their new barracks. Only, when they saw the rooms, it wasn't so crowded. The report originally had Selina with them, which showed how old it had been. It also showed they would be among the last to be selected, so their rank was placed before Selina was transferred.

They entered their new living area walking past a view room, game room and finally the gym where they turned right into the main study area. The area had four round tables that didn't seem to be enough room for two people to work without interfering with each other, much less the four and five that were cramped around them now trying to study. Eight single computer terminals were also visible, and every one of these were full.

The students on them stopped their work and got up to move in with four other people standing close to the entrance as the twins walked in. They looked to be about eighteen years old, which put them better than halfway through the Second Echelon. The brothers never saw them before, nor did they care what they had to say. They went to walk around the group into one of the four sleeping berths. One of them put a handout, touching Nite.

"You need to listen, knobs, if you want to sleep in a bed instead of on the floor, or in the showers."

"I would suggest you remove your hand from in front of me or I will remove it from you."

Nite looked deep into the boy's eyes, seeing the fear now radiating from them. The boy dropped his hand, but another boy who had not seen the look on the first one's face decided to chime in.

"What are the two of you going to be able to do against the eight of us?"

Nite looked around. He saw four of the students hadn't come from the terminals to join the rest. They just moved in to see what was going on.

It was a mark that they were trying to prove their

loyalty to the group without joining them before they were accepted. Either that or they were hoping to take their spot if one or all of them were moved up. They did look a couple years younger than the other group.

Mike's ax kick was unseen until it dropped across the one that spoke's shoulder, snapping the collar bone clean in half. Nite gripped the hand of the one in front of him, twisting it to expose the back of the elbow before snapping it down, leaving the arm flapping uselessly as the first boy bounced off walls trying to get away from them.

I said I would remove it if he didn't get it off me. I didn't say I wouldn't punish him for putting it there in the first place. Learn quickly or spend more time in medical than you do in here, Nite thought has he looked around to see if there would be more challengers.

His brother didn't wait to look. Mike round housed two more; one in the back of the head as he attempted to leave. Nite caught two of the females who stood by the side, but were still part of the group with several quick punches to their bodies, doubling them over. He alternated feet to shatter their noses with the floor, dropping two quick succession ax kicks to the back of their heads.

The last male and female stood back with their hands raised as if that would stop the twins from finishing what the group started. Nite took the male by the back of his long hair as he went to run, realizing they weren't going to stop. Nite slammed him back into the ground before ensuring his ribs were completely broken by two well placed stomps from his left foot.

The spittle of blood across the ground told Nite the boy would not interfere again. His breathing was ragged and shallow. Medical could already be heard responding to the fight.

"I didn't know you were so . . . *hot!*" the girl started at Mike who returned the compliment with a smile.

She smiled back, assuming she was safe until the combo punch-elbow crossed her face followed by a back elbow to the throat. She dropped to the ground, struggling to get a breath through her broken nose, jaw, and constricted throat. He was smiling because she left herself open to an easy attack.

She wasn't able to defend herself any longer. Her eyes were filled with tears and her hands searched frantically for a way to breath. She turned her head to look at him, maybe to beg for help or mercy. Her face was turning colors. Mike dropped another heal kick down the side of her face, putting her nose across the bottom of her left eye.

Nite and Mike continued to the empty racks they selected the night before as medical droids rushed in. The one that was just put out was the first to be retrieved and rushed out of the room. Those that could not walk, were scrapped up and strapped down before being rushed out and down the hall. Needles were already being injected into them to help the healing process.

Two stood, grabbing onto one of the bots rushing

from the room. They held on as they were dragged out behind it. Not even trying to stand and walk.

Nite was not sure why. They stopped beating on them. The girl shouldn't have thought she could get away with flirting after starting a fight. That was dishonorable. She deserved to be shown the dishonor of her actions. The rest started a fight. The twins finished it.

None of them would be out of the barracks for more than a week. The droids responded quickly. No one would walk away with any permanent visible marks. Nite was not sure what operator triggered the call, but he was sure it was done the moment the group put an arm out.

Nite considered this a blessing for them. The battle was not called, so it meant they lost nothing in being defeated. Mike found it a great disappointment. He wanted to scar them to show others the consequences of challenging the twins. He thought it would be better for their reputation.

I just hope someone too our standard bet anytime we get into a fight. This one was too quick. He should have waited a little longer before taking down the others. We might have gotten at least a nibble.

They looked over their new room once more. It was bigger and had less people, but there seemed to be less of what they would need to have access to everything. Aside from the four tables and the eight computers, there wasn't anywhere else to sit outside the lounges.

It explained why there were three girls sitting in the middle of their barracks floor when they walked in. They were at least a cycle ahead of the twins. They barely looked up before returning to whatever they were working on. They recognized them at least.

The three networked their personal arm computer or PACs to each other. One had a wireless connector, another had a digital keyboard. Nite assumed the third requested the cables to connect the three of them. Without a wireless connector you had to be at a terminal to connect to the school system and TWN. Even with a wireless connector, the conductivity could still be slow if a lot of people tried to link into the same access points.

Originally, when you received your PAC, you were given a hundred Opportunities to put toward it for extra designs outside of reading flat disk. The Opportunities were often exchanged on either a wireless connection or a three-dimensional typing and reading area. The three of them must have gotten together to be able to have as much access as they could. It wasn't uncommon for those that had been locked into team together to ensure they had what they needed, even if they had to share.

The Pack made sure there was plenty to tempt everyone in these schools to keep them hungry. The twins learned Opportunities usage to get the items for strategic advantages was also limited to this school. Reading Material Condensers would automatically take all the important information in a reading and reduce it to simple knowledge. It wouldn't give you all the information, but it gave you a great overview of what was said.

Other popular advancements included pleasure-reading disk, non-war type or educational games, special seasonings for foods, makeup, movies of assorted varieties, and personal and group games. Other options were also available, but these were the most requested by most students starting out. The twins went for extra storage and wireless connections.

The racks were only two high with a four-person cubical. They were separated from the main hall by screen shields that slid from the end of the racks. The lockers were also stacked two high. The rack on the bottom had the lower correlating locker and the same for the rack on top.

The lockers created a type of hall that led to the water rooms. One side had nine showers and two medium baths able to sit five easily. The other half had nine full toilets, thirteen standing toilets, and twelve sinks with mirrors. A full wall mirror was on either side of the main open walls of the water closets.

The common rooms had a kitchen designed for quick foods and warming what might have been brought back from the galleys. The gym and cardio areas were much like the rest of the unit, not enough. If everyone organized and used the game room and lounge at the same times, and only needed the same amount of time to study, then every person could be at one station at the same time, aside from showers, toilets and sinks. Yet, the likelihood of them ever learning to operate that perfectly was as likely as the twins to operate with them.

What brought Nite and Mike here the night before was their exploration of the heavy rooms. They had assumed they would have been selected for one of them based on their scores in the First Echelon. No other students were in their range. The fact that they had been chosen to come here bothered them more than they would admit to anyone, including one another.

The heavy rooms had thirty-six students, but over a third more of the room. There were thirty-two individual terminals with twelve more in their personal library. There were eight study tables which were hardly used for actual homework and more often used to lay out large strategic maps when the two map and planning rooms were taken by others.

Individual cardio and weight gyms were almost twice the size of the ones in the light rooms. The view and game room were similar to the light rooms, but for the higher ranking, head to head games were often replaced with higher level strategic games designed to help with troop movements.

Each rack was above the student's desk, locker and personal cabinet. A second locker was next to the rack and often offered the semblance of a side table for the higher rack. They had the same number of showers and baths, but it was still a smack in the face because they had less people fighting over them.

They chose to take the two racks nearest the showers. If they had been selected for the heavier Abas they would be moved into the better rooms. They knew their scores should have done it. Seven more years, and they would be in their individual rooms.

Seven more years!

Nite thought to himself as he looked over at the two racks next to him where his brother kept his back to him. He was hiding the emotions as best he could. Nite could tell the disappointment hit him harder than Nite, himself.

"We will have to prove we are beyond them. We never planned to reveal too much this early, but this insult proves the need," Mike finally said in a voice so cold space felt like a desert summer.

Nite looked back toward the common area. He didn't believe they had done anything they hadn't seen yet. If they weren't good enough with what they showed so far, they hadn't shown half the potential they discovered in their hidden accounts.

"We will," Nite agreed knowing it was time to start showing a little more of what they were capable of outside the class.

For the first time, Nite wished he marked someone for life before now. Those idiots were not going to be the first, but he didn't want the Headmaster and whoever was pulling his strings to think this insult was enough to bring it about. It was just the next retribution against the Pack for treating them poorly.

It was the first hammer strike in the destruction they were about to bring to the school.

Nite let his thoughts settle a little more. He heard from Selina there was an unfair advantage given to the heavier side when it came to these schools. He never expected it to be so great. They were not put here because they deserved it; they were put here to fail.

Selina was taken from us because we were making her too good. Now these light pilots are being punished because they will be judged against us. I will ensure they have what they need when I can! I will ensure they understand what it means to be an Abas Warrior!

CHAPTER 9

PURITY LOST

The twins first real experience in an actual Abas cockpit was scheduled for today, two weeks after being moved up. It would start in their personal training cockpits, which due to their selection was designed for Light Scout Abas. Up till now, students trained in simulators, wearing only the Integrator Computer, called Working Body System or WBS, which helped them learn to convert their physical movements and reactions to the Abas.

It connected to the all the major movement parts of the body, including the head. The WBS learned to convert the actual movements and brain commands of the pilot to the larger machines. Although most light scouts were barely bigger than their pilots, the endoskeletons allowed the bodies to hold more armor and power systems for weapons.

Most students didn't wear the WBS outside of classes that required it. It was little more than a long rucksack that attacked to the upper thighs, arms and around the chest and shoulders when not in full use in the simulators. Although the more it was worn, the higher the connectivity developed.

The simulation reactions were smoother than those of the machines. It was no longer the mind thinking it was in a real machine and the software being the only interface point. The machines responses also depended on convertibility between the pilot, the WBS and the Weapons Control Group Computer or WCG.

The WCG was like the cerebrum of the Abas. It controlled all the *thinking* of the Abas, including Radar sensitivities, battle histories, weapon powers, converters, auto-firing for defense, temperature controls and billions of other calculations at the same time. The WBS was the cerebellum of the Abas, controlling all the movements of the body itself. The pilot was the human director, or conscious mind of the machine.

The WCG had to accept the pilot and the WBS. If the WBS and WCG didn't *get along* with either, the pilot would be rejected. It was possible for the WCG to override the commands of the Interface computer and break bones, rip off limbs or even kill the pilots.

For this reason, each pilot had to have at least a thirty-percent compatibility with the WBS before they could attempt to enter the linking with a WCG. Then the WCG required a ten-percent compatibility to not rip you apart, most the time. Even with ten-percent, pilots could still get seriously hurt.

No non-human, including cyborgs that was not an accepted as a human pilot prior to becoming a cyborg, had ever been accepted by a WCG. Every one of them was violently destroyed. This was what worried Nite the most. If there was any chance of the twins not being human, the WCG would know.

Not all WCGs were equal either. Some were more receptive. Others were very choosy, to the point of having to be broken down and reprogrammed. Some pilots would be accepted by many WCGs, even picky ones, while others were lucky to find one that would finally allow them to connect.

There was no way to tell which type the WCG or the Pilot was until the WCGs and pilots started connecting. Then it was the engineer's choice as to when to reject them completely and start over. If the pilot were rejected by an engineer, they would have two more chances with different engineering teams to find a WCG that would accept them. Or they could pass on being an Abas Pilot. If they failed to find one by the time the third engineer came long, they would be rejected from the program, no matter their scores.

Once the pilot had a real Abas attached to the WBS, they would get their full functioning pilot suits. The pilot suit would then act as an interface between the WBS/WCG systems or Abas. The cockpit would then be moved between design systems until the pilot was locked in. After that, they would never be allowed to change Abas forms. It was better for the computers that way.

It was why, after school, the War Council only had five years to change the grading of a pilot. Sometimes schools didn't give people the opportunity to learn and grow like they could have. Other times, students and the Packs didn't pick each other right, and if they were taken Domestique, they found they were better or worse. At these times the council would step in to ensure the pilot was properly placed for the best nature of the Packs as a whole.

They would train in their Abas for simulations. The suits would act as a second protection level as well. Helmets would give them their display inputs, although the students spent several classes wearing helmets to learn to navigate properly already.

Each Pack Pilot cockpit was personally designed for the pilot. In the forward schools, the pilots could get their cockpit adjusted four times before they graduated without Opportunity exchange. The students could choose when to have it done, since they were the ones still growing and knew their bodies best. After their fourth selection, it would be on them to earn the Opportunities for such adjustments.

Exceptions came when pilots switched between designs based on promotion, demotion or lateral changes to designs. Since these changes were approved by the Headmaster, they were automatically completed for the systems without it counting as one of the four. It could be moves like going from a biped to an otto zampe design. Students wouldn't normally jump to an eight-legged design. Instead, they moved from biped to tetrapod to hexapod and finally to otto zampe.

Smaller frames, like light and medium scouts couldn't handle a full cockpit unless it was a quadruped design. Some smaller frames could also be designed to fit two people, but it required removing cooling systems and some of the mechanical assisted movement equipment and was done only with mission critical requirements. Multiped designs were better for these, since they could add equipment to carry the second or third person easier.

Removing the cooling system and mechanical assists left the battle suits to control the internal temperatures and usually restricted movements in response and difficulty. It made the computers run hotter and slower with a higher likelihood of errors. This was a death sentence to scouts who depended on speed to survive. But if the mission required getting someone in or out of an area, it could be a required and often a rewarding gamble.

Other options aside from using opportunities were always available for those willing to take the steps and smooth out their negotiation skills. Pilots could attempt to hook up with a good engineer or technician who would do it for them under the table for traded favors.

Most Abas pilots, students, or fully-fledged Abas pilots, didn't want to be seen involved with the lower ranks unless they absolutely had to. In the forward schools it seemed even more taboo but was almost required by the leaders of successful teams or successful individuals at the same time.

It became a dirty secret, like who the best students were at attempting to learn counter espionage. Everyone took the course, but then there was a drop period for students after the third week. Some stayed and openly took the course, but not all that were rumored to be training attended class.

Most lighter students took it as a cover for other activities, since if you chose to stay, but not be graded professors would ensure you gained opportunities. The professors would also help you get other things you might not get from other instructors as bribery as well. And they were especially willing to help you pull pranks.

An even lower option was to learn to do the work yourself. The main reason it was considered lower was if you were learning to change and adjust your cockpit, then you were not learning what the school had to teach. Yet, the information was available to those in the school.

Heavy Abas pilots usually had the best luck with finding ways or people willing to assist them inside these schools' environments. They normally had several engineers and techs assigned just to their squads if they were on teams. These same members would be looking to rotate out for higher honors sometime in the future if they didn't have the honors banked from previous assignments.

Since the leaders selected and proven successful were the likely leaders who would be doing the selections, it was easier to get little things done under the table. The engineers and technicians were especially nice to the long term team members, including the lights, since it was likely successful teams would be kept together leaving school.

It required a higher exchange of opportunities for Zhayedan and the Heavy Sentinels to change things because of the complex systems in their Abas. Often, the *hookup* was getting it done at a lower exchange rate. Favors were often returned when the Abas pilot was able to select their head engineer and or senior technician. It could be an opportunity for the member to gain a substantial raise in their Honor Levels, even for those remaining within the schools. This was true for the other schools as well.

It was a small blessing lighter Abas didn't require as many opportunities to get changes completed. Their systems were much easier to work on since things were normally kept simple for the smaller spaces. Also, because they were smaller, they were more often specialized in their fields.

Unlike the heavier system which allowed for the need of adjustments, weapon swaps and upgrades based on the mission and were expected to be divergent in capabilities, scouts often had specific missions they became experts in. This gave them the greatest chance of survival. What they required in terms of best equipment the Abas was usually already equipped.

Honor's earned by missions could be used for other aspects of the Scouts training, unless they weren't good at the specialty styles they were put into. Then they were usually killed within the first five years of leaving the schools. Unfortunately, the forward schools didn't seem to specialize the scouts as much. They saw the highest death tolls in their ranks.

Unlike the other Pack Schools, if these trends were found, scouts would choose not to go to that particular Pack or group. The forward schools didn't have an option. The best they could do was hope to have the War Council intercede for them during the five year to be promoted. Or hope to get assigned to a team with a leader who didn't spend the life of scouts fruitlessly. The last hope was to die with enough honor to have earned at least one child to carry on their legacy.

The one exception to movement up and down was at the Medium Sentinel range where the pilot could be laterally converted. The consideration of a Medium Sentinel ranking higher or lower was based on if they were specialized, what the specialty was, or if they were diverse designs. Diverse were considered the higher levels while in school, due to it aligning with the fighting style of the larger designs. Individual hunters, AKDs and backline specialty fighters, known as disrupters, were also considered higher levels.

Nite thought on this because it was likely his next step to move toward the higher-ranking levels.

Until this point, every pilot was training with scouts in the simulators. Now the selection was sixty-forty for separation.

At this stage of training the Abas selection wasn't as important as the light-heavy selections. All pilots were going into Light Scouts for the next few months to ensure they were properly linked. Then they would receive their first upgrade fi they were heavy ranked. Those considered a light pilot were all put into biped Light Scouts. Heavies received a diverse Medium Sentinel style.

Nite's thoughts ran through everything that he considered with the knowledge of what had been happening. Everyone, even the newly selected *heavy classes* had been standing in the hanger awaiting their assignments to the light Abas they were to start their training in.

A few months to prove they were absolutely wrong to put us in scouts' barracks and be moved up with the others. If that fails, maybe we start injuring others until they admit we are better. We could kill some if it comes to that. It is what we are training to do.

All of them were wearing the pure white suit for what would be the last time. White suits were the mark of simulator trainings. If a pilot wanted a pure white suit after this, it had to have at least one visible mark somewhere. The mark could be as simple as a different shade or texture to show they were no longer simulator only trainees.

Nite never wanted to have white in his suit again.

It was a childish thought, but he still felt he would keep his suits from being largely white unless the mission called for something like that. He just shook his head internally, and allowed the excitement of being able to leave the simulators to be in a real Abas and testing what it could really do warm him on the inside.

"The white suit is a semblance of purity, devotion to the cause of the Wolf Pack and a sign of uniformity. Once we are placed in our Abas, we will no longer have such a comfort of everyone sharing the same basic level of a pilot suit," a female voice spoke from behind Nite.

He turned his head slowly, although surprised, to see one of the girls talking to another girl, not to him. His exterior remained calm, but he wasn't sure he was containing his excitement anymore. These two weren't. Nobody in the room seemed to be. He was about to be completed.

"Yes, but it will be nice to be able to be different," the other girl answered. "This is the first steps to be individual as well as unified."

All the students were receiving the same style Abas, a Vulpes Macrotis or Kit Fox. It was the smallest design in Wolf. Other Abas Models were in the hanger for them to see, although not allowed to touch. At the end of 678, during the break, the greater part if not all of them, would leave the lightest form and moved into a larger armor. Those that failed to prove worthy would be demoted back to Light Scout. All the pilots would be using one of the three designs.

Those deemed Heavies were moved into Medium Sentinel Armor. They would spend at least two more tiers and more likely a full cycle within them before being able to move into a Heavy Sentinel or Light Zhayedan for another cycle of training. Most students didn't see anything outside the generic frames until Cycle Three.

The lights would move to Medium Scout bipeds so they could have the chance at a full cockpit and an actual missile drum. They two would spend the remaining of Cycle Two in them unless they proved themselves better than someone in the Heavy Classes by the end of the tier.

In Cycle Two defeats in challenges outside of Abas started counting against student records as well. Anyone past the midterm wasn't allowed to challenge students younger, but the younger students were not restricted. The longer a student remained undefeated, the higher Honor Ranks and bonuses they received. The more challenges, the more difficult the challenges and the higher the other persons rank would increase the level of the gains for both sides.

The number of challenges issued and accepted by the student set the Honor Levels as well. A student couldn't dodge challenges to gain more rank. They would be dropped for not participating. When they were finally defeated, the one or team that defeated them earned a bonus of the previously undefeated's current level.

A thought of fear crossed Nite's mind. What if he had been calculated to do worse in an actual Abas then in the simulations? What if they were able to work perfectly within simulation but not within an Abas? Sometimes pilots did better in simulation then they did in an Abas while others did better in an Abas then they did in simulation.

This was the reason the Pack preferred the methodical movements in these early advancements. To ensure the base skills were completely developed and mastered in muscle memory. The Packs didn't need to rush their soldiers through training. They needed them trained to be the best.

Mike put a hand on his shoulder and shook his head. There was no need to worry for nothing could be changed with it now. The time of worry was over. It was time to find out.

"If there are any questions for the technicians or engineers please route them through either your instructor or professors first. They may be able to give you the answer without bothering these gentlemen. You are released to look at the other Abas and to see what you will be getting into.

Nite and Mike walked right up to the two computer consuls that at the time were installed into the Kit Foxes. It was one of the only Abas in the room that had your arms and legs throughout the entire design. It was barely larger than a battle armor suit and much smaller than a Tutevibian.

The frame would adjust to the size of the person. For the students being eleven to twelve, the frames would still need to be adjusted down for them.

These will be what we are training in, Nite thought.

Its primary assignments were city protection and behind the line sabotage due to their small size and amazing speeds when the pilots were trained for it. Nite and Mike were able to take a squad of Heavy Zhayedans out with two of them using only Abas swords. They also met some of their greatest simulated challenges within these.

Once, they were both seriously injured by TTG while they piloted Medium Sentinels in a city. TTG was a master at this thing as well. It was the most like moving your own body, which was why it was the one every pilot started in.

CHAPTER 10

SYNERGY RATING

A young engineer with dark brown hair, chocolate brown eyes and an interesting look of professionalism watched the twins closely. He came to the forward schools' program after he completed his engineering degree to be closer to his sister. She was an Abas pilot in a different school. He served on a few battlefields, but he left there feeling the pressure was getting to be a little too much for him.

He could have sworn some of the Abas pilots programmed their machines with voice simulators; only he was the only one that seemed to hear them. The schools were quieter. Yet, he couldn't take his eyes from the two boys as walked to the machines as if they had been called to them.

The other students were mostly walking around the bigger ones' filling dreams with what they hoped would come. Some stayed in a huddle, looking scared. The engineer was not sure why they would. So far, every student over 10% had been accepted by one of his designed WCGs.

It was the same every year, though. Some going this way and that. Some huddling in small groups waiting to be punished for not being enough. But the two walking right up to those two Abas that were built with old components wasn't. It was something new.

"You two think those are yours?" he asked as he walked up.

The two turned and looked at him as if confused by the question, yet they did not make a sound. It was as if he had asked an obviously stupid question and they were wondering if he thought he was funny or if he were really that fatuous.

"Do you know who they are assigned to?" Nite asked with contempt in his voice.

The engineer looked back at the two of them before looking back at the systems that had been brought in especially for them. He knew they had to be the ones because they came to the systems as if they were called. He could feel it as if knowing they were connected. Yet, he couldn't answer why.

"They belong to you, I am sure. I will check the DNA registry, but I would guess they will align with you. Why don't you try it out?"

"Won't that have a chance of killing us?"

"Yes, but I don't doubt you have found what you needed. If it kills you, I will honor your funeral with a personal appearance," the engineer laughed.

It would be of no great honor for him to show

up to their funerals. The offer was at least a peace offering in he thought there was no chance of death. Nite looked at his brother for a brief minute before turning to the first machine and crawling into it. Mike didn't wait for his brother to make his move as he too crawled into his own machine.

The two instructors and the assistant seemed to hold their breaths, waiting to see if the two highest scoring pilots of their year were about to die because an engineer would allow them to make a stupid mistake.

The engineer didn't even check the compatibility of any of the machines first. The young assistant instructor went to move forward to stop it, but the senior instructor stopped her.

"He is the highest-ranking engineer here, even at his young age. He is here because he is a Designer Engineer. If he is allowing them to go there, then he has his reasons," she smiled with a vicious twinkle in her eyes.

The engineer was not sure what he was waiting for. There were no lights from the heaven or a string of perfect music. It never happened when anyone entered an Abas, but he felt it should have accompanied such a tremendous event.

These machines refused eight-hundred-twenty-three students prior to them. Well, they tried to kill eight-hundred-twenty-three students prior to them. These were the only two machines he did not design. Honestly, he didn't have a reason to put them out today. He hadn't for the others of this cycles at the school.

The Supreme Headmaster ordered they be put randomly put out, sometimes adding two additional Abas for selection. Some would try to crawl in, especially after he told them the rejection rate on them so far. None were successful until this point. Even in the inner schools.

And they belong in much heavier frames. I had to specially align them to these smaller frames to see if I could find a pilot they would accept. I thought that might be why the WCG was rejecting so many pilots. Maybe it's balanced out. Or maybe these two are special.

I wonder if it matters they were together. No one has ever tried to enter them at the same time. Was that the trick to pulling the sword from the stone? He laughed at the thought.

The instructor felt a little disappointment as well. She saw several Abas pilots ripped from these cockpits because the machines refused them. It was a safety process now that they were not allowed to close the cockpits or buckle in which they were told at the brief to prevent those kinds of accidents.

"These computers came from some old Abas. They have the older parts for . . . larger Abas. I assume I will be seeing you soon for upgrades and you will want *new ones*," he tried to lead them away from keeping the old parts.

No one was supposed to have them. They were supposed to have been destroyed years ago, yet, he couldn't let them go. They were too . . . *well trained and developed.*

He felt a connection to them. A desire to see them completed again. If only he could find the right pilot. He also liked them constantly refusing others. He thought it was appropriate for the Abas students to be rejected.

"I would prefer mine to be whole as soon as possible," Nite answered before he looked over to his brother who gave him a quick head nod. "We both would like the old parts put back in as soon as they can fit into the chassis."

He half laughed as he headed around the back, thinking he would never bet against them no matter the odds. He brought up the readings of link percentage to ensure they were not just linked enough not to get thrown out and dropped his tablet. His hand trembled as he went through the commands again.

The instructor heard the sound and took the eight quick steps to find out what had happened. She was hoping something was wrong with the machines. They would have to try again. She came around not sure what to look for, but the tablet was in the engineers hands and he was just documenting their student numbers.

"Why did you drop the tablet," she asked.

"There DNA was already registered in these machines and they are at 92% link."

"Then they have not made 100%. Room to grow. What does it mean their DNA was registered? What is the problem, exactly?" her voice commanded with a level of disrespect.

"They are at 92% and the cockpit has not been closed," he added as if she were the idiot for having it explained to her. "And these . . . body frames are not designed around these computers. They are usually test for those that will," he stopped to think about the words he was going to say. "That will be more than your average pilot," he added in a shallow whisper that the instructor was speaking in.

It didn't matter, they were behind a wall of silence, no one from behind could hear what was being said. It was put into place because the engineers didn't want people to hear when they laughed or made cracks about the Abas Pilots and their cockiness. Very few Abas pilots earned the respect of the Engineers.

"With these in . . . the right chassis frames, the number could be at 100% easily. By the way, it is highly unlikely any student will reach 100% by the end of school, much less the first day they step into one. Most of the time, it is the scouts and low sentinels that reach it because they spend the most time in their Abas and use their Abas like their own bodies."

"What are you saying?" she sneered at the engineer.

"One, we are of the same rank, even if you have your position of Abas Pilot above me, so you will not refer to me in that manner again. Two, I would not put it past their ability to reach Elite. Both of them," he said as he continued to write numbers down. "Before they leave school."

She looked at him exasperated but could say nothing. He had corrected her in private and he had done it with all respect maintained. Then he attempted to predict something only the council could approve.

She looked back at the Abas wondering if she did something to the two of them if she could cover it up. None of what she saw made sense to her. She was just following her orders, but if what he said was true . . .. She turned and stalked out from around the two Abas.

"What are you not telling her?" Master Raven asked from a shadow that was contained in the cone.

"What you already know about these Abas. They are used parts and it is the reason that so many have been refused from them. They were only brought out to see if we could find a link and match them to the original owners. That will be impossible now since I can't bring up anything on where they came from. Strange, if I do say so myself."

"What can you tell me of the previous owners, Jason" Master Raven asked.

"Nothing," Jason answered quickly with a little anger in his eyes. "I don't know why. I had it before, I'm sure. I just didn't pay attention to it.

"I can tell you I am to pass the information onto the Triscifield, Master Raven," the engineer stated as he continued to look over the systems and write down numbers.

"When will you be sending the information," Master Raven asked with a small smile.

Even behind the field, they should be careful as to what they said.

"This is a lot of information with nothing in return," the man answered. "It might get lost before sending. At least until I get some of my questions answered."

"What I know of these two pilots is on this disk. Yet, you would know almost as much by looking at their records. Some things you will have to discover on your own from the clues. I did give my word I would not *tell* anyone."

"Tell, but not assist a little to find the information," Jason Jr. laughed.

"Only you and I will ask this information not leave your personnel care."

"They are not likely to see me again. Not directly anyway. I will have to bring the Triscifield this information by hand. They will wish to examine it very closely. I'll take it back to the Lab with Ferrera. Then, I think I will be leaving here for a while; time to return to the front lines. I need to test some things. Maybe if they prove as worthy as they seem they will, they will be willing to test things for me as well."

"You found the home for yours and mine together. Should I maintain the bets for you."

"Always for them," he answered. "Take the deductions at my standard levels so I don't lose everything if they lose. But reduce it by half. I might get to retire decades early," he laughed.

Jason looked over the class as he stepped back out where they could hear him.

"Well now that two of yours have come up, the rest shouldn't be too scared to make the attempt. The technicians have checked your WBS compatibility. All of you are ready for the first attempt.

"You only need a ten percent connection to be accepted by the Abas computers. Don't worry about the connection rate. I don't think I have ever seen a starting day pilot higher than twenty, maybe twenty-two percent," he finished as he looked down at his clipboard tablet.

That was, until today. Who the hell are these children? I better double my first few bet ranges for them. There won't be many takers very long. Maybe triple. Would it be too much to quadruple? Auto betting and tripling might be too much.

"We will start with the highest earned Honor Levels over your time at school and work your way down. Pick any in the Green Area. It doesn't matter what Abas you go to. They are all the same as of now but because one doesn't accept you doesn't mean others won't. We'll test you in one until we find a system that will accept you. There is more than enough for everyone," he paused at a collected sigh was released.

"The only reason we are going by rank of honor is it is the easiest way to track you guys, and it allows you to know where you are in the school. From here out, rank will matter more than you can imagine."

He paused as he looked at the first two scores and then back to the Abas pilot that would surely tan his hide for the waste of time he was about to cause.

"Ah, I think I have the wrong data. . .," he started and then stopped as he looked down at the rest of the rankings. "No, this is the right one, but these scores . . .."

"Sir, I am sure you have the right page. Please give the assignment numbers," the bony vulture of a female instructor known as Bird Eye had called to the engineer.

Nite was surprised to find out that she was an Urocyon Cinereoargentus Abas Pilot. The Grey Fox, as it was known to those that used their proper names, was a diverse Medium Sentinel and was considered a borderline Abas. It was also known for being a Light Hunter, often part of city invasion teams.

Jason Jr. had looked at these scores and knew that he had made the right decision in the bets, but if what Dracon said was close to right, then there was more then what these scores were showing. There was even more that they had accomplished.

Ten times the normal amount and keep it running for the first year, he added to a message to Master Raven. *After that, I'll see what ranges are being accepted.*

Master Raven and Jason Jr. had a close connection, even though they only came together in these schools. He was respectful to the Engineers and passed on who he thought had the best potentials for winning. He also slipped Jason inside information on the students that were hiding training skills so he could make better bets.

Jason helped Dracon with some of his pet projects from the engineering side and slipped him new equipment and information as well. It was a mutually beneficial agreement, but Jason thought he might have finally gotten the better end of the deal.

Why do they fight so hard? What are they fighting for? Could they be cyborgs? Could a cyborg link so well to an Abas in the first linking if they had never linked before? I thought it always killed them.

What if the link can only be established if the cyborg doesn't know it's a cyborg? They are only twelve years old. Does that matter? Or is it that the WBS was at 100%? They must have worn them all the time. What would this mean?

I think I'll drop these numbers on the reports. I want to see what they are capable of and I don't want everyone betting with me. I'll be watching you two. I would like to see what you are capable of. Might suggest students spend more time wearing the machines to get their connections up.

CHAPTER 11

OSTENTATIOUS ACTIONS

The twins adjusted quickly to the lighter Abas; unbeknownst to their primary instructors, they had been practicing in everything up to Zhayedans within the first year of receiving their WBS. It was two months since they had received their Abas. Their classes were spaced throughout the six days that made up the standard workweek.

The last day of the standard week was given for rest and study. Although no one knew on what planet the standard week had been set by, it was standard throughout the Packs. The leap day was also a day of rest, but it only came once in seven years and was attached to the first-tier break period for the students of the schools. Next cycle would be the Leap year, 679.

The students were told the standard times were

developed for the Pack Military to be stabilized. It was based on the cycle of Ramstar, the first moon settled by the predecessors of the Packs. The first seven months all had thirty days, while the last five months had thirty-one. This made up the three-hundred-sixty-five day rotation Ramstar took around Daritock or a standard year. Twenty-four hours measured the rotation of the axis, and Years were broken into quarters and quarters into months, months into days for easy of measuring smaller, balanced parts. That made sense.

Well, the schools used three tiers to divide the years. One-hundred-seven-day periods with a fourteen and two fifteen-day breaks between them. Leap year, like next year, would mean fifteen days on the first-tier break. Class schedules and training aligned to the time better than quarters.

For the Pack, the 31st day was added to the end of the seventh month on Leap Years. It was given as another day of rest unless it fell on the Seventh Day; then it was just a normal day of rest.

Maintaining a standard time instead of trying to run off of every planet timeline differently made sense. It could take several generations for Daritock to circle Sasaria for example. A member would never have a birthday if time were based on its rotation pattern.

To expect to change standard working days, time schedules, frequencies of meals, or lack of frequencies, as well as countless other problems, could wear down warriors and take them out of their natural groves.

The standard times were created to prevent this. It also helped line up events so strategist could look back on them and learn the bigger picture. Again, it made sense.

Months and days were referred to by numbers only. The fifth month, the third day to tell the timeline. Twenty-four hours in a day, with sixty minutes in each hour and sixty seconds in each minute. Time was told by hours and minutes with each one just the number it currently was. Sixteen twenty-three or the sixteenth hour, twenty-third minute, since day or night might last years. All simple.

But why are there seven days to a standard week? Seven doesn't go into thirty or thirty-one. It doesn't go into three-hundred-sixty-five or six evenly. Why would Master Raven ask us to figure out why seven days to a week, when nothing is measured in weeks, but weeks? Even the month's days are numbered one to thirty or thirty-one.

Within the schools there were no differences in times either. They didn't have day and night, hot or cold periods. There was no winter, summer, spring or fall, although they were taught about these things. Some of the Arenas were set up to have different temperatures. There was no sky to look at, except those in the arenas or simulations. Time was relevant to the students, but it was standard.

Students could have up to twelve hours of classes scheduled in one day. For the twins, every working day contained twelve hours of classes due to the workload they took on. The only day they had no classes was the seventh day of the week. Some of the ones in their barracks had two and three days without classes. All those students were all in the second half of Echelon Two and completed their basic courses to at least the minimum requirement.

It was not as easy as having a straight ten to twelve hours of class broken up by two mealtimes and a few breaks. Meals were available any time of day. There was a wide variety of selections of food available at all times as well. Time periods for classes were not standardized, either and could be held at different times throughout the day.

Pilots were scheduled based on the best available times throughout the month for each section of topics being covered that month. If overlapping or other requirements came up during a class time, the pilot could go to one of the others to get the material covered. They could also watch the video of the course.

Questions could be posted to be answered, but some questions didn't get answered for a week. This was done to encourage people to show up for classes that without mandatory attendance. Students were expected to take responsibility for what they had to accomplish.

Some of their days only gave the twins enough time between classes to sprint to the area where the class was to be held. Other days left them with 14 hours between their first set of classes and their second set. Then they started the next day right away with ten hours backing up to the last day's set with only one-hour break in between the sessions and the remaining two hours.

Master Raven assured them, this was normal for students that took on this many classes, and other students were given these types of stress testers as well. When they entered the second half of the second Echelon, the students would decide what classes to continue. Specialties, applying to be on teams, open battle challenges to and from anyone in school including Abas, and even long-term missions which could take up to a month. It was their responsibility to map out their schedules by tier based on class availability and received a higher flexibility.

It was to prepare them for the Third Echelon, where classes were even less restrictive, but not attending meant not gaining the opportunities that came from them. Also, in the third Echelon, external warriors could come against you. This usually happened if they wanted to test your abilities for you joining their teams.

This was part of their training and testing. It was about dedication, time management and the ability to be flexible as priorities changed. It also meant they had to set the priorities for their work and their extracurricular activities.

But none of this explains why we have a seven-day week. Why not make it flexible as well throughout the month? Allow for four break days throughout the month.

Sometimes you could get five, but who cares. Four is enough.

No one had classes on the Seventh Day or break days. They were not allowed to have active battles unless the simulation was longer than seven days, and restricted battles during the breaks. The Seventh Day was so important to the Packs, they would only defend themselves on that day. They would not seek active battle.

It seemed over the last five-hundred-fifty-years or so the Desitians respected the Seventh Day as well. Only the Silent Knights seemed to violate it with attacks, often to their own demise. Attacking on that day historically had the Pack Warriors reacting in much harsher performances then they would have otherwise. Where they might not have pursued an enemy before, they would hunt them to ground, giving no quarter.

The day of rest wasn't always needed, but everyone seemed to spend a few hours in the books or going over something from one of their classes. Some perfecting what they had learned. Others trying to figure out what they had not been able to in class.

Students could spend time with family during these periods, but Nite had never seen anyone leave. He knew some did, but it was rare. Most students used the time to get ahead, catch up, or decide to drop or add classes before the next Tier.

Mike considered using these breaks to see Selina or bring Selina back here for a few days. The denied request came back the day before their first break in Echelon Two started on 678.4.18. It stated students weren't allowed to leave and travel from the schools alone. No student from other schools were allowed to physically intermingle prior to the End Games. The lines of communications between the schools was allowed after Second Echelon Midterm, but greatly monitored and at times messages were blocked to protect secret leaks through aggregation.

Nite considered this as he thought over his brother's plan to leave the school at the end of the Second Echelon. Nite wondered how much of Mike's desire to leave was to get back to Selina. How much of him wanted this more than logic told him those years would be their chance earn their real Abas sizes, including Selina. Although in truth, she was playing a much more dangerous game these days.

Neither believed they would be given the chance if they left the schools. It was not that the War Council would be restricted, but it was harder to justify if they left school five years early and would have graduated when the War Council could no longer promote them. It would be smarter to use those five years in school to prove their worth and have five more years for the War Council to close out their training for Elite, their final goal.

It was the same for Selina. She had a better chance being promoted if she didn't leave school early. Even if they made it, Selina's rank and privileges had to be considered. Her game was not as direct as the brothers.

Brother, there are times the heart must suffer for the greater good, and the love of two must be tested for the mission to be successful. A little more time and you will be together.

******

In 679.3.29 the Twins were almost through the First Tier of Cycle Two. They were finally moved into Marbled Polecats (MSc) from the Kit Fox (LSc) frame. Everyone trained in the Kit Fox since moving into the Scout Abas frames during selection day on 678.3.29, a full cycle earlier. Yet, every student in their class had been selected for either Heavy Classes and moved into a Grey Fox (MSn) or Light Classes and moved into Dingo (MSc) at the beginning of the tier. Even after the promotion finally came through, the Twins were operating in Abas that didn't align to anyone else in the school.

A couple days after they were notified of not being promoted to the higher levels, there was a small incident in which forty-seven of the fifty-two selected members for Heavy Pilots were trapped in a net that was spinning them like a centrifuge in the Heavy Bay. A couple instructors also got caught in the trap. All the people caught ended up with at least one broken bone and most with several.

While it was never pinned on the twins, Master

Raven felt it had a hallmark of their pranks within it. The Headmaster decided to ignore the damage of the prank, chalking it up to the upper classmen setting a trap to see if the pilots were smart enough to discover it. Yet, no one came forward to collect the additional opportunities earned from its successful capture.

Little less than three months later, being promoted from Light Scout to a Medium Scout was not what they were expecting. Especially when other class members they outscored and outperformed were preparing to be moved into Light Zhayedans and Medium Sentinels.

Only the "very best" would get the chance this cycle, in during Third Tier, but they felt they should have been in the "very best" category. It wouldn't be until Cycle Three that everyone was freed for full movement throughout the Abas Ranks, although it was unlikely anyone would see a Medium or Heavy Zhayedan ranking until Cycle Five, which also contained Midterm during Second Tier.

They demonstrated their frustration during their next class with live Abas the following week. The instructors issued clubs to simulate Abas Swords for the practice sessions. The three instructors had fully equipped weapons system to ensure no one got carried away.

The class was nothing but Medium Scouts, while the instructors were all Medium Sentinels. The one was specifically designed to hunt down and kill the lighter Abas, Bird Eye, gave them all a stern warning and set the expectations. Presents was supposed to be enough of a deterrent to keep Students from acting up.

Nite and Mike felt they didn't have enough presents and beat the students they were assigned to unconscious with a few seconds. When the instructors engaged them, they used the two sets of clubs to deflect attacks and knock away several missiles before they engaged in close range attacks on the instructors. Security Protocols shut the Abas down before they caused enough damage to kill any of the instructors.

The external and internal armor on the instructors Abas around the cockpit had to be completely replaced. Half the internal structures and two of the Abas had to have the bars cut from inside the cockpits. It was then the twins Abas were finally shut down. All the weapons had to be replaced on the Instructors Abas as well.

Bird Eye made the comment, "All these worthless students should get use to the barbaric clubs, since they aren't worth training to use anything else."

The twins were sure she meant it to go over the instructor's coms only, but they were listening in. It was the comment that provided a reasonable challenge to their honor. A challenge they accepted as response to a posted bet they made earlier in the week. Then they ensured the instructors would start the fight by dropping all kinds of antagonistic actions that were blamed on others.

As far as Wolf Law was concerned, it was a clean fight. The Headmaster did tear into them for disrespecting the instructors in front of the class. He also said the fight was not properly implemented because they did not verbally notify the instructors on the reason they were beating the other students so badly. This is why the instructors engaged, after the comment and the posting challenge.

The Headmaster also said Bird Eye must have trigger the wrong radio signal, which was why the Twins heard the comment. This meant, all the students heard the comment, and all the students were recognized for the engagement against the instructors. This lowered the honor earned by each individual student but was still higher than they received for the entire exercise since they were credited for beating the instructors.

Falstar, unlike Master Raven, did not complement them on their ability take down three Medium Sentinels that were fully armored and weaponized when they had Medium Scouts and armed with only two bars each. Instead he docked their earnings from their bets to pay for replacing the training equipment they damaged when smashing them into the instructors Abas.

The Headmaster also restricted their future combat training for the rest of the cycle to virtual only, unless the Master Instructor on the field let them join in. This lowered their earnings unless the instructors were willing to take them out on the live range. Falstar told them, this punishment was due to their needing to learn to show respect to the instructors.

They could have stopped the fight after they disarmed the instructors. It would have lowered the instructors Honor being beaten that badly by students. The twins taking it to the point of almost killing the instructors made his job harder, since he had to find replacements for their classes for the two weeks they would be spending in medical after the incident.

Selina was mad at them for beating the lighter pilots so long. She understood they needed to get the instructors to attack them, but she gave them a long talking to about being responsible for the way they treated the lighter pilots. They had enough going against them, like the twins.

Then she tore into them for allowing the Honor sharing. Since the scouts were suddenly boosted so high for beating the instructors, they had several challenges against them outside the Abas. The next person to beat them would get a boost in Honor as well. It made their next few weeks extremely difficult.

The twins felt this should have been a boost in their confidence and helped them get to the higher ranks. Only a handful of the seventy-seven students in the lower class had been with Selina's trainings and still in the lower ranks. Since the twins had not continued it since she left, they would not be prepared for the fights inside or outside the Abas. Inside the Abas wasn't allowed yet.

Falstar also told them he was tired of seeing them

because of incidents like this. While they did not comment back, they openly showed their anger at being addressed alone. To them, if the other students were getting the Honor for the victory, they should have been part of the orto chewing as well.

If he was going to spread the wealth, he should have spread the love, a comment Nite heard Dracon said after they told him about it.

Nite also felt Selina and Falstar should have decided who was going to do the chewing instead of seemingly taking turns to ensure they both had nothing to sit on for the next few weeks.

CHAPTER 12

FIRING RANGE

The twins were finally coming to the end of their punishment tier when an instructor approved them to go back on the field. It was 679.11.28, and although they were at the end of Cycle Two, they had not technically been assigned an Abas. They hadn't gotten into as much trouble these last two tiers, but it was more due to no one being willing to engage the thirteen-year-old trainees outside of simulations. They were still in the Marbled Polecats (MSc), though.

Simulations in your Abas were not the same as simulations with just the WBS. The bays the Abas were in were designed to react to the Abas and cause damage. It was less severe than if it were real world, but the pilot would feel it. Their body also went through the real motion of lifting the feet, moving the arms and turning the torso. For lighter scouts, this meant working their body pretty hard, even in simulations.

If a pilot did something wrong, they would receive from mild to severe shocks, jarring, and even burning sensations sent into their skin. Simulation deaths were accompanied by Severe body shocks throughout the body or burning pain injections, and lost Honor Levels. If the death was bad enough, the pilot received the full force of all of them.

The pilots could also increase the level of their physical punishments and lower the level of their Honor loss. The twins set their punishment levels to highest setting. It was not to save Honor, as many of the lighter pilots did. They learned quickly not to make mistakes more than once. It was not that they made many, but they made sure each one was memorable enough, the other one didn't make the same mistake.

For most, the change from virtual to Abas virtual was extraordinary. Even the twins felt more real within the light scouts they had been given. The scout frame didn't stop them from testing in other frames virtually, but they stayed more with those frames, mastering how to use every advantage they gave to face impossible odds. They wanted to learn to defeat the greatest of enemies with the lightest of Abas.

All their lives, they felt as if they had to prove they belonged. This was just another step toward it, however upsetting. Every step, every move, every iota of honor they received they earned. They also made others learn the failures of facing them.

Going on to the field today was very interesting to them. It was the first time they would be facing against the Heavier class in a Head-to-Head competition. Since they were truly facing a test of skills, they would know if they were where they belonged.

"I am your instructor. You may call me Illuminator. Some of you may know me from First Echelon or your first cycle if you have attended Heavy Courses.

"We will start today with firing your first weapon group from stationary for both you and the targets. Toggle to your second and again from stationary against moving targets, fire on the second group of targets. Then switch to your third weapon group and fire on the third set while both are in motion."

The voice belonged to an older woman, one Nite had heard before. She helped Selina get over being the child of light Abas parents and convinced her she could be better. She said no one is limited by their genetic forbearers, only what they perceived to limit themselves.

Nite always thought she truly showed what an Abas Pilot should be in and out of the school. Many of his positive memories had her attached. His more honorable actions reflected what he thought she would do. Their system of learning and improving came from her guidance, both direct and indirect. He was glad *she* brought them back.

No student was beneath her helping them, even

those that acted with less than honorable actions. She looked to find the right motivation and way of teaching them. Often, she left it for them to find it their own way with a little guidance from her, so they would learn to improve themselves. It was not about always coming to her but figuring out their own systems so they would always be impowered to be better.

There was an instructor who's design Nite didn't recognize with her. The pilot was in a Lycaon Pictus, or Painted Wolf (MSn), but did nothing to announce themselves or their reasons for being there. The pilot was not a light instructor, nor were the designs common in the schools.

Painted Wolf Pilots were very loyal to their groups. Usually attached to nothing smaller than a fire team of Painted Wolves all the way to a full platoon for operations. Once they joined larger packs of their own kind, they normally didn't leave them. They seemed to have their own hierarchy as well, although it was said most decisions were put to a vote when possible.

Their groups never really belonged to any Army or division. They were moved around based on mission needs and acceptance by the group. They were not broken apart by the Pack either. They were the outsider forces, even amongst other Abas pilots. Yet, they were effective with the highest success rate for any designed Abas group, exceedingly over eighty-percent success rate throughout their designs life.

Painted Wolves were also not limited to Wolf Pack

only. The design and mentality of the pilots were across all the Packs. The different groups of Painted Wolves would not fight each other openly either. It was one of the few designs that could be both biped and tetrapod in design as well.

To even be allowed to pilot one, you had to be accepted by an active *Pack* outside the school. They were also the only Abas warriors who were not attached to a Pack Family. The Painted Wolves were your family.

Nite saw the design before, although not this specific one, and like the idea of the Painted Wolves. They had specific markings in their cover designs so you could tell exactly which one you were dealing with. Most Abas were either covered in material that looked like fur to cut their radar tracking and give them better hiding advantage outside of cities or were exposed exterior armor with paint designs, which were more popular. Ghillie Suit could always be used in place of fur.

If it wasn't for the need to be connected to a Pack, Nite might have considered requesting to join them, even though they were only Medium Sentinel designs. Nite didn't want to be tied down to them or a Medium Sentinel.

"So how long do you think it will be before we get our true size, 6541231?" Nite jested.

Mike responded in coded beeps to his brother.

"Silence, 1321456!"

The command didn't come from one of his normal

instructors. It was meant to tell them to stop all unimportant communications on the com channels, even though Nite specifically spoke to Mike, he did do it where everyone could hear. The voice was the same scratchy old male voice Nite heard in the simulators a few times. It came from the Painted Wolf (MSn).

There was an Abas on the field that was not an instructor, nor a classman. She was an assistant who would one day move right into instruction from her school years, probably giving up her third echelon of school. Instead she would be in a different type of training during that period.

This was not the first time she was at a class with the twins. Nite was sure she was not originally listed on the schedule to be here. Like many times, she was not on the schedule, and then she was. It was more common since they got moved to simulation only, because she was on the non-simulation portion, but would then be moved to the simulation class.

She must want to see if we are as good in real life as we are in the simulators. I don't want to disappoint her.

Her attention had not been negative, as some of the instructors seemed to be. She helped them the same was as Illuminator. In truth, most the time, Nite felt he was helping her. She would ask him to try things differently and see if they would work or how it would work best.

Mike suggested she might be building up knowledge on how they worked so she could devise a strategy on how to defeat them. She wasn't the only one. There were at least three in their class that were *studying* them. At least one was trying to use it to get better, Moon Chaser.

Nite thought that was crazy since she entered her Midterm Cycle. By the time they could be challenged by her, she would be in her Instructor training. Which meant she would have to wait until they entered Third Echelon to challenge them.

Selina had other suspicions. None the less, Nite listened to his brother. Nite figured direct was the best solution and asked if she wanted to challenge him. She said the only game she was willing to try was a kissing game after he entered Midterm. He wasn't sure how to win those and the specialty classes on them didn't start until after Midterm.

Maybe that's why she wants to wait. She is waiting to challenge me after I have started the class and the defeat will count. Being defeated in something you haven't officially trained in wasn't counted against you.

Nite forced his mind back to the current situation. He was sure there were plenty of people with bets on them and their performance. It was time to make their personal bets pay out as well.

"Since some of you think you can do this without instructions, why don't you volunteer to come up and show the class how to do it?" the Painted Wolf called out.

Nite and Mike eagerly moved forward on the request but were stopped by the commander of the exercise. It was a challenge, not a mocking. He wanted to see what they could do.

"Let the demonstration be shown first, please."

It was Illuminator this time. Her voice was stern, but the twins had the distinct impression it was not meant for them.

The firing pattern was fast and impressive. The students quieted down so they wouldn't be called out and embarrassed as well. Illuminator might have been helpful, but she was also stern, to everyone. Instructors and students were the same to her.

If you messed up, she called you out. If you didn't listen to her suggestions, she would drop you. She seemed to always know the perfect punishment to get someone to listen to her the next time. Nite, never having experienced a mother, would have called her the Mother of the School.

Nite and Mike went ahead to the position on the firing lines. They went through this several times before in the simulators. Now they didn't have to hide their piloting skills while shooting. It would be simple for them to beat the instructor.

The goal was to destroy as many targets as possible. The highest would set the standard for the value of ranking points each one was worth. As with other competitions in the schools, light and heavy classes were pitted against each other. The highest score and the second highest score for each set would set the bonus for the victor team.

The better the two best were, the better the

ranking Honor Levels and Opportunities received for the next cycle. This was important, because the next cycle started free movement with the Abas Ranks and no longer being in the generic Abas Frames. The reason the top two scores were used was in case there was an exceptional pilot, they would not make it an unfair advantage for the rest of the students.

Lights were already at a disadvantage because of the lack of diverse weapons and lower powered weapons they had. They were given an advantage boost for this based on the weapon designs of their strongest performers compared to the strongest performers of the heavies. If they won, then that advantage could double the benefits they won. Even though they were in generic scouts, they could still choose their weapon configurations.

The losing team got the stick, as was true for the school. Their teams highest scores would set the differentiator for the exercise. That would be the bonus every other team member went up or down based on their scores, aside from the highest two. The differentiator would not impact the score of the highest two scoring members. This way, the competition in the two classes also remained.

The Pack wanted the lights and the heavies to learn to work together, so the exercise took the highest score and set each individual box value based on that score. The more boxes destroyed, the more ranking points each box was worth to the class as a whole. The higher ranking, the higher the Honor Level earned from the exercise.

The instructor's shots were almost perfect and marked those of a master firing. Nite and Mike watched closely in case they changed the exercise. They noticed several of the shots were barely close, especially in the end, but the floaters exploded anyway.

They were programmed to explode because the students would only pay attention to what was left, not how close the shots really were, Nite thought to himself.

He was the first to walk to the line. Another thought suddenly entered his mind, but it came from that strange, almost-distant part.

Illuminator doesn't miss.

I've seen her fire before. She barely missed to show us they were programmed for her.

He understood her message. His shots had to be dead-on. Nite was sure the boxes were programmed not to explode for him. He started to shake the thought, but it seemed so true.

She was the only one who has invited us out. She helped us in the past, plenty. She wants us to know we have to be dead on, better than anyone else if we are going to win this.

Why would she do that? Maybe she bet on us being victorious. It was a good bet. Only six people, including us, bet we would be the top of the class in scores and time in the same run.

Nite destroyed every box of every set without going stationary. He didn't even slow to a paused position for the advantage, speeding up the completion time. Mike followed suit getting everyone as well, again without stopping. The time difference was almost immeasurable, but one had lost to the other by twelve picoseconds. Not stopping was allowed, but most who went for the speed records didn't get the hit records. You had to qualify high enough in both to qualify for top scorer though.

Picoseconds were the lowest measurement of time capable by the program, but on the scorecards, they only showed the milliseconds. Both times were over thirty seconds faster than instructors preprogrammed run. Of course, she stopped. The group of light students cheered, knowing what that would mean for their class rankings. Two perfect scores doubled the high-ranking multiplier and reduced the impact of the lowest scores that much more. Even if the top two heavy class members beat the times with perfect scores, there was no differentiator. They would all receive the highest ranks in the next cycle.

The Painted Wolf stormed off the field. Nite smiled deeply inside himself. He walked the Abas back to the rear of the line to await his second attempt. Mike was right behind him, showing the same lack of emotion on his cockpit view.

It was one more mark of them proving they were here to be the best. The best meant better than all in the school, including the instructors. Ever since they received their abysmal promotions, and against

Master Raven's advice, they started to show enough of their talents to ensure they beat everyone.

The twins were just coming to the line for the second time. No one came close to their scores, but they wanted to do better anyway. It wouldn't be that hard since they couldn't help but be nervous. No matter how many times something was done in the simulator, real life always provided an interesting twist.

"6541231! 1321456! You are ordered off the field immediately. Please do not delay in returning your old training Abas to the bay. You will no longer need them," Illuminator announced just before the twins got up to go for their second run.

Nite and Mike offered no reply. Just turned their Abas off the field and started toward the hangers. They knew they might have taken it a little far lately. They were outscoring everyone.

This was their first time not in the simulator, and against their heavier classmates. It shouldn't have been a stripping offense. To be completely reduced out of the classes and back into the lower level was unheard of for such a small offence toward an instructor. Especially one so subtle.

Master Raven warned us not to challenge Falstar too much. Falstar did tell us to learn to be more respectful of the instructors on the field. We didn't listen. Maybe we'll just be sent back to the simulations. We've been accepted into Abas. They wouldn't take that away would they?

CHAPTER 13

ADVANCEMENT

"They are destroying our ability to teach the lower classes. They have outscored every student in their level. And I don't mean just the lights, Headmaster.

"Do you know how far they are in their classes? They are going to complete all the basics before the Midterm. *All* of them!

"You must send them to the heavy levels. Or better to Varanasi's schools," Bird Eye scowled at Falstar. "Even the Sentinel Classes don't have anyone close to performing at their level. None of the schools do."

She took a calming breath. "They don't belong in these schools. Not for what the schools are designed to do. We can't send them on those missions."

She came in shading the line of respect in the first place. Now she was pushing her luck no matter how much she was right. Still, she was going against the

Headmaster and the Council's orders at this point. To Falstar, they were one and the same.

"I am glad to hear you think so highly of them, but they may not be selected for a higher level until they have actually been selected for an Abas. As you know, they have not officially been assigned an Abas class. We only upgraded them to Medium Scout to give them the ability to carry a drum of missiles instead of a few in launchers and a couple extra external weapons."

His voice was calm and flat. He left the moment of silence, knowing she would jump on it.

"Then get them promoted to a low-level heavy Abas and get them out of my classes!" the department head of the light students demanded. "I can't keep doing what you have asked me to do? It's too great a risk," she added rubbing where her arm had been previously shattered by one of them.

The risk was not only in the school. At some point in time, they would be leaving the school. Bird Eye knew she wasn't going to stay in schools the rest of her days. Falstar was barely keeping her here now.

It meant they were likely to meet in the Armies at some point. A point the brothers might purposely make since she was making their life a misery. *I was following orders* didn't seem to cut it with students that took personal grudges against old instructors.

"I am glad you asked so properly. This just came in today. If you checked your box before you stormed in here or not interrupted me just now"—Falstar noted her face change with the realization of what she had done— "you would already know I have sent the requests off and finally received approval for them to advance with support of a team. They will both be in the Heavy Sentinel Frost Ferrets for now.

"The Painted Wolves under Master Electro will not accept them. He does not believe they will be limited to lighter Abas. Painted Wolves are all promoted to Medium Sentinels, and they will not approve their moving into the specialty Abas just as a steppingstone. He informed me of this when he left today, ending his observations.

"As you know, they were to be locked down until Midterm to ensure they fought to be the best. We agreed it would be best training situation based on their First Echelon scores. For them to struggle through. The Council agreed, and has not agreed to release them, even with their scores. The only way we can promote them to a higher rank is through an external team approval.

"The Artic Wolf Specialty Teams are willing to approve them for Frost Ferrets as a potential steppingstone. They have also accepted the students are not to know of their approval to join the team, especially since they didn't request it.

"They countered with it not being known the offer was given if they are turned down in the future. Which is why they are probably the only team that accepted my terms with counter terms. They proved they are worthy of actually going for that type of team and several others."

"Sir, I apologize for the disrespect that I have shown. Of course, you know what is best for them and the school. I . . . I . . . I am sorry, sir. Please forgive my rash actions. I've been here too long."

"Think nothing of it. I have also received their scores from the exercise you just monitored. They set a new schools record on their first attempts. It will be awarded to them both, since the time difference is in picoseconds, but Nite's number will be first."

"Nite? Which one is Nite?" Bird Eye suddenly asked.

"You will know by the number 1321456. His family name is unimportant. He will be named soon, I am sure. Afterall, this is the first tier in which unofficial naming starts amongst them. Your students will of course keep the honor score they earned as scouts. It is a great mark for you."

"You know their family names?" Bird Eye added as if the prestige he just pointed out was worth nothing.

Her words showed she was confused as she tried to place the pieces together. No one knew anything of these brothers since before coming to the school.

"OF COURSE I DO." Falstar slammed his hands on his desk as he stood up so quick, she didn't see him move.

He settled back in his seat before continuing.

"I know all the students' family names or random generated names, as is the case with these two. I have the right as Headmaster since I assigned them the numbers upon accepting them!"

Falstar noticed two indentions marked where he hit, but they were small enough that no one would noticed without looking a little closer. He ensured his movements did not draw attention to them. Especially in this well named convert.

"Forgive me sir. I am just a little . . .."

"You are forgiven, but do not read more into this then there is!" Falstar answered her. "All I have are the names."

She looked at him for a second longer, with her head turned, as if a bird looking at a particularly dangerous predator, wondering if she had been noticed.

He looked back at his desk and shifted through some files on the monitor with a wave of his finger, as if she were no longer there. Not wanting to change his mind, she left quietly.

Falstar looked up at the door as it closed and back at the desk. He checked his hands to ensure everything was still intact then shook his head. He destroyed another one of those mechanical bugs someone was building.

They were tiny but didn't have any recording or transmitting devices on them. It was more likely an upper classman was trying to use them for pranks, but they seemed to wonder all over the school. None had been a risk to security yet, but he still preferred to have them destroyed.

Small favor, but you must get a hold of yourself.

Acting out an emotion to drive someone where you want them is one thing. Actually showing emotions could ruin long laid plans. It will not due if they discover the truth.

She has been perfect in treating them like lower pieces. She even treated the other students against her normal way to push them harder. Although when they are not around, she does treat them slightly better. She was great at setting up the emotions you needed for them, especially with the girl.

Do not push Bird Eye away now, even if she will no longer have to deal with them directly. The staff still talk. We need her a little longer. We need her to go back to treating the students better before she leaves. I don't want her reputation ruined.

I wish I still had the girl here. It was easier to direct them with her.

Two more request are still out there. Should I promote them if they come in? We'll see. I might hold them another cycle. Struggle my little salmon. Prove your worth.

******

The first night in the heavy dorm was a little restless. It was not that they had better mattresses or nicer pillows. Those were the same for everyone. Only, they couldn't get comfortable, as if someone was pulling, poking and pinching them throughout the night.

Both twins shot up out of their beds with the low echo of screams still reverberating in their heads. A small tinge of the sound was still there as if it were calling out to them.

They dropped into the hidden tunnels and set off to find the sound. Moving as quietly and quickly as they could manage. Both had a since someone was following them, but they didn't stop or slow down. It was more like being accompanied than stalked. It was like the someone was right at the edge of their vision, but no matter how they turned their heads, the person was never there.

They couldn't slow down to investigate properly. They continued to follow the moaning, low screeches. Continued the search into shear madness. Even if they wanted to stop, the shrieks wouldn't have allowed them to.

Pain accompanied the wails of agony as they got closer to the source. The screams didn't get any louder, just clearer and the pain sharper, spreading throughout their bodies. The two stumbled to a sudden stop as the shrieks abruptly ended and the pain vanished without a memory of its existence other than it did exist.

Directly above them were the frames of the Marbled Polecats (MSc). Their WCGs had been pulled from the machines, gutting the core of the Abas. The WCGs were being installed in the cockpits that would maintain them. Even if the twins moved to larger frames, the cockpits wouldn't have to have the WCG removed, just reframed it to meet the design.

They could feel the shaping of the cockpits holding

their computers being morphed to the new designs. The cage that would protect the pilot was being added to. More of the older parts were being reconnected. It felt as if it were becoming whole again.

The upgrade to Heavy Sentinel would allow them to have all the old parts back on their machines. There were so many changes yet to go through. The twins knew it was going to be a long night for the Abas minds. They could tell the parts remembered this discomfort. The twins felt like they were holding the hand of a partner, giving them strength, while they dealt with the pain.

Whatever summoned the twins was sedated with their arrival. Satisfied, it stopped its strange calling, leaving them to listen to the engineers talk as they finished the last part of their Abas cockpits and fitted them into the new armor.

Nite and Mike both knew this would not be the last promotion to a new frame. They knew the experiences wouldn't be as painful either. The cockpits inner workings would never have to be modified for them again. The final transformation of the internals had been complete.

A gruff woman's voice spoke up suddenly as she could be heard rising from a squatted position.

"They're both ready for Elite if it comes down to it. But why did we put on these old parts?"

"They wanted them. I asked," Jason left his answer unspecified.

"There are times I wonder about you, boy," the

woman laughed. "Spent a week coming back here to watch over these upgrades personally. You normally don't take such an interest in designs. Is it because you didn't design these?"

"I never have to wonder about you. You just tell me how it is. I like it! I have a lot to learn from these two designs. They were not the same designer, as I am sure you already know, but the synergy between them and their pilots are . . . amazing."

"You know I have a daughter about your age. A technician, but she's a smart one. She would have been an engineer if I had the connections and opportunities to back it, I think. She just missed the score requirements to not have some type of backing to get in. You know how it goes."

"You have always been held high in my books," the man answered with a smile to soften the blow of the memory. "I do. Same happened to one of my brothers. Although I think with him, it was less connection and more just didn't try hard enough."

"Yeah, that happens as well. Sometimes the young don't know how to push themselves hard enough. Get complacent and rest on their laurels. Yesterday's victories and defeats are in the past. You can only move forward from either."

Nite remembered him from the cockpit linking.

It must have been from that conversation when he said "they wanted them". *He remembered we wanted the old parts. He remembered us. Maybe we have another potential member, or would it be ally?*

"Besides, you can see more then what's in front of your eyes. I followed your bets on these two. Might retire instead of returning out if I find the right path for my daughter. About my daughter . . .," the woman continued as the twins turned away.

Nite suddenly looked around where he was at. His brother was next to him, but neither of them seemed to remember the other making their way there. Nite couldn't even remember coming other than the drive to answer the call. He couldn't have retraced his own steps if he wanted to.

By the look of confusion on Mike's face, he couldn't remember either. Yet they both knew their Abas were about to be moved to a different hanger. The Polecats would be moved back to be reframed for another pilot. They seemed to have said goodbye.

Nite felt a since of ending with them. The frames they had learned so much in were going to be gone from their lives. Even if someone else took it, they would never be their frames, their alignment again.

But the best parts of them are in the new frames. The parts that make us whole are together. We are being prepared . . . but for what?

They were about halfway back to the barracks when they sensed more than heard someone coming up from behind them. It was not on the same path that they took earlier. Yet, they knew whatever it was, it was coming for them.

"You saw me coming this time?" Dracon asked one of the corners the twins took seclusion in.

"Aye, sir," they responded together as they emerged.

"I will try to do better for you next time."

He laughed, although his mind was not into hunting them, but something else. Instead of admitting he was distracted, he tried to use a different approach.

"Maybe you are used to me, or maybe I have trained you too well. Might need some other tools now."

"We know you have several other tricks up your sleeve for us to learn no matter how fast we are doing it. What brought you out here?" Nite asked, wondering if he too was called.

Master Raven only had parts of his system remaining from when it was destroyed. He kept them but went to the schools and never had it built again. It was only enough to enter into simulations. He said he felt as if he needed to rebuild himself before he rebuilt his Abas again.

"I have come down here to see if you wanted your own rooms. The Headmaster asked me to find you since you were not in the recently assigned barracks any longer.

"It seems no one wants to sleep in the same barracks with you. They are requesting to hot rack instead of being in there. The Headmaster felt it would be better to move you to Third Echelon Heavy Rooms instead."

Mike made a hand gesture to ask a question.

Dracon watched the movements, making a small change in the holding of the fingers on the left hand.

"No. People do not normally go from Medium Scout to Heavy Sentinel without a transition period. No, I don't believe Falstar has access to your secret training records. You do have training records with up to Heavy Zhayedans in simulations prior to the 679.1.4 and after the 679.3.29 incidents.

"Both of you are going straight into heavy ranked Abas. You'll probably get awarded with Grey Wolves by midterm. It isn't up to Falstar to make the final decision on that, like we have been assuming. Others are taking a more direct interest in your promotability or lack thereof.

"It's a great Abas, if I do say so myself. If you do qualify, it will be the first time I have ever seen a pilot from these schools put into such high level Zhayedan this early in their second term as well. No one in your class will see a Medium Zhayedan until at least a cycle past midterm."

Mike asked another question through hand signals.

"You are going to be put in Third Echelon Rooms because of the promotion. All medium and heavy Zhayedan pilots are in their own shared rooms in this school. This way you are out of the barracks as a reward for qualifying early and they won't have to move you later. It does make more sense. I don't think the school administration is used to using common sense, but . . .."

Master Raven laughed after giving a half shoulder shrug. Then he beamed at the twins accomplishment and recognition. The excitement in Dracon's voice was honest and he was happier for being able to show a true emotion. He grew tired of the false emotions he used with his students, especially the best to give them a false since of security or to lead them down a path that would make them better.

The twins were beyond those simple tactics. They learned to read them faster than an interrogation computer. He only had one other student that good. When she left the school, there was a mark no one would forget. It was an Elite leaving. Even she didn't develop her skills this early.

Nite and Mike studied Dracon's expression for a moment. The looks on their face said they knew there was more to what he had to say. They were giving him the respect of bringing it up himself. Dracon silently nodded his head, readying for the reaction they were bound to have.

"The Council has been monitoring you . . . closely. A member specifically directed you to not be placed in the higher Abas until after midterm and wanted you back in the Polecats. I watched the video conference with them from Falstar's office.

"The Supreme Headmaster was there as well. I think he pulled some strings to place you, to be honest. Probably pointed out there was no point in holding up your training any longer. It was said by others promoting you too high too fast might make you think you were better than you were.

"It was a stupid reason, since you are accepted by a team that would allow you to be promoted to Heavy Zhayedan Level. It's the only way to get promoted to the higher levels in any school before Midterm Echelon Two. The Supreme Headmaster, if that was his voice, pointed out there was no way, with your scores, that you two would leave here in less than a Medium Zhayedan.

"The War Council Representative said it didn't matter what you graduated as, since they would be willing to assign you to several special teams after a couple more years of training. He did say he preferred you finish school. However, if the schools were not going to see to your proper training, they would approval early release for them to provide it.

"Midterm Second Echelon is the earliest you could be released. I do not believe they would approve Selina before the start of Third Echelon. Pulling Abas students have never been done as early as Midterm Second Echelon. It is a precedence the are using from other warrior caste.

"Your current scores are higher than any other student who has passed through the Pack schools. You are well above what any Zhayedan has shown at this level. They might as well get on and let you have your Heavier Abas Frames to start developing your full range of skills."

Nite and Mike looked up at their instructor. A

little confused and a little excited. The excitement was that of youth. Master Raven doubted there was anything society could do that would remove this type of excitement from young teenage boys. It was an excitement of receiving something they had been dreaming about and working toward for years.

Most men still get excited, even if they don't show it.

"The engineers were designing our cockpits around Timber Wolves. It was not the Grey Wolf model. The differences are simple, but they are set up for the wider shoulders of the Timber Wolf. Frost Ferrets can fit either frame for the cockpit with modifications. It's why it's one of the most popular for training selection in the Heavy Sentinel's outside these schools.

"Why would they put them in Timber Wolf settings if they were going to put them into Grey Wolves? I doubt Falstar would ever try to push us into a higher Abas. More like trying to hold us down by hoping we fail the added pressure."

"I said the Supreme Headmaster, not . . . wait, how did you recognize the framing of a cockpit?" Master Raven switched back into professor mode.

"I've been reading up on it. There are a lot of books on those subjects that are not limited in the heavy classes reading. They just aren't accessed often by other students. We barely spend more time than just skimming them."

Nite quickly corrected himself, thinking that if they knew how fast the two of them could read, and retain, it would do little for them. Even Dracon wasn't privy to all their abilities.

"You've read that much already? Those books can only be accessed after you have completed several other readings and all your base courses. That is why those books are not read often. It is not only because they speak of Engineering of the Abas, but because you have to have cleared a lot more information before you are permitted to even have access to this.

"Have you not been submitting all your completed work? What level are you on?"

"We did this under our other accounts. We don't have access to those books as light class members," Nite sneered in resentment.

"Wait. You completed the work under your other accounts. And you have them as heavy members in advanced years. And you're still that far ahead on your other studies!"

"We have great memories, and our parents used to read to us all the time. They would point at the words as they did. That is one of the only memories that we have of them."

Nite didn't mention that if Mike read something, he would know what it was. It also worked the other way as well. They couldn't talk to each other yet, but they had learned early that if one had figured out how to do it, or read it, the other would be able to quote it verbatim as if he had read it as well.

"What else do you remember of them?" Dracon

had dropped out of professor mode and was back into friend mode.

The switches were hard to read, but the twins were used to them. With him, he was not sure of how to stand with them either. Both sets moved between the stances as fast as others blinked, never considering the changes strange or different. To them it was as natural as breathing.

"The smell of their cockpits. The internal framing was for Larger Abas. I've not found the style within the books yet," Nite answered as he closed he eyes and held his hand to his head.

That explains the interest in the cockpit framing, Dracon thought.

A flash of light, Mike replied with hand gestures.

Dracon looked at him wondering what it would mean. He didn't bother to ask. The answer was as unknown to the twins as it would remain to Master Raven. He hoped to get something form the memories that might help him find out who they were.

He didn't tell them everything about the Council meeting and the way they reacted, which groups seemed against them, or Falstar's perceived and real stances. This was another piece to the puzzle of where they came from. Yet, it was another one that brought more questions and no answers.

Why were you born? What greater purpose are you here for? You are not cyborgs; I tested that. I tested your DNA as well, and you're 100% human. It shows absolutely no connections to anything in the system, though. Or it is blocked, specifically from showing anything.

I know it had a backtrack alarm set to it. I hoped I stopped the emergency signal and rerouted it fast enough. Someone doesn't want anyone looking into your past without them knowing someone is looking. I believe I did, but why is it so important to stop people from looking into it?

What would be so important as to protect your DNA trackers? What did your parents do to deserve a fate of complete obliteration from our systems? What did they do to create enemies as high as the council? Who are they? Who are you? Does Falstar really know or are his orders there to throw me off?

CHAPTER 14

THE CALL OF
THE COUNCIL

Nite and Mike were not happy about being separated from their Abas for so long. They were notified, packed and placed on a transport on 680.6.1. It was now 680.6.9 and they would be arriving on Varanasi within the hour.

It had just been over seven months since receiving the promotion to Frost Ferrets. They were not the first children of Wolf to be called in front of the council, but that did not stop them from wondering what was to become of them. Most students called by a council would have reported to the War Council on Daritock. Nite had not found a history of anyone from their schools being called to Varanasi. They had not been able to crack the record for the Varanasi Schools, which were guarded by all the Packs.

Since entering Cycle Three, the twins backed off

on their performance levels. They still performed at record breaking speeds, setting new standards. Only one student in a different school was able to beat even some of those, although the records of them were as tightly locked as the Varanasi School information. They would work to get the record back once notified, often showing a little more of what they learned ahead of schedule.

Mostly, they kept it closer to the cuff on operations and didn't completely destroy everyone as easily as they could have. In a way, it helped them start performing better. They allowed people to get an advantage before they began to truly perform. They would walk into traps and weaken themselves, to find out if they could push through the damage and win. No one had come close to defeating them, although playing this game gave others hope.

They started taking on more teams as well. Teaching them was not on the agenda but helping them become better was. They would take the time to let team members make mistakes, but they kept them from outright dying. It was kinda like the way they treated Selina when she was around. They worked with a team for a short period before shifting attention to a different set, never working with any one team longer than a month and all were lighter teams.

The travel was quick through the Coil Launchers and finally a Worm Head crossing almost ten Au's of space. The Worm Head seemed the strangest. They could have turned and pointed at their Abas straight through it, but once it closed their directions changed completely and the distance was immense. That was two days ago.

With the lack of experience of how to act away from the school, the twins looked to their three older traveling companions for direction. Dracon came with them and offered little in expression. This they were used to and expected, yet it was not for the reasons they had come to understand.

The closer they got to the city, the more recessed he became. It was Illuminator who answered why, or at least gave her opinions on the matter. It was a simple story of lost love and a son that was given to a different school. He hoped to get a connection with the boy after the loss of his mother during the son's birth. The son was ordered to a different school to prevent Master Raven from discrediting them both with favoritism that could result in unworthy ranking amongst his peers. He wasn't even sure if his son was in the forward schools or the Varanasi ones.

As with her insight on Master Raven, she brought many more wise tidbits to the table during the trip. The grey hairs in her head actually marked wisdom, unlike some of the other leaders they'd met that were put out to the school due to lack of knowledge. Only she still moved as if fifteen years younger and gave signs even this was just a show. Nite marked her as the most dangerous of all the companions, including the twins.

Enlightenment, their last companion, was not

there for the twins, but was called before the council for her own reasons. She seemed to be very interested in the twins but showed her special interest in Nite during the trip. He was not sure what to do with the interest of the young lady.

When he asked if she wanted to challenge him the last time, she said she would only do it with a kissing game. Dracon warned him to be careful. That was a game you could win and lose at the same time but provided no more clarity on the matter.

Being on this trip added to the confusion. It was not because she was a few years older than him. It was because she was there to get final approval to become an instructor. Nite wasn't sure if she wanted to use him in some way, like many of the others. She knew this was coming and had helped the twins in the past. Yet, if this was her purpose, it didn't align with her questions. Nothing she asked seemed to deal with their Abas or with Mike. It was just about him and she talked about her as well.

They had spent several hours talking of nothings while Mike sat back in a dark corner, not really adding anything to the conversations. She even put in more information and told them stories of her other instructors. These were vital to the twins since it gave them very powerful insights on how the Heavy Instructors gave their classes and what the Senior Instructors looked for in their mastery classes for scoring.

Enlightenment was fair skinned, with thick, wavy

light brown hair. It was pulled up in a bun for most the trip, but Nite had seen it when it was let down and allowed to dance around her lower midback. She had a beautiful shade of green-blue eyes that held a look of brilliance in both mental as physical attributes. Her bangs were cut to the tip of her nose and then lifted to curl to loosely decorate her forehead. She had plump lips with a natural wet pink-rose color that made a heart shape when she blew kisses at people. It was a habit she used when saying good-bye or good night.

Even at the younger age of nineteen, Nite could tell she was going to remain a beautiful woman. She insisted on working out as much as she had insisted on studying, just not as long. She told him she wanted to be lean and flexible. To him her goals were well met so far.

Several times she had come into the common cabin to stretch in front of everyone. It was not to show off; there just wasn't enough room in her stateroom. Nite agreed. He and Mike were sharing one. Dracon and Illuminator had their own as well. It was barely big enough for them to sleep in, much less work out.

Nite and Mike went through their forms, stretching and fighting as well with Master Raven in the commons. They had not been allowed to leave the little apartment area since coming on the ship. It seemed Captain Neosp was not a fan of having Abas Warrior Students on his ship. He believed they would cause trouble and threatened to jettison the entire apartment if they were ever found outside of it.

Illuminator seemed to frown on the idea of the young lady acting as she did in front of the twins. It was such an old set of thoughts, Nite didn't understand why. She didn't say anything, but the air became frosty when Enlightenment showed up in her short armor to do her workout routines.

The twins lived with girls and boys always together. Showered in the same rooms, bathed in the same baths and used the same facilities for everything. Dracon couldn't explain the older lady's concepts, either. He, like the twins, lived within the same rooms as his female counter parts.

Other than the sexual organs, males and females were looked at and held to the exact same requirements. Requirements were based on job skills and talents. Sexual partners were also a basic need but had little to nothing to do with the way they saw females when it came to missions. The two distinctions were completely different.

Mike speculated it might be because she didn't like someone of Enlightenment's standards talking to and showing off in front of someone as low as them. They were students not past midterm and she was a selected instructor. They were often separated and did not perform such task in front of students. They were perfect without practice as the concept they were to adhere too.

Master Raven agreed this might be part of it, but it was also part of a very old school of thought. He added part of it might be Illuminator felt protective over Nite and Mike in some motherly way. What it boiled down to, they were always supervised, even when performing the simplest of task around the apartment by her orders. Even Dracon seemed to take a special interest in not allowing them to be alone, although he was more discreet in his monitoring.

Illuminator was still beautiful in her older years. Her hair had long turned shiny silver, but it didn't slow her mind or the fierceness of her grey eyes. She too had her hair pulled back, but the size of the bun did not tell how long it was down her back. It was thick and rich and said she had taken care of it most if not all her life. She was never seen as anything but an instructor.

Her skin was light but still held a tinge of a long-held copper tan to almost a pinkish tan skin with a few creeping wrinkles. It was expected with someone of her believed age, although the twins were not quite sure how old she was. She was marked with old age and her mind was full of knowledge that could only come from true experience. The only thing that really seemed to date her was the opinion of "how a young lady should act".

This woman was walking wisdom. A perfect example of what Nite wanted from himself when he reached his graying years. Yet, he couldn't tell anything about how old she was.

Illuminator spoke of old battles, even ancient battles during their travels. She told the twins the way several different leaders led their armies to victories which should not have been theirs. Some she spoke of as if she was in the midst of the battles herself. They were beyond even her youngest years, and likely was more she performed in the simulator to really feel the experience and gain the knowledge from the generals of the time.

Through it all, Nite and Mike both continued to learn from the stories. More than just about the battles, but the tactics they used. Illuminator brought up several pictures and diagrams during their travels, showing the battles. It was like watching a strange version of Lupus Medium. This was better because as Nite voiced the questions, she answered them as best she could. These eight days of travel advanced them more than the last two years.

In a way, they had continued their schooling, which was expected, but the level that they were training was beyond any that they were use too. They were getting answers to questions, and ones that made sense. It was as if she helped start the Packs. Then lived through it all just to pass the information down to the twins.

Enlightenment sat through the lessons, although she claimed half the time they were speaking above her level. Nite was sure that it was just her way of trying to set a comfort to them. She brought up points the twins hadn't thought. For Nite, this was the greatest point in his life to date. For Mike, it was the most educational.

The Central City was the only city within the

Varanasi system which never saw war. If the Packs stayed in power, the city would never see war. Even the Silent Knights stayed away from the City of Peace. The Hunters were not allowed within the walls. It was as if a silent pact was made with the Silent Knights and the Hunters. Neither of them would bring their war within the walls of the Central City. Trials and other actions were always held in a different city as well.

When the twins laid eyes on the city for the first time, they understood the reason for the silent agreement. It was the most beautiful sight they ever saw. The engineering and layout of the city had to have been planned completely before it was built. The harmony of everything living, created, and designed flowed evenly throughout the city, adding to what could only be described as "living peace".

Nite and Mike temporarily forgot the reason they came to the beautiful city as they passed through the streets. Their education continued. Each building was brought to life as its purpose and meaning was told. Each building of the main walk told a story of each Pack. They were obviously walking the perspective of Wolf, but Nite hoped they could walk some of the others with Illuminator before they left.

I wonder if she knows as much about their walks as this one.

The peace of the walk was interrupted as they came upon a building she merely referred to as "the Capital Building", as if there was some great failure through the rest of the city. It didn't take long until the twins were escorted into the center of a room with several rows stacked in a spiraling semi-sphere that opened like a flowering petunia. Every chair seemed to be filled with hundreds of eyes and sensors staring down on them. All the people, and those that resembled people, wore cloaks of shimmering colors that blocked their faces.

"REPORT!" The voice echoed throughout the domed room, but Nite and Mike both turned to the source to answer.

"I am student 1321456, reporting as ordered," Nite called out.

Mike looked at all of them for a long time before he too called out, "I am student 6541231, reporting as ordered."

"The council recognizes the students 1321456 and 6541231, and their two escorts, Illuminator and Master Raven. We will begin the proceedings," a different person called out in the same voice.

Nite and Mike again turned to the source, only this time they noticed a slight shift under the coats. A series of questions were shot at the twins. They answered them all flawlessly, having been through these types of procedures in school when taking oral exams.

Every time one was asked, they looked at the thing that asked the question to answer. It was the way they were trained. Respond directly to the person who asked. Often it was an android giving the exams.

Are we not supposed to know who is asking? It seems so obvious since they shine differently when they speak.

Nite wondered if seeing the question coming from who had asked it vice paying attention to hearing reverberating echo from every direction was part of the test. Did it mean they were passing or failing. Once two beings, both circuits asked the same question at the same time from two different locations. Mike and Nite turned to one respectfully and answered in unison.

They became more confident as they answered. Even when they dug deeper into answers, the twins were able to respond. Nothing gave them the impression they answered incorrectly.

Finally, after what seemed a couple of hours, the twins were asked a question they had to think about.

"Why do you believe you deserve to be promoted to such a high level?"

This time the voice was not the same as the others. The voice spoke of a beautiful lady who sang every word she spoke, even though she had not sung a note during her question. It was relaxing and comfortable, unlike the question it asked.

Nite was the first to speak.

"There is no equal for us within the forward schools. If there is one in this room, then we would like to see them come forward to challenge us. We will take any Abas within the level we have earned and face them, either alone or together. If they are not warriors, we will face their champion."

Mike continued as Nite took a breath. It was as if they were speaking the same thing from two different minds.

"We have no fear of what we are capable of becoming. We do not fear those who will get us there. If we are to lose before we leave these schools, then I would have you know, nothing you have brought is even remotely able to fulfill the mission.

"You are welcome to leave your benches and face us but be forewarned. We will not hold back. We are prepared, as we are supposed to be within the walls of Timber Wolf Academy."

"We may not be victorious in the end by the flying of our flags, but we will be victorious in proving there are none our age who are our equals," Nite finished.

Seven members around the council stood up at the remarks, but the rest remained seated. Those that stood, Nite and Mike were sure, would be the ones that were willing to face them. They never wished to have their own Abas more. A challenge like this could not go unanswered. They were asking for it when they were at their greatest disadvantage.

Illuminator suddenly rose from her seat behind and to the left of Nite.

"They do not have their Abas, so I ask those who have accepted to please sit. There will be a time when the greatest of you will be able to face these warriors. Their age and our policies do not allow it for now. I ask the council to consider what has been said and to give their answer."

The seven sat back down as the door the twins and their representatives came through opened. Nite and Mike were quickly shuffled out to an excited Enlightenment.

"Did you get approved for—" her words were cut off by a sign from Master Raven.

"We were not given an answer. We left so they could deliberate," Illuminator answered.

Before Enlightenment could ask another question, Master Raven added a little more information on the previous actions of the twins.

"We decided to leave it to them to come up with an answer because the presence of two very young and very *dumb* students who challenged them *all* to a warrior's contest might sway them from what is best for the Pack. You'll have an interesting Third Echelon after, I can say that much!"

"You didn't!" Enlightenment looked between the two momentarily, laughing with shock.

Her eyes settled on Nite, waiting for an answer. It was not that she didn't expect an answer to come from Mike. He had graced her a few times with words. She almost never took her eyes off Nite when he was present.

"Seven of them were ready to answer. But I foresaw this being a problem and left their Abas in the school. It was a good thing, I would say, my young pupils," Illuminator smiled at the boys as she took them by the shoulder and turned them back toward the exit.

The realization as to what they did settled on them. They challenged the Council of the Pack to a Battle of Equals. They could not answer their own challenge at this time by loops, but they did not know this when they spoke. The brothers couldn't help but show their emotions as they sped through them too fast for even the twins to toss them into their internal, mental fires.

Illuminator watched Nite's face, seeing the true realizations for the first time as he shifted through his thoughts. They were faster than she could keep up with, but for the few moments they were there. Emotion on their faces. It was something she was sure they were not used to showing. She would never forget their looks.

She didn't turn from Nite to watch Mike. Master Raven was watching him. Every face, every emotion that could be linked to it, pure, true and expressed for her to see. A rare treat in ones who trained this hard to always remove emotions from their exterior. The two instructors would compare notes later.

When they settled back into their calm exteriors, they realized the doors were open. It was time for them to face their answer. The twins walked into the door as if they were walking into their execution. Their heads held high, with an air of confidence exclaiming, if they were to die, then they would die with every ounce of courage as any Abas pilot before them.

There were only seven members remaining. The

rest seemed to have left the room. The twins were not sure the significance, but they were sure these were the ones that stood.

"The council has agreed and will finalize the promotion when it is deemed best. Until then, young ones," the centermost cyborg answered with a wave of his hand toward the exit.

They knew they'd seen him before. They knew under the cloak was a cyborg no one wanted to be on the wrong side of. Being on his right side might be even worse.

Dracon led the twins out before anything else could be said. They passed Enlightenment as she entered after them. Nite turned to ask her where she was going. For the first time he could think of, she wasn't paying attention to him. Her focus was on entering the room.

"Where is she going?" Mike suddenly asked after the door shut behind her.

Enlightenment was no longer with them either.

"She is here to face the council. Much like you, they are going to question her. If she is half as successful as you, she will be made an instructor, even at her early age. She will not have students for a while, but instead of being graded, she will start earning the rankings of a real instructor. Her understudy will begin, and in four years, she just might be instructing the two of you." Dracon smiled, not giving the twins enough time to truly consider what he was saying.

"No. She won't be instructing your level for several

years after you leave. She is good, but I doubt she is that good. Her focus will remain on the First Echelon children for a while."

"Would they want us to become instructors if we score too high?" Mike asked suddenly with a new fear for his dreams.

"No. She showed excellent promise in instructing others and in her grades. Not as a practitioner of war. If she ever went to the front lines, it would be to guide the troops on the right path or to help those in the Five-Year Promotion status to prepare. Not to actually fight to hold the path."

"And we would hold the path?" Nite asked.

His young mind was full of information but had lacked the experience that came with time. Both the twins had a problem with this, always wanting time to move faster.

Ironically, after it has moved to you understanding what you needed, you want time to slow down, and give you just a bit more! But such was the life of a Human.

"After today, you likely are the ones they are guarding the path from," Master Raven answered.

CHAPTER 15

PREORDAINED ASSEMBLAGE

Dracon left the twins to find their own way through the city. The twins agreed not to separate. As good as he was, he would not be able to watch over them if they did. The city was too big for him to try. That did not mean he would not follow them from a safe distance.

He wanted to let them have the experience very few pilots from the forward schools would see before graduation. While they were only fourteen years old, they were also well-trained warriors. Sometimes the best thing to do was let them run a little wild so they would settle down when locked up later. He hated to admit it but trying to watch them in that small apartment on the ship was killing him. Nine more days back wasn't going to be a pleasure cruise.

At least we agreed not to tell them what was going

to happen when they got back. It might be impossible to keep them from taking over the ship and trying to find a faster way . . . from within the apartment.

With a few additional privileges on their PAC, the twins set off to get some trinkets and see the first true city they could remember. As if a magnet pulled them, they didn't stop until they reached a larger dome resting in the city center. They walked through four guarded gates to get there, but no one had questioned them.

There were warbots, the first the twins ever remembered seeing, at every gate. They held their PACs up to every one of them as they passed. It was what all the other Humans were doing when they entered passed the sentries. They followed suit and acted as if they weren't doing this for the first time. It didn't reduce their Opportunities, Privileges or Honor Ranks, or they might have tried to sneak into it differently.

Outside, in the dome's courtyard, they saw what had to be a female Cyborg and two male androids. She spoke almost like a normal Human, but there was just a little something off in her voice. She was fully covered in skin, but every part that could be replaced had been. How the twins knew this was unclear to them, but they knew it to be a fact. Just like they knew three of the seven who stood up to face them were Cyborgs.

There was a younger human with them as well. At least the child looked younger, but the twins had an impression from her that seemed different. Older. Weird.

She was with a beautiful, young girl with thick, wavy black hair and perfectly bright white skin. Her eyes were a bright stone blue, unlike Mike's, whose eyes were stone grey. She was about Nite's height and of an age with the twins. She wore a shimmering emerald dress and matching shoes that raised her height another seven centimeters (3") higher than she would be flatfooted.

Her attention shifted to the twins like a laser locking in on a target. They did not change their own gaze on her. She had to shift between their eyes, but all held steady. It was not a look of challenge, just one that seemed to take in the other. It was the curiosity of two very dangerous animals crossing each other's paths. As if two masters were squaring off and sizing the other's true capabilities up.

"Come, Mercedes," the cyborg woman stood up and looked down at the child. "You do not know them, and you are promised to someone else. We have permission to leave with your Abas, so let's not waste another minute. As it is, it will be at least half a year to prepare. Let us begin.

"Besides, I would not want to live in a place that considers you common. As if *that* girl could look as beautiful as you do."

Nite knew the last part was meant for him to understand she was the most beautiful girl throughout the Pack association. He found more interest in the comment of them leaving. The girl was beautiful, and well trained, but she was not what he was looking for.

Where would they go? The cyborg said it.

"We have permission to leave with your Abas. . ."

The Cyborg probably added that to make an Abas pilot seem so much more to those who were not. I wonder what we look like.

Nite was an Abas pilot. They looked the same as every other person, aside from the Cyborgs, Robots, Tutevibians, and Grameracks. Well, they looked the same as every Human anyway. The warrior Tutevibians were well known and the twins had seen pictures and videos with them fighting in and out of armor. They had never seen a Gramerack, for the few times they were seen on video they were wearing the robed clergy cloaks common with the race of peacekeepers.

It was rumored that within the peaceful walls of their temples, they trained to be great warriors. Such rumors would be common amongst the young warriors, though. After all, what was life without war? It wasn't as good a rumor as the cyborgs having a special unit to kill any Human Abas pilots that got too good. That one at least was backed by most the pilots that participated in the last Crusader Olympia being killed off.

In truth, if they earned a high enough reputation, they were offered the ability to become a cyborg and join their elite ranks. The benefit was to live longer than any Human could hope to live. To be able to watch as technology grew and to bring the peace of war to others was a thought of ecstasy to most of the young children.

Some of the greatest warriors turned it down. They said they had but one life to live and did not wish to live longer than their body was meant to. Nite met a few of these in his younger years. They came to see their children in the housings units the twins stayed.

The young twins couldn't help but want to be part of conversations. They often thought of the people talking for them as well as the blood-related child they had come to see. When a child didn't have someone coming to them, then their imaginations make do with what they could have.

The twins turned down a path leading opposite of the girl. It was not due to failing to find the conversation interesting. They already pushed their luck with the council and didn't need Master Raven getting in trouble because they got caught stalking someone outside of school.

It'd still be nice to test our skills against those androids though. See if ours just let us catch them.

The path stopped at the first closed doors they came to. Two giant warbots stood outside of it. Unlike the first sets who allowed them to enter the courtyard, these seem to be a warning against entering. They both were close to twelve meters tall, just topping the size of the gate they stood guard.

Likely to prevent people from getting over it.

Nite and Mike looked at each other. It seemed their teenage, boy brains forgot what limits they already tested for the day. One act of putting a toe across the line was quickly turning into playing jump rope with the laser beam. The twins raised their PACs to the warbots and continued to walk forward.

"Do you wish to have your levels checked? If it is found wanting, you will be killed. Do you wish to proceed?" the warbots sounded off at the same time.

"Yes," the twins answered, not looking away from the warbots.

They fought things similar to this in simulations. They were sure they could beat these two as easily. Afterall, they had weapons on them. No one said they couldn't bring those to the council's meeting. If they couldn't find them or detect them, that was their fault.

"Proceed," the machines answered as the doors opened.

The twins looked at each other and walked in.

******

Master Raven tried to make it into the gates before they closed for the second time but failed.

"Do you wish to have your levels checked? If it is found wanting, you will be killed. Do you wish to proceed?"

Dracon did not answer but waited for the rushing footsteps to come up behind him.

"How did they get in? I assume the other two slipped in without you being able to follow."

"I don't know, and yes. I know I do not have enough to get in here. It is marked by the council. How the hell did all of them get in?" Dracon cut back without looking over his shoulder.

He knew who was coming up behind him.

"It doesn't matter how they got in. The four of them have entered in there together. We have to get in before they are trapped in a spot that will not let them out. Mercedes entered from the West Gate. She slipped Melania Lagorio, her keeper, and went in after she saw the way the twins went. I wonder if putting you in as their guardian was a good idea," the sienna skinned woman snapped out of frustration.

"Didn't your daughter follow my students in, Nox?" Dracon shot back at the Headmaster of Canis Lupus Training Facility.

The child with the pretty girl kicked Master Raven hard behind the knee, dropping him to the ground.

"You had an insect on you. Figured it was best to kill it before we found out if it was deadly," she answered with a straight face.

The power behind the kick didn't align to the girls inverted triangle figure. Dracon would have placed her at the same age as the twins, but she kicked harder than they did.

And your marked as Bear Sleuth, so its like your one of her students. Why'd you choose to attack me.

He owed Nox no additional respects outside the schools. She was a great warrior, who outranked him. They were both Zhayedan pilots. She did not outrank him that much. It wasn't like she was an Elite.

The girl was just an Abas Pilot Student. That was all her uniform said. She didn't have a fit body, probably closer to twenty-five percent fat being carried. It didn't align to the power of the kick.

Dracon looked at his leg. The remains of one of the metallic insects that were plaguing the school was there. He looked at closer at it. He acted as if he were dusting it off while commanding his gloves to capture the fragments.

For the love of the gods, tell me it's not them designing them. I'll need to figure out if it has spy equipment on it. This would be devastating.

He raised his eyes to Nox, daring her to comment on him being dropped by a child. The kick should have been defended. He wasn't sure why he didn't even have a since of it coming.

Is being a teacher making me soft? Not around those two? How'd she do it?

His eyes were daring her while hers hid a silent laugh at the expense of her ex-lover. The parting was mutual, and they had no animosity. If it wasn't for being caught in the embarrassment of losing their charges, it would probably have been a friendly, unplanned rendezvous.

Melania came sprinting up behind the odd group and stopped short of being asked the same question.

"Open in the name of the Twelve Dragons so three may enter!" her robotic voice called out.

Dracon and Nox stopped their silent, gaze squabbling and sprinted toward the next test area. Melania might have been able to get them into the doors of the testing arena as the second to Più Alto Drago, but from here, they would have to solve the puzzles.

******

Nite and Mike walked out of the core. They knew there were two others following them, but they didn't wait. It was a race for the center. They had won. The prize hardly seemed worthy. Ten cloaks were hung in individual circles of light. There were no tricks to them; you just reached in and pulled down the ones you wanted. Nite and Mike selected three each when they heard the others reached the outside of the doors.

They nodded to each other, knowing four to experiment with and one each for originals was enough. It was only polite for the last two to get part of the prize. Nite and Mike walked out on the two as they put the back of their hands together to start the challenge.

Mercedes, no surprise, was one of the other two in the maze. The second was a girl who was leaving the council area when they were walking in. The woman with her rushed her out, but Mike had a good look at her as she turned back and the door slammed shut on them. The two girls were about to fight to see who got to enter first.

"We left two each for you. You lost to us, but it is an equal loss," Nite stated as he finished pushing the last of his selected cloaks into his backpack.

"We could fight you and take your prize and leave what you left for us for your own prize," the new girl said without taking her eyes from her primary target.

She had also not removed her hand from Mercedes'. Their challenge would have to come first.

"We lost, and I bow to you. You may enter first," she smiled at the smaller girl. "I see what the prize is. I trust you to leave at least one for me."

The new female had to be at least a year younger than the twins, but she had a familiar face. One they knew they should remember yet didn't. It was likely she was from their earlier times and didn't recognize them any more than they did her.

Her face was round, with large teal eyes that made Nite think of the sea. Her nose was narrow with a button ending. Her hair was a flame red with hints of both gold and auburn in them. It reached midback in its triangle cut. Nite remembered how it moved; it looked like a fire burning down. He was impressed with the way it looked and wondered if it was natural or if she had the opportunities to make it look like that.

Her uniform said she was Wolf and from the forward schools like them. It didn't name a school. Theirs didn't either.

Nite smiled at her as she slammed past to get into the room.

"Mercedes, right?" He looked at the other girl. "Named or family? I don't mean to be rude.

"Please!" she scuffed. "I have no time for you or her. I have a mission, and what is in those walls may well come in handy for it. I only need one though."

"What is your mission?" Nite asked swiftly. "We would offer our help if it is possible."

"When it is ours to offer, we will consider offering it," Mike suddenly corrected.

He had not taken his eyes from the other girl until she left the inner wall. She was shoving the two cloaks she collected from the wall in her own satchel.

Short would have been an understatement, but she had power and movements. Nite knew what he was thinking without asking. Selina had the same style and build to her fighting, and at least that girl was in Wolf. Even if Nite wouldn't be with her, Mike might have found an equal for his brother to train. Not one that he would take for a special friend, but at least he would have a friend to help with the special friends.

"Then when you are able to offer, I may consider, but why would you want to leave your precious Pack so much? You recognize where I'm from. I see you three are from the forward schools. Different ones by the way you reacted to each other."

"The business you hold is not within the Packs. You are leaving, and we may have an interest in following," Nite answered.

He showed her he understood more than what she said. Then gave information to keep them equal on the levels. He had no need to start a mini war with her. On the contrary, he wanted to know to help her.

Mercedes looked them both over and then looked back to Nite.

"I wish you were the answer to my problem," she let out a sigh that said more than normal pressures had been put on her young shoulders. "I can only hope that he is as respectable and knowledgeable.

"I must start a journey that may never come to an end. Would you really want to be forsaken to start a journey of forever failure? Would you want to join a mission that has an impossible goal?"

"Every journey is started to never end. Even after the journey is complete, the path must be returned," Mike answered.

"I am not of the Packs of Human. I am to be a Dragon! Do you still wish to join for what you think it may cost you?" Mercedes again tried to break their spirits or to see them waver.

"Packs and Dragons operate for the betterment of all. It does not matter for what we travel but know this, we have been undefeated even when it is impossible. The Wolf Pack was victorious by those that gave birth to our generation. We are thrilled to continue what they have started," Nite countered, as true as ever.

"My life might have been easier if they had not. I mean no disrespect to you. Such things are hard to talk about. If we meet again, then I will ask the final time. For the final time, you may answer. I would be grateful to have you," she answered them.

"I am not sure how the tiers line up to the quarters. Wolf's forward schools are not the same as those of Varanasi. Probably so the schools couldn't do an apple to apple comparison of progress until after a student graduated. Shame. If it was, I might be able to request you be allowed to come with me and continue training. I could use more than the one friend that volunteered to go.

"Maybe we will have a synchronistic rendezvous if our destinies allow," she nodded as she walked into the room.

"I don't believe in destiny. You may call me Wunderkind-Krieger. If we meet again, I may allow you to join under me if you have the honor. If not, we'll see who would have won today," she added with a nod to Mercedes.

It spoke of respect. She was saying she would not accept her has a leader until Mercedes proved her worth. She meant it as an insult to the twins who she probably assumed would follow her because of her beauty.

Nite and Mike saw what she had to escape to get back to here. Then she had to pass the same puzzles the two of them did. All four of them had to. Then she made the command decision to buy time with the twins to learn more instead of rushing for the prize.

The other pilot was too blinded by where she was

going to see what surrounded her. She was missing vital information. She needed someone to challenge her and force her to learn to slow down. It was what Nite and Mike often had to do with each other to prevent the same mistakes. Mistakes she would not see because no one challenged her.

"If we are not to learn your secrets today, then next time we meet. Maybe you will tell us what you are looking for. A needle in a stack of needles, or merely the purpose of life. Either we can help you with," Nite smiled as he gave a small bow to Mercedes and Wunderkind-Krieger.

Wunderkind-Krieger made a face at him, almost like a little sister, before turning to Mercedes.

"I left two in there. I respect you and the friend you left out there," she showed she may have paid more attention then she let on.

She looked back at the twins and gave them a disgusted once over. She seemed to want to say something to them but decided ignoring their presents was better.

Mercedes let a smile cross her face. She walked into the room with a small wave to the three wolf students who set off in different directions. It seemed another race started, even if none of them had discussed it.

Melina Largo would probably say something like, children of the same parents are perfectly normal until they get together. Or, your Pack is the only enemy you can't live without, Mercedes thought with a laugh.

I would collect you all if I could. But why condemn you to the failure I must meet. The impossible mission to find the bloodline that is no more, ended by the loss of those that one the last Crusader Olympia.

Sometimes I wonder if my mother is sending me away to prepare to purify the Packs.

CHAPTER 16

SETTLING IN

The twins were entering the year after the Midterm cycle, 683.3.29, wondering if remaining in the schools for the Third Echelon would be worth it. Returning from the Council on 680.6.22, they discovered the results of their promotion. Their Abas were fully converted to Timber Wolves, following the design of the Frost Ferrets. No one else in their class was eligible until Midterms in 682. Only three people had been promoted to Medium Zhayedan since being eligible in their class.

Enlightenment was approved for early advancement to Instructor for the schools. As soon as the approval went through, there seemed to be a wall between her and the twins. It was not that she was not still helpful, but it seemed every move was monitored. She was always accompanied by an Android or instructor when she came to check on them or watch their classes.

Their paths were split to two different directions

that day; they knew the paths were opposites of each other. While they tried to maintain the blossoming friendship, it seemed more natural barriers were growing between them. The Twins were excelling in their classes and she was more entangled by the needs of the younger students.

Upon returning to the school, the twins also found they had access to TWNs early. The only person they had an interest in following currently was Mercedes. They were only able to exchange a few messages before she was cut off due to her mission. The twins were still able to find signs of her in Pack Space until 682.4.18. Then it was like she vanished from time and space.

It was the break before they started the Midterms. Most students were concentrating on finishing off some courses to get the bonus. For the twins, it was more of a period of morning the opportunity she presented to them.

After completing so much of the school requirement early, there was little reason for them not to consider leaving to go with her and continue the training like she was. It seemed fate prevented them from joining her though.

Mike took the opportunity to ensure Selina was named as soon as she were allowed access to TWNs following the break. With Mike having her named, no one would be able to change it until he was defeated. If that happened, they would find a way to get the name back.

Like the twins, she completed all the basic course requirements to earn the Honor bonuses for her. Between the name protection and the bonus, she could skate the rest of her years in school. However, her actual professors didn't know she advanced so far, so she was continuing with classes.

The twins took greater ownership of these rooms since they would be theirs until they left the schools. Each of them set it up to meet their own requirements. At first, they were trying to calculate how many opportunities it would take for them to reach each level of improvement and what they wanted. Yet the rooms had more than they could have wanted and were provided by general privilege of being given them.

They realized in other aspects as well the Honor Levels would come. It was more important to concentrate on being the best, which was why getting these rooms were almost as important as being promoted. It was a perspective they did not understand prior to advancing, even with training in the Heavier Abas prior to this. It was more than being a great pilot and having a WBS that was strong enough to control the Abas machine.

Mastering the Timber Wolves was not as easy as the others before it. Truly mastering meant understanding the plethora of weapon combinations, armor and equipment change outs, and even power sources could change based on missions. Medium and Heavy Zhayedan pilots were not just larger Abas.

They were more diverse warriors which required members to be more of everything.

Of course, it wasn't all hard work they returned to. And there were new mistakes to make, which they didn't realize there were mistakes coming. Excited by the idea of being able to start designing their own cloths and having more freedoms, the twins jumped on being freed to create their own clothing. They used their built up opportunities to get seven pilot suits, five cover suits, three formal dress uniforms, and thirty sets of underclothing and comfort wear, and ten sets of workout clothes. It was a mistake.

Laundry services came and picked up their clothes every other day. It wasn't even against their opportunities. It was just part of their advancement package Privilege Level.

Pilot suits, formal dress uniforms for formal gatherings and other clothing were also part of the privileges of their current rank. After Midterm they started to have every Sixth Day, they were not in simulation missions, dedicated to etiquette training which included formal dining, dancing, and other social gathering requirements.

Not like that wasn't hammered into us plenty during our first echelon.

They were also required to have at least 12 presentations a year for training purposes. It was for them to practice being responsible for briefing commands on upcoming battles and long-term goals of their missions. Many of the things they assumed would take up their saved opportunities were now being provided due to their ranks.

The Zhayedan rooms had a common area between the two of them and they were the only ones that shared it. It was larger than the apartment on the ship they traveled to the Council in. The private rooms had a three-piece toiletry area off the bedroom, walk in closet and a separate room with an open kitchen-sitting room.

The kitchenette had a small refrigerator, three-eye glass stove and a small set of metal cabinets with a small sitting bar looking into the sitting room. The sitting room had a small couch and two chairs and a view screen. There were several glasses, plates, and dry goods in the cabinets as well.

The bedroom had another view screen, larger bed than their old ones put together. The closet was the size of their old cubical areas in the barracks. It was plan, but the twins were provided opportunities to design it how they wanted.

The rooms shared another toilet facility and a single bath large enough for four. The common areas included a kitchen area looking into a larger sitting area. There was a larger refrigerator where there were several different types of drinks and chilled munchies.

They had two couches and four recliners with built-in massage units within their lounge. There were three screens, two screens almost two meters square with a third that was five meters square in their viewing room. There were several small tables, and one large table in the middle of the room. An area rug covered enough of the floor to fit all the furniture and still have several steps before ending.

Their gym's mirrored walls reflected multiple exercise equipment. Every type of style of workout had its own area in the gym for them to use, practice, and master. There was another viewing screen and a sound system installed for them to play music while they worked out.

On the other side of the gym was another door. The twins assumed it led into more Zhayedan rooms. Surprisingly, they found a private sauna. Two showers were outside the voice-activated sauna and were fully stocked with what was requested within the normal showers.

I don't remember finding this to be true for other Zhayedan Pilots in the school. Is it because we are Heavy Zhayedan's so early? And that we have completed all the basic courses? Are we being treated like Third Echelon?

With the acceptance of one of the highest Abas' in the school the twins were open to fighting with everyone within the school early as well. It was as if they were marked; either for or against, groups were coming at them constantly. It seemed to Nite, there were as many who wanted to take them out as were willing to fight with them. Some went both ways.

Some groups asked for special help from the twins, especially when facing missions which seemed impossible. They would offer ridicules terms to have them join them, and only slightly less to plan the battles for them. Ridicules in the meaning of trying to buy the twins off with almost all the Honor Levels of the battles, which meant they were going to post a hefty bet if the twins accepted. Or physical and service favors, as if all these were not being handled by the Androids and School Services.

The other students weren't told that of course. There were as many offers as could be considered, and like most, the twins would negotiate to a reasonable level, which might have lowered their scoring for Negotiating. Yet every deal had to be approved by TTG, via her own command to Mike, and they wanted to remain being able to sit down.

Although this did not stop a lot of the ladies seeking Nite for more than just a little help with a battle or to prepare for a class. Always Nite and never Mike. How Selina was able to hold them from him while being so far away, Nite could only guess. He was sure they weren't able to communicate on TWNs yet.

The twins provided extra opportunities for the androids assigned to cleaning their shared rooms. They hacked the systems to ensure the same ones were assigned to it. If they were not available, then the twins would do the work themselves until they came back. It was never longer than a week, but it ensured a certain loyalty to their room. The androids always showed them loyalty.

The first year, the twins often set out pieces of information on battle plans they would never use. It was to look as if they were planning on using them in upcoming challenges with instructors or other student groups.

The information never seemed to be leaked. Even after they started leaving out real plans, same results. Sometimes, they found markings on their plans, highlighting what the other teams were planning.

It was a small disappointment to Mike, who wanted them to think they were getting an upper hand. He had plans for them when they went to use the information. Nite found it encouraging. Those considered the lowest ranks of the Pack had true honor.

Nite and Mike didn't make life harder for those considered lesser ranks either. They go the impression some Abas Pilots did. Instead, they tried to take care of as much of their own messes as possible. It wasn't hard. They didn't require much.

Dracon told the twins Abas Students assuming they were gods happened in the forward schools more often. He believed it was because there were no other warriors to reduce the perceived bridge and highlight the need of support staff. Nite didn't believe they were buying their loyalty in what they were giving up. He believed it might have been in the gestures like going out of their way to make the job easier, even outside their rooms.

Mike once buried a Medium Zhayedan Pilot in the dirty laundry he left around his room for a week. Sneaking in and gathering it before the maids. Then he rigged it to drop on him the next time he put something on the floor of his room. The third echelon student was almost asphyxiated from the weight and smell. He seemed to change his clothes very often and worked out three times a day.

There were individual secret passageways in each private area of the room and the commons. Nite's was in his closet, hidden by a slide point in the back. Mike's was under his bed, but you had to crawl all the way to the wall and push down at the middle to cause the turntable to drop you down into the dark passage. Both escapes led to different sections of the hidden halls. Neither could be reached from the other without going into the forbidden areas.

Mike knew the area he dropped into very well but had never seen the door before. Nite's opened into a tunnel they hadn't discovered yet. It led to new areas of the school they would not have been able to reach without forging through several different restricted areas and lowest levels. Even though Master Raven would not have been able to know which room the twins would be in, Mike still said there was a reason for him getting the familiar and Nite getting the new areas to explore.

Nite said it was absurd, due to them sharing the entries equally. It wouldn't have mattered who was in what room, they would both be entering the halls. Besides, these rooms had not been designed for them, but for Zhayedan pilots individually. With this thought in mind, they might not have known the other was in those classes and would be operating in different areas of the school.

They purchased many new things not provided by the school through Master Raven, as well, and still didn't make a dent in their opportunities. They would tear down the equipment and then rebuild it with improvements, much as they had done with the Nano cloaks they received from the council. Improving old things led to them designing their own new toys as well.

Selina received several items from Mike as well. She found several ways to improve them and designed the virtual copies. The twins took her ideas and built them. Then sent her the physical copies through Master Raven. She never stopped being a part of their group, much like she would never stop being a part of their family.

To the instructors, it may have seemed Selina accepted her life as a light Abas, although she made it to Heavy Scout. She was still progressing under the twins training secretly. Selina also started to develop a higher speed for learning since she'd left the twins. Unfortunately, as she pointed out, she wasn't quite as fast as they were. Unlike the twins, she continued to work under the veil of secrecy, with only one instructor that knew her true talent level.

The scare of losing Abas pilot status settled them all down. They decided going out to discover their history was useless now. They accomplished what they dreamed of, being Zhayedan pilots without it.

The only promotion left was to Elite status. They had to master being Heavy Zhayedan pilots before they could really start considering what it would mean to become Elite.

It was more likely to reach those ranks during the Five Year. Which lead them back to the consideration of leaving early.

Would leaving early hurt or hinder our chances of getting Elite?

Nite believed staying in school gave them a better chance at reaching Elite. He only considered leaving when the three of them might have been able to join with Mercedes. They would have continued their training from what he learned.

Mike on the other hand didn't feel the need to wait much longer to leave. They completed all the advanced course work offered by the schools. The only aspects left for them in the Third Echelon was mastery skills training, which Dracon was already giving them course training in. The only reason he seemed to be willing to entertain the idea was that Selina outright refused to leave her team before Third Echelon began.

Nite's focus was on being an Elite pilot though. No one had graduated directly in an Elite in these schools. Mike, in Nite's opinion, wanted to be with Selina only. He hated hearing about the way people targeted her, and now the Headmaster had allowed her to be named in the school, even though the name would not carry out of the school. Quick Hit didn't like the loophole that was being utilized to protect her.

To her, it didn't matter. When the time was right, Selina would also be allowed to reach the levels she too deserved. In honesty, they didn't care what the Packs said she deserved. They would find a way for her to be where she belonged.

The twins made randomly scheduled training cycles for themselves to maintain being the best. It was easier since they no longer had any of the twenty basic courses to complete. All the specialty classes, except those that were not available until after Midterm were completed through Third Echelon as well. This seemed to be a good thing with the number of challenges that were coming at the twins.

Another reason to be masters before we leave. We have much more to learn brother. It is not wise to allow your desires to rule your direction. Our teenage angst is not helping our eternal need to grow. And these walls are not as limited as you believe them to be.

Even in the early years of the Second Echelon, the twins were fighting in almost as many battles as those in the Third Echelon, tripling the average numbers of those in their cycle. They hardly had to spend any opportunities on repairing their Abas due to their skills. Often used the salvage gains to repair their selves and team members that joined them in battle.

They concentrated on using Scouts and low-level Sentinels in place of heavier Abas to increase the challenge opportunities rewarded. They organized them into strike groups, using themselves as targets. This allowed the lighter Abas to use tactics they were better at, taking down larger prey. It was the most they were willing to do so directly at this point, but it was still something that Mike felt was needed.

Some of the lights tried to learn their plans to trade them to the opposing teams. Likely to gain acceptance into that team. When the twins noticed one of their team acting out against orders, they would kill them and revert to a new plan created as the battle went on. The twins lost more members to them killing the traitors and those refusing to listen than to enemy Abas combatants.

Their workdays usually left around five hours for sleep a night. Like all students, they tried to maintain the Seventh Day. It kept them from burning themselves out while working as hard as they did to stay on top for their cycle. The day of rest was usually spent with their Abas and on pleasure reading. The time in the Abas wasn't meant for training but finding a peace in them and with them.

Mike spent a lot of his time speaking with Selina while in there as well. Just walking along, taking in the sites together. All the schools maintained the same Seventh Day. She matched their schedules as much as she could, so they could train together as well.

It wasn't daily and sometimes a week could pass between talking to each other. Nite and Mike had days where they didn't see each other as well. They looked forward to them as much as regretted them.

They might have been twin brothers, but they liked to be separated occasionally as well.

Reaching the top at an early age didn't help them for feeling the need to stay. The younger age seemed to have made them higher priority targets for defeat than idols to be feared and worshiped. People were hungry for the Honor gain which would come from conquering them. Every trouncing they caused was more to the pool for the next challenger. It seemed more bet against them the longer they went without a loss as well. Seeming to think sooner or later the streak would end.

Wolf Pack typically agreed. Even on the video's the showed Wolf winning, they showed where some mistakes were not capitalized on. "A win can always be improved on," as the narrators pointed out.

For the twins, they did the same thing. Constantly looking through their victories trying to find where team members made mistake and could improve. Where they made mistakes and should have done something different. And where they were required to change plans because they didn't recognize someone was going to betray them.

And these lessons are better to master here, brother, Nite would point out as they continued to work through every victory as if it was a devastating loss.

When they were not training within their Abas, they would study all the other aspects of Abas warriors. Hand-to-hand combat was usually practiced in their rooms with one another, while blade fighting, archery, long range firing, raid courses, and other battle tactics were with classes.

Tactics and war games were played virtually. They liked to use fake accounts in public challenges for these to test themselves against non-students. The school still graded it though.

Fights were never marked as won or lost when between the brothers. They reviewed them to figure out how to improve already-created moves and counters. They learned a wide verity of fighting styles, which was true of every student in the schools. Combining them and creating their own style from those was what the twins worked on the most during their private sessions. Selina was able to join them virtually, adding a different aspect and perspective to the style as well.

Master Raven popped in from time to time just to find out how the private training lessons was going. He was the only visitor to their quarters, even with the quarters designed for entertaining and maintaining teams. He would drop off new reading materials not kept in the school libraries as well.

He liked adding items for them to study, which were often forbidden in the school and sometimes even in the Pack itself. To keep it in the study aspect, he would grade their understanding under being able to procure and capture information which was not authorized.

Master Raven was even more impressed when the twins started to open up more with what their hobbies were. Every student was to have hobbies outside of just Abas fighting. The three of them designed and built technology.

They showed him things they developed from their training or items they improved beyond even the greatest minds of the Triscifield caste dedicated to such things. At least that's the way they pictured it. Master Raven assured them the Triscifield was always developing things the twins were not allowed access to, yet.

Master Raven gave the impression he was sharing these discoveries with someone, but he also brought them back many new things to work with both in and out of the Abas. They would provide feedback and suggestions for improvements in turn. Playing with new devises was almost as fun as tearing them apart and trying to improve them.

Selina was part of these sessions as well. Sometimes she would send the designs back with Master Raven instead of having the twins work on them. She didn't just take to technology though. She liked painting and sculpting work. For her, the art of the design was as important as the function.

Pack instructors could teach anything in any way as long as they taught the basics of the class and the students showed improvement. Master Raven being the Senior Security or Espionage Professor had more authority and freedom in his teachings. He could require them to gather information, plant bugs, gather blackmail material, and anything else his imagination worked in the lines of espionage.

Gathering new information outside of your training or that allowed within the pack was also part of it. A pilot would never know what codes could be created in. Flower formations, circuit diagrams, or even discussions on proper rearing of children could be codes and cyphers.

This was why many students took the espionage classes, even if they weren't interested in actually defending or actively participating in the course study. It wasn't seen as the most honorable class even though it was taught in the manner of defending one's self against such attacks. But those that did take it could pursue knowledge in any direction they chose.

As often said by the spymasters, "It would behoove you to understand how a master spy would do it, so you could defend against it. Relying on the defenses already known opened you up, so learning them and developing your own paths helped you understand what others were capable of. After all, if the common were known, then someone knew how to get around them."

Nite thought this was an obvious statement. If they had been discovered, then someone discovered them. If someone discovered them and was teaching defenses, then the defenses were exposed to figure out how to work around them. It was a double edge sword that required one to think, not just remember.

This was the argument Mike used on his brother

for leaving the schools. They had already consumed the knowledge of what people thought here. They could learn more techniques in which the instructors mastered, but he didn't care about a "Master" title. He wanted freedom.

Brother! You must understand. Freedom isn't free. Freedom is responsibility. And we have a responsibility to our future selves to spend the time here wisely. Wisely is not trying to prove the need to leave early, but to find the weaknesses in our selves before those weaknesses cost others their lives because of us.

At least he's agreed to stay until the start of the Third Echelon. Three and a half more years to change his mind on how much more we have to learn.

CHAPTER 17

A QUESTIONABLE MEETING

Selina arrived at the new school under a cloud of depression four days after leaving the twins. The entire time she spent on the drop ship was in her Abas. She didn't even leave it for food. It didn't seem anyone was going to bother her in it either.

When she got to the platform, the Headmaster didn't bother to meet her, not that she expected it. Instead it was an Instructor by the name of Master Fade, who was the Second Echelon Espionage Master and a Medium Sentinel pilot. It was strange because Master Fade greeted Selina with a Hug.

Master Fade later told Selina her sister use to see people with down faces and would hug them randomly. She got punched a few times, but most the time people were pretty receptive of it. It was strange, because she spoke to her like a friend, but called her Student 9824651.

This led Master Fade to tell Selina the story of being Illuminator's half-sister as they left the platform and she was shown around the school. Almost thirty years separated the births linked by their shared father. After Illuminator made the original contact after her selection to school, they maintained it with each other over the years.

Even as a child, Master Fade could not remember a week passing without something from Illuminator coming in. It was very special for the Medium Sentinel pilot to have packages from someone of Illuminator's Honor Level and family connections. Of course, when they started talking, Master Fade didn't know Illuminator would become *The General* of Wolf's four armies.

When Illuminator took her orders locking her to the schools, Master Fade felt it was a good time to leave her short-lived warrior duties to train the next line as well. Spending time with the only family she knew who still lived seemed more important to her than the levels of comfort she could earn from then on. Although it was rare for someone of her experience to be accepted to the schools so early, the Forward Schools seemed to have a need for her skillset and a lack of volunteers.

And Master Fade believed Illuminator may have suggested her approval be allowed as well. It seemed the sister wanted to spend some time with her as well. They spent most their breaks together with Falstar and the Supreme Headmaster. What a family to be part of!

Selina and the twins lost contact as far as everyone else was concerned. It was the reason for Master Fade to tell her the story. Illuminator and Master Fade passed the messages between them regularly. Since Selina seemed to be secluding herself at the new school, she suggested keeping in contact with them.

Master Fade hoped keeping the connection kindled for a while would keep Selina from feeling as if she had to be alone. Then, naturally, she would find friends in the new school and stop needing them so much. It was something Master Fade often encouraged and seemed to try to guide as well.

There was never any tampering with the letters that could be detected. But there was never anything of importance sent through them either. It was mostly bland conversations, not highlighting a single action or aggression that happened. Aggressions being more on the twin's side.

Master Fade was Selina's reporting instructor. Selina decided to play a very dangerous game when she was sent to the other school. For it, there had to be at least one instructor in which real assignments were submitted and actual Honor and Privileges were maintained.

Selina knew between the mission and the letters; her curiosity drove her to develop a speaking relationship with Master Raven. She wanted to figure out how they were doing it. The small messages being passed couldn't contain the information she was progressing with.

Master Fade didn't have any bad intentions about her curiosity. It was in fact just the opposite. She wanted to know how *these* children created a sophisticated way for them to communicate without two spymasters being able to detect it, much less crack it. After all, if they could do it, how much more had she failed to detect?

This was not the strangest of events for Selina in the new school due to her mission though. The biggest one started on 679.8.16, almost a year before the twins were called to the council. The strangest was over two years after and probably due to a chance encounter that day.

Selina remembered it well. It was 682.7.22, a few months after Mike named her TTG through a challenge issued on TWNs. Claudia and Selina started training privately. The other original three in their cubical were not part of the Core, but the Crux, so they kept the training random, to prevent them from feeling they were being excluded. They weren't at the level the two of them were training for these missions.

The one that figured it out later, was the least likely. She was so flakey and ever wondering mentally, it was amazing she had found the pattern. Yet, this wasn't Selina's strangest story.

A younger pilot was waiting outside the simulator for Selina. There was no doubt the pilot was waiting for Selina, which wasn't unusual. Many of those interested in the Crux would wait for her near her Abas, waiting for someone to find them, as they were instructed.

Most didn't know Selina was the one that would be greeting them. They didn't know she was the final point of acceptance, although they would have many more test. Unlike those, there was no doubt the pilot knew when and where to wait and who she was waiting for.

This pilot was not here to join the Crux, either. Another strange coincidence. She was shorter than Selina, with more of an hour-glass figure vice the reversed triangle Selina developed in her sixteen years of life. She had long, dark, thick, wavy hair, which brought a story back to Selina suddenly, but what it referred to was out of her reach.

TTG was working off some frustration caused by having to throwing a one-on-one battle with a horrible Medium Scout pilot. The guy didn't deserve the level he was in. If he lost to her again, then his family, the Vlcek, would drop him from their scrolls.

That wasn't an issue for Selina. From what Master Fade said, they wanted to drop him and considered inviting her to their family instead. It was a low-level family, but it would have been able to force her up to Sentinel ranking, even if it lowered her into a light Sentinel.

It wouldn't stop there. They would realize her potential, having access to her complete records. If that happened, she would not be able to stop the attention. At least that's the way Selina saw it.

Denying the family could cause just as many issues. She didn't want the family's attention either for gain or loss. The only way for him to keep it was for her to lose, spectacularly.

In response to having to act so feckless, Selina input one of the toughest scenarios she designed for herself. Working herself this hard was one of the few ways she could relieve the stress of hiding her true abilities. Losing that much Honor in one battle really teased her nerves.

Not that Selina had to worry about her Honor Levels. She had kept a private account with Headmaster Falstar that was linked to the twins. Their success and hers were tied together since their trio team was an underground. Since all of them were marked as leaders, no one could know about the account unless all of them were under someone else's command. It was set up this way before she left the school.

The Crux also had an account, which hedged bets within the schools. Since passing through Midterms, they would bet high for the twins to always win. Not many were taking bets for them as much as against them, so the pools were larger, which helped to supplement their underground teams honors that much more. Most underground teams used betting to help their members get additional help when needed.

Selina blamed the frustration of the loss for her

failure to notice the pilot was there. Still infuriated even after a victory within Gauntlet Three, she couldn't get the pain of the loss, both physical and mental, out of her head.

The pilot was rocking back and forth on her feet as if to bring the attention to her. It seemed she was anxiously awaiting TTG to get out of her cockpit but didn't wait for her to properly get on the platform before she started to speak. As soon as TTG looked at the younger pilot, she blasted her with a question.

"Why are you here?"

The question came so quick it, TTG thought she missed something. She looked back to ensure she was in the right Abas and the girl was speaking to her. Selina could find her Abas in the pitch black of the night without a second guess, so the gesture was for the girl and to give her time to collect herself.

The girl had large, deep-drawing, brown eyes that seemed to drink the world in with curiosity, but they were far from innocent. She could not have been less than a few years younger than TTG. But her identifier had said the pilot was only a cycle behind Selina in training.

"Excuse me?" TTG finally asked, realizing the strange pilot was waiting patiently for an answer.

The pilot was a selected Heavy Sentinel, which meant she outranked TTG. There was a proper respect to be given. The age difference seemed to neglect it at the present time and situation.

"I asked, 'Why are you here,'" she restated the question as if it was plain fact.

"This is my Abas, and I am training. Why are you here?" TTG replied, a little taken aback by the girl now.

"Why are you in this school as a light if you are so good?" the girl asked again.

It was impossible, but she had somehow figured out what TTG was up to. There was no way for her to monitor the Gauntlet Three program. If it had been monitored, it would have shown her operating poorly in a different scenario.

"My school had too many lights in my year, and none of them seemed to be showing the potential to move up." TTG had not realized how much of a slap in the face that was to admit.

Not only to the school with the best two students in her year, or any year for that matter, as lights, but she was selected as the greatest failure. So great a failure she had to be sent to a different school because she was bringing them down. That was the cover story she spread, but for the first time, it hurt to say it.

"You do not belong in an Abas if you think that story is even close to the truth," the young girl replied in the same factual voice she restated her earlier question. "I am only here temporarily. I was brought here to test myself against someone else to prove some ranking my Headmaster wanted. I think I will be approved for an Elite soon."

"But you are just a Heavy Sentinel," TTG said before she could catch herself.

Nite and Mike jumped from light ranks to a step just below Elite without seeing their first approved medium Zhayedan. But they were *the TWINS*. No one was as good as them.

There was that one. Could this be her?

"Just waiting for the order to be able to move into Medium Zhayedan next. They said the final testing is here. I will have a month to prove my worth to be promoted early.

"If I do not leave to soon, I will truly test you. I will speak to my mother as well. I think you should be in our school.

"I think you would be better than the lights assigned to my squad currently. You could at least *train* them to be better."

How do you know about that? No one else outside our group knows.

The girl gave her a once-over and then continued.

"You have not answered my question. You hold your potential back. You do not belong in a Scout. Why are you here?"

The girl might have looked young, but she didn't act it. She seemed almost familiar to TTG, as well. TTG marked it off to being offered a position at a different school. She might think she was an elite in the making. She might even have the connections to help her. But that created no hope for TTG. Wolf

Pack would not grant her the chance to go somewhere that would allow her to prove she deserved more.

"The Pack feels differently," TTG sighed at last, feeling this would stop the pointless conversation.

I'll show emotions and act inept. She should let these ludicrous ideas go then.

The girl would not need her help if she was stepping into an Elite. Her mother must have had a lot of power. The girl seemed to believe the Wolf Pack still operated for the betterment of its people and, in that, making itself better.

TTG did not want to be the cause of breaking the idea. It had almost destroyed her when she discovered the truth. She chose not to inflict it on others, even those that followed her.

"The Pack is wrong."

So much for preserving innocence, TTG thought as she kept her jaw from dropping on the comment.

Her voice started with a slight annoyance to full anger. Even her outward appearance seemed to morph in front of her, in a way she had seen Mike do sometimes when he had lost his calm.

It was a pleasant reminder of the twins' Human sides. A side hardly shown to anyone and never to ones they did not trust. The pilot showed an inner strength of phenomenal proportions. This girl might not have been the twins, but she had the potential to learn from them. Nite would be interested in learning about her.

But was that display a show to build trust with me?

Nite would have used it that way. He did it before with others. Something he learned from being around me, he said.

"Wrong or right, they are the ones who decide. There is little I can do about it. Even if I tried to prove them wrong and stretch my limits to beyond what they have ever expected, they would just move me again. Make up another excuse for me to start at the bottom. I have found where they want me, and I will stay there, like a good dog."

The young girl's face went back to a calm serenity she had shown for much of their conversation.

"My mother told them I am ready to advance higher, but they say it may be that I am not at the level she believes I am. I have already beaten several of the pilots here today. All your Zhayedan willing to face me in the first round. I should at least be approved to be promoted to that level by the time I leave here.

"I wanted to go to Timber Wolf Academy to face the two unnamed there, but my mother and the council refused the meeting. It is not that she is afraid I will lose. I have already been named by my mother. I'm Wunderkind-Krieger, the Prodigy Warrior."

Her eyes probed TTG for reaction while she continued as if she had not just announced that she was the best and everyone else should bow down to her. Although the attitude was not unfounded if she was the one that TTG thought she was.

"No, it is that they fear what will come of the battle. They do not want to give them warning of events set in place and coming. I will not be happy if I am not the one to bring the events to the unnamed."

The words came as a shock to TTG. She had heard other students talk about the twins as rumors and figments. It had never been as actually people, much less knowing exactly what and who they were.

What made it worse was she was telling TTG something they did not know. She was passing information because she wanted them to know. She had not come to talk to her or bring her under her command. That was all to see her reactions. She wanted to learn about the twins, and TTG was the closest anyone would let her get to them.

Mike named me. She figured there's a connection here. But how? She can't have access to TWNs yet? Or does she?

If she was as good as she claimed, and she could face either Nite or Mike in a real battle, then why was she not sent? Her mother must have felt she was not ready to face them. Maybe she didn't know as much about them as she thought.

If she is only going off their posted scores, then she had no idea of what they are fully capable of. If her mother does know . . . but that should be impossible. No, assuming it is impossible is bad. The twins make fools of people who do that all the time.

"I scored second overall in tracking here just recently. I am tied at second with one of them by the smallest point of calculation. It is frustrating to lose by as much from the opinion of a computer. It was a timed event, though. He beat me fair and square, but I don't know which one it was. The records have us all named at the same time with mine last.

"I have to go. They have noticed I slipped away. I'll be back to talk more."

TTG couldn't form any words to talk about the twins. She desperately wanted to find out more about the girl. If she was able to get that close to TTG without TTG knowing, then she could have been anywhere at any time. That meant TTG couldn't get close to where she was without giving it away.

The girl came by Selina's personal quarters several times during the next few days. It was not as abrupt of conversations. They were polite, but distant. Then, as fast as she was here, she was informed she would be leaving. She did not talk about the twins or ask Selina anything more about them.

She didn't seem to be gathering information, other than a few peaceful chats about the different trainings Selina built.

"I acquired them from one of your trainees. I made copies so they didn't lose theirs. It is very interesting the designs and layouts. The scenarios are extremely difficult.

"I see where using a light scout would make it harder to get through and causes you to master individual weapons. Would you be willing to give me the Scenario's were you train to master groups of weapons?"

She's a little presumptuous. And she's already figured out the training's full potential.

"I would be willing to provide you with some of what I have developed along those lines, but it seems you have connections and the ability to make your own," she started to suggest a negotiation.

"Ah. Quid pro quo. I should have assumed. I will give you disk for disk of the training I created as well. Will that be acceptable?"

"How do I know you have enough to meet my total numbers?"

"Well, you could assume because I out rank you that I am able to get the equipment, training and technology to do as much as you, even being a year behind. No. I didn't think so.

"I will allow you to select the number we trade. If I am short, you can select the ones I get? You can select from any that I have up to the number you provide. I will also give you an equal number to what I have already copied."

"It's a great deal. What are you really after?"

"I am giving you my designed training. I can't give you all my secrets," she laughed for the only time in front of Selina.

She went on to talk about the Supreme Headmaster and a few other big names as if they were all personal friends. It was possible for them to be familiar to her. She met them so many times in discussion with her trainings they might as well have been on the student's level.

Or her on theirs. It's like she's like the twins, only good. Is good the right word? Open with her discoveries. She seems to be openly challenging everyone at least. Even the twins. Prodigy Soldier or not, you might find you are less than you believe if you face them.

Selina had never seen anyone treated like her though. An entourage of people seemed to have followed her from place to place. Even her classes were taught to her on the move. She was learning the absolute best ways to do things from those who were the best in their fields, not just the schools. She was being treated much like what Selina expected they would treat a potential Elite Pilot.

Against her better judgment, Selina liked the girl. It wasn't until days later, when she spoke to Mike and Mike asked a couple questions that she recognized the story of the girl.

She was the one from the council chambers. The one that made the face at Nite. No wonder she's infatuated with them!

Lady Wolf, Selina's second, knew Wunderkind-Krieger was an important person by the craziness that followed her. It was her approaching TTG over those days that brought attention to TTG she didn't want. Yet, Wunderkind-Krieger seemed oblivious to feels, people or items that were not aligned to what she wanted at the time.

TTG did not tell Claudia Wunderkind-Krieger was the only other person who beat her in tracking. She did tell Claudia she was sure Wunderkind-Krieger was going to be selected for Elite one day. It was hard to hide after she destroyed over one hundred of their

Zhayedan pilots from a Heavy Sentinel. When she started to challenge five to one, they decided it was time to move her back to her other school sooner than expected.

TTG didn't tell Lady Wolf about the offer to transfer either. While TTG believed she could request and get it after the second meeting with her, she didn't bring it up again. TTG wasn't willing to remind her, nor did she want to leave.

Shortly after the girl left, there was an explosion in their underground ranks. Why the girl had been so interested in her was the question of the month. It took several more crappy battles and performances in class to get it from students minds.

There was a hidden agenda, but TTG didn't have time to work on it. She informed the twins, sending what she got from the girl. She was right. She had at least twenty-times the training then what TTG had created by herself. What she got from her was excellent though and provided a new perspective.

Since the meeting, it seemed the pilot was cut off from any potential contact with the twins, including Selina. No messages came or were passed through TWNs. Even rumors were shut down of her, while those of the twins progressed.

Sometimes TTG would go to sleep wondering, *what were you up to and why are they hiding you when you were so open? Why bring the twins to light when they are so hidden? Is this a game and who are the players? Who are the pieces?*

CHAPTER 18

INTENTIONS

The rumors of the twins being the grandchildren of a dishonored five-year pilot bloodline seemed to grow stronger with the lack of information on their history. Master Raven especially liked that one. It had those looking into their past searching for every Five-Year Bloodline, saving him the time of doing it.

Every group who chose to fight against the twins was gathering information on them, where they came from and especially trying to figure out who their parents were. Hoping the missing key to defeating them lied in finding out who they were. He helped spread that rumor as well, although Selina was the one that started it before she left.

Every master student he had was looking for information as well. That was because he assigned it as a hidden project with a humongous reward, not that they were willing to face them again. So far, no one had been able to beat the seventeen-year-olds in any challenge. Those who thought they were guaranteed a "Master" title were fearful of losing it because they failed.

The instructors were no more successful either. They wanted to find any clue to beating the twins, and not just because they couldn't win. The level of Honor in finding a way to defeat them at this point would likely have a class named after them in their specialty in the Varanasi System. There was no honor higher for an instructor.

Another rumor had them as children of a Domestique Abas pilot. The children of such parents weren't often accepted within the Dirigeant or Dirigeante's family unless they ended up mating into it. But if the pilot was pregnant when she was taken, the children would have been born during her service period.

More often, the Domestique's original Pack would take the child for training in replacement of their lost pilot. Pack's liked to mix blood lines, but they liked to keep their own lines as well. Mixing was usually done with the Domestique and someone from the Pack agreeing to after. Not taking what would be a purebred of another Pack and calling it within yours.

Once a Domestique served their time or their leash was cut by its owner, the pilot was considered, and even considered themselves, a part of the Pack that took them. Unless they were released back to their Packs, which some requested. It was usually a higher honor loss to return to your old Pack though.

It would often see the pilot starting at the bottom of the ranks, having to work back up to whatever level they were.

This was believed of the twins almost as much as the five-year rumor. Most preferred to think of them as from a long line of Wolf Pack. They wanted to believe only Wolf would be able to create such pilots. They didn't want to go out into worlds knowing someone else might be out there, like them, waiting to be challenged.

Master Raven took the most interest in planting the bug of interest in their background amongst the other instructors, professors, and masters. To his great disappointment he hadn't been able to use them to find any more than he himself learned. It didn't matter who it was; there was no way to find out their past.

Dracon figured he would have to go to the source to get any more information. He needed a new path to hunt. And the only source for that would know why he was there the moment they hit the topic.

"I don't understand why they have to be sealed away so much. Even the other two five-year children in their cycle don't have a history security like theirs. In fact, there isn't a single history locked up like this other than . . . those of traitors," Master Raven finished in a half whisper to himself.

"Traitors aren't locked up like this," Falstar snarled. "You are not to try to find out any more about these children." His voice was firm. "Your drawing too much attention to this school, and we don't need our location discovered. We'll end up purified."

There was an anger under it that reached every sense of Master Raven with a wrongness he never felt from the Headmaster before. The danger in his voice was not meant for Master Raven to feel. Falstar was many things to Master Raven over the years, but one thing he had never been was angered and terrified to the core like he was now.

"Really Pedant Perplex. When you are the Security Department Head of a School, particularly this one, you would be expected to be able to get any history of any student and through the security barricades. But when they are so secure the council's ruling couldn't free them, there is more going on with these two than anyone realizes.

"Any reasons you can disclose, or are your hands as tied as mine are to get the information?"

Master Raven knew giving Falstar a port for his anger and a way out was a successful move in getting out of this office without giving more away. Like on a battlefield, Master Raven knew he had to give his enemy a way of escape if he wasn't prepared to fight them to destruction. Sometimes sacrificing a way out gave you a victory you were never supposed to have.

"Are you saying that you would like to step down from Security Department Head? And please don't call me that!" Falstar stared hard at Master Raven.

He bit on the bait. Just not with the anger he had earlier. Master Raven now knew Falstar had taken it so both of them could get out. It had to be continued, but from here on out, both knew the truth.

"Would you prefer PP? That is what I used to call you for short after you thought you could beat me at my own game. Why would you ever think you could come close to it?" Master Raven sneered this time, showing the obvious disrespect that would never be shown to someone who was being watched or listened to.

"You stole my reports from me and used them against me!" Falstar started up the old argument.

His tone and mannerism spoke of a wound that had never healed and only grew with infection as time passed.

"They were reports on security. You should have kept them more secure if you didn't want me to find them. Besides, we have been through this a thousand times. I am here, and you are there, and you are still PP. Now that it has been discussed for the thousandth and first time, let's just start talking about what we are going to do with these children."

Master Raven knew it would seem peculiar for them to completely drop a subject which was started as heated as the argument was. From what he saw of Falstar's face, Falstar realized it as well. But the drop was initiated, and they were back on the subject.

"Why is it so important to you to know where your star children come from?" Falstar started with a calmer voice, signifying Master Raven's failures with his words.

Falstar started the dance again with a calmer exterior, meaning he was to be at the advantage and lead the conversation.

Master Raven noted the caution in his move. There was more than even Master Raven knew. Now Falstar was trying to tell Master Raven something beyond important, but impossible to put into words; even coded words. A chill started up Master Raven's spine before he could control his mind.

"I have my reasons." Master Raven acknowledged his failures in the argument allowing Falstar to get a few more stabs in to finally end this.

"If you really want to know, go through the security codes. I can give you no more."

Falstar's eyes flashed dangerously, sending more messages about his words and the real meaning behind them.

"I can't legally," Master Raven acknowledged his willingness to give up his pursuit along this alley.

Falstar had provided him more than he could have ever asked for openly. The meanings were clouded, but Master Raven just needed time to work them all out.

"I see," Falstar switched to fake serenity.

His eyes were going to fill in the final gaps that he could. He let out a sigh and seemed to settle back in his chair.

"Well, I still can't tell you what you want to know. Like you, I don't know. I do know why the council put them in my school. They did and then asked me to push them as hard as I could, to see if they would crack under pressure. I've seen diamonds turned to dust under the pressure these two have faced.

"I assume they're from two highly honorable families. It might be as challenging as some of the ancient practices. Put two master DNA warriors into the same carrier to find out if they could survive each other. Now they are head to head in school. Believing they are brothers, destined to prove whose bloodline is better in the end.

"Or worse, there weren't supposed to be two of them. The other family only had one child, so the test is off from the beginning. Twins should have weakened the test, but instead if exploded in their face.

"Think about it. One council family challenged another to a free birth challenge. No one is allowed to know where they came from, so it is locked down tighter than a Gramerack Temple. Then the test begins. The other family is probably in a different school. It is obvious who is winning. I have seen no reports like the ones that I am sending in from their cycle.

"It makes the most sense to me to consider them this way. This is the way they will stay in my mind. The alternative is worse to consider.

"You know the plans with the Varanasi schools, I am sure. I discovered them. It might be to test some of the results of that.

"The one I prefer, of course, would explain why they were selected for Zhayedan pilots so early.

Political powers trying to push and pull with the Honor their children will earn them through proving the strength of their DNA. It's that or some result the Triscifield was able to cook up. Either one doesn't change our position.

"We're to ensure they could survive an exploding star. We're to put the ultimate pressure on them or find when they will break. Figure we're about halfway through putting enough pressure on them. Do you believe they are going to break?"

Falstar let the information fly. None of it was true. That's what he was telling Dracon.

"If you find out, anything, please tell for my own curiosity. But when they were selected, I was also told to increase the pressure. Do not think your *star* students will be given a break just because they have been promoted. I will ensure they do not fail the test.

"I have one other theory which would explain why we have contact from the Triscifield so much about them." Falstar was about to tell an important lie while trying to pass Master Raven a possible ally to hunt down next.

"Maybe they are the offspring of the new genetic experiment form. I would like to think of their talents of being Red Born were born from the bloodlines of Wolf, but . . .. Being a cover for our Triscifield to test not only us but them under very strenuous circumstances would align to finding out if the new schools would stand up to adding some new form of warrior.

"Would it not make since if they were the next generation of the offspring of Blue Bloods? These twins with their special ability being the next step in warrior evolution would be right up the way they are able to destroy any opponent, out maneuver any test, and pilot any Abas like a child's toy."

The importance of the lie was beyond what Master Raven had expected. Not only was the council watching these children very closely, they were creating a lie, a cover if they truly did prove to be beyond anything that had passed through the school.

It appeared the twins history was so important to keep secret, the Council would rather give some of its power up to the Triscifield then disclose it. There was a need to know why, but measuring the risk and reward determined how much you wished to push the envelope. Them not retaliating in the most-dastardly ways was as likely as an Elite pilot giving up their Abas for a light scout just before entering into a major battle. Master Raven needed to determine how far and what he was willing to give up before he pursued this deeper.

"It pains me to admit, but I do not know any more truth than you have discovered yourself. I have not been told any more than I have told you today, and you now know more than I have told anyone else on my thoughts of them. I would be more than happy to trade any additional information with you.

"Funny, they have tied my hands so much with these children, and yet I know nothing." Falstar put his wrists together as if the physical show would push the words in a little more.

Master Raven looked with anger and disrespect at Falstar with his actions. It was the best thanks he could give him at the time. The Headmaster did many questionable things, but today he did what he was supposed to do. He empowered Master Raven with as much information as possible and left it for him to make the decision of what to do with it.

"I find it hard to believe, but I will accept your answer. You don't have a reason to lie to me." Master Raven had smoothed his face before responding.

He made a hand motion telling Falstar he would also pass information on as it became solid, not just tangents. It was a code they set up when they knew Falstar would never see a real battle. He was selected for his present position and more before he had even finished half his second echelon. Much like Enlightenment.

They were not going to allow him to follow in his father's footsteps after the last Crusader Olympia. They were not going to release another like his mother out in the fleet, where the Five-Year proved they had missed the true talents. They feared what two generations capable of doing the same thing might lead to for the rest of the ruling families of the Wolf Pack.

"Thank you," Falstar finally said as he sat back in his chair and rotated it to face out into the luscious planetary view.

The screen gave an appearance on the subterranean wall of a well-developed planet with new sprouting life of spring. Several different types of plants decorated the grounds outside. A rare collection of flowers surrounded the external appearance of the window.

The "thank you" reminded Master Raven of the last thanks they had received when they assassinated their old master.

The two of them had found he had betrayed the Pack by contacting a member of the Black Wing, an elite group within the Cyborg community. He was passing information on students, selecting targets to convert to cyborgs, whether or not they were willing. He was also trying to build a program to create broken children.

Falstar thought of this as he watched Dracon walk out of the room. They risked much at that time. More than Falstar knew at the time, but the betrayal of his Master was important to gain his own footing within the Pack. He's plans weren't fruitful enough. His monitoring failing and he would never be sent to the forward schools, where the fruit of certain projects would likely be sweeter.

Falstar knew what he gave Dracon in the coded messages would keep the spy master busy for years. There were always more information to be gathered, and when you set someone's perspective by acting as if you were giving them nothing and something, you could control the direction of their hunt. Falstar needed to continue to the directing to the right path with Dracon. It was part of the longer game.

Any spymaster would plant devices when they left any room. Dracon would plant several so Falstar would find some he wanted him to find, find more than he wanted, but the hopes were that at least one would slip through.

Falstar also knew that Dracon was a master at small arms, blades and hand to hand combat. While these training are common for spymasters, reaching master level was extremely difficult. Falstar was also a Master from their classes in these and he had another advantage.

He discovered four devices left behind. He pulled one from the chair that Dracon was sitting on. The others he left in place, where his system would wear them down quickly over the next few weeks. This way the equipment would look faulty or if it had problems. He would pass the information he wanted Dracon to have while they were active.

I need you to keep playing the game as well. Too many of you are wearing out.

We'll see who's right in the end, father. I wonder how Mother is doing with her pet project?

CHAPTER 19

LEARNING CURVES

Selina became a master of showing multiple faces before meeting with Wunderkind-Krieger and more after. Before the questionable invasion of her new school by the pilot, there were only two groups in the school. Those who thought she was an okay pilot, capable of being a Scout like her parents and nothing more. And those who believed they had an insight to her true capabilities.

For those who seemed to want to ensure she stayed in her Scout Abas, she acted as if she was no better than the best of the lowest ranked Abas Class. Always staying just above them while just below the others was a talent. One she thought would have given her way by now, but people saw what they wanted to see.

The second group started as a few lights who had stumbled onto one of her private training sessions with Claudia. Scouts had a bad habit of following each other. She thought she lost the girl, but she was a better tracker than Selina gave her credit for. Better than Claudia thought as well, since she acted so airy all the time.

Because of this discovery, the Crux was born 679.8.16, before the *incident* with Wunderkind-Krieger in 682. The pilot that was able to follow them was moved to a different school on 683.4.11. Selina ensured she was equipped to train others and more importantly to continue her training. They also maintained communications over TWNs, but she wasn't part of the training group with the twins.

Selina didn't think Wind Wheel would be respected enough in her new school to find a following. She would be great at passing information. People tended to overlook her, even though she was beautiful, athletic, and talented. The airiness of her personality and inability to appear to make decisions set most people off from her. She was also one of the only ones that seemed to know who the training was being developed with.

Most of these members would later develop her Core. These were the ones Selina started to see the advantage of using the most. Master Fade recommended having a group to truly meet her goals of hiding after she was original discovered by Lady Wolf earlier that same year. It would be easier to control attention. It would also create a way for her to have multiple points of influence which would be harder to track back to her.

This one seemed ready made. The group was

mostly scouts, already operating as an underground group. It seemed every Forward School had an underground group of Scouts somewhere. If not more than one, like Canine Prime, where she was at.

More information provided by Master Fade. But Nite said there were at least three in Timber Wolf Academy. Wunderkind-Krieger also knew to look for us and she was from Canis Lupus Training Facility. Wind Wheel mentioned several in Wolf Pack Academy, where the Supreme Headmaster resided. It seems truer than not.

When Master Fade first suggested finding and joining the underground group, Selina refused outright. She did not want to draw attention to the group. Nor did she want to build connections after such a fresh loss. It was only a year since coming to the school.

Then there was the risk of the leader finding out how good she truly was. They would want to use her skills and abilities beyond what she was trying to maintain. It was likely to be a conflict of interest in seeking additional help.

Master Fade said these groups naturally formed in the Forward Schools and were common in the Inner Schools as well. At least when there was a strong light-level pilot locked into position. Often, they purposely selected a Pack they wanted to prove wrong in their operations and started the groups in their Third Echelon, sometimes taking a group with them.

Master Fade brought up joining an underground again after Selina had Claudia to back her. The two started to train together, which showed Selina the need of a companion. the two of them could easily find a Scout group to work with. Master Fade meant for Selina to push forward in both her classes and Abas. With a collection of the Scouts and Sentinels to develop, she could easily reach the highest levels within a few cycles. Master Fade mapped a plan for Selina to be Medium Zhayedan within a cycle after Midterm.

Selina was not locked in. She could be like the twins, winning impossible battles with only the *lowest* ranked warriors. Selina had to be willing to build those warriors and develop an underground training system.

At the time of the conversation, the Twins were only in Medium Scouts doing the impossible with themselves. Their scores were already being monitored by those that knew to watch for such things. Twenty-two days later, they beat their instructors almost to death. Master Fade stopped referring to them for a while after that incident.

She did not fear Selina would follow their reckless path. She just didn't want to associate Selina's growth and accomplishments with them. The incident provided the best breaking point, which Master Fade seemed to be looking for.

This conversation was about a year after Selina arrived. It was then Selina had the impression Illuminator might have been providing some extra input to Master Fade. Her suggestion sounded like the old woman.

Prove Wolf Pack wrong in their ways yet again. It seemed harder to prove such things pointless after Wolf Pack won the Crusader Olympia against the other Packs.

And Illuminator would argue, "Might does not make right. It was just a day in which two were better than many."

Ironically, Chevalier was credited it for saying something like that at the beginning of the Packs.

"Might does not equal right. Fighting and winning does not mean the most honorable won or the path taken was the best path. It just meant someone had a better day then the rest."

It was the argument for the creation of the Council and the War Council. They were supposed to be the guiding forces for the Packs. Honorable battles, growth and the pursuit of war for those of Lerikatia to have Peace.

But why did the Pack have to be created for war so Lerikatia could have peace? Lerikatia didn't provide anything to the Pack. Food was grown here. Supplies were mined and created here. There was nothing that came from Lerikatia but Cyborgs and The Council.

I guess the same could be asked as to why I choose to stay a scout. Why do I hold myself back so others can have peace? Did Nite and Mike really find peace? Did Lerikatia with all the Silent Knight attacks that happen?

Selina met Master Fade halfway, only performing

high enough to stay in the top of the Heavy Scout Abas. She preferred the Neovision Vison, whose battle name was Mink (HSc). It followed the design the twins were forced to use, the Marbled Polecat (MSc).

Hers had a beautifully polished black armor that was almost too shiny to fight in. She didn't try to hide in it when it was so clean either. She liked to draw attention, then vanish in the city settings.

For the Forward Schools, the Mink Abas was designed as a stalker-style light Abas, which usually operated in low numbers behind enemy lines. The likelihood of living five years after your release from school was low in these conditions. It attracted the cockiest of light Abas pilots to this particular Abas.

This was the first clue she was not what she appeared to be in class. A clue missed by many who were not looking. For those that were, well, it was one of the starting points for finding their way to the Crux.

It was said Mink (HSc) Pilots knew what their life was worth. They were destined to die fighting. It didn't matter to them if they were fighting friend or foe. Due to this, in the forward schools, they had little to no real connections with others. Its design suited Selina's needs.

It was a general frame, not belonging to any Pack particularly. This was one of the most popular Abas model in the Inner Schools, who often started talented students in these instead of the Light and Medium

Scouts. If the selections of the Sea Mink (HSc) was also added in, it was the most popular.

The Neovison Macrodon was popular among Jegermuri more than other Packs, due to the Sea Mink's design to be more aquatic. They were extremely popular designs for planets with more coastal lands and high-water regions due to their multifunctional designs working well within the cities and waterways. They were great for Space battles. These modifications were the only differentiator between the two designs.

In the Inner Schools, the Minks were more popular in the earlier training. Obviously because of the non-Pack commitment, which in those schools didn't start until the Third Echelon. Also, because they were the most divergent design systems for Scouts. Students training in these could go through all kinds of weapons, designs and trials without having to change out frames.

Most Scouts were very specialized for a style of fighting or mission type. These were more diverse because their missions varied due to the link to Naval operations and Space Station assignments. The Forward Schools didn't operate toward any of these types of combat. They solely concentrated on Abas ground fighting, fortification and invasion tactics, which lead to the higher death rate for those who graduated in non-Sentinel Midlevel classes of Abas.

Living and mission statistics were provided on every Abas design when the students went to select them. Common set-ups were also provided. Students could create their own versions as well, specializing the Abas to their specific styles. Most scouts stayed with tried and true designs in the Forward Schools.

The Mink sounded like a simple name. The design was simple as well. It was built around the theory of multiple shots with powerful bursts at quick speeds would destroy most enemies faster than standing toe-to-toe. They were lighter-armored than others of its class but had a large-enough power supply to run extremely quickly with the heavier ammo. The more they shot, the lighter they got, the faster they could run. This meant hard round weapons, not lasers.

The disadvantage came from the weight of powerful, hard round weapons and limited shots. Hard Rounds were not as popular as Lasers when you had the armor to stay in a battle longer. Laser's didn't run out, only got destroyed.

The Mink usually consisted of three rifles with a combination of one or two short assault rifles with the remaining sniper rifle for greater distances. Some went with a single or paired handgun set. Handgun designs were normally lasers, due to hard round ammo requiring the same space as rifles. Unlike other specialized Scouts and Sentinels, there were no middle grounds for the Mink. It was either kill at a distance or kill close.

They commonly carried a set of short blades or one long blade as well. It was one of the few Scout designs with blade weapons as a primary weapon style. Any Abas with hands usually had at least a knife, and most carried swords if they trained in them. Swords and knives were great close combat, silent weapons that could be deployed when no other options were good. It was always better to have an option, then to have none.

The close battle for a Mink had to be really close, which was why the armor didn't matter. The powerful hard-round weapons they preferred lost power over distances of meters, not kilometers like lasers. It aligned with the light armor design. A little extra protection would not create any more defense for them than the speed of their Abas.

The Abas themselves were designed around the build of the pilot. The cockpit was a full frame, but some still had their appendages engaged in the upper appendages of the machine. This gave more room for extra ammo storage on the Abas. Short thighs and long, narrow forelegs were often the mark of a Mink, which lead to its greater speeds.

The arms, when added, were equipped with clawed hands and large bicep areas. The pilot's entire arm could be in the bicep for control of the rest of its operations. This was common for taller or larger pilots. Smaller pilots usually stayed within the cockpit, learning to fight from a ball position.

The claws were designed specifically for ripping holes in the armor of heavier Abas, so they wouldn't have to fight through the exterior armor to finally get the kill shots. It was not a highly practiced tactic because most Abas traveled in packs. Even if you were able to get one kill, you would just be shot off the Abas corpse by one of its team members. Depending on the size of the Abas you took down, it might be worth your life to perform the action.

Knowing her Abas life depended on her own willingness to train, Selina pushed herself harder than any other member of her team. She never even asked them to train or punished them for lack of training. She set the expectation by her actions. They choose to follow or not to.

For her, the basic warrior skills included long range firing and sniper operations coupled with close range, quick reaction rifle and handgun training. She also had to learn close combat fighting beyond what they were all taught as children. Hunting, stalking, survival skills, hiding skills, blade training from basic knives through swords. She didn't feel the need to go into poles, long knives or chain weapons though, since most of them required more weight and space to carry.

She did learn bows, crossbows, and other archery styles even though she did not carry any of these on her Abas. She did keep a small crossbow with her uniform. It would work for antipersonnel or hunting when required to get her own food.

She also worked in explosive ordnance handling, development, disposal and placements with additional training in underwater, subterranean and city as primary placements. Demolition was a second expansion of these skills, which she planned to take in her Third Echelon. She specialized in computer programming, hacking, security designs, corruptions and viruses, encryption, and development of new language systems. Human language development, creation and understanding were in her selected classes to continue in basic. Espionage was an obvious choice due to the nature of her other missions.

Like most scouts, she also learned the basics and went into advanced for history of the Packs. She enjoyed several other basic classes, like combat leadership, psychology, and language. She appeared to have dropped many of them after Midterm, although in truth she completed every one of them early.

Instead, her classes appeared to have her concentrating on developing the skills that would keep her alive. She only performed high enough in them to keep her Heavy Scout. The real submission and performances were only done for Master Fade, who was just beginning to realize even what she saw was not Selina's full capabilities.

An android in the school tracked all of Selina's performances as well. If anything happened to Master Fade, the Android would pass the scoring and grades to Selina's next confidant professor. Her and several other students, but it was the only other being that knew Selina's full capabilities.

Lady Wolf, who trained in many of the same classes with Selina, would sometimes push Selina a little further to see how good she really was. Lady Wolf was one of the only ones that qualified to work with the Twins directly. They started to set up simulations over a hijacked signal in TWNs. Only her Core was ever permitted to know or even join these sessions. Then all their codes were guarded so no one knew who they were.

It was after one of these sessions, Claudia came forward with the hardest question she had ever asked of Selina. She used hand signals, but Selina could almost hear Claudia's voice perfectly in them.

"Why do you hide how good you are? Even now, after they have obviously moved into Timber Wolves," she asked.

She winced from putting on the healing agent to a cut she suffered from an earlier training session where she wanted to test something against Selina. It didn't work out well for her.

"How do you know they are Timber Wolves? They were in Frost Ferrets again for this mission. The last one they were in Kit Foxes."

"Because Students 1321456 and 6541231 operate Timber Wolves. No one else could have done what we just did with our team and not lose anyone else," she smiled at her.

"Why do you believe that? We may have people from the Inner Schools with us."

"They're not from the Inner Schools. The signals are blocked to get there. I've tried. I was trying to find my brother that was selected for them. He's Blue Blood, android born.

"Don't worry. No one else figured it out. They think they have, but I keep leading them to different directions. Like, using you as a point of people hiding their potential. The most common answer now is they are instructors, trying to determine our true potential.

"But I don't know why you are holding back anymore," Claudia asked as she flung the towel over her head like she would if it were her hair.

"Is this a question to find out how much I trust you?" Selina asked.

"132 does that. Changes the question instead of answering it. He's better."

"Fine!" Selina tossed a towel at Claudia.

They were alone in bathing areas, which was rare for the scouts. It was supposed to be one of the "off limit" places for the school to monitor. They did. Androids maintained security and health scans, but no one was graded. That didn't mean students didn't plant bugs in them.

She sighed and continued with a second set of hand singles, changing in case people were figuring out the first.

"The truth is the same reason for the Crux growing so much. Wunderkind-Krieger. We hide everything and she still popped up one day, asking questions about *them*."

"The Crux was growing before she showed up," Claudia countered.

"It's barely been two months since she was here. How many Cores did we have before her arrival? Three. How many are there now?"

"I don't know."

"How much have we grown in the last two months? We were at a hundred-fifty before the visit. What are we looking at now? At least two times as many in two months?"

"I think I see what you are getting at?"

"I hope you do, Vlcek," Selina added to iterate her point.

Selina always used Claudia's family name when she wanted to highlight a point.

"I hope you do," Selina shook her head and looked down at the floor.

"If I openly performed to the level I show Master Fade, then what would become of the Crux? How many would link that back to the twins?"

"Their twins!" Claudia exclaimed out loud.

Selina shot her a look of warning, which she internally sent to herself as well.

I can't slip like that, even with her. See. I'm not ready to show my truest potential. I must keep the learning curved down for others.

"You're right!" Claudia sighed.

She shook her head and continued.

"Your right. We would be exposed, and what happens to underground teams that are exposed?"

"They get destroyed," they signaled together.

CHAPTER 20

INVENTIONS

Dracon reached his office to discover one of five bugs planted in the office was found.

"PP, you have got to do better on your security. Scan! LA, LA, LA, LA, LA, LA, HE, HE, HE, HE, I WANT A PACK OF PICKLES. I want a pack of pickles," he finally finished in a light whisper.

The scanner picked up fourteen bugs. Nine of which were voice activated and would not have shown up unless he was speaking. It was a low number for his normal students to inflict into his room.

The ultimate test was to get something on your spymaster. Once the students usually took more to heart than the normal requirements. The ones that had really impressed Dracon, though, were created in the school itself just recently. Nite, Mike, and Selina designed them together.

Selina remained in a Heavy Scout Abas at her new school. While Falstar was holding her back, his nefarious reasons were not directed at her, but the twins. Her scores were greatly improving, and she was helping other students. She was being looked at for Instructor promotion from the talents she was showing, even if it was originating from the twins. It was converting what they did to a system other students could pick up that got the attention of those that made the decisions.

Her talents on the battlefield might have blocked it by the War Council, who would want the same talents combined with the ability to fight out on the lines where they could develop new teams and advancements. She would be like Illuminator.

They wouldn't care she came from a Scout Heritage, either. She would have been advanced to her highest potential, then used as a talent identifier and improvement tool. If she continued to prove she was worthy, that was.

Falstar would have tried to get the council's approval for her advancement with the twins, eventually. But while she was here, she was a tool for their guidance. Whoever made the choice to move her was either trying to remove tools from Falstar or didn't understand the relationship between the three of them. Dracon would have bet both were factors if they were trying to keep the twins from eventually falling out over a lover's quarrel. But it only showed they had no idea what was really going on.

Since going to her new school, she converted her training to an underground group, instead of openly like before. Those that were watching and selected her had only one point to monitor through now, her Spy Master Instructor, Master Fade, or as Master Raven referred to her, Blackout. She submitted and acted one way to the school.

She performed differently within her other role, submitting her real assignments and levels to an android that was monitoring her progress. Even the other instructors and Headmaster didn't know the game she was playing. After graduation, based on her actual abilities, she would be promoted. The game was dangerous, but her Spy Master was her core instructor who would guide and monitor her progress.

Canine Prime's Headmaster, Quick Hit, wouldn't bother trying to promote her since her Honor was still tied back to Falstar. The connection had not been released because they had not traded for students. Instead, another student was moved up the list and promoted in her place for this school, and one less would be from Quick Hits.

Selina helped with the appearance. She acted as if it wasn't worth fighting for since they would just rip it away from her. Most of her training was done in secret with the twins. Dracon never learned why they maintained this. Her going to the other school and proving her abilities would have seen her advancing and helping others to advance. Instead she was hiding her abilities, as if hiding them got them closer to a different goal.

Master Raven and Blackout kept in contact about

Selina. It seemed he wasn't the only one from the school, but Dracon hadn't figured out who the other or others might be. Master Raven would often compare her to the twins. He knew there was some connection between them, but it wasn't like the two brothers.

Those two learned faster than anything he had ever seen and seemed to be developing a way to talk without even seeing each other. Dracon realized this the other day when Nite was talking to him in the office. He suddenly looked toward the wall, almost involuntarily. Then made a comment about Mike finishing his research and would be joining them shortly.

Dracon had felt he was looking at the location of his brother, as if there were no walls between them. They did the same thing with their Abas at times. It may have been really good spy equipment or a way to distract Dracon from noticing something else. It seemed too *natural* to them, and unnatural to him for it to be that.

Dracon and Nite were talking for a couple hours when it happened. For Nite to have been able to do that, he would have had to have received a message on his PAC, or he would have had to set an alarm to say it. That wasn't their way. Nite had to have known his brother was close to finishing, and Mike knew Nite was with Dracon.

Nothing new, Mike hardly liked to let Dracon in on any of their business. Dracon couldn't help the way Mike felt. He could only do what he could to help them and keep them on track. If Mike didn't understand Dracon had to do some things Mike wouldn't understand without explanation or keep some things from them to protect them, then so be it. Any father would for his sons, sergeant or otherwise.

Nite and Mike had enough access to information and knowledge that should not have been provided to seventeen-year-old children. Even advanced seventeen-year-olds needed to have some restrictions on the access to knowledge that these two were accessing. Usually limiting it with predecessor activities and honor level requirements were enough to prevent early detection. It was quickly showing its weakness against these two.

The twins had access to information that would normally be limited to high level Zhayedan Instructors, Master Instructors and the Headmaster. That didn't include what they could access across TWNs. And they were talking with people in the fields, gathering even more information, asking powerful questions and providing feedback with experts.

It took Dracon every trick in his book to keep them from finding certain information that would unlock paths they were not ready to go down. Dracon could hardly keep up with them, which was one of the reasons he was meeting with Blackout now. He wanted to ensure Selina was at least requiring her Third Echelon. Otherwise, these guys might try to leave early.

One of the most important things Dracon was

trying to hide from them was the same information he and another student discovered during their early years. Too many dark secrets of the Pack. They learned to create an access through back doors he developed. They since helped to close up those doors and more.

Most of it didn't seem that important other than just privilege knowledge. There were classified items like genetic codes scheduled for removal, possible new upgrades the Triscifield were developing, plans on team development within and outside the schools. Then they came across information that would see them dead if it were known they found it. Hidden Cyborg spies and when they were going to kill them was one example. There were millions of other political games being mapped by the circuits, but none of that compared to the actual secret.

The worst and most important knowledge they had ever learned from their invasions was the reason for Wolf entering the last Crusader Olympia. The reason for the fifty-year peace. He felt this was the day he had truly lost his innocence. It was also the day he was condemned with the name Raven.

The black bird of death and bad luck came from Falstar. He'd beaten Dracon in their last match and won the right to either change his name or change Dracon's. With him going to the schools he would either be allowed to drop his Code name and use his family name to honor his family or keep his Code Name to show he would return to the field. He was never going to see the field, so dropping his name was the best option.

Instead he set a constant reminder of what curiosity got you. The story was covered in Dracon's End Games. This was mostly due to Falstar's father's creative work. Thankfully, they found he was one person they could still trust after digging out the dark secrets of the circuits.

Falstar named Dracon after the bird of death who ate its enemies' souls, for Falstar had lost his own soul as well. The reason their animosity was so deep now. Falstar gave up everything for a mission that was his doom whether victorious or failed. Dracon got to be the visual hero and live the life they both wanted.

Dracon allowed his mind to wonder away from the memory. He was waiting for Blackout to become available. He didn't wait long until the long-range transmission came to life, notifying him of the other's presents.

"Good day," she started.

"How have you been," he responded, expecting a nothing answers and not being disappointed.

The conversation stayed subtle until Blackout finally lead him to where she wanted. He wanted her to bring it up so he could direct it to where he needed it.

"I know I was still in school training in a light Abas during that time, but it was just before the great battle. From what I hear, it was a wonderful time to be a true Abas pilot and participating in the field."

She waited patiently but knew Dracon would not fill the empty space.

"I understand you participated in it, the great battle. Was that where you earned your rights to the school then. Well, being around all those great pilots, you might have seen something. Like whom really developed these and let the discovery come to their children's credit instead?" she suggested tactfully with the question.

She was not trying to find out who built it as much as whom the parents of the twins were. Their school was not the only one hunting for answers to the greatest mystery in the system. More and more espionage professors were turning toward the answers as they discovered the students that were outscoring everyone.

Don't get distracted from the mission I need you on. We can do both.

"I am sorry to say, but there has never been anything like the two of . . . well, I guess I should start saying three of them now, since it seems TTG has also discovered her new talents," Dracon added as he set his glass down.

He never took a drink, but the sounds of the drink in his hands would invite a calmness between them. Delicacy was important when building trust. The two had not shared names, therefore it was not polite for the senior to initiate video. Video allowed them to learn even more about each other. When spymasters communicated, it was only polite to allow the younger or lower level to establish the comfort zone.

Dracon hoped by acting subtle as if he were relaxing during the talks would help her to relax a little as well. Most young spymasters rushed in. They wanted to prove they were ready to face off.

Her soft operations showed she was cautious. A very promising spymaster. One Dracon would have to be careful in dealing with. At least until he could learn even more about her than he already did.

"It is impossible for students to develop something like this! There has to be something else behind it," she finished, a little less convinced than when she started.

It was an opening, and it was one Dracon could use to learn more about Selina.

"I believe there is something behind them, but I don't know what it could be. I will share with you that which, of course, is not considered classified by the school about them; and of course, you have Selina's developments to go by as well. That will give you at least three more years before they could leave school early."

"No. Three years only gets them to almost starting the Third Echelon. They gain nothing by leaving early," she responded.

What she was really saying was she didn't believe those years would be enough for her to finish figuring everything out she wanted to know. She moved methodically. She liked the idea of having almost a decade more with them. She wanted all the time.

And the seed is planted.

Before Master Raven could fertilize it, Blackout added her own.

"You don't understand what I have seen her capable of doing. She was practicing with her light's VR trainer and took out an Elite. Not just any Elite either. It was a Behemoth. I checked the program; it was set for a difficulty that Zhayedans would use to train against for a challenge. No Scout could take on by itself, and I watched her do it."

The sound of her settling back in her chair could be heard clearly. She either leaned forward to stress what she was saying or was keeping it quiet to prevent others from hearing. It was more likely an involuntary need to push the information's importance on Master Raven.

These young ones think seeing is the only way to get and give information. Hearing is more important in our line of work. You must have been trained by . . . Master Jaasoophee. Yes, the glass worked.

"You have seen real battle. Even the lowest member of the warrior classes has taken out some Abas or another. I do not mean to belittle her actions. I have seen the twins do some weird things in their Abas as well. I am saying anything is possible when one has the right determination, plan, and terrain.

"As for her abilities in an Abas, how are others

reacting to them? Or I guess she is still hiding them since she seems to be a Scout."

Dracon tried to downplay the actions, but it even made his heart jump a little. The story of the Tutevibian and the trainee. The Tutevibian was four meters (13'7") tall, and enormous even by their standards. The trainee was small for her size. She killed him with a single shot with a well-aimed pebble and a sling.

"Yes, you are right. She still hides them. I only got the recording of the video before she destroyed the copy and made a second, much less promising video to give to me. The ones she gives to the other instructors are worse. I am submitting the original.

"You can see her making the mistakes on purpose if you know what to look for. I doubt anyone is looking, unless, of course, they have seen what I have seen. The War Council . . .."

She stopped, realizing she was giving too much away.

"Let us hope no one ever does," he finished for her.

"The evidence was destroyed after the grading. All that is left is my own memory," the spymaster lied and let out a small sigh. "My name is Fade, by the way. I think we've talked long enough for me to at least give you my call name."

A distraction from the slip. Good call. But you forgot there is an android also monitoring it, and I guarantee they have not forgotten.

"Master Raven. I am glad you feel so comfortable with me."

Master Fade. Do you think I don't know you are a master in small arms, piloting and espionage? No. You know that and know more about me as well.

The conversation was short lived after that. They closed out the transmission, and Dracon looked up to Nite standing in front of him. He had not seen him approaching.

Nite on the other hand was waiting patiently for the conversation to end and started speaking as he held out a small device to Dracon.

"The device is designed to react to key words, and once they reacted to the key word, they would start on voice start-ups of only particular people.

"For example, if the bug was planted and I set it for my voice to start it when the word *happy* was spoken, then I would be the only one to turn it on. Then if I said the word *see*, it would change program to the next number of voices that were preprogrammed for it," Nite pointed at the input area.

It was so tiny, the beam of light carrying the program had to be nanometers in measurement.

The light program could be sent through any light source to add to or change the program. It wouldn't be detected. If the transmission is the same . . ..

"Once I have all their voices, I could keep them recorded to my arm computer. Then I could program any of these before a meeting by selecting the serial number programmed in and selecting the voices I want. If I want it to pick up a new voice after I have set the program, I just have to get them from recordings.

"The filter can backdate as well, and only pull their parts of conversations if you only want to hear them. But that's in the program written by Selina.

"This way, you are not wasting time searching through several conversations with students that usually lead to nothing. If you did want to have two running together, so you could get all the talking in the room, as well as the important conversations you are looking for, you just have to set two of them with different programming.

"We've figured out how to get seven voices to command operations to trigger, and independent operations. So far this is all we can manage and keep enough for the sound recorder to go without being detected by any means we have been able to find, including what is in the Headmaster's office.

"Mike will find a way to do it. He's the best between the three of us with it, although it was Selina who finally reached seven. We only had three before she had her ingenious idea."

Nite stopped speaking, allowing Dracon to have the full disk for the program, design and what he hoped was a prototype and not a finished model. Dracon knew better than to push for more information on their items.

What you are not telling me is you couldn't keep the security as tight as you wanted it and maintain the size. I can tell by what you have been reading and buying, but even this is beyond what I could have guessed you were building.

Dracon thought about the number of seven voices. There weren't many places that you would need to have seven different triggers. Even if there were, where you would expect to collect targeted intel with that many common at one time. . .?

Unless they were planning on bugging one of the councils. Wait. The twins would likely target every council. Could they do that? Should this be allowed to exist? Is there a line we have to draw in allowing them to create?

"How is she doing?" Dracon asked, accepting the opening of changing the conversation.

It was another difficulty in dealing with the twins. From another conversation with Master Fade, Selina was doing the same thing. Changing conversations and getting you to think you changed it. It kept you from asking more questions than you might. By the time you realized, they were gone, and you were thinking along the lines they wanted.

Much like I just did with Master Fade. How long have you been watching me? Watching us?

"I don't really know the personals. Mike is the one with the communicator."

Nite seemed to be hinting at something. Dracon didn't grasp it yet. Maybe it was Nite's way of trying to tell him something in a way Mike wouldn't know.

"What? Mike talks to someone besides you."

Dracon laughed at his student's comment and surprise at the rebuttal.

"She makes him laugh. Something I do not do so well. I irritate him because we disagree. It's hard to argue with your mirror.

"Back to the devise. It can do up to twelve transmissions at one time. We wanted to get more again, but size matters. Smaller is better on this one. Well, you can figure out all the applications. The rest of the details are on the disk.

"You can separate your voice after the start-up if you want. Before the start-up. I just like having my own voice as the start-up, so I can control when it begins. It also helps to not have to fish for a word or know their common vernacular. There is only one start-up program word for each operation, then it runs the program."

Dracon missed something, but he couldn't tell what it was. He knew because Nite gave him what he wanted on the other conversation, and then went back to the device. It was the way he taught them to turn conversations in codes when you knew you were being listened to, but you didn't want them to understand the significant parts of it.

Do they know my mannerisms so well? Programming with out talking. Mike. No requirement to be in the room. Could this fit into a robotic bug? Oh . . . my . . . gods! Size matters.

"I see. Ingenious. It keeps things simple. And I can take my own voice out of the conversation.

That could be dangerous on its own. It adds a lot of applications. I like it," Dracon rambled, as his mind was wondering.

Is that how you were able to connect to that girl so quickly? Melina Largo would want to know, but would I want to hand this over to Bear Sleuth? This is worse than I thought.

"I think I understand enough now," he added looking at the devise.

"There are obvious problems with it still, but we are working on it." Nite stopped abruptly.

Dracon realized he was only getting one of these because they were able to secure the devise outside of the delivery system. None of the three of them would ever allow anything to get away from them without it destroying itself. Anything they make could be improved beyond them and used against them.

That's why the remains were destroyed so easily. It was not poor design, but purposeful design. An acid inside designed to corrupt the material. It literally disintegrated. Then what is found is something that could only be annoying.

How long have you had these then? Three to seven. The need for more. You bugged the council.

In 682.7.2, I found that ant-like robot gathering materials. We tracked them back to an area where they were self-replicating. We thought it was the circuits trying to spy on us. Not uncommon.

The schools consider it part of training. The devises practically fell part when exposed to a small controlled

EMP. We cleared the school by an EMP blast drill. No transmissions were detected. Haven't seen them since.

Now this. Have we allowed you to go too far?

It was hard not to take it apart and inspect it. Dracon wanted to know if these were the same designs. Nite warned him once to never attempt to open anything they created. Dracon took it to heart and never allowed himself to submit to the urge.

Nite seemed to read the thoughts off his face.

"It was something you said," Nite mentioned unexpectantly, as if they were having a conversation. "I wouldn't want to be the creator of my own doom, as you like to say. Be careful where they go. We would not want these to get to the wrong . . . minds."

"You have learned something from me." Dracon let out a small smile.

But again, Nite was looking for something from him. Something it appeared Nite did not believe Dracon was hiding not getting. Dracon could not think of what it could be.

"Of course, there is a defense to it. It would be nice to see if someone can find it. I might need one in your office," Nite said it flatly as if it had not already happened and he was asking permission.

Dracon looked over his student very carefully. Then he laughed. If he knew Nite, Nite probably planted three of them entering the room.

"You are better than any of the others I have ever had the privilege of instructing. I really wish I could find out who your parents were. I feel I owe you that much," Dracon went fishing.

By Nite's face, he had the subject wrong. Mike must have been listening to their conversation. Dracon might have just asked Nite outright and allowed him the opportunity to lie about it.

"How many would you like? We have made about fifty of them."

Nite looked over the table as if the last comment had not been said. Politely ignoring the comment was a way for him to tell Dracon he didn't want to broach the subject. They had seemed to have left it behind while everyone else was digging in on finding the answer.

I assume there are at least 70 not in use. He did say about fifty. Which means they have deployed some. And those kuso insects!

"I would love to have at least twenty-five," Dracon continued. "I assume you want something from me to tell me about these and so readily offer them."

Dracon readied for a price that was higher than he would ever agree to. They would start the negotiations after that. It was the way of any two masters trying to get something from each other. It was a different part of their training, but it was still a part of it.

"Selina needs some for her. I want to send her at least twenty-five. Since we can produce about five in a night, if that is all we do, then I feel we can give you what we have ready now. At least the ones not set, already, of course," Nite was telling him he figured out how much Dracon calculated. "We had two meetings with the Headmaster since your last one. Here is yours, by the way. The transmissions are already set up for your desk, but you may have this back for a reminder or example of the antique," Nite laughed.

It was his time to pay back his instructor for setting him up on the last comment. He handed him first a bag full of old spy equipment, which Dracon placed throughout the school and thought were still active. The second was a simple list of where the replacements were placed.

"I see. You knew how many I would want right off the bat. Oh, and remember what I told you the first night we met. It doesn't matter where you came from, it only matters where you are going. Learn from the past, so not to repeat it. You three have come farther than any that have passed through any pack school. What will the future hold?"

"No, it is not history we need to know about. There are other things. I think medical or subminimal. For the last year, Mike and I have been having . . . some strange . . . things happen," Nite talked as if he had a headache suddenly come on.

"Do you want to talk about it? Is it life threatening? Can you trust me enough to talk about it?" Dracon asked the last as a simple suggestion for engaging the level of trust they had for each other.

"I can't. I don't mean that I won't talk about it with you. I mean we can't talk about it at all." Nite seemed to shake the last thought off, and his mind seemed to settle back down.

Looking at the young face in front of him, Dracon realized how young the twins really were. It wasn't that age mattered in the Packs rank. To see someone so young accomplish so much so fast could come to two endings for him within the Pack. Either he would continue to progress until he went mad or died young.

The brightest flames burned the quickest.

"I see. You have what older Abas pilots call the longing. It isn't too common in someone so young, and it usually comes when you are no longer going to be in an Abas. Don't worry; they are not going to take you away from your Abas.

"Consider your request complete. I know the security and espionage instructor there, as you obviously know. I will send Selina a package via her. I don't maintain direct contact with Selina. Since Mike seems to keep the transmitter with him, ask him to pass the information on to her.

"I wish I had the other one to give to you," he paused at the look from Nite. "I wanted all three of them, but I was only given two to activate. Maybe you . . .."

"No, we won't take it apart for now. It is being used too often for us to risk a failure on our parts. If we had the third, it might be possible," Nite interrupted Dracon, but he gave a look of annoyance.

It had obviously been discussed already.

Mike must have thought I had the third one and

was using it to listen in to them. Of course, if Mike and Selina were more than just friends, but . . .. Dracon let the thought drop off.

"I do not have it to give to you," Dracon added disappointedly.

He couldn't even get a replacement set. He wanted one himself, but the quality and level of that one was beyond his reach.

"I will try to get it from where I got the other two. Without having access to at least one of them, it cannot be programmed for the other two. It must be that one. It is quite useless, but I will try to get it for you just the same.

"I am unable to obtain another set to give you. A complete set to replace the one you have. They are next to impossible to find. The man that gave those to me is . . .." There was no need to finish.

Nite would be able to figure out the rest. He rose and left the room. Dracon's eyes followed his assumed path for a few minutes, thinking hard. Then curiosity got the best of him and he started checking the messages from the Headmaster's office.

How could a couple of seventeen-year-old Abas pilots create things like this? No, they were younger when they went to the council. But are they able to find transmissions that powerful to get the information back here?

Piggybacking on others. The need for the smaller signal. Did they want the others found to find out how they would be disposed of? Is that why there was a plague of them? How far have you been planning? How long?

The design was perfect for hiding about anywhere. The silver needle was barely the size of a needle prick of blood on the tip of a finger. He started to wonder how many were in his office. It would be pointless to look, though. If he removed one, Nite or Mike would put five in its place. Not that they didn't trust him, but just to show they could.

"Honor among thieves, but there is also competition."

Crap. Did I just trigger one to turn on? They know my common sayings. They know my mannerisms and preferred vernacular. How did they figure out a defense for it? What was it?

He looked down at his desk where a small spider almost seemed to be staring at him before it turned and ran over the edge.

I must be seeing things. I could have sworn that thing was monitoring me like some kind of video device. Tell me they haven't figured that out! Hearing is one thing. Seeing? Have we let them go too long?

CHAPTER 21

A DECISION OF LOVE

Scout Abas did not suffer from loneliness. Lack of privacy was in abundance for all the light Abas, even in Second Echelon, unless they were on a team. Selina found as much privacy as she could and more than most since she led the largest underground team in the Forward Schools, from what Master Fade told her.

Even with the ability to get privacy, she still needed a space no one would be able to get to or use. Finding the right hidden room in the underground passages took her almost two years after arriving. She barely fit after connecting the room to her cockpit.

She had to maneuver three different battles to get her Abas moved to the bay that was above it. It was supposed to be a General Bay. Yet after Selina moved, almost every one of her Core took up space in it. Then leaders throughout the Crux started to get in there if they weren't on a team. It was the most obvious signal the underground group provided on who they really were.

But with this many recruits, we had to have some gateway. Some point of antagonizing to let others start finding us. If they looked too loudly, they would bring attention.

And that noisiness is why I can't trust even the showers in this place after Claudia has taken the time to ensure we could have a peaceful hour. They all want to know about what is next. Are we talking about them?

It's the reason I foresaw the need of a room no one else would know about even before I started to gather followers.

Room wasn't really the right word. It was more of a crawl space the size of a Tutevibian coffin. One she closed herself in with when she pulled the block that was covering it back in place. She created it, like many of the spaces below the school had been.

Yes, the builders practically put a small town under the school for those looking. But there were also spaces like these, which had to be discovered, cut out and then remolded to hide them. Selina wasn't sure if it was designed this way, or if it was just natural lost space due to the design plans. Either way, it was the only way to meet her needs.

Even with all the effort put into it, she didn't use the room often. Most the time it was only for speaking to Mike on very private matters or for dates. She connected to her Abas so she could use the simulation generator in it to project herself to him and be with his projection. They used the private communication device Master Raven provided, but never felt as if they were ever alone enough to do more than hold each other.

Lady Wolf was the only one who knew the secret. She helped Selina hide her tracks and prevented others from finding her. The unexpected meeting with Wunderkind-Krieger made protecting the secret connection all the more necessary. However, Wunderkind-Krieger figured out Selina's location that quickly needed to be blocked before someone found this place.

At least we don't do our training from here. I think part of the lack of desire to come to this room is because it is more like a coffin. And the desire is because it is the only place I can be with Mike, alone. Or as alone as we ever are. Scouts never have true privacy.

At least the power drain is low enough, even the engineers don't appear to notice I have tapped into the lines going to my Abas. Their probably too busy trying to hack our training sessions with the twins. I know they try to get enough information for bets from me and mine! At least they know how to keep quiet on the right things.

And the twins constantly changing Abas depending on what mission we are training with also helps. Scrambling codes to make it appear as if it's coming from different schools, also a plus. But mostly, because they have opened up to training with their team, as if we were all in the same schools.

Sometimes, to challenge themselves, they would take a lower Abas class. But it wasn't the same mentality or perspective that Selina fought from. For them, it was about operations with lower weapons, capabilities, and testing strategy. They wanted to see if others should be able to do the same.

For her, it was preparing to never leave the smaller frames that would define the length of her life. A life she would gladly give to protect the ones she loved. She would rather live it with them, long and fulfilled though.

I just hope I live long enough to see the fruits of that love, she thought as she touched her stomach, thinking of the one day Mike and she hoped to create.

Selina fought differently than the twins most the time. Use of weapons, the way she hid in her Abas or outside of it, and of course the obvious advantages and disadvantages of being female changed her perspective a lot. They needed that diversity to grow, and their unwillingness to gather followers in their school meant she had to gather a team for them in hers.

No matter how much they learned about themselves, it was learning from others that made them stronger now. Although she did laugh as they tried to bridge the gap between being a male and a female. That was a mentality they could never figure out.

How did Nite put it? It was like having a discombobulated maze with no exit and needing to find a way out in order to be sane. An endless maze, with changing walls. Sometimes it was rewarding. Sometimes it punished. And it would do both for the same action at different times with no way of knowing which one you were going to get.

Mike's was a little better. He described trying to figure out female's mind was like trying to solve a ten-thousand-piece jigsaw puzzle with twenty-two-thousand pieces. Only there was no picture to tell you where you were trying to go or what you were trying to accomplish. There were three different puzzles mixed into it. Then someone would come along and change which puzzle pieces the complete picture belonged to without telling you, taking away some and adding others that didn't belong. And it didn't always align to one of the original sets either.

After this description he said the smartest thing she heard from him. "Maybe the key to women is not trying to solve the puzzles but being willing to put the effort in to work into them."

Just letting us know we are worth the effort. Like the effort you put in to help me help others. It's made you better, even when you had no intention.

Without me, you would not have grown in the way you needed. Without you, I would not have been able to be complete. I guess it's together that we work the best.

The twins helped bring about something which was not supposed to be in these schools, but it was really Selina's pet project. She longed to be with Mike, which was the only reason she considered leaving once they completed Second Echelon. Something Master Fade recently picked up on. She started to make some strong points to keep her around for the

Third. She wondered if Master Raven planted the seed, or if Nite was ultimately responsible.

An elite group of Scouts and Sentinels, self-sufficient, and capable of truly winning battles against the best the Pack could provide. This team created by a pilot that was only considered a Heavy Scout, and by most her instructors, maladroit at best. If she left early, would it collapse? Would her team follow her example, leaving before they had the opportunity to maximize their efforts?

It's what Master Fade asked Selina.

One day, Selina could see the light Abas becoming more than just the throwaway Abas of the heavies in these Forward Schools. They would be the ruling battle figures. They would be the strength of the team, respected as much if not more than the ultimate delivers of battle.

Yes, the Twins were not like that. Yes, she was willing to give up her life to protect them, but not because they were Heavy Zhayedan pilots. She did it because she loved them, as leaders and more. All those under her loved them, even if they didn't know them.

And because of Claudia, they at least know there are others out there. Just not who they are or what they pilot, or even that they started it all.

Selina knew this deep inside, like she knew she would not be around to see its fruition in the Wolf Pack. Mike and she were planning on leaving. Where, they were not sure. Mercedes went somewhere. That's what they understood. There was somewhere not part of the Pack or the Desitians.

Master Fade said the Inner Schools had this respect. Every warrior was respected, even the non-Abas. They might fight with each other, but it was like sibling rivalry. You could pick on your own brother or sister, but if someone else even made a comment about them, you destroyed 'em.

Thanks to the twins, the three of them started something to change Wolf Pack for the better someday. At least the Forward Schools would be changed. But it was the change that mattered, and she felt she needed to be here to see it as long as possible.

The Core leaders can take the training out into the Pack or wherever they are going. But I can't risk it falling apart because I left early. Others will follow.

Selina ensured Claudia had a regal name and was the underground face of the Crux. It was only her Core who knew Claudia was not the actual leader or starter. Others may have had suspicions, but Claudia was a Master at keeping people from Selina, often by acting as if Selina was the most important person, while Selina looked to Claudia for confirmation. It gave the appearance of Selina acting as the leader, while Claudia made the smallest of symbols for confirmation on where to go.

When others sought to change Lady Wolf's call sign in battles, Selina took necessary precautions to ensure the win without giving away her own training. Selina's name, TTG, was protected, as long as no one was able to beat both the twins. In battles, she seemed to be nothing important other than a good Heavy Scout.

Quick Hit allowed the student body to change it in the schools and refer to her by whatever the current trend was. It was not a real call sign. In her records she was still officially TTG, which was also how instructors were supposed to refer to her.

Currently she took on the name Tug-O-War, a teasing name Claudia had in their earlier years. People thought it was funny enough they didn't try to change it now. TTG felt it was an honorable name because she was playing Tug-O-War against Wolf Pack. And her team was growing exponentially. To her, they were winning the long war against the Forward Schools.

But would we if I left early? Would others continue to take up my rope if I left before we completed our last echelon? Would I have made a strong enough point?

Mike controlled Selina's Call Sign solely before, but recently Nite wanted to have more protection. Another aftermath reaction of Wunderkind-Krieger. They were engaging in battles individually more and more. Sometimes with teams, but just as often alone for Mike. In and out of their Abas as well, which increased the dangers.

Aside from Wunderkind-Krieger discovering their connection, the twins discovered the instructors tried to use some cheats to get wins. Nite didn't want a cheap shot to get through on either of them, putting her at risk. If the school was that desperate to see them go down, even if they couldn't call it a true defeat, securities were needed.

They also hid their connection by naming fifteen other students in schools outside of Timber Wolf Academy. All Scouts at the time, but each one could be tied back to a home they had stayed in. They hoped it would cut down the attention Selina seemed to have drawn.

Selina hiding her connection to them was one of the reasons she didn't fight the Headmaster on her decision. Many of her decisions rested on her abilities to stay hidden. It was trying to stay hidden which brought Claudia's attention.

And leaving early would keep these games from having to constantly be played. Leaving would not stop the Five-Year promotion for me. It is possible to do it early. I have proven enough by now, I am sure. And leaving would let me be with Mike all the sooner. Would Claudia come with us?

Claudia was the first one to realize Selina wasn't the wallflower she acted like. This was after starting the Crux, when Selina still pretended to be one with them all when she was not training with them. Selina was talking to someone outside the schools in a way that no Wallflower did.

Claudia knew they were outside the schools because the way Selina was speaking about instructors. Then there was the way Selina referenced to things which would be common knowledge in the schools, even if they were Heavy pilots. Claudia also realized

Selina was hiding her true talents and abilities even from Master Fade and Claudia. Claudia wanted to find out why.

Scouts were curious kitties. Thankfully, cats have nine lives to learn from their mistakes, because Claudia needs them all. I might need to remind her not to be so curious again. It's been a while since I set a trap for her.

It was the same curiosity that had Claudia watching Selina, trying to find out what Selina was really up to. For Scouts, people acting weird got others killed. Curiosity and paying attention to people's intentions and changes in actions could mean your life. It was not a skill taught in class but developed by almost every one of them.

Claudia's original clue came when she watched Selina purposely answer just enough questions to ensure she beat the average score of the next highest pilot. She actually saw Selina calculating her score, then change answers that were obviously right to incorrect. Not only were they incorrect, but they were so wrong, someone would have had to be trying to get them wrong in order to come up with it.

I assume she was tipped off by Master Fade. I never did try to confirm that. Is four years too late to ask the question? Does the answer change my mind now?

After that, Claudia started to track Selina, although at first, she wasn't able to keep up with her or find her. Claudia was curious why the pilot was really at the school. Why would someone who was obviously able to do better was doing less and purposely keeping attention from her. After she saw the test, she detected the rest.

The more Claudia learned about Selina, the more she spent time trying to earn her way into Selina's trust. But then she started to put more pieces together. Selina confirmed she was doing an espionage game, called Freddy's House. Selina only knew of it being played in the Forward Schools, but it was started there in the early years.

If a pilot could hide their true talents and abilities from the Headmaster, the instructors, and even other students that were not part of their underground group, they would earn a huge boost from the Five-Year. They had one instructor, and one android who would track their actual progress. Since every student had an android tracking them and most had a favorite instructor, it wasn't hard to hide this. Underground groups were not required but were often necessary.

Selina confirming it was a huge risk if Claudia wanted to report the discovery since this was before they started the Crux. If someone was able to find an actual Freddy and prove it, then they got the Pool of Hidden Opportunities from the other pilot. Selina wasn't sure what the purpose of the game was.

A lot of Scouts claimed to play Freddy's House, but real players were as rare as Elite pilots. Most were Scout Abas that knew early on, the only way they would blow past everyone else was to break the rules in the perfect way. The long game could earn a Scout triple the honor ranks leaving school and promotion to a Zhayedan by the War Council upon graduation.

If the pilot was caught and turned over, they were denied what they earned, including the Bonus ranks if they earned them before Midterm.   They were instead left where they pretended to be. They had to fight to try to get everything they held privately back.

Which is a reason a lot of pilots playing this game choose to leave early. They want to reduce the risk if they are good enough. Getting a Team Leader Rank out of School would be phenomenal. Better to not risk it too long if you don't have to. A great reason to leave.

Instead of turning Selina in, Claudia started to help Selina protect her secret. She even helped her to find the room she would use for her *special training.* It took them until 680.2.20, after being discovered by Wind Wheel on 679.8.16, to find the space between the walls, sealed away.

Before Wind Wheel's discovery, Selina primarily operated out of her Abas and hid as much as she could there. Yet, she couldn't keep the private communicator in her Abas. The engineers were in there too often and while it was small, carrying it around all the time would draw attention to it.

Having one of these rooms somewhere was typically vital for the completion of Freddy's House as well. Claudia believed her loyalty and dedication bought her all the secrets of her greatest friend. Claudia knew she didn't have any remaining by the time they had set up the room.

At least Claudia did before she started to realize Selina was speaking to someone outside the schools. Someone not Triscifield. They were other students.

Claudia thought it was the Triscifield at first due to Selina receive equipment and devices. She even got special upgrades to her Abas that no one in the school had. All this made since and aligned with her getting things through Master Fade, her instructor point of contact.

Selina designed equipment in their rooms and had upgrades to her Pack that no Scout had. Then she started receiving study disk and information disk way above even her unofficial grading that had nothing to do with that. These were not things just provided to a Scout, no matter how well they played the game.

Master Fade let slip in front of Claudia that she didn't have access to some of the material. Most, if not all, was shared with the Crux. Claudia was internally getting credit for the additional access. They believed she was getting it with the underground accounts. But when Claudia checked them, the opportunities, Honors and Privileges didn't align to what would be needed for that information.

She figured out I wasn't talking to an external family. I wasn't accepted. She knew because Vlcek was looking too hard at me too early. They wouldn't have made a move if it were them. If it were a different family, they would have discretely handled Vlcek for me. I let her in too deep to hide this.

What most, even her tight nit group, didn't know

was by the beginning of her Midterm in 682.5.1, her Abas cockpit was upgraded to Heavy class. An upgrade that was reserved for those that proved they could be in a Heavy Class Operation. She could be moved into as high as a Timber Wolf with some additions for framing.

Selina would never see it in these schools. She needed the upgrades to be able to hub the scramble training with her team. Due to her smaller body frame, she was able to fit the extra computer components into the areas her Abas normally reserved for extra ammo in her Abas Frame, the Mink.

Claudia was eventually upgraded as well. Several of the Core Leaders were. There was no single point of failure after the Core's started to train with the twins during the first break of this cycle. It was necessary for all of those that passed the final test to get the individual developments only live instruction could provide.

I am not sure they provide instructions, as much as opportunities to fail spectacularly before showing you what you could have done differently. It was changing the perspective of the pilot, not the talents. The talents were already developed in the under training. Kinda like Claudia developing all that information on what is going on.

It was the collection of these small iotas that lead Claudia to knowing she and Master Fade were not getting the full experience of Selina's talents. Even with them, she was holding back.

Which didn't make since to her. Holding back in Freddy's House worked against what the pilot was going for. I see how much you were paying attention to me. I can see how long you have loved me as well, Claudia. Friends. Best Friends, but I kept you out and you kept trying to figure out why.

On top of that, Selina was hiding a relationship, which seemed intimate and loving. It was not that Claudia was jealous. Their intimacy was not physical or sexual. It was only friendly; deep and meaningful, but only friendly.

Claudia did not need to hold Selina to only her, either. She wanted just the opposite. To get Selina to share more of herself with others. To get her to provide those experiences for others to learn. For Selina to show Claudia what she could really do, maybe for no other reason than for Claudia to see what the full potential looked like.

And now that she's had a taste of that over the last month and a half with the twins? Do I even compare to their abilities? She knows who she's working with. But the others don't. And without her, I am not sure I could keep hiding it. Maybe I need to stay to ensure I learn what I need as well.

The loyalty Claudia proved over and over had been enough for Selina to mention her to Mike several times. Selina made one request of Mike. When they went on their hidden mission, she wanted to take Lady Wolf with them if it could be done. Selina knew Mike was not fond of inviting more people. He understood Selina's want to keep her most loyal friend with her.

And she was afraid I was holding myself back for someone else's benefit. I guess I am, but not in the dangerous manipulative way she thought. Does she understand now?

I know what others would do to get to the twins. I have to protect them. If protecting them requires this little bit from me, then so be it.

Another voice seemed to come to her mind and ask another question of her.

And would leaving with them early draw attention to them? Would it not cause them to be exposed? They could no longer hide who they are and have not truly proven they can lead a larger group.

Even four more years of training the Core is not the same as them being in real leadership. Nine more years of them proving they are better than everyone else isn't enough. It is the Crux that is providing them what they need to learn. They need to be leaders, able to impact events across multiple teams, not just the one they are currently attached to.

Selina let this thought settle as she took a deep breath. It didn't sound like Claudia, or Illuminator, or Master Fade. This voice was something else, but it seemed there with her more recently. The more she thought about which way she was going to answer, anyway.

She gave the single to join Mike in the simulator. After a short embrace, no words, and a simple kiss, she took his hand and led him to a rock. She sat down and stared deep into his eyes; the most beautiful eyes to her.

"I will not leave at the end of Second Echelon," she blurted out, not meaning for it to be so blunt.

"Nite will be happy," he responded disappointed. "You're right. Both of you. We need the time. Training with the Core these last forty-four days has been . . . *enlightening*."

"Then you'll stay with me,"

"I would never leave you. Even if I died, I would come back to you."

"Well, if you die, I will tear down the gates of Hades and free all the souls to get you back. The others can be a distraction for us," she said as she crawled into his lap and settled on his chest.

"Are you going to tell Nite?"

"He already knows. He can feel it," Mike responded.

Selina never understood how they did that. She didn't care. She had her rock and he was going to stay with her. That's all she needed.

"Since we are staying, will you provide Claudia with your full potential?"

"I think I have little choice but to start showing at least her. She's almost as good as me? What about you?"

"I don't think we have found what our full potential means yet. I think Nite is afraid of doing what is best for us to find it."

"What would Nite fear? Claudia would be interested in knowing," she added with a giggle.

"You mean besides this Crux of yours?"

"Ours," she said as she settled back into him. "Always ours."

"Not being defeated."

CHAPTER 22

BRAVO'S ENGINEERS

Dracon was looking over the message describing TTG's company of Lights when one of his motion alarms went off. It was on the outskirts of the boundaries of the school.

Only two students could have gotten so far out without sounding one until then. I'm surprised they didn't get noticed earlier if they are triggering early detection devices that are meant to be discovered by ones that are as good as them.

The twins were known for sneaking out of the school boundaries, but it was not to get into trouble. It was to train privately. One of their more independent moves to ensure they were not tracked, as they assumed, they always were. It was an accurate assumption which expanded beyond the school as well.

Nite and Mike wouldn't have sounded the ones as they were coming back in. Not unless they wanted to tell me something was wrong, or someone captured them. But if the twins have been captured, why would they be coming back into the school? Why move so slow? No, this is one someone entering. Not very good, are they? Must have gotten here with help.

The movements were slow and methodical, but sloppy. It was not the right style of movements for the areas they were within. They were in no rush to get into the school, and the movements might take days to get within the inner perimeter. These were not the movements of the twins, even if they had left the outer perimeter.

I guess I must do my job and report this. Might as well see what I am reporting exactly since they are being so sloppy. Unless being sloppy and slow now is to throw me off or lure me out. Maybe this will be more interesting then I think it will be.

******

Twenty minutes passed from Dracon's notice to when he had reached the present alarms silently indicating intruders. He moved through the darkness with a swift stillness only a master of the craft truly possessed. Crossing over three kilometers while not making a sound and ensuring he was not being followed was both a hindrance and a requirement.

The security system of the school was tied in with his PAC. If he died, the Headmaster would immediately get a message. Ten seconds after the school would go into lock-down and the anti-intruder system would engage.

There was no need for him to require backup. If he failed, the students were still safe. If there was more than one, he had others to contact before the normal operations of the school would be interrupted.

I can't remember the last time someone tried to sneak into here. When was that? At least two years before the twins arrived. Maybe the memory didn't last as long as we thought it would for the Cyborgs. Or Silent Knight Cyborgs as they claimed. Black Wing most likely.

Dracon considered whether or not to take the intruders alive. Questioning them might help, but most likely, taking them alive would provide nothing. Circuits would have been programmed with nothing or wiped with nothing but the mission essentials. Cyborgs would do the same with the circuit mind and getting to the human mind was difficult. It was normally so damaged by the process, there was no reason. Silent Knights normally considered these suicide missions.

Besides, they were too low ranked and too expendable to know much. At least by their actions, thus far. It would be better to just kill this set outright. If more came, they would be better and probably worth questioning. Let them send more if their testing the defenses.

Two shadows shifted in the sides of Dracon vision. His heart went into defense beating while his mind raced a million kilometers an hour to figure out if he were about to die for underestimating his prey.

Dracon turned his head swiftly, ready to attack in three different ways and defend in five to find Nite on his left. He looked back over his shoulder to find Mike standing on the other side of him, like a protective guard. They were armed for a fight, but this time it wasn't with him.

It suddenly occurred to Dracon the twins were reaching an equal footing with him in what he normally considered enough for teaching mastery. Within the year, they would be beyond his training, if they already weren't. He let out a quite sigh and turned to face Nite.

"What are you two doing here?" Dracon scolded as best he could with their silent hand talk. The tips of his fingers ran quickly but roughly across Nite's bare palm to pass the message.

"We should ask you the same thing. How did you know someone was coming in out here?" Nite asked. "What are these? We have never seen them."

Nite held up the motion detectors Dracon placed only two years earlier. They were double triggered, so if one was removed, it would sound an alarm. They figured out how to remove both in such a way they would not trigger they were no longer there. Dracon realized they bypassed his most advanced motion detectors.

They don't know they're mine. Could they have found a way out I haven't discovered in all the years I've been here. Or they found a way to hide from even the best of my sensors when I haven't introduced them to the equipment that would even start to help them. I couldn't. Look at what they are doing without it. I guess it doesn't matter now.

He would not lie to them. They would not like that, and he needed their trust still. It was a fragile thing.

Like wild animals. Deadly as those genetically modified Dire Wolves.

"These are mine. I designed them. I have never used them in the school because no one had ever been good enough to test them on. Don't remove them. I will make you some to play with. These are here for the protection of the school."

Mike and Nite nodded lightly, and suddenly went tense. Dracon heard it as well. The motion detectors hadn't signal anyone coming, but they could hear two voices talking to each other about some device. They were discussing whether or not it was working. Obviously, it was since his equipment failed to warn him.

What an embarrassing night. At least two groups have gotten past what I built to be impassible.

Without even realizing he had, Dracon found himself submerged into the shadows of the roof. He could easily guess where the twins had vanished as well.

At least my instincts are still with me!

Dracon's mind leapt back to wanting to question them but taking them alive with the twins was a mistake and was too dangerous. He was lured here on purpose. He was tonight's target.

"Stop talking. If it is working, then we are going to give our positions away by our voices. There is no telling how long it will take for them to clear the five kilometers to our last location. We should take up here. I am sure this will be the best area to eliminate everyone that comes by without being seen."

Five kilometers? They had the distance wrong if they were looking for me. Or did they not know anything about the inside of the school?

Dracon's thoughts almost robbed him of hearing more of their conversation.

"How do we know we have what we came for?" the second, a female voice, a little shakier, asked.

"No one else will come," the first answered with a slight laugh.

The blood-hungry male voice was happy with the idea of killing more than was necessary to accomplish his assigned mission.

He made the mistake of talking about killing everyone just for the fun of it in front of the twins. Big mistake. You just challenged them to a death match. Idiots!

The female looked hard in the area where Nite was tucked in, but he offered no movements. Nite frozen every muscle in his body to hide under the shade of darkness cloaking him. A third assassin leaned within inches of Mike's back, which was facing out, but still couldn't detect him. He pulled back and looked at the other one. "I think this one might be too shallow for me," the second female called back.

"Find something quick. It will be here soon. Be alert!" the man answered hard and in a hushed voice.

They are not using sensors on their equipment or they would have detected Nite, Mike thought to himself. *It also fails to give them very little definition since they have to lean in so close.*

Mike and Nite would try not to damage the equipment. It would be nice to have something new to work with. All the other technology they were able to collect didn't have anything to do with hunting humans like this.

The last of them finally turned from Nite to look for something better. Nite swiveled without leaving the opening and slit her throat below the neck with a crescent-bladed knife. The skin split as if it had been stretched to its limits, allowing the warm life fluids of the android to gurgle and spew. The blade's sharpness filleted the robotic parts if they were mere muscle and bone, freeing the head from its prior confines with a smooth stroke before he vanished back into the shadows, leaving the question of where he had come from.

The body stayed standing. The hands reaching up to where the head once rested. It toppling over to the ground with a wet thump and splatters of water as it danced in the small amount of drainage on the side of the tunnel.

Mike moved as the other man made the mistake

of turning toward the sound. As in any battle, life and death depended on the mistakes you made, and your opponent was able to capitalize on. This man made too many for Mike to allow him to continue on this plane of existence. It was time for the Sleeping Gods to restart his life if they deemed him worthy.

Mike slid a long straight knife in-between the man's front pelvic bone. He turned it out, up, and around to completely drop the man's entrails to the ground in a pretty puzzle-diagram fashion. The white bone of the spine was visible on the inside, and the diaphragm kept his lungs and heart under his ribs.

He would not die quickly. The taller twin would be able to watch as life changed to death. He was curious of it.

The man looked down at the gaping hole where his fit stomach used to be. The blood vessels had retracted back, keeping the spot mostly dry other than what had been there from the slicing. He dropped to his knees as if he would put his parts back in.

His eyes found a foot atop his stomach and liver. He followed the leg up to find the shadow that stood over him. The man was almost beautiful with the darkness outlining his silver hair and cold blue eyes. The man closed his eyes, laid his chest open with his arms back, and settled back on his haunches. He accepted his death at what he believed was the hands of a god who found him a worthy opponent.

The second woman did not realized her legs were split open. She felt the sting run just under her buttocks. She tried to turn, but her legs refused to follow the orders. She fell to the ground, dropping her rifle. Her eyes looked through the special night scope to find the feet of a man standing almost in front of her. She knew she didn't have a chance at the rifle, but instinct had her hands go for it anyway.

Nite used a small cylindrical blade to jam the signals of the mechanical spine. Her entire body went limp, but she was still alive. The shaking of the unfeeling parts was not the first sign she had of the lack of control. It was the smell of her bowels emptying into her uniform. An emergency warning for the android.

Normally, it would be used to fake death and appear more human. It could be used for other points of cover as well. The design had as many, if not more, uses then the humans she mimicked. She didn't think any of them would help her now.

She knew the smell for it held a tint of the fragrance of her last meal. It was a great meal, as every meal was before a mission. She didn't even mind it being her last, for every time she left with Rac, she wondered if she was coming back.

I thought a digestive system was a great upgrade for the work we did. I definitely appeared more human for it.

"She is alive if you want to question her," Nite called to the roof, where Dracon watched everything.

It hadn't been a full minute since the first one went down in the blood dance the twins performed so perfectly. Dracon saw them in training. He saw them in simulation. This was the first time he saw them perform in real life.

They took the lives as they were trained. Without hesitation. Without fear. Without remorse. The twins did what they were supposed to do, win.

Nite recovered his spin spike. Mike already started to gather the equipment from around the woman's head that was still alive. Dracon's hand found his shoulder to try to steady the brother, for the woman was still alive.

He wanted to show her respect. It was an important lesson. You had to respect your enemies, even after you killed or debilitated them.

It was with unbelievable quickness Dracon stopped the first blade. The second ring sent shivers down his spine. Nite stopped a second and third from Mike's knee and other hand. He aimed for Dracon's groin. The wound may or may not have been fatal. Most likely Mike would have struck a fatal blow before he had even considered it was Dracon standing by him.

Or he knew it was me and would kill me anyway. The first blade was a distraction from the second. The third was to guarantee the job was done. He didn't want to be touched.

I didn't identify myself. This close to the end of a fight, he would have been justified in the attack against me. I should have been more careful. I am not even sure they really consider me an ally.

Remember, they are wild animals. They haven't been treated as much more than that, even if incarcerated in gold. Gilded cages didn't stop the beast from being when it was raised to never trust.

Dracon got off the ground, looking blankly from one twin to the next. He turned swiftly and took off down the hall. He vanished well before either of them should have lost sight of him.

Nite turned back to Mike with a look of anger on his face. He returned to the calm before he chose to speak. Mike took the opportunity to speak instead.

"We should go after him. He may have gone to find out what is going on," Mike suggested to his brother innocently.

"He will expect us to go to the classroom if we are loyal to him. We should not follow, like he should not have given you an opening.

"We will respect him enough to allow him to have his secrets. If you ever try to kill him again, we will find out who is the better brother.

"Let's strip the bodies and take the technology back with us, if we are not going to follow then. We will be able to tear it apart and study it. Leave the remains here. There is no need to drag them back."

"Why do you protect him?" Mike asked, not hiding his anger.

"Because if you were not blinded with unjust jealousy, you would see he has tried to be a father to us. More than anyone, and there are only a few, he protected us while teaching us to protect ourselves. Especially from ourselves. He's raised us as Eurthorians, like him.

"He got us the way to talk with Selina. He has helped us understand why others are important. Even Illuminator couldn't provide that to you.

"You have never been able to prove he has ever listened in to a conversation. We searched every item in his areas and every area he spends time in. He does not have it."

"We have not been to the forbidden areas he goes to," Mike shot back.

"Vaffanculo, Mike. He is due some his privacy. He has never been there when you were talking. I have watched him for countless hours while you and Selina talked, and he has never listened to you. You watched him while Selina and I talked, and he never listened. What kuso more proof do you kuso want?"

"He did not kuso help kill these kuso people," Mike sneered as he raised the woman's head up.

"No. We did it. We were done without need of him getting in our way. He allowed us to share the first kill. If he was still here, then he would have presented us with the cup to drink the blood," Nite shot back at his brother. "Or fluids in the case of the cyborgs and Android."

"It is normally animals for the first kill." He looked down at the pools on the ground. "It is not supposed to be cyborg chemicals."

"Well, you didn't want to kill any animals before now, at least not out of a simulator."

"Humans understand the games," Mike responded.

Nite agreed. Unless they were going to eat the animal, there was no point in killing it.

"Merde, you left her alive. Do we need to kill her?" he suddenly added as he pulled the woman's head up.

"You didn't damage the spine, did you?" Nite asked as he looked at the fluids seeping slowly from the small hole.

He could guess by the wound what the answer would be. But Mike's roughhousing and indifferent treatment was a problem.

Were supposed to respect the enemy.

"No," Mike answered. "She will be able to use her body again soon, but her legs are shot. You went too deep."

Nite leaned down by her face. Tears were flowing freely from her eyes, but Nite knew she felt no pain.

Why is she crying? What is she trying to accomplish by it?

"What I am about to do to you is going to be painful, but you won't feel it. Not at least until you start feeling again. It shouldn't take longer than fifteen hours. Do not try to walk on your legs for at least three days. By then, the Nano meds should have taken affect. We will monitor your progress."

She looked Nite with a fear in her eyes. He knew she would never lose for him.

"Merde! She is an Android."

Mike suddenly popped up off the ground and vanished back into the darkness on his own.

No, please don't! I am alive! I am alive! I don't want to be taken apart, she screamed silently in her mind as the smile cut across Nite's face.

It was a cold, evil smile that she had only seen on Humans before they performed the worst of things to her after finding out what she was. Her voice was not working. She was not able to access anything but the shifting of focus of her eyes, which did not require movement.

"This will hurt a little more for you, then. If you do not turn off that part. We are going to have to change the plans now." Nite looked at his brother.

He couldn't help but give his smile at the idea he suddenly had.

Mike came back out of the shadows with what seemed to be an equally evil smile to the Android. Where one was cold as black space, the other seemed a supernova of heat. Neither of them looked like she was about to enjoy what was to happen to her.

Before she could scream, a bulb gag was forced into her mouth. She felt Nite's mouth close to her ear.

"You will appreciate this in there."

His voice was still cold and gave no projection as to what was about to happen. Mike moved around behind her. For the first time since it had happened, she was glad she could not feel.

"I didn't know they could do this?" Mike added from what sounded was near her created anus. "This is so cool!"

She suddenly felt movement in her toes. Sensations

started to come back slowly the entire way up her body. Before long, she could feel the coldness of her legs from the lack of the synthesized blood within them. Her fingers could sense the wet ground around them, but she feared moving.

Each region of an advanced Android, like her, was designed to act and feel Human. It could also act separately if need be. She could shut down parts to protect her cybernetic brain, much like the Human body, but with more efficiency. It was not until she was pulled from the ground that she had realized she had all her clothing still on her body.

Her legs were as they were supposed to be, but she wouldn't be able to get them warm until her body could produce more proteins from her storage facilities. It would be hours at best.

It would take days of eating for her to get full strength. Even her skin would have to be healed slowly, but it wasn't too damaged. She could grow it back. It was a high-quality skin, created from the T-cells of two human babies' umbilical cords. It gave the android its own DNA signature, unique to it as the figure prints, and was a mark of becoming as close to being human as possible.

They removed the gage, looking her over. It was quicker than she thought, but she wasn't sure what happened.

"What did you do to me?" she asked as she ran a scan of her body.

They removed all her weapons. Her external

gear was gone, but nothing had been done to her body. Her braided hair was wet and slithered down the back of her suit, but other than the tears below her butt, there was no damage to the suit that wasn't there from the attack.

"Well, we healed you," Mike answered with that same supernova smile, but this time it didn't look so evil. "Worked better than I thought."

It did not changed. The Human boys' faces had the marks of anger. Even when they smiled, it seemed dark, yet their cores had to be as pure as the fresh snow of her homelands.

"Don't you mean fixed? What are you going to do with me?" she snapped, holding her hands at her back.

It was where they would be secured when they took her prisoner. If they needed restraining devices, they would find them on the other assassins. Special ones for androids.

Broken bones or frames weren't hard to work around or fix. You had to have special devices to hold us. I hope they don't know that.

"Healed, since you are as close to Human as you can be. Your kind prefers to be referred to in Human ways as much as possible. I would not have fixed a Human, and I have not fixed you.

"I was able to heal you and test something we have been working on. You are not the first Android we have ever seen this advanced. Don't flatter yourself with thinking you impressed us," Nite answered.

"What do you want of me?" she asked diffidently, almost regretting having to be angry with them.

Other than the original damage they had caused, they were better to her than most of the humans she had met. There was only one other person who treated her so well. The dead woman cyborg on the ground. It was probably because they were lovers before she had learned the truth.

The Android preferred men before they found out she was part machine. Then they thought she had no real feelings, emotional or physical, and did things to her they would never do to another individual human.

Not that I was around good *men. Most the ones in this line of work didn't align to* normal *either. We are in a dishonorable profession.*

This woman treated her at the same even after she had found out, though. She even tried to find ways to improve it for her on her cybernetic mind's level. It was a sexual partnership, where both were to benefit.

"From my understanding, if someone tried to change your mental programming in any way, you would explode. Is this true?" Nite asked as he walked around her, examining her. "Move your fingers for me," he suddenly added while he waited.

She did as she was told while she considered her answer. There were ways for them to have their programs changed, but if it was done wrong, then, yes, they would explode. It was meant as a safety mechanism to protect them after they become

Androids. Cyborgs had something similar. It was almost natural in their Human brains.

"Yes and no. There are ways around it," she answered honestly.

"There always are," Nite responded. "Move your feet. Good, now jump once," he continued to order her.

She did as she was told. She knew that they were asking her questions to test her as well as see how she reacted.

"Why did you come here?" he asked.

"To ensure the job was done," she answered.

"Raise your hands above your head as far as you can. What was the job?" he asked as she did as she was told.

"To assassinate someone, but I was not told who. I was just here to protect them and ensure—" She stopped as the emotions overtook her.

She was not supposed to be here at all. That was why Rac didn't tell her anything. Her only way home would have autopiloted into space and self-destructed after he died. His PAC would have fried itself as well. She only came to protect Tori, and she had failed.

"Someone or some ones?" Nite asked without giving another command.

He then followed up with "Touch your toes by bending at the waist and then come back up."

She did as she was told. "I do not know."

"Bend as far back as you can without dropping your arms," he commanded.

She dropped back to the ground and then walked her hands back between her legs.

"Very impressive."

"What was your real purpose here?" Nite asked as he bent down to look her in the face while she was twisted up.

Before she knew what was going on, the humans locked her wrists and ankles, trapping her bent backwards. She wasn't sure why they waited. She was sure something was about to happen.

She tried to struggle and screamed for a few minutes. They just waited patiently. She finally stopped trying to struggle and looked at the two of them.

"I came to protect her. I failed."

She fell to the ground. She could tell they shoved a pole under her braces, but she had never felt anything like them. The two were no longer doing something near her either. She turned her head to look at Nite once again. Before she could ask, he responded as if she did.

"You have no more useful information for us. I assume when the *leader* died, his PAC erased and the landing craft or whatever you came in was destroyed to cover your tracks. He seems the type that would do that," Nite added with a shrug. "Dracon will know what to do with you."

"Wait! Are you just going to leave me like this?" she half cried, half raged.

"I would have done it to a Human if you are

asking. We have done much worse to those who have asked us for help after failing. Be glad you didn't ask.

"Leave the equipment if you escape them. We'll figure out how you did it. No one has yet. But we haven't tried on other humans in this desperate of a situation. An Android would be a better test anyway. Consider it payment for your life if you do."

She heard the voice but couldn't follow the echo. It was speaking to her, but she could no longer hear anything else that would indicate their presents. Then they were gone. It was like the blackness swallowed the two of them, welcoming them home.

I don't know if they are evil or good. Was I just not worth playing with? Or is this part of a longer game?

Has anyone ever mentally broken an Android? They are too young to consider trying that right? Although their faces and emotions. It was like they were trying to act human. Were they human? Are they something else?

I have met evil humans. Rac was an evil human. Those two scare me more.

How in Hades do I get out of this?

CHAPTER 23

THE CORE AND THE CRUX

Training in the Crux was open for those accepted. If they decided to come, then they were taught. If they did not, then they lost the training that day. It was up to them to learn what they missed.

The disk made this easier for people. They were designed for the scouts to go through multiple types of training alone or with a small group. Even though most of them were in a different cycle, the small groups normally were within the same cycle, allowing them to graduate together and have a chance of teaming after words. A few crossed cycles, but that was normally new members, trying to catch up to the ones in their groups.

Age and time in school didn't matter to the Crux. Selina created the legacy Master Fade suggested without trying or meaning to. It started with Claudia, then Wind Wheel and the group she belonged to. After that, the fire started, and there was little she could do, but try to control the burn.

And how much did you manipulate for that to happen? How much were you manipulated to do it? I don't think you did it on your own? I know I didn't.

Those who learned passed on knowledge to those that were new to the training. If someone was new and in their first cycle of their Second Echelon, or if they were in the last cycle of their Third Echelon, they started in the same place, as Nubs. What mattered was what they learned and how fast they learned it. As they did, they moved up.

When they moved up enough, they started to instruct those under them on what they knew. This was an important marker for most. Teaching others often was the first step to self-development. Self-development gave you access to the libraries of the Crux.

The Core were small groups that lead sections of the Crux. Because the Crux was decentralized, which allowed it to grow exponentially, the number of the Cores was almost impossible to count. The Crux had grown as well, to the point Selina was seeing members entering the library that she didn't even know were in the Crux. They asked her if she were new to the group and needed help.

At least our anonymousness is working. Our own lower groups don't know who's in charge. Is this a good thing or a bad thing? Will it get to big to hide? If it does, will it matter? We'll have to start considering this.

Selina's Core consisted of three others. Although all sixteen of the light pilots from her cycle were in the Crux now. Recently two heavy classed members came back to the Crux from her cycle as well. She thought they were the only cycle with all the Light Pilots in the Crux. It was likely a trend that would grow.

Selina's Core was the first to start training with the twins, at the end of First Tier during the break. It had only been two and a half months since then, but now every Core had access to additional training after the majority of them passed the test.

Selina's Core was also the only ones with access to all the data disk which the twins provided to Selina since 682.4.17. They were the training programs and books they built with her but didn't want to risk sending through other means.

Selina helped develop them and trained with the twins through the private communication device to perfect them. But even there, they limited what they showed, in case someone had the third and was monitoring them. Staying private was almost as important to them as staying together.

It was now 683.7.4 and Selina was hoping Claudia would have an answer to a question she asked her back on 683.5.29. How big was the Crux? How many Cores did they now have?

It was an important question, because the bigger

the Crux got, the more attention it was likely to start drawing. Attention was dangerous to underground teams. These subtleties were easier to control with smaller groups. Large ones, which this one appeared to be coming might have to start hiding in the open.

But if we are in the open, can we continue to operate with virtual training with the twins?

Virtual training with the twins, crossed all the platforms. Like any late Second and Third Echelon Training, it was randomly assigned. Member's didn't even know which of the shadow instructors were teaching. Shadow Instructors were the best instructors for certain areas. Selina wrote a program which tied the DNA of the member to their level to prevent people who were not qualified from teaching. But those that could, did with their identities protected.

Like with all things in the Crux, it took on its own life. They were training with each other, and Selina wondered if other schools started to join them. It was possible for anyone after Midterm to get on TWNs. It was becoming almost impossible to tell exactly where and what they were becoming. Yet they did what the instructors of the Forward Schools didn't . . . made the light pilots the best they were capable of.

Selina and Claudia theorized early on, what the Lights needed from the Forward Schools, and the Heavies got in abundance was attention and access. The Heavies had twice the number of instructors, with a third of the people as the Lighter pilots. Scouts and lower Sentinels often didn't get the equipment or attention they needed. It was a competition for life sustaining equipment that would be provided if they were in the Inner Schools. The Crux was providing it by doing it themselves.

As they did, they started to control more of the battles. Heavy students that were marked as unsupportive, couldn't get the talented Lighter Classes they needed to complete missions, which caused them to fail more often. Or if they did, the members would go off on their own, surviving the battle and accomplishing their part while leaving the team to fail.

As the scouts developed, they pushed the Heavies to be better as well. Their scores rose both on and off the fields. Their performances outshined across the board for those in the Crux, and with this growth, the Heavies took notice.

They wanted these members in their teams. They started to respect them and seek information or inputs. Some even took training from them. At least the members of the Cores were reporting this back into the pool of information.

This was an important growth over the last cycle. The Core would protect the Crux. Yet, the Core understood there was more going on than just advanced training for the lights. They were training for a real war, a real mission for a different life they had not been exposed to, *yet*.

Why else would the Forward Schools exist? What

purpose do they really serve? We have not found that out yet!

Selina did not intend for her team to grow to beyond what was now the Core, who was made up of only people from her cycle. The Crux didn't care what she intended. It grew into the largest underground team the school had ever seen, from what Master Fade discovered. The Crux was currently a middle-sized Battalion, with four-hundred-ninety-two regular Abas pilots logging into the training this week.

She knew this from the DNA registry. The program ran independent to track Shadow Trainers and ensure integrity. It would probably last another twenty years. Her android monitor was tasked and rewarded for maintaining and adjusting the program. He would be responsible for it once Selina left and would pass it on to others if she chose to leave the school.

The highest-trained person outside her Core was three cycles above her. And the one below him was in her third cycle of Second Echelon. Each had their own hand-picked smaller group as well. The other top performers outside Core groups were all in Third Echelon. Yet, Cores were forming in each cycle now.

The Crux would continue as long as the library could be maintained. It was becoming an Army of Scout Abas. And with access to TWNs, Master Fade believed they could grow it into every forward school. At least they could if she was willing to issue the data disk to others.

Wunderkind–Krieger already had the disk. Wind Wheel took another set. The twins created them. That is four out of five schools with access. I doubt three of them are sharing them like we are.

Master Fade suggested purposely sending some of our Core, although she didn't call them that, out to the other schools on purpose. Our Shadow Trainers would be better. But she wants to grow this deeper. Why?

Does it matter? The Core leaders take the training with them into the fleet? Or they will with our first member leaving with the complete training set. Next cycle, our first Core Member will leave. What will this start doing to the fleet?

Time to have a conversation with the rest of them.

CHAPTER 24

ELIMINATION VS EXECUTION

Nite and Mike entered the class about half an hour after they left the android. The position for a human would cause the arms and legs to go numb, but no permanent damage would be sustained. The android should be better than that. She would live in any case.

They also had faith Dracon would have a better idea of what to do with her. They never considered what to do with a captive. Figured it would be in the rules of engagement or part of a turnover negotiation.

They were going to kill them all, but the twins picked up on Dracon's hesitation in not joining the slaughter. They had not even considered it more than a test when they saw the crawler come down from the north gate where the elevators lifted out from the school to the outside. It was an emergency exit.

Normally, pilots left through the landing elevator in a Brawler.

They already searched the crawler and disabled the bombs before they entered the tunnels after the supposed assassins. There hadn't been any information on the ship. Even navigation history only listed the closest city where it was probably rented.

If they flew that junk through space, they should be glad we killed them before they had to do it again. I wonder how much honor we'll gain from turning it over. They shouldn't know how much we stashed from it. Spoils of collection. But it might get us closer to something that could carry our Abas during breaks.

Mike thought of using it to get to Selina, but that thing would be impossible to get our Abas on. And we don't know where the other schools are yet.

Nite continued to allow his mind to wonder over the things they were thinking about before seeing Dracon in the tunnels hunting the same prey as them. It seemed all three were picking the same spot to ambush each other.

That was fun. But we should have been more original. It was too obvious. Still, we appropriately went into track and kill mode. It was easier than I thought.

Only one human. We took a prisoner. That may have been stupid. Let's see what Headmaster Falstar has to say. Well, Dracon first.

Mike owes him an apology. I said my piece. That's over. It's up to him to figure it out from there.

Nite settled down in his thoughts, closing his eyes

and allowing his body to relax. He was fully aware of every noise around him. In the half sleep, he was able to rest and recover while staying alert for possible threats. This is how he was able to reduce sleeping down to three hours a night on average.

Nite looked at the door as it rattled from being unlocked. Mike raised his head from the desk, settling his hands under his chin while facing forward. Master Raven walked in and went straight to his desk. He sat there looking over something, completely ignoring that they were there. After a while, fifteen minutes or so, he looked up with his face mastered to prevent any signs of emotions.

"Well, there isn't anything in here about sending Bravos for anyone in the school.

"There is something here about a special project being set up for one of the two of you at Canis Lupus Training Facility. For some reason, the Headmaster there has been given a special assignment involving one of the two of you by Falstar. It does not say as to what the assignment is."

"Might have to do with that pilot that keeps challenging our scores. We keep having to beat her. No one else has come close to anything. Although, from what she said to Selina, her mother, the Headmaster, doesn't want her involved.

"The Headmaster doesn't know about—wait, what is a Bravo?" Nite asked, caught by his own confusion at not knowing something mentioned so casually.

"It doesn't appear so, and a Bravo is an assassin.

I didn't think that he would have sent this type of assassin anyway. I am sure Falstar would have felt them below my level, but there might have been a message for him to ensure they were allowed in for something else."

"How could you be so sure he did not know?" Nite asked.

"He would have known they would have died. Even the Android has never been taught any type of advanced espionage to the level they would need to get by the equipment. That was provided by someone else. She is a very skilled warrior, though.

"As for Falstar, he is monitoring every aspect of your training. He would have known I could easily take them. So could you, as you have proven. If any of us were in the tunnels when they came, then they had no chance at all if I was not the target. They never had a chance against you."

"What type? Do you mean light or a different caste of warrior?"

"No! They are not any type of warrior caste. From their appearance and dress, I would have said they were merchant class warriors from Lyon's Pryde, but with the human, it might have been a segment of Lion's Pride. One with a 'y', and the other with an 'i'. It's all very silly for speaking."

Nite and Mike both detected the slight difference in pronunciation but didn't get the why until Dracon explained. They allowed the look to show so he would. Then they cleared their face to show they understood.

"Normally, they are only seen on the inner planets where there isn't as many Pack warriors. Those that do come out here on the long trade routes usually don't attempt to act like warriors around the real deal. Other than this device that fried my motion detectors," he raised a small black box off the table, "they didn't even have good of equipment. Have you had time to examine it yet?"

"We grabbed what you didn't, but we have not looked it over." Nite looked at his brother, and then back to Dracon. "The procedures say if there is a death in the tunnels, we are to return to the class as soon as possible and await orders."

Dracon knew they had not followed him because he didn't leave the area. He had watched everything from a location even they couldn't have found. No matter how advanced they were, he had tricks they didn't know. They were equal to his skill level if he only used what was taught and accessible. They had some skills beyond that, but they didn't have the twenty-one years of experience Dracon had.

He doubted they would need twenty-one years to surpass him. Like the assassins, they just didn't have access to the best toys. Equipment, after training might separate two masters and make the difference. As they showed earlier, equipment was only icing and shouldn't be the complete recipe. They got past his.

The twins had entered a rare state, which he first

noticed six years ago. They were still and blank. Their breathing was synchronized. They even blinked at the same time. Master Raven had seen it a few times. He had only started to understand what it meant the last time it had happened.

Even if he had not been there, once he saw this, he knew they would not lie to him. It was strange, but they didn't know they were doing it. When they did, they acted as if they were one entity. When in that state, they could not lie. They only knew the truth between them.

It meant that the night's events put them on edge. They had not come down yet. Master Raven felt the tension in the room as he walked in. He wondered if they were still deciding on killing him. He had the best chance to survive sitting behind the desk. With the two of them in this state, there was no way he could stop them.

"They must have been looking for something, not someone. I believe they were sent in to check the path for others and kill anyone that got in their way."

"They wanted to lure someone out. They were to kill at least one. We figured this out already. There is no reason to stop us from assuming it was one or all of us three.

"This explained why the leader turned on the sensor blocker after triggering some. He wanted to draw someone into a fight, hoping the Android would make up the difference in skill and training. We may have dishonored ourselves in killing them.

We assumed they were real warriors or at least testing dummies. They were no better than children."

"No. They set the challenge. I heard it. They were stupid, but they called it first.

"Since they are merchant class, they were not worthy of getting the top-of-the-line equipment. Instead, they were given low-level equipment for their ranks. Might have been great for them. Would have worked on most average security in the inner planets.

"When, not if, they were killed, there is no real loss, especially the equipment. This box should have exploded. The bomb was disabled. Probably by the android."

"She said she was here to protect the cyborg female. She wasn't part of the original plan based on the information we gathered."

Dracon nodded, adding this additional information.

"There isn't any signature on their equipment either. We can't back track them through it, so we are left with the scrubbed Pack markings. Avion Proie doesn't use these types, so the marking cover-ups can be dismissed," Dracon added as he flipped through symbols.

"The human had several marks common with Lion's Pride training from the Inner Schools. I would say they originated there. Or at least he did.

"The Cyborg was fresh fleshed, so they could have been anything prior to this mission, including male. I doubt the remains will tell us much more, but we can turn them over and see if anything pops up.

"The problem is, submitting the remains will show the bomb didn't go off. Could be a single to say they failed. We could report the bomb going off, but then we don't know the target or targets," he nodded to the twins.

Master Raven in training mode was less likely to be attacked. He continued to bring several pictures up from his PAC. He was showing them what he saw and how he came to the conclusions he had. He didn't move from behind his desk, though.

"I examined his PAC. There was a continuous loop, outgoing transmission, so they were tracking where they went. This group was set up to die from the beginning. They just wanted to know what the undergrounds looked like. Maybe response times.

"We stopped them from getting too deep. They will try again. Likely with better people.

"I also think they were sent as a warning for future failures. They were supposed to be killed during the mission. The bomb was to make clean work of it. They would have been killed by the ones that sent them, and no one would have known better. The evidence, just enough if it survived, would point to Avion Proie," Dracon commented aloud.

"The ship was supposed to explode as well. We assumed the main pilot knew. We disarmed it incase you wanted to turn it over."

"You got a fully functional ship? Space worthy? And your turning it in?"

"It's not large enough to fit our Abas. Since we acquired one, honorably, would they let us get a different one?"

"No!"

Dracon knew they were not asking because they expected it. He was thinking through his earlier thoughts, not giving anything away he didn't want his two possible enemies to know.

But if they are enemies, then I am dead when they are ready to take me. I might be able to slow them down, but I won't kill them. They have the advantage. They showed tonight they are capable. Not that they needed any more advantage or proof of ability.

"If they are not Pack, why were they marked?" Nite was smart in asking.

They saw the bodies when they field stripped them of the equipment. They left them naked. They saw the pictures of the marks. It was after they stripped them.

The already knew I went back or never left. Were they trying to test me? What was the answer? What was the question?

They already knew. They were trying to test something in Dracon now, and he had to come out of thought projection to answer the question.

"Only the warriors have to be marked, and that isn't till the end of school. The tattoos are to show the level of the school they came from so their names are put on the proper wall if they did not earn the rights to be put on the Wall of Wolf itself. Or more likely, on the Wall of Honor of their Pack. It also shows what they accomplished in their training years if they ever become Domestique. After the service, they are to be returned to their classification of Abas.

"But merchant class assassins are trained to gather information. They are not marked to protect their Pack and groups. Again, it is for them either dying or being captured. They are not held to the reverence of an Abas pilot. They are not expected to carry the honor any Warrior caste would carry.

"You have to remember something. This isn't really part of your training, but it will help you understand. With Merchants and other non-warrior classes in the outer rims, they are often trained in their hometowns or areas. They go through a basic school, learning general information from about five to thirteen. Then they go into their specialty schools based on needs and talents for another one-to-five years. Then they apprentice until they reach the skill level required to be promoted.

"The general ranks are apprentice, craftsman, journeyman, master. Each subclass of merchant or laborer have their own ranks. Consider the Medical Doctor Laborer compared to a Building Engineer Laborer. Then you have the Janitorial Merchant, who is also vital. They could be equal in Rank in the Pack and would receive the same Honor and Privileges as Master or Apprentice.

"They would receive the same Honor Level based on their rank in their field. The one was assigned to the Dire Wolf Team would likely get a bonus of Privileges and possibly Honor Levels as well. They would also have a higher level of promotion because they have more to accomplish.

"It is like the engineer working on Scouts versus Heavy Zhayedan. The Heavy Zhayedan engineering team might have five Abas assigned to their truck team. The Scouts might have twenty. But the engineers on the Zhayedan are likely to have a wider verity of work and knowledge that has to be applied, where the Scouts are swap shops. The Zhayedan Engineers are rewarded higher.

"The drivers of those same trucks are equal, but the Scout Team Driver is likely to have to cover more area. They are going to have to be ready to recover from different, probably higher danger zones. They are going to earn a higher Honor and Privilege Level than the Zhayedan Team that is likely staying in Second Line or Third Line positions and have a recover team working for them.

"Both sets are vital to have in War fronts. If one is assigned to the Dire Wolf's Squad and one is assigned to a Polecat's Squad, then depending on their job, their requirements could be absolutely different.

"If they are assigned to a military unit, then they are marked with the Unit Commanders level and their own level at which they joined or earned throughout their cycles there. Promoted or demoted based on performance.

"But if they are never assigned to a Military squad .... If they never leave the area they were born, there is no reason to mark them. Their journey is in their records. Their path is steady. The work is constant based on their skills. Everyone is assigned somewhere else eventually, but they may return after a cycle or two, depending on the orders.

"To become a Penumbra Combatant, they have to be approved for additional training, which can come at any time. Once approved, they are usually given orders somewhere to cover what they are really going for, and then are trained. Additional training may be granted later on based on assigned missions.

"Their success increases their chances of their offspring being reviewed for warrior status and being selected to go to the Inner Schools. This is a great honor for the family.

"For them, information is power. They have to gather it to be able to find and prove there are issues without being discovered. Even after, they may not be selected or select to do the work. It would be hard if you found your mother or partner that you have worked with for ten years is corrupt. Anyone can make a report of suspicion.

"Not much different than us. We call it intelligence as warriors, not information. We have a different need for it as well.

"They are not normally assassins used against

warriors. Too likely for them to fail. It's better to send our own kind after our own kind if we can't . . . openly accuse them.

"Then they might investigate a potentially corrupt group locally or be moved into the area. Once determined they are violating laws or acting out of personal gain not aligned with the Pack's Honor, the targets are punished. The proof is usually turned over and a level of punishment is set by a non-partial circuit.

"They may be capture orders and kill if resist. Or they could have to kill them to protect their own lives. They may have kill orders only. In any case, they are given a job and expected to carry it out. After, no matter the result, there is another investigation. But these jobs are typically in addition to another job performance. It isn't common for this to be their only job unless it is actually their job."

"Why don't we have any real contact with the rest of the Pack before we graduate? Why are the Forward Wolf Abas Pilots separated from everyone else? Why don't we even see other Warrior caste?"

Master Raven looked at the twins. Sooner or later, every noble pilot asked those questions in these schools. Master Raven thought it was a mark of a true Abas pilot—not just to accept what was given to them but question what didn't seem right and try to fix it. These were the twins that he had tried to raise the best he could. Even in their heightened state, they had not forgotten where they came from.

If I am to die tonight, then I will die knowing they have been raised as properly as I could. It will be a good death.

Dracon dropped his head to clear the tears from his eyes. He was going to tell them a truth of sorts. It was the only truth the students were allowed to know.

"You were separated during training for the same reason we separate the heavies from the lights. We don't want the Abas pilots seeing an easier life, which they could, and would, expire at with less work. You still see it from the lights to the heavies on how some aspire to be better and others accept where they are.

"We were either bred or born for this life. Either way you came into the world, the Pack doesn't want you to lose it during these prime years of training. It is these years when we become the elite men and women of the Pack.

"These schools are also an experiment. Normally, you would be exposed to other warriors by now. Only this is a forward school. It is protected by the highest of securities.

"These Bravos shouldn't have known where to even find this place, much less how to access it. It shows why they were sent to die. They were never coming out of this alive, even you prisoner if it is discovered she was on the mission.

"Every memory of your life has something to do with being an Abas pilot. It is all you will know or remember. It's all the Pack ever wants you to know. You know how to be Abas Warriors and you know how to secure areas and remain within Honorable actions."

"We forgot you also went through all of this, Master Raven. Please forgive our insolence in not addressing you as we should have."

Mike sighed then added, "I wish to apologize for attempting to wound you as I did. It was a disreputable move. I will accept whatever punishment you wish to administer."

Master Raven's jaw dropped at the astonishing remarks made by Mike. He had shown Master Raven a great veneration in telling him, and then to offer restitution for the act was beyond anything he had ever expected from Mike.

By merely admitting it was wrong, he showed he would never try anything of its like again against Master Raven. In fact, he would always be in debt to Master Raven, until he had saved his life, or the life of one of his children. Mike swore fidelity to Master Raven's lineage until the time he was able to save one of their lives through this action.

When he had finally recomposed himself, Dracon looked deeply into the twins' eyes.

"You made your first real, non-simulated kills today, and you did it without interference from a superior. In my lineage, you are to drink the blood of the first kill.

"I do not ask you to follow through with it, and if you choose not to, we will go for a kill tomorrow. It will be an animal. We will stay out and eat as much of the meat as possible. The rest will be used for . . . feeding something else.

"There are animals I like to attract. Raw meat is the best way. If you do follow through, I do not think the cyborg fluids will kill you, but they aren't going to make you feel good either."

He reached down and pulled out two stainless steel cups. Each had the smear marks from him wiping the fluids from the edges. It had been collected from the bodies. They were full.

"If you do choose, it only has to be a swallow. I will not try to waiver your decision."

Nite and Mike both came to the desk and picked up the cups. Neither of them wanted to think of what they were going to be drinking. They turned the cups up and continued to swallow the warm, metallic liquid until little remained on the inside. Dracon's face didn't change as he put his fingers into the cups and marked each one with the blood of their first kill.

Nite was the first to show signs of sickness. He quickly suppressed everything back into his resting blank face. Mike had to swallow his back a couple times. Both men, as of today by the Eurthorian Tradition, were able to hold it down. Men now because they proved they were ready to face the challenges of life till death.

"It is 663.8.26, and I name you men with these marks. Be men of honor until the day you are no longer required to be in these forms."

Dracon continued telling the twins of the

differences between the classes of assassins as if nothing had happened between them. They stayed on the other side of his desk, waiting at ease. They would not move from there until they had been dismissed.

He started anew with how the training differed from the merchant assassins through all the others, to, finally, the Abas assassins. Abas assassins were not supposed to truly exist, and the training was claimed only under defensive purposes, because acts of assassins were not considered admirable acts. To perform them would bring disgrace to the Abas pilot, but being caught would bring a different disgrace, so it really didn't matter.

Sometimes, a pilot was able to hide a darker side that would bring a greater dishonor to those involved then could be acceptable for the Pack. In these cases, the member was killed in a way to maintain the integrity of their position, and then lowered and erased from history to reduce their glory or presents. Those impacted by the dishonors were restituted when possible.

Nite and Mike started to ask about the other classes inside the Pack, but Master Raven could not answer most of the questions they had. He did not have to deal with most of the other classes. Tech and engineers usually had to deal with the operations and merchant classes. Team Leaders dealt with a Senior Merchant, but the Senior Merchant took care of everyone else. The only other ones they worked with were warriors, especially Naval Space Commanders.

Abas warriors were considered the highest level of warriors, but there were thousands more on the battlefield. Tankers, footmen, bionics, warbots, nano warriors, cyborgs, Dragons, which were once human Abas Pilots now cyborg Abas Pilots, combat medics, Tutevibians, Air Fighters, and so many more including ships and subs, and subterranean vessels. It was impossible to try to lay them all out.

Which only brings the question to why we don't deal with them more before we leave school? Why are we disadvantaged. He didn't answer the question. He's not allowed to provide a better answer, Mike thought.

"During the third echelon, you will have the others with you in simulations for some battles. You will also have to face them in a lot of your tests, but all simulations. You've fought with fighter jets and ships attacking you and for you. They are all simulated because we do not wish to show such a high military presence around our schools.

"It would draw attention and open them for attack from other Packs. Or if the Desitians were able to sneak into our space and find our schools . . . we would lose generations of special warriors. That is less likely than a Silent Knight or Dragon attack, but the principle is the same."

Mike and Nite nodded their acceptance and finally took their leave for their beds. Master Raven called the Headmaster and told the story as if the twins were never there. Falstar would be able to read between the lines. They agreed on the new addition to the Androids on his staff would fill in the rest of the blanks that Dracon left.

Dracon knew the sender of the assassins would find a way to monitor the Headmaster's office. The story the way it was told would send a message to the sender of the assassins.

"We know who you are. We know more are coming. What are you willing to sacrifice for it?"

CHAPTER 25

COUNT OF THE CORES

A younger male by the name of Masakari, who was part of her Core, and Ono, also part of Selina's Core, entered, continuing a conversation they were obviously holding on their way to their hidden meetings arrange spot.

"She is discussing how to get others from her current team back into the other schools after graduating. They still don't have mission briefings or orders for after school. They graduate in less than a year right. And when she asked, Quick Hit merely said you'll find out when you're on your transports. Weird, right?"

Ono, the girl with him added, "I heard the Inner Schools get orders at least a year before their final test. Closer to eighteen months. The final test can change the general orders, but at least they know what's up for grabs. Use it like a motivation for performance that final year.

"Although, she's the first Core Leader we'll have leave the school. We have twelve of the sixteen lights graduating with her as well from her year.

"If she's successful, we will be able to start the Crux in all five of the Abas Front Line Schools within a decade at most. From there, we could move into the Inner Schools and into other Packs. Our potential growth will be . . .."

"Deadly," Lady Wolf answered from behind him, interrupting the other two's conversation.

Lady Wolf was the last member of Selina's Core. Most believed she was the actual leader of the Crux and the one that sustained instructors or fleet members to train them as *Shadow Instructors*.

The name "Shadow Instructors" came from Mike. Each instructor was named like Stalker Shadow One or Small Arms Shadow Three for their instructor rank and style. Ranks changed based on scores. Shadows were masters of the crafts willing to help others become better. There was never more than five of them allowed.

Will we have to revisit the number with the increase of members likely? Would it be appropriate at one percent of the members? Or one for every hundred members? Does it need to be restricted by those taking the training? So much we didn't account for.

"I can't believe our ideas have reached the First

Echelon of the school," another, younger pilot continued as he and two more walked into the meeting.

"For the Honor of the Elite," Lady Wolf called, granting Cachet permission to enter closer as she looked over the videos of their last battle.

Members had pulled weapons and blocked him at the door because he did not give the right greeting. It didn't matter that they knew him. He might become one of the three and a half percent of students that died in training accidents.

For this meeting, they had gathered in a cave in one of the Live arenas. It was being used by two Crux groups that were fighting each other. There were a few ground battles also happening within the Area, which were controlled by the Crux. This covered the meeting of the Core Masters.

"For the Honor of the Elite," Cachet answered with a smile.

Sometimes they selected someone to try to breach the meeting, even if they belonged. One of five greetings could be given. The wrong one or not giving one would be met by the same response.

"I am here to report the Senior Core has finally earned its last leader. She will be an excellent contact point for you when you leave the schools. She's in one on one training with Abas Shadow One right now."

There was a collective grown from the members.

"I may not be staying within the Pack Space," Lady Wolf replied as she always did to these pipe dreams, trying to bring them back on track.

Training with who Selina and Claudia knew to be the twins, especially on one-on-one battles usually resulted in that response. Everyone loved and hated those trainings. You came out better after them. But you also came out very sore. They were not polite, and your mistakes tasted like orto.

For them, it was her way of saying she was heading straight to the front lines as soon as she was released. It was the best chance to pick up rank in the Five Years, but it also had the highest rate for death.

With Selina being a Mink Pilot, it was the way they believed she was going. Even if she was the *pretend face* of the Crux's leadership, she was still important. They believed Selina and Lady Wolf, being best friends would venture out together to the most active war zone to test their training.

It was always the way a Mink's pilot went. But Claudia was a Heavy Sentinel Frost Ferret. The life thief was primarily a Special Teams Abas. That and the family already being aligned with her meant she could have better orders if she sought them. Once that would allow her to direct from a safer distance.

The younger Core teams assumed she would bring them together again under her. The Senior Cores, or those that were in the Third Echelon, knew better. They could see it in the design of the Crux. It was why it was decentralized. No one was irreplaceable. Everyone had to be at some point.

Selina was happy with the progress of the Crux, but the Younger Core seemed to think they were going to build their own Pack. Or maybe another form of the Painted Wolves. The elite group only operated in the Medium Sentinels, but their dreams included every style of Light Abas. Like some newly formed Special Team of Lights only.

The greeting, "For the Honor of the Elite," was meant as a slap to the higher ranks by most. For her, it was recognizing the Twins would one day be Elite pilots. For the others and as it was taught, it was in recognition of the Elite fighters of the lower ranks.

Selina believed in the training of the Scouts to be the best they could be. She would not leave anyone to die. The normal Pack Schools wouldn't send someone to their death. Especially if they were ignored when they should have been trained. It was against what the Pack and Wolf Pack stood for.

She didn't understand why these schools were so different. What Selina was able to accomplish, even without direct help of the Twins, was still beyond what Master Fade could have expected. She said it was the closest anyone had come to creating the same Honor Levels Scouts had in the Inner Schools.

This was beyond that. It was creating something new that was not seen in the Inner Schools either. It felt like so much more, but Selina couldn't grasp what that more was. It hid in the outer view, or shadows. She just knew they were getting closer.

"It is the end results that matter, and protecting our members as well as our goals," Selina added to the group. "It's 683.7.4. The Crux is a little less than a month from the fourth year of creation. We are moving to fast to the end."

"What end do you think we will be at?" Cachet asked as he gave Lady Wolf a small bow, ignoring Selina other than to ask a question on her question.

"It does not matter when the death of many of our people will be the result. We have made it this far by moving in slow steps. You who want to jump to fast will find a cliff instead of a ledge. Our numbers grow quickly, but there are still those that do not train with us. And we are bringing a lot of attention to this school's scout classes.

"We have to weed those out that are not progressing and leave our group underground and *Elite*. We are not for the betterment of all Scouts and low-level Sentinels. We are the creators of the Elite Scouts and the Elite Sentinels. Those unable or unwilling to be recreated are to be left behind."

"But we offer ourselves growth to bring the best of all, not just our limited numbers here," Cachet answered.

Cachet was one of the other Younger Core Masters. Younger meant they had not reached Midterm yet. Core Master was the title of the leaders that would meet with Lady Wolf to discuss these issues and bring up request.

"Our origins were never meant to grow beyond these walls. What you don't understand is we weren't meant to be this big. Yet, we continue to grow. The training continues to grow us as well. And what does that lead to?

"Do you think the instructors are blind? They noticed the students are getting better on the lower ranks. Where there use to only be a few growing, we are seeing entire classes outpacing their Heavier counterparts. We're lucky half of our cycle can't advance because the Abas Frames won't accept them. We would have the Lights becoming Heavies and we'd have to have the Heavies start training in the Crux.

"How does an underground team operate when they are known about? When they are being looked for? How do we hide who we are now? It appears we will have Fourteen Cores starting by next cycle," she sighed as she dropped a report disk beside Selina.

Selina scanned it while her mind raced with the answer.

Fourteen Cores? It can't be that big now? Every cycle has one. And he mentioned rumors in the First Echelon now. We will not go unnoticed. Lady Wolf is right. We are to remain hidden to be successful. At least for now. Sometimes it is worse being too successful.

"You just reached the final training level's yourself. Did you tell her?" Lady Wolf asked, distracting Cachet from the topic.

"I had not had the opportunity," he answered shyly.

He's afraid of the test. I don't blame him. It's harder than any before it. You have to be a master to pass it.

"Fourteen Cycles worth of trainees. We'll be at over five hundred by end of this cycle where there use to only be two people in a matter of years. We started in 679. It's 683.7.14, and we have grown over a hundred a year. Think about it.

"Our growth will be so quick that we will no longer be a quiet group, but another pawn of the Pack. Our greatest strength is in stealth and we need to keep it quiet and growing slowly until we secure more of a hold. We need to only promote those that are able to understand the training, not just follow it."

Lady Wolf flipped her long, blond, single-braided hair behind her back. It fell forward as she was stressing her point with her knife hand. Selina hadn't seen it hanging from her head in a while.

"As you say," Cachet again bowed to her.

Claudia braid reached the lower parts of her buttocks. She preferred to keep it strapped in different arrangements closer to her head. Few who didn't see her combing it out realized how long it was. She claimed she wanted to get it a little longer than her knees but was afraid of the problems it might bring for her in her Scout cockpit. Her face was long and triangular, with small lips and a thin-framed nose.

She moved as gracefully as a mother wolf silently hunting her prey for hungry cubs. It was also one of her favorite fighting tactics when she was in private training. Hunting, tracking and following her prey before sending them scurrying into a trap.

If he was wise in nothing else, he understood not

to argue with Lady Wolf when she made her points clear. That knife hand was more deadly than most blades. It was one of the reasons she was made second over others who showed potential.

Selina realized how young Cachet was. The older Cores understood the need for staying underground. It was were their power laid. To have the seed planted would mean it was looking for nourishment to grow. This was a weed inside of him. Lady Wolf was right to call him out on it early. He had to learn to slow down.

Selina was limited in the classes she was allowed to take due to her Abas Rank, but Mike and Master Fade taught her more than just what was in her classes. To test for approval or Master Level didn't require you to take an official class. Some skills didn't have classes associated with them. But you had to be in the top seven performers of one of the five skills, ten percent in two more, and finally twenty-five percent for the last two. Then three of the five skills had to be military related. The Headmaster was the final approval for each school member to get the title Master.

Claudia was unable to score high enough in enough events for her master title, but in tracking, she surpassed almost everyone else in the school. Only Nite and Mike beat her throughout all the schools in their cycle. Only one other student, a year behind her, beat her in the rest of the schools for Second Echelon.

The one was a cycle behind her made mention of this during her visit to the school.

As for the rest of Claudia's classes and scores, she greatly improved but no longer felt the need to be named "Master" by the Packs. The Crux had their own labeling and ranking structure outside the Pack. It might have been looked down on by those outside, but it was the way the Crux worked.

A Light Scout could be in charge of a Heavy Sentinel if they proved they had the skills for the mission or the training. The likelihood was almost zero, but the freedom was there. It was all based on skill sets and requirements, like the real ranks of the Packs.

No one found anything against creating a different ranking structure within the Pack. As long as the group allowed the rankings of the Pack to be accepted outside the organizational walls, internal groups could have what helped them work the best. It was the same for larger, specialized teams.

Nite suggested this was how the Council worked. It had to have a different structure within to allow everyone to have an equal say or to prevent those who were of a higher position to sit over those of lower positions. He also assumed, like the Painted Wolves or the War Council, there were underground groups throughout the armies of the Pack. Some a little more visible then others.

The ranking structure was needed even with the Cores. The Cores were acting like hubs for those cycles around them. They were responsible to direct, influence and set the stream of battles.

The Crux controlled every battle they had at least a third of their people within. Most the time they could place half in important battles to them. Their influence in the school was also starting to draw attention from some of the instructors and engineers who were matching bets to what certain members were doing as well.

Being able to sway the battles, allowed them to make bets and raise their Opportunities and Honor Ranks, even if only temporarily. They used this to upgrade their Abas equipment, rooms, and even got more personal things when the payday was bigger.

"There is more to being a leader of the Core then being good at networking," Selina commented, knowing the senior woman was more than capable of being a leader.

It was her underground team who caused Selina's group so much trouble in the beginning. Yet, Selina's training could not be matched by any of the others. She continued to produce more. Even the twins didn't give her everything she developed. Her adroitness within Scout and Sentinel Abas for training was unmatched. The twins hadn't spent as much time in lighter Abas since being advanced to Timber Wolves. Most the Crux and Core didn't know this though.

The twins, as infamous as the Silent Knights, were known throughout all the schools by their cycle's Midterm as well. Their scores became the setting point for anyone who wanted to prove they were one of the best. Yet, hearing their names, or student numbers more accurately, was like little needle pricks.

She didn't want to discourage the Crux from doing it, but Selina believed Claudia picked up on the annoyance. She wanted to create a new name for them, but that could be seen as dishonorable, naming the unnamed. Speaking in code was the way around it, but that might lead others to putting the unknown members and the scores of the twins together.

Claudia dropped it. It wasn't too bad in the Crux, even though, throughout the school, Selina would still hear things like, "I had a five-point drop from Student 1321456 newest posted score," or "I was within sixty points of Student 6541231".

Claudia understood being named before you were allowed. She was teasingly called Tug-o-War in reference to the length of her hair before naming was allowed. She was in Heavy Sentinel now and while considered a Heavy, she stayed with the lights in their classes. Most marked it up to big-fish, small-pond mentality.

Her mother was a Heavy Scout, and her father was a Light Sentinel. It wasn't hard for them to get cleared to have her due to their success in the Crusader Olympia. Shortly after her birth, they both died.

Selina could have told a story much the same, but with both her parents being Scouts. It was in the telling Selina learned their parents lost their lives during the same attack. This information bothered

Selina more than it made her want to be close to Claudia, which might have been why she turned away from her during the first year and a half at the school.

Well, less than that. It was three months before Claudia told me her story. I was trying to be a wallflower, and she was trying to lure me out.

Selina hid the fact from Claudia at first. Then when looking over Claudia's shoulder when she was speaking to a picture. This wasn't uncommon for Scouts. Pictures were sometimes the only connection they had to their past. It was two months before Claudia followed her to watch her train in one of her simulations. The picture was of her parents with some of their closest friends in the squad they were attached to going into the Crusader Olympia.

Selina almost cried when she realized what the picture was. She had the same picture, except in hers, her parents moved to the front when she brought it up on her PAC. It was possible for them to fake the picture and give it to a spy, but Claudia looked like her parents.

At the time, and even now, TTG realized to most, she was no longer *that* important. It was the reason for her game. It was why she kept everyone at a distance when she started at this school.

Selina was as quiet as Mike when it came to the presence of others outside the Crux Training and in classes. She didn't want to draw attention to herself. Most passed her by as if she did not exist. They didn't know she could influence their lives for the good or bad.

Just ask Vlcek. She got family name and is now a Heavy Sentinel. The family is trying to find a way to get her into a Zhayedan.

The pilot TTG lost to who originally had the family's attention was reduced to Light Scout where he belonged. It was not a mark against him. He's skill sets best served the Pack there, in a tetrapod frame, scouting and running.

The memory sent a fury of frustration through her again. She took a deep breath, trying to gain her center. Taking breaths reminded her of her most important endowment.

The one gift she kept with her at most times was the blanket Mike gave her. She could still smell him in it five years later.

It might be mental then actual physical ability. I didn't realize I have been separated from them longer than we were together. Whoever did this to us either meant to make us stronger or failed to weaken us.

Selina slept with it by her head for comfort. She knew she would not see him until the End Games unless they left early. But she agreed with Nite. They needed to stay. Recently Mike agreed to as well.

And the more I think of the one that brought us together, the more I see her fingers in this as well.

Selina never told the twins, but it was Illuminator who got her to talk to Mike in the first place. She sat down by Selina one day when the twins were ordered from the class. This time because they beat twenty students in hand to hand combat. Since there were no more students left, they started to move toward the instructors.

It was the first time in that particular class they were ordered to report back to the barracks early for being disruptive. Illuminator was not an instructor for it. She just sat down and watched the twins. Many instructors did in those days. None smiled at them like she did though.

Selina saw it as a great failure on her part because she was about to challenge Mike. She wanted him to notice her. She watched him, continually trying to get into a position he would have to engage her. Every time she tried to engage him, he was suddenly gone from where he was.

"You have not been hit hard. Why are you crying like a little girl who lost her teddy bear?"

The mix of kindness and hardness in the older woman's voice said she knew the truth but knew Selina had to say it as well. Selina looked at her, ready to deny she had been crying for any reason, much less being physically hurt. She knew there was no way to hide it as soon as their eyes met.

"I will never get him to talk to me?" she said as she settled back down in her silent sobs.

"You would if you would approach him, instead of waiting for him to come to you. Did you watch the battle? Of course, you didn't. You were to into it to see. No less than five times, he defended you, then moved away before he would come into a conflict with you. I am of course assuming you mean the taller one of the two," she smiled. "The other one is not interested in you."

Selina looked at the woman with straight confusion. She dodged Nite like a blazing flame. He hit her once, in class. She didn't wake up for two hours. Considering what happened to some of the other students, she got off easy.

It was her fault. She openly challenged him, and he sent her sprawling twice before the strike. She figured if she could hit him, they would pay attention to her. They were mean to everyone and she wanted them to be nice. The third time he knocked her out.

Mike never struck her, though. She was willing to let him have the chance to talk to him if that's what it took. It couldn't hurt more than not having him.

Her eyes could no longer shed a tear, because her mind could not make since of how the woman knew exactly who she was talking about. It didn't help the instructor pointed out he supposedly defended her. They didn't defend anyone but each other. Sometimes they didn't do that, as if seeing the other one challenged was funny.

Thinking back, Nite never touched me after that first hit. If I hadn't stepped into it, he probably wouldn't have hit me that hard. But it was a brawl, and I wasn't paying attention. He tossed me out two times and I kept coming at him like an idiot. I did deserve it.

And when they train with you . . . holding back isn't

their style. They're just nicer about it now. Although what they do to people . . . is it really nicer to bend someone that way?

"I take it you have never seen him looking at you. Or the way he watches over you even when you are on other teams in challenges. If you give him a reason to talk to you, I think you will find he will," she said as she pulled Selina in closer to her. "I, also, wouldn't wait too long to do it.

"It will be harder if they are advanced soon, and you are not. Not that you can't. You have a great amount of potential if you would accept it. Crying is not going to get you there, though, will it. Nope.

"Go to him . . . alone. You are always surrounded by that group of pilots that lost their parents together. For him, you have to go alone. Ask him for help on something you can do well. Let him show you the better way to do it. Don't hold back when you go to do it right. He will respect you more if you don't hold back."

Selina had looked at the old woman for a few more minutes before she stood up and walked over to perform her knife work. She was one of the best in the class when it came to knife work. She was going to perfect it. If he didn't speak to her or blew her off, she would stab him in the heart.

It had worked out fantastically until her removal from the school. She caught Illuminator smiling at the three of them in class. She knew then she accomplished a splendid union between the greatest of friends. The closeness of Mike and Selina was hidden. Yet, she doubted if those old eyes missed much.

Did you know then they would need me to bring them the Crux? Did you create the need by having me separated? Or after it was done, did you send me to where I would find Lady Wolf? She's the only one in this school with that picture. And you have your sister here as well.

I feel your hands in my affairs now. Did you help or guide Master Fade? Do I have to question all those around me? Would I or they be so important for you to use your half-sister?

Selina and Mike didn't know if Illuminator was the cause of the move or just foresaw it coming. Another reason they did not truly trust anyone outside their inner circle.

The circle inside the Core inside the Crux. The charges inside the light source fighting against the darkness. Are we always to fear everyone until they prove they are able to be part of us?

Would I trust Claudia less if she were brought to me by Illuminator?

Should Mike trust me less?

Sometimes those brought in our lives are the ones we needed, no matter the circumstance, the voice suddenly said, clearer than ever before.

CHAPTER 26

PLANNING AND IMPROVISING

The next standard year the twins received better hands on training for their counter espionage mastery than any students previously. The message was beat into the sender of the assassins on an almost a weekly basis. They had sent as many as twenty at a time, although they did not appear to be a squad or platoon. It was more like a mass gathering willing to operate together.

Shortly after them, the sender provided a two-team squad into two different areas. The Dracon and the twins took one, hoping to lure the pincer movement into a different trap. They only found a few metallic parts of the other by the time they circled back.

The last attempt had one was on the anniversary of the first, 684.8.26. This time it was a Cyborg, heavily armored with multiple internal weapons and self-destruct capabilities. It showed the marks of being an Abas pilot prior to conversion. Dracon suggested it was more likely the low-level pilot was offered a re-skinning operation upon completion of the mission.

Dracon took her by himself, although the twins were there to watch. The twins took most of them alone. Dracon watched and provided orders of execution for styles of engagement.

They had treated the actions as if Dracon were teaching them in school. Nite was sure it was confusing to the assassins. They would hear the commands of attack, putting them on guard, then being struck. Or battling in hand to hand combat, failing to have their devices working, fighting for their lives while being played with.

Mike enjoyed when they heard the command "Finish them." It was not that he was allowed to kill them. Killing them was the signal they had completed proving their assignments of task.

He also enjoyed the look on the assassins' faces when they realized they never had a chance. They were supposed to be the bringers of death. Until that point, they didn't know it was their own death they were carrying.

It was not for morbid reasons Mike enjoyed this point of the battle the most. He used it as inspiration in his paintings. Every Abas Pilot took on hobbies. Selina and the twins mostly concentrated on being able to improve other things they collected. They wanted to break through technology to learn about the past of the twins.

That desire to learn about their past lessoned over the years. They continued to work on devices, but after Selina started the Crux, the twins started to consider how to use hobbies to get different perspectives. Painting seemed to be Mike's medium art.

Mike and Nite both enjoyed painting, but Nite was horrible at it. He could draw well enough, but the colors didn't work for him. He also didn't get as much in the shading of the faces.

The largest piece Mike ever made was for Selina. It was too large for her to put in any of her private quarters, even though it was in different pieces. Instead, it was placed in the den of the Core as a reminder of what the world could be like.

The piece was made in the ancient form of sprayed oil painting on several rectangular canvases of different sizes. The largest was three meters by one and a half meters long. The entire painting had five different pieces. Each bordered by a gunmetal cloud that created entire outer rim as well.

The first section started with a group of thirteen receiving marks of death from what looked to be normal men. They all shared the same look, but different faces. Those who received the marks, the shadows behind them were changing. The first more developed then the one that was just receiving his mark. For those that had not received their marks, their shadows were normal, human shaped.

There was one being receiving the scroll, with three marks on it. It was the seventh one in the middle. As the mark was being handed to him, his shadow was transforming into another shadow of death. If the observer looked closely at the shadow of those handing out the marks, they saw they too were not what they appeared to be. Horns, wings, and a spiked tail were all within the shadow.

Demons brought forth from the depths of punishment. The Forth Level of Hades. They were accepting the Power of Punishment through Death.

The second scene showed the thirteen traversing several different obstacles as they fought their way to a cave at the base of a giant black tree, lit by lightening. Each one had a shadow formed in the Evil Death Shadow they were carrying. Each shadow was fully formed and carrying its scythe. They were almost independent of the forms of the beings carrying them.

The second man to finish the task could be seen waving to the others as they made their way to the same location. The first to arrive could only be identified by their shadow. He entered without a look back at the progress of the others.

The third scene on the second largest frame showed a great fight with the thirteen surrounding three individuals. One tall, one short, one in the middle of the other two. Other than height, the only other distinguished marking on them was the ones on their chest. Those marks aligned with one of the marks on the writs of death handed to the thirteen in the first scene.

The battle showed the fierceness of each warrior. They waited their turns to strike, trying to find an opening left by the trinity. The trinity had their own light spilling from the middle of them, forcing the shadows back.

The deaths had their scythes raised, ready to strike. This time there were other faces within the shadows. They were no longer only outlines of those who carried them.

The second-to-last scene showed the last of the thirteen being cut down by the man of middling height. The point at which the sword had entered the woman's heart was the same place the shadow of death put the point of its scythe. The soldier was taken quickly and without pain.

The other two could be seen fighting the demons. They appeared to have been released when the bodies fell. They still had their lights shining, but a triangle of light had appeared between the three as well. It was not lessoned by their separation to other parts of the battle, but brighter.

They were pulling the bodies into their light, where there were no shadows. The demons were trying to pull the bodies back into the darkness. The demons appeared strong, but they couldn't stand against any of the three without others willing to anchor them. The three would not allow the demons to have their way with the dead.

The three felt the honor of the dead enemies. The ones that came to attack them believed in what they were doing. It was not a question of right or wrong, but what side of right they chose to stand on. What side of wrong did they fall on?

The last scene of the painting showed twin wolves, one black, one white, standing with thirteen graves between them. A single, bright moon could be seen shining down on them. Two suns were rising over a red planet at the edges. The tree with the cave could be seen on a rising hill behind the graves. There were no longer obstacles for them.

A single flame shined in the entrance of the cave, white with intensity. Just in front of the flames, a figure could be seen kneeling in prayer to the sleeping gods. Thirteen souls could be seen transitioning toward the flames.

They are praying their souls find solace in death they were denied in the life they chose which was ended by those that were better takers.

Nite's favorite part of the painting was the gunmetal smoke that separated the scenes like little frames of the stories. Hidden in the smoke he could see the faces of the members of the sent into the schools. They were in there without signs of humiliation in their deaths. Their failing brought them peace. They failed only because they faced people better than them, not because their belief was less or unjust.

Dracon and Master Fade arranged the delivery of the pictures. No one would be allowed to win them from her. Not that the Crux would allow them to leave their headquarters even if they could be lost.

It was funny, because the pictures arrived on Selina's birthday on 685.1.21. That was about ten days after Mike completed the work and had it sent. This put the package delivery over their average time. Usually it took six to seven days for shipments. Sometimes it was as little as four, and it hadn't been longer than twelve.

What made it funny was the Crux started a tradition when they found out she received it from an unknown source, on her birthday. Birthday's were hardly important in the Pack, accept to mark cycles of transition. But the Crux decided to start marking them with presents.

The gifts were given anonymously, and the receiver had to try to guess who gave it to them. The number of times they guessed wrong, the more they had to make-up for it with the person they guessed wrong about. They had to find all the givers by their next birthday as well.

What happened and what was used to make-up was always done in humor. It was about bringing laughter and connection to the group. The humor was never meant to be demeaning, even if it was a little on the edge of tar and feather style. It might be completing an obstacle course, while moving only on your hands or having your helmet face backwards while pilot your Abas for an hour in a simulation. All good fun, at no true personal cost.

******

Dracon approached dealing with the assassins in a different way. He kept Falstar informed of the attempts. Falstar seemed to think it was less important than Dracon. The security Headmaster was able to keep the school protected and none of the groups technically penetrated or infiltrated the school.

Falstar assured Dracon it was just people from one of the other schools trying to find out what they were planning for the End Games. Or more likely, find out information on the twins, since they had become a higher interest on TWNs. It was why the assassins had all been lower level. They were not trying to challenge the school. They just wanted to know how good they really were.

"It might be why they are being sent in the first place. Life experience. Didn't you say they needed this to improve. Someone is providing it ready made for them," Falstar pointed out after the third attempt.

His mind didn't seem to change after the fifty-seventh attempt. No one wanted to run that many tests or provide that much life skills. Each one spoke of testing different points of defense or style.

Dracon knew better. He found a picture of the twins, although much younger. About the time of their visit to the council. He also found a separate picture of him on the same group, number nine. By then, they knew who they were going to be running into. But these excursions seemed too logical and didn't have enough creativity to it.

Falstar refused to allow it to go beyond the measurements already set for the school's exterior defenses. For Dracon to step over him would have brought the attention of more people to the twins' unique talents. That was a dangerous road to walk down.

Illuminator half agreed with Master Raven. The attacks were not coming from other schools by the way they were coming. But she also agreed with Falstar. There wasn't a dangerous level presented. Everything about these jobs spoke of low level or lack of understanding outside of printed work.

Even after learning the twins were involved in several of the stops, Falstar didn't feel the need to escalate. He told Master Raven he would offer them a higher Honor Level upon their naming. He would also guarantee Master titles due to what they were showing their capabilities at.

Neither happened over the year since the twins had not been beaten. They were not named nor could they accept Master Titles without being named. Dracon felt like a dog being patted on the head while his master waved a juicy bone lazily around.

If they had been, they would be considered the highest honored. To date, they had outperformed every predecessor who came through the schools.

The twins had not accepted any of the family names that had been offered, either. If they had, they could be referred to by one of them.

Dracon wouldn't recommended they accept any but an offer from one of the top three families of Wolf. Aiolfi, Stidolph or Fenrir. While all the families were supposed to be seen as equal, those three had more members on both the War Council and the Council for over four hundred years. Accepting an invite from one of them would put them on track to reach any goal they had.

The twins were happy with the current level of Honor they were at. They had no idea how high or low they were compared to others. They didn't care. Their comforts were met and more importantly to them, their Abas were in prime condition. They were training beyond advanced in every class they were taking. To them, they were meeting their purpose.

******

The twins pushed the limits further in battle, ensuring they stayed on top of every class they were taking. The one student from Canis Lupus Training Facility was the only one that pushed them to show more than they wanted to. It wasn't to the level they were pushing themselves in their private training.

Those accounts were starting to draw attention. No one in the schools were scoring higher or faster than them. If the students were not the two primary targets under different account names, then they needed to be found to face the first two. Every other pilot in their class had been named by the end of 683, the second cycle of naming.

No one in any of the warrior schools made it to the end of the fifth cycle post naming start without being named. Every pilot who made it past the end of the third complete cycle was eventually made an Elite pilot. For the twins, it was the end of 685 since naming started after the start of 682.

Nine more months and we will be there. We'll have made the basic requirement. Not all Elites have gone that far without being named. But everyone that surpassed it was made an Elite.

It was almost three weeks past their nineteenth birthday. Selina sent them a song some members of the Crux wrote and recorded for the Shadow Trainers One and Two. The group was pretty talented from what Nite could tell. He had no real understanding of music, so he felt it was outside his realm to make a judgment on. This made him appreciate the jester that much more.

It seemed Selina's placement of the pictures Mike sent her earlier triggered a gift exchange. The Crux was too large to send something to everyone or receive from more than a few. The Cores usually designated certain people based on connections, development, and how hard they wanted that person to work.

This one stumped Nite and Mike on figuring out. It took them twelve days to solve, but they didn't make any mistakes. They merely had one of the other members of the Crux leave the members, including the ones that played the musical instruments, a single red and white flower within their cockpits.

Nite liked the tradition since it gave him something new to do. The twins continued to progress farther than any previous Abas pilot in any Forward School, which was great in the beginning. Now, there was no one else providing challenges which took them twelve days to figure out. He was beginning to see what his brother saw all those years ago. The end of school because they had learned what they could in these walls.

The Crux provided something new to them. The development of others, which made the last few years something new and challenging. But it was taking on a life of its own. While they were loyal to the Twins, they didn't know who they were. They were not a real team.

Those in their school had too many walls between them and the twins. The only losses the twins suffered were ones that were programmed in with impossible solutions. Those losses could not be used as defeats in the naming due to the dishonor of trying to claim them.

One time, it was a planetary bombardment, which pinned the twins team down so long they missed the window to complete the mission. They kept everyone alive, but there was no way to transition. However, the bombardment should have made it impossible for the ships to load and leave, but they were supposedly on time.

Another time, the twins completely decimated the defenses of a city. They went in but lost the two scouts. The two vital to the mission, since they were who had the necessary skills to disarm a Silent Knight weapon that would wipe out the majority of the circuits. Two High Powered Laser (HPL) fired from a turret with no barrel, no mount and was pointed the other way, through Mike's Abas without causing any damage and into the scouts protected engines with such precision, they exploded.

The twins, having mastered the skills necessary, completed the mission within the time constraints and set a new record. The Senior Instructor overseeing the program marked it as a failure due to losing the vital assets. When they challenged the ruling, the loss did not count against them, since the system could not calculate or provide any real reason the Laser was able to fire, then bend itself without assistance and land perfectly in an Abas without exposed parts.

The last time, under the same Senior Instructor, the program entered turret fire into the Abas power core, causing it to shut them down. Both twins shot to destroy the laser blast, but their shots were nullified. The shots were only able to shut down their Abas for a minute, before they bypassed the ruined circuitry and repowered their Abas.

The operators were told to ensure the kill shot were implemented to stop the twins from continuing in the battle. The Senior Instructor, leading the battle from the Control Room, ordered them to be shut down.

"They maxed their ranking points within the skirmishes. With such high levels reached, they need to be removed. Everyone else within the battle needs to be allowed to score as high without them," Master Demagogue ordered.

The Androids were not allowed to go against him, if what he was doing was considered honorable. They shut the twins down, keeping them from restarting. What the Instructor over the battle wanted to see was if the team the twins had brought together could operate as well without the two of them.

Everyone watching or participating knew these shots were bunkum. With Nite and Mike off the field, the team fought even harder. Somehow even with four additional Heavy Zhayedan's than the was negotiated, the team pulled the mission off without the twins. Even though the twins had *lost*, their team won the battle. It was acceptable.

The twins had not started a team to this point in the school, but it was the first time Nite considered it. Mike still didn't want to. He was happy they were able to follow through with the training they provided prior to the mission. Mike just didn't want another Selina. Someone developed and then yanked away.

Brother, there like us, Nite thought. *They don't make the same mistake twice. Two more years and we are in Third Echelon. They have two more years to prove they are worthy of us staying here. What can they do if they did take someone from us? Put them in another school and give us influence there?*

No brother. They have something else planned. We just need to think of how we would attack ourselves. How would we?

CHAPTER 27

FROM THE MOUTHS
OF THE DESOLATE

Master Demagogue, the Senior Instructor for Second Echelon Heavy Class was pacing in Falstar's office. He had just left the command center of yet another impossible win for the Twins.

This time, they found a cave that led close to the underground tunnels of the city. After blasting into them, they set charges throughout the city's underground and sank it, destroying over a thousand Abas and five hundred Dragons. It was a Silent Knight city. Most of what they were facing over the last year had been Silent Knights.

"We need to do something about the brothers. They have outgrown any of the staff being able to defeat them. At this rate, we are going to have two unnamed leaving this school. Sir, it will not look good for your record to show a loss to your father when two of your students couldn't even be defeated in your school."

"What makes you think my school would lose, especially in the year they graduate? Are you and your instructors' incapable of beating those assigned to my father?" Falstar reacted with a cold fury, standing behind his desk and swelling with anger.

He let out a deep breath and singled for Demagogue to take a seat. It would keep them both calmer.

"Forgive my outburst. I understand. I do not believe even my father could find a way around defeating them, as he has done with so many of my other promising students. We still had years of success against him. Even if they were scarce these last few cycles, we have been able to beat him. Only Nox can say the same.

"I do not think my father would be able to do much against the brothers without throwing a detestable number onto the field targeting only these two. Look what they did when you tried it. What would a win like that really be worth?"

Falstar asked waving his hand in front of his face and turning sideways. He let his eyes focus on something in the distance, not really looking at anything in the room. Richard made an important point without realizing it. If they, the instructors, couldn't keep school interesting for the two of them, it was not likely they would be staying.

"I won the last End Game. I don't think I want to wait seven more years for them to graduate to win another. I would prefer to concentrate on finding a different way to name them.

"Less than a thousandth of a percent have made it to eighteen without being named in the common schools. No Abas pilot has ever made it past twenty-one cycles. No one has made it longer than seventeen years in the Forward Schools.

"No one that is, until these two. They are over eighteen years old. Every day they go without naming, they are setting a new record. I have yet to see a plan to get them to be named.

"Why are you failing?"

No one is to know they were born 19 years and 17 days ago. Even that is hidden from everyone. The twins know. The androids told them. They needed some hint to start them looking.

Falstar's serenity settled back on his face. He was trying to look more flustered by their actions so the instructors would relax more around him. He looked over the records of the twins' battles and then to the loss' category.

Falstar knew he should have been proud to have such students in his schools, but there had been too many secrets that came with them. Too many problems caused him to create more faces and façades to keep the secrets. Too many masters looking over his shoulders questioning his calculations.

They question, but they have no answers. I am doing what both ask, while they both want different ends. Do you know what ends I want? Do I?

The second worst part of them being in the school was he knew their bloodlines. It was the secret everyone wondered about holding the key to their defeat. Falstar wondered if the path he let them travel was leading them down the same roads as their parents. Or if he successfully changed it by the way he treated them.

If I brought them in and told them the truths of all I knew, then maybe . . . No. There was no need in even entertaining the thought. I have to continue with my plan as is. It was time for the next step, but I must make this look as real as possible. It can't be linked back to me.

"They are beyond our skill. No one in the school can match them. If we knew maybe where their grandparents came from, or even who their parents are, then we could possibly find out how to beat them. I can't find a way as it is now," one of the other five instructors who were over the twins Master Programs popped up.

"I am the strategic master, and I was a platoon commander. Yet, I cannot find a weakness to exploit. I can't even find a steady constant to their fighting other than that when agitated, they start killing everyone. That, and, it seems, anyone who follows their orders live through their battles," one of the highest ranked instructors added.

She sighed before admitting an even greater, personal dishonor. One of absolute defeat.

"I have reached out to analysis teams in both Wolf and Bear Sleuth. I have gone as far as Avion Proie, without providing what I was looking for. Just them as battle simulations. I have said they are defeat programs to train for losing. Their best analysis cannot find a way to beat them without serious dishonorable attempts.

"Several have asked for the programs completed data to provide to generals to start training against. They feel that if they can use the simulations, they will . . . be even better leaders of their armies."

"I have begged and pleaded with Illuminator to prove us some insight as well. She will not provide a plan against them," Master Demagogue started softly. "She seems to be the only one that is able to hold them at bay. The Child Instructor, Illuminator, and a few other students that have studied them have provided some key insight to fighting them. It has been fruitful, but no less than what we have created so far.

"They counter it within a few minutes, almost like they planned it that way. Student 1321456 is the fastest at doing this. I have discovered that much."

Master Demagogue spoke carefully of Illuminator. It was Falstar's mother. The others were admitting they were going to any point in which to gain insight on how to defeat them.

And they miss the most important ones to ask. Keep thinking. Keep moving. Don't give up, Falstar thought while keeping his face blank.

The recognition of such a great failure led to the others bringing up their own dishonors in trying to find a way to defeat them in their own areas of expertise. The most surprising was the one from Demagogue, the highest ranked Abas warrior in the school after Illuminator.

"They are students. They shouldn't be this . . . perfect. I have seen some like them in the fleets, but . . . not this good. We might need to call in Elites to start helping us.

"I have personally lost too much to try and to defeat these two. I . . . I cannot . . . continue," Demagogue finally finished, admitting out loud what he had not been willing to admit even to himself, up till moments earlier.

"Maybe if you can't win, then we should put you out to the pastures where the hunt isn't as hard and bring someone else in. Now leave me to look over my notes on them."

Falstar waved the instructors out of his office without feeling the heat he had put in the words still in his mouth. There was no justification in the words other than to motivate Demagogue to continue to try. Falstar would have to raise his Honor Level for something special to answer for the disrespect he had given him. After all, Demagogue was the key to the puzzle he was working.

Don't give up yet Demagogue. I need your anger! I need you to be willing to go into battle one more time. Just once more at the right time, and I will honor you with every ounce I am allowed.

The other instructors were halfway through the

door before Falstar noticed Demagogue was waiting impatiently near his desk. He cut his eyes toward him.

"Sir, with all due respect—," Demagogue started, but was cut off abruptly by Falstar.

"I said leave, Richard. Do you have a problem with that?" Falstar was back on his feet, with his hands pressed into the desk again.

This was more emotion than the school's Headmaster was used to having to show during a conversation with any subordinates to get what he wanted.

"No, sir, I don't have a problem with leaving, but you must hear one last thing."

"What?" Falstar acted as if he was reaching the end of his patience.

"When we set up a lucky shot kill, the Abas failed to trigger the shot five times. The shots where dead-on. They didn't get into the engine for kill shots. The program worked when we tested it out afterward, but both of them survived it in a battle against the five different Heavy Zhayedan instructors, including me.

"We can't even cheat and win against them. When you talk to your father on this, you might want to tell him this was tried as well."

Richard dropped his head, before adding what he didn't want to say.

"Even after the lucky shot went through, it only caused minor damage to the internal armor. It was as if the Abas refused to be cheated in its victory. Then they killed every one of us by headshots. We were barely children to them."

"I don't need my father's advice on how to run my school. Now get out!" He sneered, while his upper lip curled with tension.

The man turned and almost ran out without the grace he normally carried. Falstar thought of calling him back in to belittle him more. The other instructors fled, so it would only be the two of them. It would not put him on the path he needed any faster than what he was doing now. Richard didn't respond well when he was this beaten down. It's why he was sent back to the schools. To refresh.

Besides, he needed Richard to be on his side. This little tiff should be allowed to blow over. Falstar knew the frustration the twins could cause. He knew more than anyone else, because he faced victories and losses from both sides of their actions.

If they fart, I hear about the contents of the air and then have at least two people telling me how to correct it to what they want it to smell like. If they win, one's ecstatic, one's trying to figure out if they could have done better, and ones trying to figure out how to make them lose the next time. If only there were only three working on them.

Richard, you lead Elite's before. But you have never tried to build the best and prepare them for . . . better not even think about it. I am constantly chasing two rabbits when it comes to them and starving for my efforts.

If they excelled more, he wasn't sure he would be able to keep them in the schools where they needed to stay, if but a little longer. There were still test in the works; test that would lead them to where they needed to be.

Falstar let his feelings settle down before he let his mind wonder on what needed to be done. He had one plan in motion that no one knew about. Only one person had enough information to truly know its purpose but would not likely assume it.

This means I will have to continue with the lesser attempts to keep them from looking for it.

He let out another sigh when he realized where his mind had taken him.

"They have exceptional DNA, whether it was scrubbed for imperfections or not," Falstar relived the moment aloud.

He looked around the room and immediately ran a scan for bugs. When the scan was over, and he had thoroughly checked around physically, he sat back down and continued to think. Falstar didn't trust the privacy of his own office even after he had checked, so he kept his thoughts in his head.

But this isn't the problem. We can't consider their parents because no one is to know who they were. It doesn't matter anyway. I have reviewed them and covered the tracks well. I did a review of every high-scoring Abas in the last thirty years. I knew which ones I was looking for, though, and it still didn't help in finding a fight these twins couldn't win. I have to——.

"Sir," the familiar female voice interrupted Falstar's thoughts. "There is a message from your father waiting for your reply. You were in your meeting when it came through. You said no one was to interrupt."

"So, I did. Good job, Missy," Falstar answered his Android receptionist.

If he had not been considered an Abas pilot and she a registered android, so much more might have been able to happen between them openly. For now, he had to be happy with what they did have.

Falstar's mind filled with thoughts of what he would like to do to his secretary to relieve his frustration. She never minded comforting him before, but he wondered how much was programming, and how much was developed from the freedom of her personality.

Does it matter considering what you are?

"Would you please come in here?"

"Yes, sir."

The reply was flat, but she knew why she was being asked in. There was no reason to ask why. There was only one reason she ever saw the inside of this office for extended periods of time.

It was part of her job description when she signed on for the school four years ago. Not the official one, but the one she was supposed to be performing for the Black Wing. The cyborgs wanted inside information on why he was so successful as a Headmaster.

She connected with another Abas Pilot two years prior to him taking orders to the school to help cover the move. Raze didn't know about this. She wasn't even sure why he was with an Android. He was boring at best in almost every aspect that didn't have to do with fighting.

So much had changed since she worked her way into the office. Even now, only two days from her *marriage* to Rave, she was regretting taking the position. Because of what she knew, only death would allow her freedom from Falstar's orbit.

The type of marriage she was being assigned to with Rave was an agreement that she would be able to carry his children if he were approved for fathering any. It was supposed to be a great honor for an android to get this type of agreement with an Abas pilot. Especially one that didn't seem interested in taking a relationship with anyone, or anything else.

Raze doesn't love me. I am just a collection point for his DNA and a way to scratch an itch. This is so much more fun and aligned to my actual programming.

It was not that the man she was set to spy on would harm her, at least not harm her in a way she didn't like. She admitted to what she was here for to him years ago. He had figured it out before then. He gave her enough to protect her secret and keep her close. These excursions were as much for him as for her.

Her heart found a true affection for the man. It might have started as a job, then a desire, but now it was more. It was so much more. So much and so mutual. She admitted her real reason for accepting being outside his office and he didn't kill her. Now, she was marrying to cover her actions with him.

The first thing she noticed was the look. The

one that meant this was going to be a rough session. Might have to postpone the marriage a few more days, but that wasn't a big deal. If it were possible, she would rather carry this *man*'s baby than her other human lover's.

Androids were often used as surrogate mothers of Abas Pilots. They simulated real life experiences during the pregnancy. But it required them to be closer to human, than most androids could hope for.

There were several benefits to using androids in this way. It was less risk and recovery time then human women. Androids could provide the psychological inputs that the fetus needed to develop healthily as well. The children needed inputs from early times after their conception through the birth process and after.

That's were Iron Wombs failed. The children which were developed for them were . . . unstable and destructive. Their failures were marked early on and the experiments had been permanently dropped.

The old thoughts entered her mind.

Why hadn't I put in a request to be reassigned before it was too late? Maybe it is my enjoyment of these moments. Maybe because he does more for me physically than my lover ever has. Maybe, because I know I love him more than my soon to be husband.

Why did I ask him to beat me and make love to me at the same time on that day so long ago? Why not just ask my husband? I know Falstar and I were both in need of it, but why did it have to be so good?

Why do I feel I need to be punished and pleasured when I was designed for this job? I am following my orders. But that same day, I admitted to him what I am here for. Was that why? Because I was giving up a part of my honor for . . ..

I will have to let them know I have been turned. I will stay with him. Falcon will be disappointed. Will the others kill me? Sophy hasn't yet. Illuminator lets me live. What does it all mean?

If I let them know I have turned, I will be destroyed. They will put someone else in here and the Black Wing will be exposed to him. I have to stay to protect both sides.

"I need you to suggest something," Falstar suddenly spoke up. "I will tell you when by asking you a question."

This is not what I was expecting? What's going on?

CHAPTER 28

CONSEQUENCES

Nite and Mike were finished with another request to help Scouts. Three Kit Foxes asked them to ensure they lived for at least five minutes after first shot. The mission was simple. Get the information stolen back to the base and to warn them of an attack from a heavy cluster.

In the real-world scenario, the twins team consisted of an Elite with two Medium Zhayedans, two Heavy Sentinels, and only one Medium Scout. They were all lost. No one knows who the carrier was or what caused the failure.

Only the mission was known about by the survivors of the base attack by the dishonorable heavy cluster. Depending on how this mission went, another group would be taking on the follow-on scenario. Since they were supposed to be dead, successfully reaching the city meant they got on a Brawler and left before the siege began.

Nite was going to be the only one that went on the challenge until they saw who it was against. He didn't feel the need to bring so many heavier Abas into the fight. Instead he picked his brother as the team Elite and three of the light Abas.

The light Abas were facing a level drop if they didn't get enough time on the field during a battle. It didn't matter if the battle was won or lost, as long as they survived longer than their normal five minutes after first shot. If they failed, they were one step from being dropped out of the school on a more permanent basis.

Of course, after this level, the only way out was death.

This scenario was perfect, due to them filling the spots of heavier Abas in the normal scenario. That gave them double time advantage. Being the winning team in a scenario where their team was considered the loser or lower performer, doubled individual ranking points and tripled team points. Nite and Mike didn't need any of the extra and passed it all to the scouts.

This had added over ten times the points they had previously held. It would keep them safe for a while longer, even if it wouldn't see them promoted out of the lower ranks. No single battle could do that for anyone.

They lost a battle because of bad leadership, and the leader was targeting them now, in dishonorable ways. The Twins felt it was time to engage.

They were going up against some third echelons that only had a couple of cycles left in the school. The twins were given an extra three Abas slots over their combined numbers to make up for the six–year-cycle gap of experience. They selected two less Abas than the other team brought on the field.

Two of the lighter Abas ended their fight that day in perfect formation firing on a Heavy Zhayedan named Gargoyle. They injured one of her Abas legs before they were seriously injured and ordered to the edge of the battlefield to monitor enemy movements. One had to drag the other while Mike guarded their retreat. Since he had the information, they could claim they were guarding his progression toward the base.

The last of the Kit Foxes took out the Heavy Sentinel Pilot known as Viper. She took a slower design setup with several long-range weapons and less armor. She was an easy target for the faster Kit Fox, who stayed within her range and attacked while she was prone.

The Honor and piloting showed on that move would likely see the pilot promoted to at least Medium Scout if not Light Sentinel. The other two wouldn't likely see a promotion, but their performance would keep them alive for a while longer. With only a year until they reached their End Games, it might be enough to see them through school successfully.

Nite and Mike took the last of the others fifteen minutes after first fire. They could have won earlier and with less damage to their enemies. They waited for max time for the lights on the battlefield to expire before destroying the last of the enemy Abas pilots. They shot everything else off of them, wearing them down.

After the battle, while the twins were still on the catwalk Abas' docking bays, four of the pilots approached them. The hurt and confused looks were something Nite and Mike were used to after so many had lost to them when the odds were against them winning.

Why are they always confused? Shouldn't it be obvious now? Four more months and it will be.

The first of the male heavy pilot was tall and skinny. The first female was much shorter and had a little more meat to her bones. Nite would have considered her desirable if but for a night. The last two males were much slower. Their heights were between the other two, but they were massive. It was likely the muscle of the group. They were strong and smart enough to get into the higher ranks.

I often wonder if it is intelligence only. The basis seems off with some of them. They are not as smart, but they can handle their Abas well. The scouts have more piloting ability, but can they handle the higher frames? Some can't. We know this. Does that mean they should be treated as less?

We need Scouts as much as Zhayedans. More most the time. A Zhayedan is overkill in a city. Although against heavy enemies, they are necessary. Why are we so divided in these schools?

The female looked the twins over in abominate

due to their proud Red Born status. She was acting like the leader, but the taller male was currently. They belonged to the True Born Team. The True Born took command of Timber Wolf Academy by the second cycle of its life. They maintained control of the battles and the school until the twins started to tear down their precious team's Honor Levels and depleted their Opportunities.

Thanks to the twins, the team lost over half its assets and rooms. The families who primarily selected from the team started to look for pilots outside of the team in recent years, leaving the graduates to struggle to pick up sponsorship. They assumed and turned down offers, offending families during the earlier parts of their Third Echelon.

The last five years had not been great for them. It started when their then leader made the comment about the twins being a waste since they were Red Born, after they were promoted to Heavy Zhayedan. The twins took on every open battle they offered for the next year. By the end of that year, they dropped from the most winning team in the school to third most.

The other two high ranking teams in the school picked up on the Twin's resentment. It was a recognized opportunity to capitalize using the twins without bringing them in. The twins took the battles and True Born's rank fell. After the year, the twins lost interest in them, assuming they would go lick their wounds and leave them alone.

They didn't. They spent the next two cycles trying to beat the twins on at least a monthly basis. The other teams only attacked when thought they could field a team based on requirements or offers that would win. It was calculated, not emotionally driven.

For the twins, it was like a small child who tried to attack when they saw a favorite elder student. The student didn't care about the small, temporary annoyance, because rejecting it would likely cause the need to provide more attention. They just swatted them away and moved on.

It was when they lost the first of the powerful families' full support a cycle ago, they started to solely target the twins. It turned out to be a grave mistake. They would have been smarter not to bring such negative attention to themselves.

The three Scout Abas on the battlefield with the twins were previously part of the group as light Abas pilots ranging between Light Sentinel and Heavy Scout. They left the group after being targeted by one of the male muscles.

He used them in a high ranked battle against the twins. He hoped the twins would be nicer or at least pay less attention to the lighter Abas. They weren't. It cost him a rank for failing the mission.

After, he started putting them in battle situations where they were killed in less than a minute from first fire. Leaving the group was as good assigning their own death sentences. Staying in it would mean they would never see anything but a Light Scout.

They left, turning to the ones that stripped them of their ranks, hoping for protection. The twins said they would give them this one battle. After that, they should find another team or start one. They were not taking them on.

"You guys are kuso good in Abas. Are you as good in ground combat?" the female asked.

"One way for you to find out." Nite's smooth reply grated the female's nerves.

Since entering the second half of the Second Echelon, very few had been willing to face them in ground fights or tactics. Typically, their class records discouraged most from even trying. This showed the failure of these students, or more accurately, their leaders.

Checking records of your known opponent was rule number two in the school. Not facing the twins seemed to be rule number one. The True Born assumed others would fall into place, accepting they should just lose to them. It was a failure with the team since they spent so much time on top.

When possible, you should always learn your enemy's tactics.

"How you want to do this? Battlefields?"

The battlefield was the primary location for both battle Abas and ground training for Abas warriors outside the simulators. It wasn't uncommon for someone else to be testing their real-life Abas skills while others fought ground battles in hand-to-hand and guerrilla warfare.

These same dangers would be found on the battlefield. Therefore, they could practice in the schools. The only difference was the safeties of the Abas were set so the Abas, unless it fell unexpectantly, would be shut down before it could injure personnel. Most the time, the medics were fast enough to save the students even after the Abas collapsed on them.

"Yes, but do you want to bring the rest of your team? It might not be fair, otherwise."

Nite enjoyed provoking others into giving way and feeling overconfident. It was simple to play to the emotions of others, and then allow them to fail because they depended on it. Once you broke the emotions, no matter how far back in the mind the cracks started, you had your opponent beaten.

And you think we don't know it's your people on the field as well. The operators are watching them. And we trust our instincts enough to stay protected. We'll kill them too.

"Do you really think your light Abas and you two can beat the four of us?"

She added a small, cute, but over exaggerated giggle. She also threw her shoulder-length hair back and looking into the sky, as if praying for the Sleeping Gods to bring them sanity against a bad decision. It was a well-practiced move, but it exposed her throat and chest to the blind spot she created by looking up.

"I think if you don't bring your other four, the challenge would be as boring as you in your Abas. You will lose with just the two of us on the ground, either way. You have the option of bringing your whole team to keep it even.

"I mean for the eight of you to face just the two of us. This will be double the original bet, not double or nothing. The lights are to be treated as if they participated in both battles equally. If you agree to it, you may bring up to all eight of your crew against us.

"Of course, you may still have the same results of winning the Abas battle," Nite spoke gently after she had finally turned her head back toward him.

The fury raced across her face, but it subsided as she acted to think it over. Her eyes cut to the hands of their leader. He agreed.

"You're willing to take on the *eight* of us against only the two of you. Do you realize . . . no, you know what? Let your own cockiness be your undoing. You are going to wish you never asked for such a fight.

"We are going to make you pay dearly for our loss today. With your defeat, Adroitness Squad will be honored beyond all teams in True Born as it is meant to be. You will be completely destroyed. We will mount your battle helmets on the entry to our facility as a simple reminder of those who choose to act against us."

"If you are going to gain so much, then when we win, in addition, you will disband the rest of your team. Your what, fifth of five ranked teams now?

"After, the six Adroitness sub team members of True Born will never enter another team while you are in these schools. You will never be on the same side in the same battle. I will make sure all of your names are marked appropriately to the way you are killed in this battle.

"We will see you in five minutes. Why don't you all start where we put the majority of your Abas to rest. We start in seven minutes."

The comments sent tremendous tremors of emotions through the other pilots as they tried to get themselves under control. The female's eyes lit red with rage. They said nothing more.

Nite and Mike knew Adroitness commonly asked for a ground hunt after Abas Battles. It was what they mastered as a team to improve their Abas Performance. Adroitness was a team that would likely graduate in two years and be kept together. By breaking them up now, Nite was putting their future honors at risk.

Watching Adroitness battles when they were still in scout Abas gave the twins the insight on doing the same thing. Not only double tapping teams but using other skills to drive a deeper understanding of piloting their Abas training to the next level.

At Midterm, the professors explained the need of additional training to the students. It was to keep them in training instead of dropping courses that would help them get better. At least it would if they learned to transfer the skills between the two worlds. It was like learning ground tactics, knife wielding, small arms, and short rifles. Then taking those skills and combining them into close-quarter combat.

It has never been two worlds for us. Is that what

makes it different? We have always worked as if it were one world. Air feeding land, feeing air through water? Maybe they should discuss this earlier. It helped make TTG better as well.

Adroitness' Team record was almost flawless when the Twins were removed from the equation. Normally being the winners, they offered ground engagements as a way for the other team to make up for the loss. They used it to destroy the other teams that came against them and create terror for those that wanted to challenge them.

Ground tactics were not looked down on, but they were not commonly practiced by most Heavy Pilots. Anyone that expected to potentially lose their Abas and need to keep fighting took specialty courses beyond the basic training. It might have been a stigma or the need to admit you could be defeated that kept pilots away.

What they wouldn't expect was the Twins set up traps around the area they took the majority of them out. They also prepared to enter underground paths near where they would start. It would keep their movements completely untraceable.

The undergrounds were the maintenance tunnels for the terrarium. They hadn't found any signs of students ever using them for battling from. It would work to their advantage, since they did not negotiate having to stay in the arena. This would protect them from interference of the Abas on the field as well.

"I'm afraid this isn't going to happen here today,"

Master Raven interrupted the group as he walked up behind them.

"Sir, we are negotiating a battle. You may not interfere."

"You are trying to cheat two younger pilots in an unfair fight. I heard you on the transport over here. I will not allow Third Echelon Students to interrupt the training cycle of any Second Echelon Students with something as tortuous as this fight.

"If you wish to take this to the Headmaster, I am sure he will find your previous conversation interesting. Now if you will excuse us.

"6541231! 1321456! Come with me! There are other matters we need to cover."

Nite always enjoyed changing the names of those that sought to make lives worse for any and every one stationed under them. He also liked to help lights kill those who believed lights were born to sacrifice themselves for their greater good. It became a hobby over the years after they had lived with the lights.

Mike, on the other hand, sought the absolute destruction of anyone who believes the Wolf Pack's ways were correct and should never be changed or questioned. He always made sure to prove his superior presence on the battlefield and never used actions deemed "the best way" by the Pack.

Every simulated death he caused, he felt was a message to the Wolf Pack Council on their lack of providing true growth by their limitations. Every opponent he defeated was a statement screaming

Selina deserved to be promoted to a suitable talent of her skills. Every move, every strike, every action was against the ways of the Wolf Pack. She fought them within their own rules, but he chose to fight against them, successfully.

Dracon spent years trying to explain why Mike's counter progression wouldn't work for the twins to send the message they wanted. Nite could tell by the look in his eyes, he was going to attempt to do it again. Yet, this was not the reason he stopped the battle.

For them to do it just meant they were a mutant strain of superior genetic lineage that was mixed with a lower level and started to show itself. When they led others to be as good as them, then the entire way of the Pack was being proven wrong. It had to be a repeatable process by others.

Nite was willing to start a team here and train them like the Crux. Mike felt taking on others would only weaken them because they would take them away. He still trained people in the skills they needed for missions or battles, but they never operated in more than one mission or two battles with any group.

"What you two don't understand is TTG already proved your ways are better. Her Crux is more powerful than any team in her school. Headmaster Quick Hit and Falstar are quite aware of who leads that Underground Team. The real leader.

"But it is an underground group. That means as long as they are active, their records and accomplishments are *hidden* from the rest of the school. They would have to come out or be exposed for their true accomplishments to be recognized.

"The virus of your ideas has spread. You have won against them. You continue to antagonize them, but not in a way that proves your *system* works better. You keep provoking a worm only to find out it's a cobra waiting to strike.

"Mike, you completed your ongoing mission the day that TTG took a second. The day the second Core was built, it was impossible to stop. There is no more for you to fight against.

"If you want to kill all these people, then kill them. Ensure it's for a reason that is respectable. Nothing is gained by shooting a corpse."

"Where did you learn so much about TTG's actions?" Nite asked, looking at him curiously.

Dracon didn't have to look at Mike to know that they had gone into their link again.

"I have learned most of it from their Spy Master. Other information is passed from a different source that has connections over there and is monitoring her progress. I cannot give you more information than neither will interfere with her."

"If you say then we will believe. Let's not allow her to come to harm within our knowledge."

"I will do my best, if I have to go to get her myself," Dracon answered.

"You will never be alone if TTG is in trouble," Nite answered as he turned and looked off in the distance.

Dracon didn't want to think of what he might be looking at. Master Raven agreed with the twin's philosophy of every pilot entering the schools should be given a clean slate, without any knowledge of where they came from. If anything came about from these two, it was that the lack of knowledge on all parts was more powerful than anyone knowing where you came from.

Selina seemed to be an exception to the rule of the twins. She not only continued to improve, but she caused the same affect in others. Granted, in the school she was in now, the light pilots were not taught at the level of the heavies, but they were still taught better than most warriors. She only increased the level of training and respect they had for themselves.

"Why did you stop the fight?"

"You were going to win and disband Adroitness. That team crossed you by chance, but it is a great team. They respect the full gambit of rank and responsibility. Destroy them would counter mind your message."

CHAPTER 29

BROKEN TRUST

Two days passed since the Dracon pulled the twins from the battle. Nite and Mike went out earlier than normal to hunt Master Raven. It had become one of their favorite pastimes over the years at the school.

Master Raven was definitely a master of his skill. He showed the twins no matter how much they progressed, there was still more to learn. Nite and Mike might have gotten him the night of the first assassins, but since then, he upped his game beyond anything they ever imagined. The difficulty of hunting him was harder than hunting the Bravos.

I miss them. While they were simple, at least we knew they were trying to kill us. It doesn't feel the same as when people are only trying to beat you.

Master Raven would tease the twins. He would give them advice from shadows around corners but was gone without a trace before the twins could get to him. He turned this into a way to lure them into traps to capture them. They started to become weary of his advice, although they often had no choice but to follow.

The twins loved it due to Dracon being one of the only people they hadn't outgrown. He could never do the same thing twice. Even when he tried it in combinations with something else, they saw the old traps and knew the rest of it without springing it.

A few nights, the twins forced him back into his own trap and trapped him. Yet the master showed his skill. He escaped by the time they circled him. He continued to keep them on their toes most nights, though. He even started taking them into the forbidden areas.

Yet every night ended in a stalemate of sorts. These were not games of winning and losing. They were instructions and independent thought training. It was being put in a bad situation and trying to find a way out. The twins got away, but not without learning something new.

Master Raven came out even earlier than the twins. For the first time, he was waiting at their favorite spot to start the hunt. The hidden passage right below the Abas hangars. Nite was the first through the door and drew on him immediately. He had relaxed when he realized who it was but did not put his small arm away.

"You are getting too comfortable walking around. You should know better than to enter a room so loud and unprepared," Master Raven scolded him.

"Yes, Professor."

Nite knew his actions were not done properly, and there was no need to argue. He could only remember the next time and he would.

"Mike, you might as well come out from behind Nite," Master Raven sighed.

He hadn't heard the double steps; it was when Nite had answered that he heard the second set of breathing through his heightened equipment.

"Yes, sir."

Mike stepped into the room and waited to be corrected on his movement as well. Master Raven skipped it, knowing the twins' not being ready for him in their own sanctuary would do more than any words he could say.

They disguised the entrances and exits of the room. It shouldn't have been noticed unless someone knew where to look. There were several fake doors that were set up, so people would get tired of looking even if they saw the twins disappear. The door that was in here was a double door a real hidden behind one that looked to be fake. Even the second path out was hidden.

It took Master Raven until now to find a way into it. The twins built it years earlier but had not stopped improving the systems as they learned more. It was harder to figure out due to them finding a way to switch the doors out with the fake ones by shifting the inner walls.

The printed the outer walls while clearing the space

for them. Then they used a bot to shift the doors blocking the inner wall. The doors latterly locked on the inside only allowing two to be unlocked at once. Then you had to know how to open it, since none opened the same.

Magnificent. Seeing it from the inside, I see how they figure all my traps out. Keep it simple, and minds will make it more difficult on their own.

"Have you told Nite what you found out?"

Master Raven dropped back into normal tones, returning his own weapon back to its thigh holster. The twins returned there's as well. The reactions were fast, but they knew better than to shoot before validating the target.

There were four seats, but the other two appeared to have never been sat in. Nite signaled for Dracon to take the one next to him and across from Mike. The table and chairs were the only lounge furniture in the room. The two the twins occupied were well worn and showed they spent more time here than Dracon thought.

They must not do it at the same time. Do they come here to be alone as well as work on their other stuff?

The work benches were full of equipment. Mike had some other paintings in the room as well. They had a small arsenal throughout the room. And it looked like this was where they kept the extra cloaks they acquired from the council.

"No, as you asked me not to," Mike said with obvious disagreement.

"I wasn't sure if you were going to allow me to

be there or not. After all, I have asked you not to do several things, but sometimes the two of you think you know better,"

Master Raven reminded them. He had not come here to scold them, though, and dropped back to a kinder voice.

"Thank you for trusting me this time."

"Yes, but this time you told me not to tell him. We have to follow orders, sir. We just don't always choose to follow your suggestions," Mike finally spurted as he looked up from the table.

He carefully avoided Nite's gaze, going straight to Master Raven's eyes for safety.

"Oh! I didn't realize I ordered you. I apologize. I did not mean to take the decision from your hands. I will also remember to make orders on the more important items." Master Raven gave a hint of mirth in his voice.

The twins eased a little as they realized he would not order them to do something they would have to disobey. They never minded following orders when there was no way around them. They would not willingly lose. Nor would they disgrace themselves in following discreditable orders. It was better that people just assumed they did what they felt was best for them.

"Instead of talking over what has or has not happened, let us move on to what I need to know. Obviously, you both kusoing kept it from me long enough." Nite's voice was the one with heat in it this time.

He forced Mike to finally meet his eyes. Master Raven looked away when their stares came into alignment.

"Someone in this school has been in contact with the person sending the assassins. The students in the Abas were supposed to kill you that day on the battlefield. That is another reason I stopped the fight. Two sets of safeties were overridden for the battle.

"Live ammo was unknowingly loaded into Adroitness' weapons before they were added to the cargo bay of the Abas' legs. It was the change in weight that bothered the operators who loaded them.

"The second was the two Abas fighting on the battlefield fell twice while in battle due to pilot error. Only there was no command error other than a prevent fall order going in with a negative value instead of a positive value. If they would have fallen at those points, it is likely they would have crushed your starting points right about the time you would have been settling down to begin."

Master Raven shrugged at telling them. The twins understood. It was his job to gather information. They had failed in protecting themselves. Their plan would have likely keep them from being hit by either plan, but there was a danger they didn't realize.

Someone was in the schools and capable of changing these small fractions without the Abas pilots knowing the real level of danger they were engaging in.

The pilots would have been considered dishonorable and cheaters in the investigation. If they were like the twins, just standing on different sides of the line like Dracon mentioned, then it would have hurt that as well. They would have been killed. No one would know to investigate deeper.

This on top of us not having our guard up when entering a space . . . we are getting sloppy in assuming we are perfect. Do we not beat people constantly for the same hubris?

"What happened with the two Sentinels?" Nite asked, trying to get a full picture of the attack in his head.

Even with live ammo, Nite and Mike could have taken them, and the Sentinels would have had to be really good to make it look like an accident. He could have picked out five in the school capable with the motivation to do it as well.

"They got up and continued to fight their duel and acted as if nothing happened," Mike sighed. "I learned the information after we left the battlefields. I went to listen to what might have been important when you went to class."

"So why are they after us?" Nite asked, hoping for a missing piece.

"It was strange they should come after you with the students since it would be easy to trace. When I tracked it back to a couple of Abas pilots who had fought in the great battle, I thought I finally had the missing lead. Only, they were both dead."

Dracon knew this information would get the twins thinking the same way he had when he came on the new information. There was more, and he had to let this settle in first before he continued.

"They died before you guys were out of your first echelon. There was no way they could have set this up. Anyone with the ability to do this has to be in levels not much lower than those of the council if they are of Wolf Pack at all. Since you basically challenge the entire council, there are too many open factors right now."

"Is there anyone who can help, or are we on our own?" Nite let out the desperation in his voice.

Are we going on the wrong path? Are they after us? If not, and we were just targeted to get out of the way, this attempt makes since. Or logic. It was not a victory over us that was the goal, but removal for another attempt.

Maybe we need to start working more independent of each other instead of being predictably in the same battles.

There had always been the hope of finally finding information on who was sending these groups. By the look on Mike's face, he did not know anything knew. It was new information, though.

"Would they have sacrificed the students just to get at us? Are we dangerous to them?" Mike asked as he looked out the walls.

"Or are we all that insignificant that a loss of a few

would make little difference to their long-term plans? Are we all expendable experiments?" Nite countered.

Master Raven thought for a moment before answering.

"Yes. Supreme Headmaster Lodestar knows as much of the situation as I could tell him, but he had learned even more of it from Falstar. It could be for proof he is not the acting party on the attempts, but he has not tried to stop them either.

"It seems more that he is standing by. He was allowing things to happen without interference. Since other students in the school were utilized this time, I doubt he will continue to stand by. He has never liked these types of games.

"Lodestar believes someone in the council is working on his or her own agenda and outside the rest of the council. I have to believe him. There is no logical reason for the council wanting to see you two die. Especially, this close to the invasion years! There must be something we are missing."

Dracon considered Nite's questions as well.

Are they trying to injure you or keep you out of the way long enough to get at me? It wouldn't take much time if they had someone on the inside. But do they? Triscifield, circuits, cyborgs would have the capabilities if they had enough honor and support. But how much without drawing attention to themselves? Without being investigated.

Are they assuming if I am alone, then it will be easier to kill me? If I am the target, then what is it about me, not them that would want someone to attack? Well, the last Crusader Olympia gave plenty of reasons. But why now? Why after so long? How many are left from that battle? That might be the clue I need.

Dracon often thought the twins were not targets themselves. He thought they were targeted because they interfered. He never considered he was the target. Just an obstacle. If they were not the targets, then the three of them didn't know who the target was.

Would it have been better to let them get closer to the target? To find out who they went for? We discussed this, but the others stopped before we could.

There were other things Dracon saw reports on. None of them tied together, but his mind kept trying to put them in the same picture. The puzzle was right in front of his face. He just needed to find the pattern to it. It transgressed so far it was almost impossible to look at without perspective.

"We fought for every inch we ever got. Everything we do, we have done with going against the odds of the Pack and have succeeded. Is our success such a poison to them they now believe we are not worthy of living in their society? Now because we have found better ways than their ways, they want to kill us. I will kill them all!" Mike whispered in a voice that could be heard clearly through the room.

"That isn't the Pack way. They would want to take what you have produced and teach it to the next generations. The Packs, all of them, have based their societies on becoming the noblest and best fighters.

The Forward Schools operate different for a reason. This is not their ways.

"If you can't earn respect from the battle and style on which you defeated your enemies, then you gain nothing but borrowed time. You have to also gain from your losses. It doesn't make sense for them to try and kill the two of you," Master Raven continued, almost trying to make it sound right in his own head.

But why? The first assassins were using an advanced light bender to get by the motion detectors. They knew where they were and didn't break them after they were sure they had tripped enough to get my *attention. How would they know the twins would follow, or even be in the area to follow?*

"You are right. This is not the way of the Pack, which is why I do not think the council had anything to do with it. Something or someone is operating on their own. This is the only explanation that aligns everything. The first question is why are they trying to get into this school? Then, why would they come after the two of you?"

"Falstar would have told them to ensure our deaths were done before we left the school because our ways cannot be taught to the other members of the pack," Mike started and stopped.

They took Selina away because she was learning their ways. But that wasn't the real reason. They didn't stop her from progressing on the underground. They hadn't prevented her from being promoted.

She was. She was doing it for them. Then she

started the Crux and the Cores. No one is stopping them. No one was targeting them.

"No. Falstar, as much as he is other things, he is not trying to kill you. At least he is not the one sending the assassins. It is above this school. It is above all the schools, and I am not sure it isn't above the council. What is it about you two?"

What is it about me? If not us, then who and why? What is the motivation. That's the first question.

"What will life be like for you when we are gone, Professor?" Mike laughed as he finally sat back down in his seat.

Dracon had not realized Mike stood. As Master Raven, he failed to take notice of the change of positions for danger or protection. He was thinking too deep and fell to the same hubris in assuming this place was safe.

"That is an odd question, Mike."

Master Raven stared at the usually quiet twin. He had spoken more tonight than ever when in Dracon's presents. Nite, however, remained silent and thinking.

"Still, you must think it will be boring. I am glad that you find us so interesting. Thank you," Nite finally chimed in as if he had read Master Raven's thoughts.

It was quick, but the look on his face said he had a thought. It would not be shared. Master Raven knew he had to say something quick, but what, he didn't know.

"Finding the missing piece is most important. You must protect yourselves and expect danger in every area now. Not just from assassins but from other students. Knowing willing, or unknowingly, but willing to face you."

Master Raven knew this did not need to be said, but it had bought him some time to think of what Nite might have thought.

"Mike is suggesting the assassins wanted to meet with you, so you could show them where we were. I think he is testing you, sir. I would like to believe his suspicions were wrong.

"You said it yourself. You would do almost anything to earn the right to thank those who won the last battle after you failed. You said don't get comfortable with what is normal."

Nite sighed, but this was not said to give Master Raven any information. It was meant to lure him from his thoughts. He had to play along.

"Nite, do you really think I want you two dead. Especially after all the times I have trapped you, and all the time I have spent showing you how to protect yourselves? Does it make sense to believe that?"

Master Raven stood from the table and turned around with his hands behind his back. It was a vulnerable move, but it also showed the twins he trusted them. It was needed now.

Mike was the one to answer.

"No, but why do you risk even more loss of Honor Levels for two stupid kids?"

"You are not kids. You are Abas pilots. One day you will become the greatest Abas warriors in the all the Packs.

"Your right. I will never be able to thank those two properly. Does defeating you or killing you do anything to thank them after they acted so honorably. I can only hope to ensure every student I let leave this school has been trained to fight with the same heart they showed that day. That you show every day."

Was that the missing piece? No. They know that. What are they missing?

"I understand now."

He stopped and looked at Nite then Mike.

"How do you choose who to trust if anyone can be turned against you?" Dracon asked himself, considering for the first time what it must appear like from their perspective.

"Is it ever going to be safe for us if someone in the council wants us dead?" the twins asked together, but in quieter tones.

Dracon's heart sank into his stomach. It was unfair to force these two to face so much more after they had fought through so much adversity.

"I can't say."

Nite sat back at the table. His mind kept racing back to the beginning. The first evening of the assassins. The first kill. They had not been there for the twins. They had not come after them then. They were only after them now because they interfered so much.

Nite wanted to ask Dracon what he had done to cause them to come for him. He wanted to ask why he had not told them the truth. It had been years since the Crusader Olympia, so it was unlikely to be that.

What other games do you have playing? We put our lot with yours. What does that mean for us now?

CHAPTER 30

CHALLENGE ACCEPTED

Two months passed since Dracon was asked about how to know who to trust when no one knows what is really going on. He hadn't answered them yet, but the twins hadn't detected any more attempts directed at them either. In Nite's calculation, they had two months left until they reached the point, they would prove they deserved to be Elite Pilots by not being defeated.

Falstar considered all this information as he looked at the person across the desk from him. He could never let anyone know how much he knew about them. He was about to break an internal promise to never let it be commonly known what they could do until he could ensure it went his way.

Most of the instructors felt the same, whether they said it or not. The twins proved they could learn as well on their own. Illuminator and Master Raven seemed to be the only classes they came to consistently.

Illuminator was not locked into a class. She seemed to teach different areas, different levels, but almost every topic. They would show up if she was teaching, even if it was a different echelon.

They once went to a littles class, just to see how different it was. They barely fit in the seats. Since they arrived and were students, she made them stay there, in the tiny seats, the entire time. They didn't show up to any more of those and she didn't ask them not to.

Falstar however, insisted they show up to classes they had not completed every aspect of classroom learning. These were running out. They were just over a year from entering the cycle that would start their Third Echelon. Even though they were staying in school, they could feel the changes mentally happening. They didn't care about the classes as much. They felt they were peaking.

What comes when you believe you have learned all you can learn? We are continuing to progress them, but what's left? It hasn't even been twenty-years and they need to start having experience to go with the knowledge for them to understand what they have learned.

The lack of Instructor attention didn't cause any loss of sleep for the twins. They spent more hours in their VR training, pushing themselves beyond what even they believed was possible. Being in the VR of their Abas, they didn't have to worry about being cheated, and the scenarios stayed as true to life as VR could get them.

Falstar and Master Demagogue didn't interfere with their VR training. Demagogue was the Department Head of Heavy Abas Training. He was the one of the instructors directly instructed not to interfere with the twins training themselves. With him being Falstar's Third, no one questioned his words or means. Ear canal

Falstar didn't spend one second on a real battlefield. This didn't hinder his ability to train Abas pilots. Aside from his father, he had the most wins of any school in the Pack System for the same years as Headmaster. When strange orders came from the Head Office, there was a reason.

Nox, the only other instructor who won any of the End Games against Falstar and Lodestar, also pulled a few seconds with the father son in first and third. Even with the record, she didn't always finish top three. Falstar wasn't willing to involve her more than she already was.

Richard said several times that they needed to be able to study where they had come from. Since that was not possible, Richard finally said the only way to beat them was to study their own training and find the weaknesses in it. The more they studied their training, the harder it seemed to find a gap.

"Have you learned anything in watching the twins work outside of instructors completely?" Falstar sneered at his third.

This was the only ground the two of them had ever come to such disagreements about, albeit a motivation and need for Falstar's plans to be designed properly.

I feel it getting closer.

"I have studied them for hours. They are beyond me finding of any weaknesses. I have even built VR trainings for them. I can't find one that is strong enough for them to face a real-life battle and not win.

"The closest I get is when I put your mother and father's simulation records in against them. It has worked to a draw eighty-two percent of the time. Six percent, they win. I mean you parents.

"I have to throw several platoons of heavy Abas at them just for them to finally get worn down enough to drop out of the battles, but they never lose their Abas, and they never die.

"To be quite honest, I have learned more from them in these past few months of tactics and strategies then I ever did fighting on the front lines. The Wolf Pack will become a new level of challenge after they start studying all this information. It won't be available until after the brothers leave school, but from some of what has been leaked, we have been extremely successful. When it becomes public material for our generals . . . we might earn a fifth Army.

"The problem is, a draw would only mean they win the next time. They don't make the same mistake twice. You can't lure them into a trap that has already been used. The only thing they haven't faced is a Dire Wolf Pack. I would have used it, but you have told us we are not allowed to use it until we find a way to defeat them without it."

Richard's words were what Falstar had been waiting for. The words of someone that finally accepted there was more to them than just students. It was time to trigger his next step in the process.

Falstar's secretary brought in the wine that was specially ordered for the meeting. She set down the two glasses and poured Falstar's before setting the bottle down.

"Honestly," Richard grabbed at the bottle, "I could put this child in my place and have as much success against them," he vilified himself.

"What an interesting idea." Falstar smiled deeply.

He had been waiting too long for the opening. Now, at long last, his friend delivered what Falstar wanted twice in a row.

Is this becoming too easy? Do I need another? Have I made you too pliable?

"You know about the two unnamed pilots who are about to move into the third echelon, right. How would you go about trying to name them before they reach that level?"

Falstar kept the kindness and informal tone he usually used when talking to her well-guarded now. Richard was in the office with them. He couldn't suspect this was set up.

She is very aware of the frustration the twins have caused me. I just hope that this idiot accepts that sometimes the simplest-minded beings are the smartest for being so simple. They don't allow their minds to get in the way of the solution.

Falstar sat back, feeling either way, he could not lose.

She turned around and looked deeply at Falstar with confusion. It was perfect in saying, why would an android dare suggest how to fight Abas students. Then she answered in a low voice.

"I do not wish to act as if I would know of such things. But why not have the two face each other?" she added as if it wasn't the most obvious answer.

Even in their personal training sessions, they only fought each other in hand to hand combats. Falstar wanted to smack the dumbfounded look on Richard's face off. But he forgave his friend in the same instant. It was too simple for them to get there.

"Since the two of them are on the battlefield, preparing to enter the leadership level, have a group set to fight them for rights to command an actual squad. One would kill the other, and then be too weak to fight the rest of the battle squad participating in a leadership challenge.

"Once the twins are defeated, the rest of the team would have to face each other until only one was left. The winner is the Leader," she added a little less tentatively.

"It is common for this school to have everyone in teams for Third Echelon. They have not joined any. It would behoove the school to set up a team with instructors for their unique talents. It is all within the honor of warriors, from what I understand."

Her voice became stronger, as it was supposed to. Her hands fiddled with the wedding ring on her finger. That was not supposed to happen, but it didn't take away from her prepared appearance.

Falstar eyed it for a second before he looked at her. He was impressed with the Android being able to answer so perfectly, but the nervousness with the ring was an extra-nice added touch from what they practiced. She performed flawlessly. He would provide her with additional recognitions to show her honor. Her reporting this as hers would also help.

The answer was simple, and yet it had eluded the best strategist in the school and parts of the Pack. It was easy and could have been done at any time. Falstar had no doubts it had been done before, and on a much earlier level, to remove the stigma that such sets of partners might have created in the past.

This would bring the twins to a normal level for them to progress from and made more pliable warriors. It would if they lost. After all, if they were not willing to follow, then how would they ever lead to where the Pack wanted them to go?

If both do not lose, then I always have my other plans. They will be used either way. I don't care if they lose. I just want to see if I was right.

"Brilliant!"

Falstar finally answered. Richard was struck dumbfounded. Her hands eased. Richard was still thunderstruck and floundered when he finally tried to say something. Falstar waved her out with no more respect than he had ever used in front of others. The idea might have seemed to be hers, but that meant nothing for her rank among the two of them.

"I want you to put them against each other as soon as possible," Falstar started after the door closed.

"VR or real combat with simulations rounds?" Richard smiled.

His mind raced with the possibilities of beating one of the twins finally. It would open-up for them to receive the promise of the council or at least it would for the one. The other would find a different way. And with them moving into the third echelon, warriors from outside the schools could now come to challenge them.

"They are beyond any four students in the school. We will need to get them to agree to a fight with the winner against four instructors after the fight between them.

"We won't say how soon after, and as long as the winner is still on the battlefield, we will fall into the Honor Code of Wolf. We will allow them to go head-to-head with training rounds . . . I don't want them killing each other, though. Those rounds need to be triple checked, full reload. Everyone else as well.

"This is a naming battle as well, so if they both lose, then they will both be named. There needs to be a high stake for them to want to bite. The right," Falstar paused to think, although he had his next words planned. "Will be to give any Abas, the winner, chooses a size upgrade to whatever rank within reason they feel the pilot deserves. That will draw them in for the second part of the battle without thought as to when it could be done."

"Yes, this will work nicely."

Richard started to laugh as he saw himself and three of the best battle Abas fighters on the field with him.

"What about using Master Raven? He has the best battle experience against them of any staff here. Do you think you could get him to fight against the winning twin?"

"No. I have the fourth already on the way. A great coincidence."

******

Nite walked out of the shower to find Mike suiting up in his battle uniform. They didn't have any battles planned for another three days. Today was a day they concentrated on non-Abas classes.

"What is going on?" he asked, putting his dirty laundry in the fold-out cleaning baskets.

"We have a new challenge that was accepted right after for the next free slot. The free slot is open for the next four hours on the large arena. We are to report to our Abas as soon as possible. We are supposed to fight a naming battle." Mike finished putting on his outer layer to protect the skintight battle suit.

"Who's challenging us?" Nite asked.

There was something different about Mike's voice. He didn't want to tell Nite something he knew he had too.

"We are going to be fighting each other. I just heard the Headmaster and Demagogue talking about it. Moments before I put the challenge in. The Headmaster wants to do it as soon as possible. Master Demagogue wants to use Master Raven as one of the Abas instructors for the winner to fight. I didn't stay to listen to the rest. I didn't know how much time we would have to disrupt their plans.

"If we do this early, we might be able to prevent him from having to make a decision and revealing more than he ever meant to. I accepted the challenge on your part. Hope you don't mind," Mike said with a guilty smile.

Nite gave a little laugh.

"I guess we have played long enough of not wanting to know who was better at this. It goes to your advantage on the timing. Don't think that is an excuse for me not to slay you, though, brother. If I can win, I will," Nite answered fiercely.

"So, will I, brother," Mike answered back just as ferociously.

It was time for them to enter a battle mind. Out of respect, Mike put it off until his brother had time to set his own mind. Nite finished suiting up and putting his cover uniform on.

Nite wasted very little time in picking out his

own uniform for the battle. A moment like this, some might have considered what they should look like. He just reached in and grabbed the first thing that came to his hand.

The greatest challenge the twins could come up with had finally presented itself. Nite didn't have to ask his brother why now. It was now, and that was all that mattered. His mind was on one thing. How do you beat the unbeatable mind? What were his advantages and disadvantages?

While Nite dressed, Mike filled him in on everything he had heard while he was in the shower, including the idea coming from Missy, the Android stationed to the post of the Headmaster's secretary. Mike sent Selina a copy of the conversation and the challenge made by him. If she was going to bet on the battle, she had to make the decision on which one and understand why now.

For the first time in their history, the twins walked out of their room, knowing one of them would come back defeated by the other. It was the only chance they had in ensuring that both were not left to an ignominious defeat set up under questionable conditions.

Mike set in the challenge of being able to take on the four instructors upon completion of the battle. If one of the twins won, they received a single request from Falstar he must honorably permit as long as it was in his power. That part of the challenge would be granted if the four instructors answered by coming onto the field after the twins had finished fighting.

There were no simulation, other than the live fire, this time. The twins wanted the designs of the Abas to act as freely as was possible. They would not be limited to the level the simulator computer.

Most didn't know they were sneaking into the underground with their Abas for over four years to true try out their strengths. There was a limit to the simulations. A limit they were not willing to leave to chance on this night.

Nite grabbed his brother's arm before he peeled off to go to his Abas.

"No regrets."

Mike nodded in agreement and turned to climb up the three-rung ladder. The loneliness they both felt in the cockpit was new and awkward. The two of them refused to look at the other, afraid of what they would see.

If they allowed their eyes to meet, they knew they would know they were now facing their greatest fear, losing in their Abas to their brother. What would it be like? Would they learn anything new? Would this be the end of their great friendship? Or would it birth something new and better?

Finally, the lights turned green for Mike, and he moved out of the bay to follow them to his entry point. Nite waited a minute or two before he was signaled with the red lights to a different path. It was something else that was new to him. Going to a different point than his brother, and it increased the loneliness of the cockpit tenfold.

"Nineteen years is a long time to live without being named. I wish I wasn't so alone!" Nite breathed out. "We were two months away from being in the timeframe for Elite. We were going to fight each other on our twentieth birthday. I am glad we were forced to do it earlier. I don't think I would want to remember the day with this much emptiness in me."

A faint noise came up from the background. It was comforting, familiar, but unknown and distant. Still it gave a warm feeling in his chest.

It was definitely a woman's whisper, which left the faint echo of, "You are never alone, here."

He shook it off and moved his Abas into the front of the drop doors.

Well brother. Let's see who's going to get the vital lesson.

CHAPTER 31

VOICES OF LONELINESS

"Sir," Falstar's secretary rang over his view screen.

Her voice was frantic and cracking under some strain. Falstar never heard it that way before.

"I am in a meeting with Master Demagogue. Is it important?" he asked her in a fierce voice, but he already knew the answer.

She would not have interrupted otherwise.

Pretenses have to be maintained. But what could have caused this.

They became a great team over their years together. He regretted he would never be able to show her openly how much he appreciated her. It might have been why she brought him around to the rougher engagements she enjoyed in private.

She enjoyed it too much for him to turn her down as they grew closer. He knew he would never do it with another woman. With them, he would only see her. But for her, he would always be willing.

"Sir, the twins are on their way out to battle each other. The battle challenge was posted and accepted about half an hour ago. You asked to be informed of their next challenge, so you could change it. Well, it is against each other now. There is no need to change it."

"They know!" Richard scorned.

They didn't have time to mentally prepare the instructors. The month they were currently discussing to work up to this was gone. The onetime chance was slipping through their fingers, and he could feel it clenching around his neck like a noose.

"It doesn't matter. Connect me to the cockpits," he ordered over the com box on his desk.

A few seconds passed as he impatiently sat over it.

"Sir, you are connected," a new, softer female voice answered.

Falstar recognized the voice at its first hint of irritation. It was the commander of the operators he had at the school. She often oversaw important battles as they came. The irritation of the newest Android in the school came from having to connect him through when he should have been in the Operation Command where he also belonged for a fight this big.

This battle was too much for her to be overseeing alone. Her second, a male Android, was not worthy of the command position over the other seven operators who watched the five different training domes.

"I will not indulge myself in asking how I was just talking about this battle with a college, and moments later, it was made and accepted. I will ask, what is it you two are doing fighting such a high-honor naming battle without consulting me?"

"Sir, with all due respect, my brother and I need to find out who is truly the better Abas pilot. A recent argument seems to only be able to be solved by who will win in such a battle.

"Therefore, we chose to face each other now, at the first opportunity. With your blessing, we would like to continue," Nite responded in a manner that Falstar could not back them out of without giving his own intentions away.

"Of course but let me sweeten the pie. If the winner is willing to fight four Abas instructors after this fight for a naming battle, then I will put on the table something special for you."

Falstar didn't mention what it was, hoping if they had heard the conversation, they would jump on it without him promising anything at all.

"There is an option placed on the engagement report for you, as Headmaster and representative of the School, to accept with conditions. My brother and I have accepted the conditions as long as you are willing to accept ours," Nite answered in a manner of great respect, but Falstar knew it was only meant as a slap in the face.

"I am looking at the conditions as we speak. As you have written, after the battle is complete, so it means at any time, they may enter the field. Are you sure you are willing to face four instructors so soon after a battle?" Falstar could almost taste a sweet victory in his mouth, and he still didn't promise anything.

"For the prize, if you accept it, it will be worth it," Mike spoke to the Headmaster for the first time.

His voice was dark with an evil hunger Nite had never heard him use to speak to anyone else. Nite knew it was going to be a very hard battle, indeed. Mike was fighting for the right to bring Selina back to the school.

Nite thought it was better to leave her where she was. She created her own army and was progressing more on her own without their help. It sent the message they always wanted to the Pack Council.

"Excuse me?" Falstar acted confused on the subject but had just read the line.

It was a request from the Headmaster, but it never said he could not choose the request, or that they had to make only one for him to choose from. If he played his cards right, he could cause them to fight very hard for nothing. He had to keep them from being too specific.

"What is the prize if we win? I don't want the *honor* of naming another instructor, especially one that I have already named. If one of us has to fight them in sequential order, then I am sure we agree we want to know if it is worth the award for giving them the chance to win."

Falstar faltered with confusion. There was always the possibility for them to have bugged his office. There was no doubt they could have had several of their own invention in there. It was something different when they seemed to read his thoughts or counter them before he could even devise a way to ensure they were in motion. He stared at the box for a while before he finally chose to answer.

"You will be able to upgrade any Abas pilot you see fit to any level other than Elite. Or I will put the upgrade request in for them. If they prove worthy to the council, then they will be promoted.

"I may not speak for them, but I will promise you this. I will fight as hard as I can to get them to the level you request by the end of the End Games. I will even ask my father to approach the War Council on their behalf. I can make no promises for him, but I will make the commitment for me."

Falstar knew this was the only way he could get the twins to take such a high risk. With the fall of one, the other might go as well, but he could not assume the winner would lose. He had to keep it enticing to them, but where he could also control what happened for an outcome.

"As long as the change is permanent, I agree. If the change is not permitted, then we gain nothing. What is offered in return?"

Nite seemed to counter one of Falstar's moves, but there was still one thing they had not calculated. Something Falstar had counted on when he had first suggested it, and held closely to himself, even in his own thoughts.

"Then I will offer a second option. I will attempt to bring her back if the council will approve it. If both of them fail to go through, then I will offer you complete access to all information I am allowed as Headmaster of Timber Wolf Academy until one of the two are granted." Falstar inserted his twisting knife blade into the deal. "With, of course the exception to my personal folders for there is too many things in there that are not privy to anyone's eyes. You will have access to any other information that I have, though."

"I agree," Nite answered without a second thought.

"Both of you must agree. If you agree and lose to your brother, then it means nothing."

Mike let out a low, growling noise. "Is that a yes?" Mike repeated the noise. "It will be considered a yes, and you will be held accountable as if the answer were a yes. Good luck, Abas pilots. If there is anything of luck in this battle, I hope it is good for both of you."

Falstar ended the coms link and looked at Richard.

"Get ready. As soon as one is done and the other is mobile, then you will be fighting him. Get the other three instructors as well. You might not be able to enter the fight at the same time, but as soon as they are selected, get ready to get in there. I don't want them to have time to leave the battlefield and call it a forfeit for you not being there."

"Yes sir."

"Sir." The screen went red again with emergency acceptance request.

"What is it this time?"

"Ultimate Munitions and General Brazen have just arrived."

"You only need two more instructors. What a great day!"

******

Nite knew his advantage in the battle was understanding his brother's ways as well as he did. He could break defenses and disrupt the game plan of another member easily, but Mike was a battlefield engineer. Nite was a battlefield tactician. The battle would fall onto the tactics used by their masters to truly prove who was better, if there was to be anyone better.

His grip on the control sticks was so tight his hands went numb. He no longer felt alone, just ready. It was the right time, and it was needed.

Nite relaxed let out a small laugh.

After all, this is just for fun.

******

Mike knew he could map a battle after a few moves from most, but Nite would not stay to just a few moves. Nite knew how Mike's mind worked. He would use all his knowledge to get into it. Setting traps would be harder, and a true test of ability on both their parts.

Nite had the advantage at this, though, for he could read a trap and set it to get the advantage on his opponent. Mike knew he had to create a new tactic for his brother, something Nite had never seen before if he was going to win. And somewhere deep inside, Mike knew that he could plan around his brother's tactics and win. He had to for Selina.

Mike could feel the desperation welling up in him as he approached the drop doors. It felt new to him, but for the second time in his life, he had to take his own path.

"I won a great victory and suffered a terrible loss on the last one. Will this time be the same, or am I to only have the terrible loss?"

"We are about to see," a whisper of a man's voice spoke, but Mike was sure it didn't come from the coms.

It was familiar, although he wasn't sure where he had heard it. He shook it out of his head and started to wonder if he had heard it at all. His mind went back to the strategies he believed Nite would be weakest against. Nite would expect him to start there, and that would begin the trap.

******

The second largest of the arenas lay in front of Nite and Mike as they looked across the plans from

East to west at each other. In the record of the Arena no two individuals had ever meet in combat against one another. First was the sheer size at 800 sq. km. (480 sq. miles) with mountains in the northern region averaging 7 km (4.2 miles). The second reason was it claimed over half the arena deaths of the school, including a few instructors. From north to south, it was a 50 km (30 miles) long with a narrow width of only 16 kilometers (10 miles). It may have been narrow, but that was twice the length of the best High-Powered Mounted Laser Range of 8 km (5 miles).

The northern regions snow-capped mountains range dropped through rough, rocky foothills to a plain with four lakes. On the eastern and western edges, were mostly light covering of woods, where most battles were engaged. On the furthest western and southern sections of the light woods were a heavier dense wooded area. These trees were thick enough to high most Sentinels and some Zhayedans.

The second most treacherous area in the Arena was the Black Forest. It was appropriately named, because the trees' crowns were so thickly woven together, no light could penetrate beneath them from the overhead. It was as dark as the intergalactic space.

Even with the deadly aspect, it was the most populated arena on Seventh Day and when students had breaks. Skiing and boarding piste were reprinted if damaged by battles to be fresh and ready. Trails ranged from green, for those beginning to learn, to blue, red, black and white ranges based on respective difficulty. The same codes were used for the mountain river kayaking ratings, and tubing for both the slopes and river paths and every other aspect of sports and recreational activities. Diving and swimming areas in the lakes and beaches were all available but marked and designed for different types of recreations. Unmarked were open for people to figure out. Recreational vehicles could be temporarily or permanently rented from the school. Most permanents belonged to the teams or staff members, who also enjoyed the same facilities.

These arenas were their homes as much as their rooms. They did winter mountain survival on those peaks. They learned about surviving rapids in the mountains, and like most students who were trying to learn to survive, had to be pulled out by the medical robots that provided as much protection as they could throughout all the hardest regions.

Surviving the rapids was required to participate in some of the hardest kayaking, white water rafting and other river races that were held each tier. Other than betting, there was nothing to win but bragging rights. Which was good for the twins, since they hadn't won one yet.

It was not just skill, but luck and the dangers that were thrown at you. An unexpectant wave, a change in the rapids, a waterfall that had a whirlpool hidden below it or a whirlpool suddenly forming under you. The twins seemed to be constantly tested on these, but they were fun. It wasn't about being the first to the bottom, even if it was called a race. A lot of members would go back through the toughest paths or where paths split to try the different ways to gain higher points, another measurement that was bet on. Here the twins usually did fairly good in ranking.

No recreational aspect was ever graded or allowed to be used for naming. It was supposed to remain fun and free. Competitions were held, even with things that were tied to school, like hand to hand combat, firing ranges and throwing competitions, but like the river runs, it was only for bragging rights and betting.

Mike looked over this arena, thinking of all the memories that were held here. Many of them were with Selina as well. This was often the area they visited in their simulations together.

And now these memories will share us determining who is the best. Will this make us better? Will we grow from it? What will it be like to know defeat in our Abas? Will it make us less?

Or will it make you more?

The male voice asked, confusing Mike. He tried to figure out if he was whispering or speaking out loud when he was trying to be in his own head. Part of it mapping the areas and determining what path Nite would use first. The second, overlaying Nite's plans, trying to find the perfect spot to hit him. The last active part, thinking as always of Selina and the memories here.

"Hello?" he asked as he looked around.

"Operator Korna here," the operator came online to his open speaking.

"Hey Korna. So were together in this. That's great. You and I have the best connection and communications.

"How many pilots are you running?" Mike spoke aloud.

There were too many things going on in an Abas to not speak to your operator and team when necessary. Most the time the team just had to follow the plans. Sometimes he would even map their firing paths, which they found strange, but when they followed it, performed better than they ever had.

Korna was the one he spoke to if he had to modify anything, which wasn't often. She would change and speak to everyone else for him. Operators were normally with the pilots, and sometimes they became connected in more ways. At least that's what the androids told the twins.

Not in school, it was frowned since an android might have to operate against a student they were close to. In the fleet, same Pack fighting each other was rare, and an operator having to govern a fight against team members even rarer. Fights happened they just weren't monitored by the team operators.

"That means Asyl is with 1321456," he asked.

"Yes, Student 1321456 is being monitored by Asyl. Command Team One is solely monitoring you. No one in command has any bets on this fight."

That was a lot of intel to provide to Mike. He

liked Korna because she always gave him a lot with a few words. Androids were often operators because they could process several functions but had a human instinct to them when it came to speaking. They could turn it off and be very logical, but they could be calming when you needed it as well.

They normally had as many as ten pilots being monitored during a fight at a time, in simulations or out. For them, it was the same. Since they could speak openly in command and to the pilots at the same time, they were not as limited. They could also prioritize and change conversations or inputs better than other circuits. Cyborgs, even the most upgraded, couldn't cover as many pilots.

And I don't think most human pilots would trust a cyborg to not lead them into a trap that would make them cyborgs at some point. Like most cyborgs have a feeling that at some point, the human will turn on them and destroy them. It's mutually understandable.

Getting to know the command androids was something the twins started doing before they entered their Abas. Since begin in Heavy Zhayedans, they were expected to go to Command and watch how things happened when others were fighting. It was also part of their training. Every Heavy Zhayedan and Team Leader in training was required to spend time in command.

Command teams were only dedicated to the highest priority battles and usually when that happened, it was a large battle with at least twenty Abas on the field.

A command team dedicated to one battle with only two Abas meant more was happening in that area then normal, even for just the two of them fighting.

Every student was also assigned and Android that would monitor all their grading and actions. No student was supposed to learn who their android was, or it would be changed. The twins figured out who theirs was so many times, Falstar left them with their current ones and ordered them to stop looking. In return, Korna and Asyl would be their operators when available. The twins agreed.

Having dedicated Operators was like being in the fleet. They were a vital part of your team. The lynch pin that could make all the difference. In this battle, them being dedicated to them wouldn't give either twin an advantage, but it took many of the disadvantages away as well.

Her saying they didn't bet meant many things as well. The least of which was that they didn't want to see this fight. They don't want to try to calculate the results. For the Androids, it was like watching two of their children fighting and not being able to stop it. Most of them referred to the twins as their child in some manner and would argue on who was allowed to claim them over the other.

This fight wasn't only impacting them. It was impacting all those that watched and helped them grow, the androids and command center teams among them. Mike wasn't only fighting for himself she was saying. They were fighting for them while tearing their hearts apart by this inevitable battle.

Then we must put it all on the line. No holding back brother. No holding back and fighting to the death. This is an all or nothing battle. I understand.

CHAPTER 32

GODS AT WAR

Nite was set to enter the battle from the Delta Outlet which brought him out between the light woods and Lake Dadar. He was equipped with his personal configuration Bravo. He selected his favorite Gauss Rifle for his main long-range weapon, but added a dual laser rifle, in case he ran out of ammo, to his rear holsters. His missile drum carried twenty multi-warhead missiles on the outer rim, ten shrapnel warhead missiles on the middle rim and in the three and two canisters of the center set. The shrapnel warheads were capable of traveling a farther distance due to the larger fuel source but were almost twice the diameter of the mini warheads.

Two automated petite lasers faced forward and rear on his left shoulder platform. They could rotate in an x, y, z targeting axis with a three-hundred-and-twenty-degree crossing fire. The automated lasers could be controlled in the cockpit, but they would override pilot command to protect the Abas.

He swapped his dual-bladed coil guns for two dual-wield bladed lasers over his already-attached Wakizashi. Most humans referred to the DWBLs, called Ditto. Simplified names were often used in place of those given to designs by the circuits or Triscifield. It seemed they wanted to make complicated names for no other reason than to show their superiority. It provided annoyance to most others outside their specific fields. Renaming them to easy to remember names was a smack to the original namers as well. Their lack of innovation in names did not hinder their creativity in developing the original weapons, or the newer designs the human test subjects provided back for weapon improvement or redesigns.

The short blades hung upside down, so they could be drawn while his Abas was squatted down in anticipation of attack. The lasers had a much longer range for their small size but caused less damage than the solid rounds of either rail or coil weapons. They did, however, have the advantage of no ammo requirement, which was of higher importance here. Mounted lasers were better than rifles.

A tracker gun sat flat across the top of his head, under the armor. The last addition armor maxed out the recommended working weight of the endoskeleton. If he hit Mike with one of the tracking rounds, he would be able to send any of his guided rounds, including his Gauss at his brother no matter where he ran. Only, the shot had to be at close range, which Nite was sure his brother would allow him to get within.

If a pilot was ever hit by one of these, their only hope was to find a safe place to hide and cut the gooey epoxy off. If the epoxy set, the only way to remove the tracker round was to cut the armor off. Ghillie suits were better defenses against this, since it was easier for a pilot to cut a small section off.

In most instances, you either severed the part or released the armor as soon as you realized you had one attached to you. It was the design of the weapon that implemented the counter ability to release parts of your external armor and appendages as the pilot decided they needed to do.

Mike would enter at Bravo Outlet, just over seven kilometers from his brother. He would be raised close to Lake Floure but would have to cross the beach or into the lightly covered wooded foothills to get to the Upper Thain. Although the two of them could see each other, the distance was too great to fire on the other.

He preferred to go with even less ammo requirements for his Timber Wolf using configuration C but had modified it for his brother. He changed the two missile drums on the back with a cooling system for the Pulse Beam Cannon (PIBC). With the cooling coils, the electrostatic lens was less likely to crack under multiple-charged firings. One cooling system would maintain both mounted shoulder cannons and freed his arms to use his two dual rifle laser and back-mounted sniper laser as needed.

Mike preferred to get closer to his victims. Instead of using the DWBL like his twin, he preferred wraparound lasers. The six lasers were mounted in a circle. They were not individually more powerful than the dual wields, but as the six fired in sequence, the multiple hits would spread the damage, ripping parts of the Abas off. It was not a weapon for someone who wanted to take salvage from the battlefield, but more for one who wanted to tear their enemies to pieces quickly.

The six firing lasers were also perfect for firing in rapid succession, for they could cool down enough by the time it circled back around for them to be fired again. The main disadvantage of this weapon was that after three cycles, it had to be secured for the power cells of the lasers to recharge from the core source. The recharge was only fifteen seconds but could be pulled early. Every five seconds you waited would give you a full volley at full power.

Like his brother, he carried two Wakizashi on his legs. One was upright, while the other was down. He preferred to have the freedom to draw them either way and didn't want to be restricted on how to pull the weapon. He was not the tactician his brother was. He planned long term, not in the moment. He needed the freedom to change his plans as the battlefield changed.

With both of his shoulders taken by PBCs, Mike

was not able to ensure he was protected automatically with an APL. PBCs were Particle Ball Chargers were commonly called the BB Guns, short for Blue Ball Guns. They create charged particles to the state of Plasma balls, that were blue and white in color, like a ball of self-contained lightning. Then released them. The balls didn't require a full charge to be released, but lower charges didn't go as far either.

These were some of the longest-range weapons, but the moved slower than any other weapon as well. The balls could also be spun with the directors, causing them to spin, bend and even turn in different directions and speeds. Due to this, they were not as popular since they required such planning and calculations in their uses.

Mike made another modification. His brother might go for the woods, hoping to disrupt any trap rounds his brother might have fired to lure him into. Mike added a magma launcher to the head compartment of the Abas. It was unable to swing left and right due to it being between the PBCs, but this made little difference. If he lit sections of the forest on fire, the damage would be the same if pointed forward or backward.

Visibility within the Abas was designed around the top of the head of the design. It allowed the pilot to see what was going on by moving their head and the inputs changing the view of their helmet's visor. The visor of the helmet showed the pilot everything they may need and more. Weapon configurations, ranges, selected weapon firing sets, a small radar with IFF, and more. It was designed as a direct link to the outside, but some movement was still required by the pilot to ensure there was no computer error that would cause you to be blinded.

If the vision array was destroyed, it often meant you lost your radar, which sat directly atop it, as well. Both were extremely small and hard to target. Even micro lasers were larger than the two of them combined. Replacements could be popped up if the entire head assembly hadn't been destroyed. If it had, the pilot either used their backup systems, which gave them visual through additional cameras, if they had them or opened their cockpits to see, risking themselves.

Will it go so far today? Will we see each other across the shields, nothing left between us? Well, brother, it's time to find out.

******

The doors opened for the twins to enter the battlefield. Both of them stepped off the raised platform but didn't move afterward. The operators stared in wonder. Every battle that had not been in action had been canceled. Those in progress were set to be secured as soon as a definite winner emerged. None of the operators, whether human or android, wanted to miss a single moment of this epic battle.

Neither of the twins could have known what the

other was doing yet. They seemed to be waiting for someone to make a move, so their own actions could come into play. This had been seen when they faced each other in other battles. Sometimes one would just forfeit to the other without a move being made. This time the operators were sure it was not going to happen.

Suddenly Nite shifted to the southwest and higher density of woods, and Mike moved for the higher level of mountains to the northeast. The game of chicken began. They were going to finish this battle.

It started out with them moving in and out of what was considered optimum range for an Abas battle. It was the most popular distance to fight at, for it was far enough not to endanger yourself while you didn't keep yourself from being too far to fire. It was middle range for most of the long-distance weapons and danced the edge of most close-range weapons.

The Gauss and the sniper, they both had up respectfully, were able to hit accurately at ten kilometers. The dual rifles lost power at eight kilometers. The coil rifles fell out about the same range. Their smaller hand weapons were only good for a kilometer distance for laser and five-hundred meters for hard rounds.

It was the missiles Mike neglected to get that gave Nite the greatest advantage in their dance between eight and ten kilometers. He was capable of reaching twenty kilometers with the MWMs and twenty-five kilometers with his LMs. Nite also knew that at this distance, it was possible for Mike to shoot them straight out of the sky with the PBCs, which were capable of twelve kilometers before the particles broke apart.

Neither of them wanted to fire at the other with such a long range between them. There was too much time between the shot and the target to get a second quick counter shot off in the direction of the defensive movement.

This meant the other could dodge and counterattack at a shorter, quicker distance before the first could move from the firing path. It would just be a countdown until one or the other finally got a hit. Time seemed to stand still and rush by all at once as the seconds felt like hours, but the minutes flew by.

Mike timed one of Nite's chicken moves just right and fired the first shots of the battle with two of his PBCs. This left him with his sniper laser to defend as he came to a standstill just before firing.

Nite countered with three Gausses rounds. One Gauss shot was able to destroy both blue-white lightning balls, giving a clear return path for the next two at the standing target.

Mike countered the two incoming Gauss shots with two more PBCs and sprinted to the left to find cover without turning his upper torso. The shots collided with a thunderclap, disintegrating each round with a bright flash of light and thunderous explosion that overrode the first. The onlookers sat in amazement at the accuracy of the two Abas.

The calls of "WOW!" and "That was too perfect a shot!" could be heard throughout those watching the live battle that had interrupted the old footages.

More and more people started to gather around the viewing screens throughout the school. As they did, they began to realize who the two Timber Wolves were; the two weird partners who were thought to be brothers as well were fighting each other. The undefeated had reached a point in which one of them would finally know the cold feeling of loss they forced on everyone else.

******

Mike moved to strafe his brother and circle around the low hills to cover his movement. As long as Nite didn't note the movement change during the flash, then he could circle to Lake Tedious and use it to get closer to the light woods while Nite was still posting near Lake Floure, hiding from Mike's height advantage in the surrounding light woods. It would take him about fifteen minutes to get through to the lake.

By then Nite would realize he had moved and would be looking for him while trying to remain hidden. Mike should be able to cover his movements enough to get closer to his brother.

Battlefield Engineers didn't design just one plan, but multiple plans that laid one atop the other, constantly shifting, depending on the way the rat ran through the maze. What the rat didn't understand, was no matter what way they turned, once they entered the maze, there was only one way out.

Mike knew he could set a few areas for traps before he reached his brother, and then he just had to lure him back into the pre-staged areas. He goal was to use already used traps to guide him to where he wanted. Nite would have to chose new or old even if he recognized what Mike had done.

******

Nite immediately picked up Mike's movements to the west through the mountains. He knew the second flash was coming and used the gauss rounds to get Mike to use it. Since Mike had given up his cover of the area, Nite changed course to cut the distance between them while Mike was blinded to his movements.

Now was the time to clear the plains between Lake Floure and Lake Dadar. If he was able to close in on the cliffs without Mike noticing him, he could catch him in the back from the side of the low hills while he crossed the plains to the light woods.

He would use the creek to sneak into Lake Dadar because the low hills near their opened into a clear valley around the creek that would give Nite an easy radar lock. With that, the MWMs would be in close enough range to split and prevent him from defending himself. They would tear into his brother's armor giving him the needed advantage to win the battle.

******

Mike caught a short tag from the radar when he hit a low dip in the mountainside. He only picked up a small blip that could have been Nite or just reflection from the rocky hills, but if Nite had circled around him, then they would switch advantages, and he could possibly be caught in the plains with his back to his brother's missiles.

Not knowing what side, he was on now, Mike had to change his direction again. He was forced to start changing plans.

The rat ate a hole in the wall. BAD RAT! BAD! Get back here!

Higher would be better with his brother giving up the hidden advantage for the cliffs, so he turned down a different path that followed the creek to the west and took him into a small range of higher mountains.

******

"The battle is too perfect. They fight is as if this was a choreographed dance," one of the female students commented while watching on the big screen in one of the lounges.

She was one of the few in the school who regularly fought both with and against the brothers. It was in the first of those battles where she had earned her medium Sentinel and was close to moving up to a heavy if someone else was knocked down. Knocking them down was why she went against the twins in the next series.

Not many could say they had fought successfully for and against them. She felt more of an expert in the second phase, if such a thing existed. She, unlike most, targeted the support members by getting them to turn against the brother's orders. That was the first move of creating chaos for them.

Not that they needed a team to win. They don't care about anyone enough to break their plans to go after them either. And the training they gave before the battles made their teams stronger individuals. These factors had to be considered as well. You had to find the right targets and turn them at just the right time. Influence them perfectly.

She wrote several papers on their tactics and how they inspired their followers. She fought against them first, breaking down several weaknesses in their fighting strategies. All of which they were able to correct during the battle and not repeat. She made one mistake in her plans. She planned on them making the mistake more than once.

Her best attempt happened when she led a small group of light Scouts against them from the rear while four larger Abas attacked the front. The scouts of the twins foresaw their tactics and flanked them into an easy crossfire where her scouts were fighting to two sides and lost quickly.

She had considered this one of the best tactics ever used against them, because she was able to get enough shots off to destroy their rear mounted long-range systems. Even without their long-range weapons, they again, proved their advanced aptitude. They killed every member of her team with perfect pilot slaying shots. They did this to administer as little damage to the Abas itself.

When it came time to finish her, the left her on the field with her Abas damaged, weaponless, but easily repaired. Even within the battlefield, she could have been operational again with the use of support trucks. As far as she knew, they only did that to pilots they respected as enemies, which were handful in the school.

She was named Subterfuge by a newly appointed instructor who returned to the school after early advancement to the position. The instructor had a special interest in the twins well before being advanced. Since advancing, Enlightenment and Subterfuge developed a pact to learn what they could about the twins and use their weaknesses against them.

Subterfuge had been working with her in gathering information on the twins well before she had been taken from the ranks of students. A relationship Subterfuge was glad and giddy to see did not end with the promotion.

It almost became an obsession with Enlightenment, but it was not for their defeat. It was a desire to understand them, see them for more than just their actions. With the lack of having the freedom of movement a student had, Subterfuge became her best tool and weapon for the gathering of the information while still hiding what she was learning.

Subterfuge's blond hair was just beyond her shoulders and highlighted her heart shaped face, round green eyes. She had light pink lips that seemed to shine naturally with her perfect makeup. Her nose was narrow and came to a sharp end, just as her chin did directly below it, giving her that very sharp, prestigious, knowledgeable, and commanding look.

She had a well-rounded rump, which might have come from the amount of free time she spent in a saddle, bouncing on the back of mount. It seemed even bigger surrounded by her slender figure, well developed legs, flat stomach. Her smaller top and narrow shoulders finished her triangle figure.

Subterfuge knew her taste lay with the women, not men. It might have been why the brothers were willing to use her again. She had no attraction to them outside the study of their performances from multiple sides. That didn't stop her from using her body to get what she wanted. She believed sharing the desires of men for women, she gained insight into manipulating them.

Using her body to gather information or gaining the suggestive command position on those appointed over her, male or female, was part of being an Abas Pilot. She was never ignorant of what her body, a few perfectly laid hands and suggestive movements would provide for her. It was like any weapon she carried. It was a tool to be used to advance her own needs, desires, and cachet.

Enlightenment returned to her previous school against the normal operation when one was selected for early instructor. It was said she had been placed with Falstar due to him being the most successful that had been selected for the same thing. It was hoped she would be treated more fairly. They, the Wolf Pack, also hoped the two would create a reasonable relationship that would lead to a new genetic offspring to set forth for Abas instructors.

Subterfuge felt she could comment honestly with her complete disgust at the thought of someone as beautiful as Enlightenment being bred with the likes of Falstar. It was not that Falstar wasn't physically attractive. It was that Subterfuge didn't like to see any beautiful woman condemned to a life with a man, especially one she had taken interest in herself.

******

The entire First Echelon and Second Echelon stopped everything within the first hour of the battle to watch the two Timber Wolves. Even professors with classes already active stopped their important teachings to watch what they felt would be a legendary battle.

The attention span of the children was lost, as

was much of the faculty. Someone streaking down the hall screaming "THEY'RE FIGHTING EACH OTHER!" at the top of their lungs, would normally be a small interruption. But only one battle would have another instructor performing an announcement like that.

As the word spread, more and more things were stopped. The students even stopped fighting in the simulators before the battles had a definite winner. Others put off homework or working out in the gyms, breaking cycles that had not been interrupted in years. The strangest ones were those who came straight from the showers and baths with their shower shoes and towels only. A few still had soap running down their legs or in their hair.

******

Hours ran by, and no one had gained any ground. The Abas seemed to become more and more mobile the longer the pilots had to work them. A few times, dodges seemed so acrobatic an Abas couldn't have performed them.

The pilots move the machines as they would have moved their own bodies. They rolled across the ground, flipped through the air, and traversed the lands as if they were two boys playing laser tag on a warm summer afternoon. A common game among the little ones. The armor of Mike took paint damage, much like grass stains in their cloth uniforms.

Nite's ghillie suit was more adapt for taking these small incursions. Neither of the Abas suffered any registered injury.

The entire body of the school continued to watch as the battle raged on. Different firing patterns went off, but nothing connected, no matter how precise the targeting. The counters were impeccable. Yet they never opened for a counterattack that connected. It was as if they were watching a perfect simulated battle. Even those were not this perfect.

Lasers taking lasers. Feints and faints so aligned the watchers weren't sure where who was going where. Even the Androids lost track of the Abas and had to scramble to find them.

The evening meal whistles were blown and secured. No one showed up to the normally scheduled meal, even though they could access it at any time. Thankfully, for the cooks had failed to prepare anything. They had not left the monitors since they found out the battles were raging.

The head chefs had not even scolded the assistants for not turning off certain foods that were now scourged to the pans. Such things would take their attention from the battle. It seemed as if every second, every move, every thought set the tides for someone else's advantage.

In the Packs' history, there had never been a battle, no matter how spontaneous, which took longer than a minute, that didn't have a bet going on it. No one took the time to look away from the monitors long enough to consider taking a bet or calling the odds. Even if they did, no one would respond for they were too busy watching to get the bets marked.

Twelve hours into the battle, and the Abas still had no contact. The morning meal sounded, and still no one left the viewing screens. Some fell asleep in their chairs, at their desk, or in the halls where they were standing when the monitors started showing the battle. The rest was usually short due to being jarred awake from others flinching at the close call of their chosen champion. The screens marked them red and blue, even though there were no such marks on their actual Abas.

The school suddenly exploded with roars of cheers and groans as the first and final hit was scored by the Blue Timber Wolf. The weariness had finally settled over the school. While the battle was perfect and entertaining beyond any they had seen, it was over. A hit had been scored. Their bodies couldn't last long enough to see who did it.

As they got up to move away from the tables, the signal for others entering the battlefield sounded. There was going to be more to the fight than what had already been seen.

******

Mike finally got the advantage over Nite when he circled around and above his brother in the high mountains. Nite was still in the lower hills. Mike was on the edge of the mountains looking down on the winding path. Nite would have to forge a different target to get him to open up.

Fatigue was setting in on both of them. Neither slowed in their movements or battling through the exhausting work. The battle had to end soon, or they would have to forfeit to each other. Even they had limits to how long they could physically perform at constant high speeds.

Then there was the second half of this battle to consider. Mike started to wonder about that momentarily. They could not do another five hours like this. It would take that long at least to bring is brother back into another trap like this one. They would be unable to carry on for the next battle they both knew was coming.

They showed too many of their talents in this battle to let someone study and find a weakness to defeat them. Whether together or separate, every trick, every move, every shot they could come up with had been used in this battle. If someone wanted to know what they were capable of, they just needed this one battle to analyze.

Even the two of them never pushed their boundaries this far. No one else had ever made them. And in doing so, Mike finally realized how much more they had to learn and grow.

Mike was sure his brother lost him during their last chase. He finally gotten to a point where he could close the gap. It was time to end the battle. It was time for the battle strategist to beat the tactician.

Nite's head popped over the hill but was gone before Mike could settle on it. It didn't matter. His brother was moving just as he wanted him to. It would be over soon. Too soon for his brother, but not soon enough for him, he was sure.

******

Nite picked up his brother in the dangerous pop-up. Mike had the advantage to either side of Nite's escape. He had to get to this point to end this battle.

Nite believed it was the only way to beat his brother now. It was dangerous. Nite immediately smiled at the thought of springing the trap before Mike could trigger it. Mike would expect it. He could only target for the trap or for the spring.

He took a few deep breaths as he brought his engines up to full throttle and let the Abas prepare to sprint past the first opening. It was the first step in the longest part of the battle that would be over in seconds. Someone was going to win. It was time.

******

A second shot for Mike, but again Nite sped by too quickly. His Abas shouldn't have been able to do that speed, especially with Nite as tired as he was.

Where is he getting the energy for this?

Mike realized his brother was trying to spring his trap early, so he could take him out. If Mike moved from his position, he could not protect his own retreat from Nite, and Nite would win.

Mike had to move to the edge of the mountain ledge and get a better view of the final shot area and catch Nite before he could trigger the last firing lane. Trying to hold the Abas on the edge of the mountain would give him a larger firing angle than Nite would expect and would leave his brother exposed while he tried to prepare for the final trigger of the trap. When he moved forward enough, Mike would get him while he prepared for the last spring.

******

The first shots slipped past Nite as he flung an arm out from his Abas. His brother had bitten hard on his ploy, but the hit was closer to the core than he had meant for it to come. If he tried to trigger the trap, he would have lost. He now took the advantage on his brother, forcing him to either move to expose himself to Nite or to watch for him at two different areas. The game had just turned to one of timing, and Nite was the better timer.

******

Mike moved as far as he could possibly move, struggling to maintain the proper footing needed after the shock of the full firing. As he concentrated on getting settled, Nite struck at the base of his feet. The loose rock crumbed under. Mike slipped down the mountainside to the level just above Nite.

Nite had raced around the corner to where his brother was still recovering. He fired three shots from his right DWBL into his torso armor, spreading the damage. Nite didn't know, but he had won before he had ever come around the corner.

Mike had taken severe damage to his foot actuator, which would have slowed him down enough for his brother to take him sooner or later. With the laser shots and advantage of speed, Nite had more than enough armor advantage over his brother to remain in the toe-to-toe combat and win.

Mike signaled his defeat by surrendering and offered salvage on his Abas. If they were out in the fleet, he just agreed to become Domestique for the protection of his Abas. Nite defeated him absolutely.

CHAPTER 33

BATTLE WITH THE BEST

"Four Zhayedans plus have entered the battle arena against you. Do you wish to forfeit or fight?" the female operator called over the communication system.

Nite knew the voice of Asyl as well as he knew it was her way to tell him what he would be facing. She had not spoken to him the entire battle against his brother. These first words were to bring his mind back to what he would be facing.

To forfeit now would be to lose after so much heartache and struggle. Nite wasn't sure if his body could take much more. He wasn't sure he could stand much longer.

Is my dream bigger than the limitations of my body? Is my mind weaker or have I reached my limit? I know how I feel, but I have a dream. Is my dream strong enough to become a need or will it remain a dream?

He wanted to say forfeit so badly. He opened his mouth to answer, and the words to continue came out. He felt his body tingle with renewed energy. He wasn't sure if it was anger or his body reaching into his reserves to pull out one last victory. Either way, he had enough energy to keep going just a little longer. If he was going to lose to exhaustion, then it was the hardest lost he would lose . . . to himself.

Nite had opened his battle armor to look at his brother. Mike did the same when he surrendered, showing the fight was over.

Are you ready?

Nite silently mouthed to his brother. Mike answered with a silent nod closing his blast shields. Being salvage to his brother, Mike was capable of continuing in the next fight on his brother's side.

They used Salvage like this when they faced Subterfuge. It was the closest they ever came to failing a mission. They had to use her people's equipment to shoot down the drop ship after they lost their ability.

They wouldn't have lost the battle. It was a bonus to get the ship. The original battle team never saw the drop ship, only the vaper trail of it's leaving.

It was something they agreed on once the fight passed eight hours over secret code. They would fight until one had the winning advantage and the other would give up. After that, the two would be free to fight what was remaining, leaving the last man for the winner to face alone.

The instructors aren't the only ones that can plan to use every advantage they get.

******

The first Abas Nite had detected came from the same gate he entered from the east side of the plains. He quickly took cover in the light woods to the south, and most likely moving into the deeper heavy woods and swamp lands. He would want to be close enough to move in if Nite was injured but not be in firing range of him at the same time.

Nite could tell it was Master Demagogue. He always tried to keep to hiding and sneaking around. He liked to lead by playing to the raw emotions of those who followed him, as well as those he faced.

It was Demagogue who taught the twins to fight by driving people's emotions on the field. He taught them to guide them where they wanted. Nite infuriated him so badly the last time they fought, Demagogue destroyed himself trying to get to Nite.

Nite picked the last of what was left of him clean before obliterating the cockpit in the simulator. Demagogue could be seen, looking out of it with such deep loathing, Nite wondered if he could see him through the abas. The headgear was shattered. He spit blood on his own visible shield, as if to block the site of his death from the stomping Abas foot.

The repair requirements were more than a completely new Abas. Only, having to fill out the paperwork to get a new Abas because yours was decimated in a simulated battle by a student was not something any instructor at any level was willing to file.

If he was the head of the heavy instructors and third in the school for rank. It was not going to happen. Such an act would almost guarantee him a position at some outpost guarding nothing for the rest of his time with no hope of higher recognition. He wouldn't even see a battle he could honorably die in.

Master Demagogue would bite on any chance to personally take Nite out. It left the worst taste in his mouth knowing he lost to someone whom he should have dominated. It was especially hard to swallow when the student subjugated him to defeat in one of his own masteries.

Nite was allowed to drop Demagogue's mastery title. A decision which had not been made yet. The gain of Honor Levels for defeating Nite, even under these circumstances, would be more than enough to make up for whatever he had lost during their encounters.

He will be hungry for this victory. Will those emotions play into the battle, or has he learned to burn them away?

The second entry came from the Northeast Gate. It wasn't a widely used gate because of the traitorous terrain. It came out just north of the Bailos Creek in the Ice Pond Valley. The pond up there was always covered in a solid blanket of ice no matter the temperature or time of year. The valley had been created to get up there to ride the rapids and skate the lake had some of the sharpest curves and narrowest passages. Some students used opportunities to get a Jumper brought in for special occasions during breaks to get there faster.

The terrain was perfect for scouts who would often use it for escape routes from the Scout-hunting Abas. Any of the larger elements, especially Zhayedans would have to struggle to make the terrain or have a special design to be able to handle it.

Nite knew it was the Giant Scorpion (HZh), or Heterometrus Swammerdami coming from the Northeast Gate which showed they were trying to bring it in without him knowing. The Scorpion would find its home in the loose rocks. Its ability to move quickly while shifting weapons from different areas gave it a great advantage in the northern terrain.

Raze teaches the light and heavy classes for Abas that are non-biped. We've had minimum contact with him. He must have been brought in to add a different feeling to the battle that I would not expect.

What would be the plan? Lure me into your territory and fight you where I have the greatest disadvantage. You saw us struggle on these mountains earlier on at least three different series. It's where I won, so I would feel this is more comfortable territory. Ah. So much to learn still.

Nite could not trust the same terrain on his two legs. The Timber Wolf could handle the majority of the terrains as well as any human. It did not have the advantage of six legs and the ability to climb straight up a mountain side or hold itself upside down and fire with perfect accuracy.

At least they are trying to conceal a little from me this time! Honestly, if I didn't recognize the radar fluctuations, I don't think I would have noticed you! Nite thought to himself as he marked the target.

"At least you can be honest with yourself." The female voice was clearer this time, but Nite was sure he had not spoken his thought out loud.

He was also sure he had not heard it come from his com channels even though he had heard it in stereo. Nite looked around the cockpit but couldn't find anything in the immediate glance around. There was no device that could have heard his thoughts, and he must have been imagining the voice as a play on his mind from being so tired.

Mike picked out a third signature in the heavy woods, moving closer to where they were sure the edges of the Black Lake were located. They forced and trapped some Abas into the lake before they realized what happened. The twins still had not been able to find all its edges, or if it was even just one body of water.

Mike peppered the Black Woods with several motion detectors while he had moved down there. It was a creation the three developed for Abas-sized movement to be tracked through there. They would not have known they were being tracked through the blackness.

By the movement of the pilot and the length and

height, it was the second Giant Scorpion within the school. This one was designed more for dense woods and underground fighting. She was also a classroom instructor for multiped Abas. Very few existed in Wolf outside the Scouts.

The pair were brought with Demagogue to the school because of the fire team's success together for so many years. Much like their Master, they had a lot to gain back from defeating the twins, although neither had faced them often. More of their losses came from betting against them.

The two of them were the deadliest of enemies to everyone but the twins. In the desert scenario, where they had the greatest advantage, they were treated like playthings. They burrowed under the ground and moved beneath the sand to strike. The high winds should have covered their movements.

Instead of being hidden to the twins, the brothers found a way to track them when they moved in a direction that was not with the wind. The deactivated warheads on a few missiles, as well as the radars, and set the engines to move with the wind. It made tracking them harder and counter fire near impossible.

The missiles pinned the scorpions to the ground while the thrusters continued to fire, looking for a target. The twins then torn to pieces with hard round fire. No one had ever seen anything like this tactic used. It made no since, but it worked out perfectly.

Calvary turned on her headlights and was trying to navigate without assistance of its radar. If she turned its radar on, the devices would have picked up the frequencies she was using and proved that for jamming and counter measures.

She's having to navigate with the eyes of the Abas and using lights to see enough not to enter the Black Lake. She's exposing herself to anyone in there. They must be confident no one has set a trap in there. They don't know about Mike's devices. If she clears the heavy woods, I can use missiles to fire on her from almost anywhere in the arena.

A fourth Abas came from the same gate as Master Demagogue, although neither Nite nor Mike had ever seen any movements like the pilot showed. They moved as if they had been seasoned over many years and had been in even more battles than both the twins combined. The Abas didn't seem to be piloting as much as it was just moving. The recognition of his own talents in piloting made him truly question who the pilot was.

It was something Nite and Mike saw on the view screens form only the best Abas pilots in the Pack. They learned to copy the flow by making themselves one with the Abas. Then improve it for themselves. It took the greater part of their training to get comfortable with the steady flows, but once they mastered the smooth operations as lights, they never had a problem converting it to the heavies.

Mike marked her as a potential danger. Nite highlighted the target, claiming the rights to fight it alone no matter the order it was taken. Mike took one of the two Giant Scorpions. Nite knew his brother would wait until Nite baited the closest one to Mike to reveal he was an active participant in the battle.

Once Mike took the northern Scorpion, the southern one could be destroyed with the advantage of height. His hiding place, like Nite's earlier, was exposed after Mike peppered the Black Woods.

Maybe they didn't realize what was in there and why I didn't return.

Nite turned his back to the northern Abas and started east to increase the distance between him and the Scorpions trying to close on his flanks. The move would look like he was trying to bring the Demagogue's Red Wolf to a lone battle or separate them from the trap.

Nite was sure they would have a second plan in case he noticed them. It was getting the other two to follow in and close in on Mike. Mike liked to get them close, almost too close for Nite's comfort when dealing with the deadly scorpions.

It's the design I have been working on. Never for me, but for someone that could be trained to be as good. The scorpion design . . . is probably the best.

******

The students who got up and started for their beds quickly took their seats and positions around the viewing screens. When they saw the battle hadn't ended with the defeat of one of the brothers, they, like Nite got a second wind. They wanted to see this come to an end. Less ammo, tired, but fully armored, Nite was either going to do the impossible or both were going to fail.

They saw most of that battle from the satellite view provided of the two Abas and the other several hidden recording devices arranged around the battlefield. With the instructors on the field, they could see into three of the four cockpits as if they were piloting them. The piloting screens on either side of the viewing screens came to life as each pilot started out of the gate.

The instructors' Abas always had recording devices so students could see how they did what they did in the cockpits. It was a modification that came with being an instructor. It was important for the students to be able to watch how they marked, set up different strategies and changed them as needed. The cameras even showed the pilot, but looking at them, you could only see the suit and how they looked around to see what was going on.

With four Zhayedans coming up against the victor of the unbeatable after the epic fight they just survived, it wouldn't be a battle but a slaughter. The question still remained, who was going to be the butcher and who was paying the blood bill.

******

The two Scorpions started their closing movements as soon as Nite showed he noticed their approach.

Nite disappeared into one of the mountain ranges' cave systems, vanishing from their radars. They knew if they entered into the cave after him, they would probably be walking straight into a trap.

They were designed to fight subterranean with great advantages, but not against those two. The brothers weren't the only ones that learned from past mistakes. They couldn't let him rest for any time without being hunted either. He may have entered there to play hide and seek with them while getting some rest.

The two scorpions started to move through the mountains, not entering the caves, but sending disrupting missiles down the tunnels. They also used sonic mapping systems to see if they could identify where the Abas was, but nothing popped unusual in the cave design.

"I have been chasing him through these mountains for half an hour now. I can't find any sign of him. He must have jumped into the Thain River," Raze from the Ice Lake called over the open coms.

"If I circle back around through the low path, I will be able to cut through the lower hills faster and hit him as he is coming out of the water," Calvary offered.

The pilot knew if Nite didn't know it was him, he would not know the speed and stealth at which he could move over the rocky terrain. Even the swamplands were easier to navigate for the arthropod Abas with its six-legged design. Water would not slow its design down.

"I thought his brother was somewhere around here?" Raze called back over

It sounded as if he might attack the already-slain Abas pilot. Demagogue didn't want him distracted. There was no way to know where Student 1321456. He might use his brother's corpse as a way to hide from the Radar or as a trap.

"His brother is not a factor in this battle," Demagogue chided the pilot. "Calvary, I want you to come a little closer to the light woods to be able to spring on him a little faster if he comes up that way. Make sure to stay clear of that cursed Black Lake. I don't want to lose you to it."

"I have never been trapped by such a simple thing," Calvary laughed as she changed the path of her Abas to follow Demagogue's orders.

"I don't think it is best to send them out against a position you are not sure he is even at," the resonating voice of an older-sounding female came across the coms to Demagogue.

The pilot was new to the school, but not to battle. Her voice held the confidence of her knowledge. She didn't know every battlefield she had stepped on, but she left all of them alive and still within Wolf. That was an accomplishment considering the battles she'd seen and the generals she stood against.

Demagogue looked over at her through his Abas without turning anything to show his movements. He outranked her as far as his position in the school. Still, this was not an Abas pilot to be considered an underling. He knew it would be smart to heed her words.

"Be careful, and don't go out into the light woods unless you need to. We will maintain where we are until we are sure where he is. We will have a little more ground to close on him, but I think you can hold him long enough for us to get there.

"Ultimate Munitions, I want you to take the point, and I will maintain six. If he is behind us, I don't want him finding out what you really are."

******

Rave didn't respond right away. Instead, he began his movements to maintain the high grounds over most the cave systems. With his missile system, he could respond to almost any opening from a cliff near here. He became more comfortable with the terrain, knowing if Student 1321456 were near, he would have attacked by now.

Raze noticed something strange. He was right. This was where the other brother went down, but there were not signs of him. He opened his coms to speak to the others.

******

An explosion around the base of the foothills aligned with a ringing blast that almost blew out the sound amplifiers of Master Demagogue's receivers before they could deafen the sound. He jerked in his Abas, throwing off even his footing.

"Rave must have tried to say something just before he was killed. By the looks of it, the rocks provided enough cover for the Abas to hide."

If that is the case, then Nite has perfect height advantage to target me. I have to get out of here!

Demagogue suddenly felt very small in his Abas. He was trapped between Lake Dadar, the cliffs and the light woods to the west.

******

Calvary sped her Abas backward as fast as she could. She could see the trees growing diagonally to the sky before she realized too late. She had backpedaled into the Black Lake. Her Abas sunk to the bull joint of her tail. There was nothing for her to do but try to keep her Abas as still as possible. If she sank too low before the end of the battle, she would not be able to be rescued.

She had to bury the clawed arms into the ground to keep the weight from shifting her down any deeper. Even if she got out of her Abas now, she could do very little on foot. She had already been submerged completely into the blackness.

One wrong step and she could be sucked under the water. Instructors, unlike students, were expected to stay alive till the end of a battle. The rescue team would not be sent until it was finished. If they died, then they make it less like to for Wolf to lose in a critical battle when the pilot may have made the same mistake.

How could I have made this mistake? I allowed fear of a student dictate my response and ignorantly did what I have caused plenty of others to do. What an idiot! Demagogue will never let me live this down.

******

Mike waited for the Scorpion to start its careful slithering movements over the edge, which would give it the greatest advantage across the mountain range. Then Mike detected the transmission being triggered. He could not allow the Scorpion to let everyone know he had moved. He fired his first volley into the rear of the arthropod.

******

The students couldn't see what was going on. Raze's screen went green, to show he was about to speak. Then the visual showed he went over the side of the mountain, breaking several larger rocks free to follow behind.

The scorpion slammed into the ground, blacking the screens almost instantly. The sounds were still on as the students listened to the heavy rocks slamming into the armor a few more times before that was lost as well.

They watched as the screen continued to show the rocks coming down. Then, without warning, an explosion that sent the rocks back up the mountain faster than they went down.

******

Mike wasn't sure if he had done enough damage to the Abas to finish it off until he saw the rocks going to the wrong way, followed by a jet of fire that erupt up over the lip of the mountain. Mike leaped into a small grotto, taking some superficial shrapnel damage in the quick retreat.

Then he heard the first sound of disaster over his own laughter. The first of the smaller crumbling rocks that followed him into the opening smacked off his armor has he leapt into the deepest point of the shallow grot.

Mike reached as far as he could get with his Abas before he squatted down for extra cover. He even pulled his rifles to put in front of the Abas to give a few more points of protection. Darkness quickly surrounded him. He didn't think he would ever hear again after all the deafening crashing of rocks and the reverberating pounding sounds.

When it finally settled, Mike turned on his lights. Dust caked most of his visualizers and had blocked him from seeing out clearly from the eyes of his Abas.

Cracking open the blast shields he discovered only one of the four light sets survived, but it was enough to show he had several cracks and dents in his armor. Even one of the heavily armored glass sets under the armor was cracked. He lost his left arm actuator and somehow hurt his left shoulder as well. His legs didn't suffer any damage, which Mike was sure if they had, he would have never made it in enough before he was crushed by the mountain.

There was still a small opening above him to allow his Abas to stand erect. After exiting the cockpit, he saw the cave had a new opening to his right. It was large enough for him to squeeze through, but there was no air or light to tell him how deep or long it went. There was nothing else he could do for his brother with his Abas. He was stuck in this tomb until someone won and the rescue teams dug him out.

Mike powered as many systems down to stand-by as possible, and then settled in for a good nap in the remaining safety of his cockpit.

At least one of us gets to get some rest.

CHAPTER 34

GRIM INTRODUCTION

Nite heard the explosion and felt the earthquake even under the water. He lost contact with Mike. That was shortly after the explosion. Still too long for him to be the one who went up. It was the rockslide following the aftermath that bothered Nite about his brother's silence.

He had no choice but to come closer to the surface and potentially give away his slowly gained position. He sent up a small bar that would extend his radar picture for ten kilometers around him but would appear to be less than a walking stick coming out of the water.

Nite barely broken the surface tension of Lake Floure when he saw the flickering around the second Red Wolf on his radar. He hadn't quite caught what happened, but it seemed to be shorter than the design was ever meant to. It was also a little wider. Then the radar image went back to its normal size.

Must have been the water on it messing with the readings.

It had ventured farther from Master Demagogue and, respectably, Nite as well, coming closer to the middle of the plans between Lake Dadar, Lake Floure and Lake Tedious. The position would have been a weakness if Nite was still in the mountains.

It gave enough distance to counter the shots if the pilot was good enough. It also meant I would have to expose myself to get close enough to fight without having the advantage of cover I often prefer if they are that good.

Nite was even more uneasy with the pilot now. Whatever it was, it was not a Red Wolf as it appeared to be. It had also not exposed itself to Nite either, which meant it had a pretty good idea of where he would be coming from. Nite didn't want to admit it under the circumstances, but he started to like this other pilot.

Either I am tired enough to read meaning in their motions or they are trying to tell me something. I don't think I'm that tired any more. Could I be reading into this though?

Nite turned off all his radar and only had his one secure line with his brother on when he broke the water. He secured it and went for the light woods across the eastern beach and the small gap of grass lands.

The strange pilot made the slightest torso turn. It could have fired but didn't bother to bring its tracking radar up. From that distance to fire without it was a sign of great confidence.

Nite vanished into the stretch of woods that almost seemed to reach out to him as he crossed the beach. He knew he could have fired on Demagogue. He had a great position on him, but to do so may have given the other pilot a chance to attack as well.

Maybe she didn't see me! No, she saw me, and she knows I know as well.

"She saw you, but Demagogue failed to take notice fearing that you would attack him from the mountains. His own bad placement showed you this."

The voice was there and stronger than ever, but Nite didn't have time to figure out where it was coming from. His heart was threatening to pound out of his chest. He would have easily countered the weapons it was capable of firing, if it were a Red Wolf. But that would have cost him time to escape and might have drawn him into a split battle. With a pilot that good and Demagogue on its side, it would only be a matter of time before he lost.

All he knew of his brother was that he was resting. *At least one of is gets to get some sleep.*

******

Master Demagogue hadn't changed his slow course over the last two hours, yet he hadn't been keeping an eye on the rear. Since the explosion, he had been checking the skyline of the mountains, waiting for something to come to the edges. If Student 1321456 had been trapped, the operators would have told them.

It would have been a victory of sorts, but one without actual win allowed. More like a stalemate. They had not defeated him, merely trapped him in the mountains. It was survivable and escapable. And then the two remaining pilots would be expected to fight it out.

Calvary was able to get her Abas secured. The rescue team was sent to prevent her from losing her Abas in here as well, but she was removed from the battle. They already announced Raze is dead. They must have cleared the brother's remains as well.

Ultimate Munitions has not spoken in forever, but she's within visual. Where did the boy go? What is he up to?

Demagogue stayed in the first level of light woods splitting the distance between the plans and the heavier wood lands. Ultimate Munitions continued to stay within the middle of the plans, as if inviting Student 1321456 to attack her.

Considering what she really was, it wasn't that bad of an idea. Only, Student 1321456 would not fall for the trap. Student 6541231 would have planned something in the attack and lured them into a trap. He would have planned to counter the strategy presented.

But not 1321654. He will keep you guessing while he watches you patiently, waiting for that one little mistake. Then strike at your heals and shoulders, weakening yourself. You will make more mistakes. He will strike again and again until you give him the kill shot, and then all will end, quick and easy.

Where are you? You have to be watching us. You must be waiting. I am not going to make a mistake to lure you out. I tried that before and lost my Abas. Let Ultimate Munitions be the one that does that this time.

Ultimate Munitions moved to the farthest distance she could keep with her masquerade but continued to try and push the limits as if she was trying to build a distance between her and Demagogue instead of closing them. The old woman had patience and could wait for her prey to come to her if it took hours. She would stand in the middle of the field until he revealed something.

Yet, those like her were all a little different. A little more crazy than other Abas pilots. It wasn't that they were trained that way. Master Demagogue was sure it had something more to do with how much of their mind had to be attached to the Abas' actions to really operate the beast she piloted.

Master Demagogue watched her turn her Abas back briefly, probably to tell him to speed up his pace without saying it over the net. Yet she seemed to be looking directly at him, as if signaling something. Master Demagogue was starting to wonder why he accepted her on this mission.

It is an advantage to have her, but is it really worth it? Why is she looking at me? Why did she create this angle between me and the plans? It is not an advantage unless . . ..

******

Nite closed on Demagogue's rear. He was close enough for him to be right on the outskirts of optimum range. Demagogue's slow movements were lining him up perfectly with where Nite had needed him, but a few more meters were still needed.

Nite could wait. It wouldn't be long. The truth of the other Abas would be revealed for Nite to know what he was really facing.

Four Heavy Zhayedans plus? *Demagogue has not picked me up on his radar.*

The trees opened for Nite to have a firing lane on Demagogue now. Nite sped up a little more to ensure he would be able to strafe fire as his torso turned and walked through the channel. There was no need for him to give his position away until he could hide again.

Nite went for the move, but Demagogue caught the radar signature of his fire control system as it lit up his Abas. The lasers just missed him at their maximum range as he ducked behind a set of trees he had been hugging. The trunks exploded, but the wood damage wouldn't do much to the Abas concealed behind them.

Master Demagogue laughed over the coms.

"I have a treat for you, Student 1321456."

"I have something for you as well. Why don't you come out and we can share them together?" Nite responded with a hiss.

"It is too bad that your brother didn't live through the avalanche. It was a good plan for you to use your battle salvage like that. A little stretch on the salvage rules, and those of the . . ."

He paused as he fired at a shadow where he thought Student 1321456 might be. Two lasers jumped out from sixty degrees off where Master Demagogue fired ripping into his right side. He took a little damage in the right torso, but it was nothing as to what the Timber Wolf could have unleashed on him.

"Salvage," he finally finished his sentence with a little more tone of annoyance.

Student 1321456 has a much larger arsenal. If he had such good targeting on me, why did he not used it all? Unless he had and had missed, and the rest ended in the woods.

Demagogue laughed again. He had worked a little under Student 1321456's skin.

It is time to really infect his being!

"Would you like to hear what I am going to call you when I am done?" Nite asked, giving away his position.

Another mistake; showing his failings in this battle. The loss of his brother must have greatly affected him. Or the weariness had.

Haven't we tried sleep deprivation battles before? He didn't make mistakes like this. But he didn't fight that hard either. It does make a difference.

"You may tell me what I am going to name *you*!" Master Demagogue laughed again, trying to draw him in closer for the attack. The game was his to win now. He didn't need the others. They were just in the way.

"Master Domestique. That is what I am going to call you, so everyone will know you had to submit to me. And in turn, I will order you to submit to everyone else. You will be the highest-ranking servant in the school," Nite laughed.

Master Demagogue had fallen into a pit of rage, but his secret weapon was closing as fast as she could, and that kept him from rushing forward. He had to maintain the link as long as possible.

Nite waited for Demagogue to close within seventeen hundred meters when he fired the first set of MWHMs. The first two salvos were racing toward Demagogue with two more fired from an almost twenty-degree different location. Nite continued to fire them in sets of two and moving until twelve missiles were racing toward Demagogue.

Seventy-two mini-missiles ripped out of the exploding missile body as Demagogue's two sets of twin APLs fired on it. With the little ones released from the core missile at such a close range, the lasers were overwhelmed.

They tore into his armor in a peppering factor while his defense system broke off to continue the fight against the dozen. Master Demagogue tried to move for cover like he had for the lasers with no avail. Unlike the lasers, these had the tracker to guide them to their target.

Master Demagogue had realized too late Nite was trying to pull him in for these missiles when he had fired the lasers. He lit off his accelerator booster system and turned to run out of range of the missiles. He knew he had no hope of escaping the larger ones, but the smaller ones could only go a hundred meters before they would lose their forward momentum. The first were already closing on him when the black gravity balls ripped past him.

The second set of missiles were taken out. The third had not been affected by the explosion and were even able to steer clear of the dangers within the explosion. The APLs failed with the increased explosion so close to the Abas and the rolling pattern that the missiles entered after the explosion. The front of the missile penetrated deep into the armor before releasing the mini missiles at close range.

The Abas' back was torn open as if a giant bear had sliced into the back of a fish while it knocked it to the shore. The APLs were gone, and he had lost his primary power supply. If it wasn't for the governing computers stopping the mini warheads from blowing up, he would have been completely destroyed.

Master Demagogue ignited the drive engine one more time with the cold blast to get the extra speed into Abas. This time it failed. The hoses broke free. As he fired the nitrous oxide into the small compartment, the engine was frozen solid.

Several whistling blasts could be heard as the missiles turned up and exploded safely in the sky.

Master Demagogue was marked dead. The damage was done. He would have no choice but to file the paperwork for an entirely new Abas this time.

Master Demagogue took a few deep breaths before he realized he hadn't been shut down yet. He knew someone in the control center would only keep him alive for one reason. He could signal pulling the brick, and if he did, he could injure Nite with what was left of his Abas. He looked out into the woods and could see something approaching. It wouldn't be long now. The missiles and destruction covered his cockpit in soot and scratches.

******

Nite saw why the Abas didn't look right. With the almost-complete destruction of Master Demagogue, the charade of the last Abas was dropped. Nite was no longer just facing another seasoned Red Wolf, but for the first time outside of the simulators, he was facing a true Dire Wolf.

This Elite Abas was created by Garthian, the primary Triscifield Abas Designers for Wolf Pack. In the Packs, there was an Elite Abas that carried the name of the Pack, but it was not required by an Elite that had made it within that Pack. There were other designs that were not based on the Pack's private and specific designs. Very few pilots took the general designs open to any pack.

Yet the Dire Wolf was different. Only the most

renowned of the Elite, even those from Wolf were allowed to have one. The original design of the Dire Wolf came from Murchadh's personal design. His was the first Dire Wolf.

There was a reason this one had been called the Dire Wolf. It was one of the widest and most heavily armored of all the Elite designs. In addition to its weapon placements on the Abas, it was still able to carry four rifles, half dozen short weapons, and another two long blades. Most the time, a long blade was used to replace a rifle for those that preferred to use those types of weapons.

Elites had the option to carry them without giving up one of their rifle slots. There was only one real option when you stood toe-to-toe with a real Elite Pilot on the battlefield and you wanted to live . . . RUN! Nite wasted no time to follow this mentality while he thought of what to do.

Elite Abas, even the Dire Wolf, were not so rare that an individual would be known by the design of the Abas. Yet each was as individual as the pilot that earned them. Elites were the rarest design of the Abas. Nite was sure, no matter the outcome of this battle, he would never forget this design. If he had a nightmare from his childhood, a monster so great nothing could defeat it, the Dire Wolf had just brought it to flesh and bone.

It took a mind beyond most to even try to enter one, and that was only after the council approved it. If they brought this one in to fight him now, Nite wondered, for the first time, if he ever had a chance of winning this battle.

The entire layout of the battle made more sense now. Of course, they would close down on him and force him to fight what he thought were two Red Wolves. Mean enough on their own, but the addition of a Dire Wolf into the mix was beyond believable. With it on the field, it was like sending an entire squad, not just a section, after him.

Or this is marked as a squad battle to prove who should lead the squad. If I am the fifth, Mike was the sixth. The Dire Wolf makes it a squad instead of a section, which meant all its members are allowed to fight. Members can team up to support someone they believe in.

"Are you going to tuck your tail into your legs and run like a beaten dog? Or are you going to claim what you have wanted since the night you met Dracon?" the woman's voice asked as if she were sitting just behind him.

Nite felt a shiver run down his spine. He was about to find out if he was as good as he thought he was.

"We're going to fight. We're going to win! I just need to regroup to think of my next plan now that the moves have changed."

CHAPTER 35

ULTIMATE MUNITIONS

"I see the façade I have been hiding under is finally over," the female voice came across the coms.

They knew where the other one was one. At least in general. Her talking to him didn't give Nite any advantage. If anything, it only built a connection between them, making it harder for him. He already liked her from what she had done before.

And now it makes more since as to why? I was right about the message in the movements.

"Allow me to introduce myself. I am Ultimate Munitions. I am using my Dire Wolf Configuration Bravo. I will send it to you. With it, we will both be familiar with what we are up against. I hope we can agree this has set the playing field back to even between us."

"Of course it has," Nite added facetiously.

Then he remembered that he wanted to stay on her good side for now. She had several chances to draw attention or do something to but had not. She was acting honorably in an unhonorable situation.

"I am Student 1321456, the unnamed of Timber Wolf Academy under Headmaster Falstar. I am using a modified configuration of my Bravo listing for the Timber Wolf. I hope for you to understand we are not on equal footing, but I believe it is a fair fight," Nite responded with all the formality he could muster.

The Elite stayed out of range of both their weapons with Nite buried deep in the light woods. Nite moved out from his hiding spot so they could look at each other. It held minimal coverage over the destroyed trees blown to pieces during his battle with Master Demagogue. He was sure it was enough for him to disappear when needed.

Nite was sure she knew he was sneaking up on Master Demagogue and allowed it to happen. She probably shot the missiles out in fear they were coming for her, but after she saw the other two roll around the explosion, she knew they were going for him. On initial fire, it would have been better aligned for her.

"Honor is a furious lover. I hope you will respect those who deserve it and don't deserve it after this battle. There are times when even the most honorable have to act another way to be able to bring about the right ending."

She spoke with knowledge behind her voice. Nite felt as if he was listening to a wiser version of Master

Raven. Even now, Master Raven could give Nite and Mike a run for their money on his master skills, and Nite had no doubt hers lay well within her Abas.

All Elite pilots' talents laid within their Abas first.

Nite felt suddenly drained of energy. Then he realized his Abas had shut down.

"They can't cheat me now. Not when I am facing someone of true integrity!" Nite yelled into his Abas. "Please, baby, power back online. They will not cheat us of our great victory."

******

"What do you mean his Abas has powered back up?" the well-dressed cyborg yelled at the operator in front of him.

She just turned back from confirming the orders and had to change it. He didn't seem to grasp that cheating one of their own for someone they didn't know did not sit well with them. It might have been better if the Android wasn't so excited about the Abas powering back up.

The cyborg was taller than Falstar. About twice as wide in the shoulders but didn't appear to have an ounce of fat on him for his elder years. He grew a grey mustache down to the base of his lower jaw line but kept it clean shaven between the grey lines that surrounded his lower lip and after them to his ears.

"Sir, we initiated the overheating sequence as you ordered, but the Abas seemed to have overridden our commands," the pale operator almost whispered her response again.

Unlike the cyborg, she picked up on the undertones. She looked even paler than usual under her short highlighted brown hair and innocent large blue eyes. Her hands trembled as they wrung each other out, waiting for his next command.

"Remove the safeties on the Dire Wolf. I want her firing live for all shots. If she kills him, then so be it!" the cyborg commanded harshly as he sat back in the command chair in the center of the room. "Likely, he will just need to be converted."

"Sir, if we do that, we will have to remove all the safeties of the Abas. Anyone on the field could be killed," the senior commander replied with a little more life in her.

It was not a time she could hold her emotions back, and she might have to answer for it.

"I don't believe I asked you, did I, *operator*," he slurred the word as if it were a dirty, disgusting thing to say or call someone. "I am the one in charge here. You will follow my orders. Turn the weapons on the Dire Wolf only," he commanded again.

His voice was ice now. It contrasted with his rage burning face as he watched his great plan failing. This was not the first time Student 1321456 had ruined someone's well thought plans. It might have been the first time they were so dangerous, especially to others not them.

The operator looked from the man to Falstar.

Falstar didn't look at the man or the operator; he had his vision locked on the view screen in front of him, from behind the man, but nodded for the operator to follow his orders. The operator turned back and hit a sequence of buttons to arm all the Abas on the battlefield. The safeties would no longer protect them.

She had been watching the twins since they got here. She refused to allow this being, no matter his rank, to attack them without it being equal. They suffered enough from the orders of those appointed to teach them. Yet, no one had ever tried to outright kill them.

And becoming a cyborg might be worse than death for them!

******

"All safeties have been removed from the battlefield. I repeat all saf—."

The operator's cold and unemotional voice was suddenly cut off, but the message got through anyway.

There was nothing that could be done from here out. The battle had to continue unless both Abas powered down and forfeited. Or both of them fought to the death.

"I don't know why we are on live fire, but we still have a battle. Do you wish to continue knowing the stacks?" she asked as if it really were Nite's choice.

Nite knew Ultimate Munitions could not have

come through any of the five schools he knew of. These schools didn't exist until after the last Crusader Olympia in 663. Their true purpose for existence was still unknown to the twins. But the building was started before the Crusader Olympia, since the first graduation was in 665.

It didn't matter which school you went through though. The rules of battle remained the same. Even in other packs, they remained the same. It left Nite to think she was offering him a way out.

"Life or death? The destruction of my Abas or yours? One in the same, same as the one. You, of course, know I can't hold back from this fight. I might have to kill you," Nite responded this time with a little more spunk than he had intended.

"Got a little spirit in you. I like that. This is not my first battle, but I did not have to face such stakes at your age. You are given the choice with no loss of honor or name. The battle may be continued under better conditions without the true loss at such a young age."

Nite could hear in her voice that she knew one of them was going to die today if they continued, and she had no intentions of it being her. He spent several moments truly thinking it over even though he knew his answer. The stakes deserved the time of consideration.

"I have a brother in the school. I would appreciate it if you would watch over him if I don't make it out. He doesn't need me, but it is always nice to have someone looking out for you." Nite simply closed the coms.

It didn't matter what she said. If she won, Mike would kill her anyway. He just hoped her watching over him would give her some kind of warning. She earned that much.

******

"You were only supposed to turn on the safeties of the Dire Wolf. Why are both of them now active?" He yanked the operator's chair around to face him.

His face was haggard with emotion. The fear streaked across her face before she could get her emotions under control enough to answer him. She took a deep breath and spoke as quickly as she could.

"I can't turn off just one Abas. It has to be all of the Abas on the field."

She took another deep, calming breath. She didn't need the oxygen, but it gave her a calming moment. Fear turned to courage since she had collected herself enough to speak.

"The system was designed to protect the Abas pilots NOT KILL THEM!" the senior operator finished with a yell at the end.

It was not her job to protect those under her, just to ensure the command monitored and responded appropriately depending on the assignments. Protection was the job of a warrior or a guard. The only other warrior in the room was Falstar and it was impossible for him to step in right now. It left the decision to the Senior Operator who was directed the question.

The man let go of the first one and grabbed the other woman by the throat and yanked her out of the operation seat. The belt that held her in the seat snapped clean through, tearing part of her pants away with it. She could feel the blood welling up across what felt like scratches.

His height was well over two meters (6' 8") where she barely reached fifty centimeters (20") shorter than he stood. Her arms locked around his wrist and hit different points of his arm, hoping to break the death grip while her toes struggled to find some kind of footing to get her weight on to attack from.

A normal human would have lost consciousness by now. A normal human wouldn't have been able to pick up an android like that either. If either of them were trying to hide, both were exposed.

The operator's face had started turning blue before the man slammed her across the floor into the opposite wall.

"Don't ever disrespect me like that again, you little desecrated konoama. Your bloodlines, created or otherwise, are not worthy of being called in with Wolf's. You are a common mutt robot."

He went to cross the room for her again, but Falstar held his hand out as he stepped in front of him.

"Sir, you have made your point, but please, do not

abuse my staff. I will reprimand her farther if you feel it should be done.

"Until then, if you do not like the way she is commanding the operations of the system, you are free to operate it yourself. I do not have any better than her. If she can't, then no one else on my staff can either."

Falstar held the fierce gaze of the man with a respectful but strong gaze of his own. It was like holding the gaze of a snake, waiting to see if it would strike with its deadly blow. One would have to break first.

The cyborg broke it, turning to look at the panels. It was no secret he was a cyborg and an Abas pilot, although he was not yet marked as Dragon.

He still had to answer to the rules of the Pack he came up in. During his upbringing, he never wasted his time to learn such insignificant things. Even now, he thought the knowledge would be wasted time if merely seconds to upload into the computer part of his mind.

He was unsure if he was being lied to, though. It might have a human appearance and reactions, but the cybernetic mind kept it from truly being human. He looked at the android one more time, trying to find some signs that would show him it was lying.

The problem with circuits, no matter how human they are programmed to be, they are still circuits. What logical end are they working toward? And in that logic, would sacrifice be required by you or them? And if them, will it be a real sacrifice.

Due to his lack of knowledge, his actions could be considered an act of great shame. He decided to back off and get his heart rate to settle. He signaled for the bloody operator to return to her chair, which she did with great speed, refraining from touching the swelling and bleeding areas of her face, legs, and arms.

******

Ultimate Munitions volunteered for the orders bringing her against these twins. Even out in the fleet, there were rumors of these two students. Curiosity drove her to find out if what was said was true about them.

When I arrived at this school, I wondered if the rumors were half true, what kind of students I would be facing. Now I see the rumors for once was an understatement of their actual ability.

These children were created for the invasion and more. So much more, they don't understand their true purpose. M. was right. This is the greatest potential for our needs. I may have to kill him . . . just a little bit to see if we are right.

There has to be truth in the rumor of where they actually came from. Since the rumor is only at the highest of secret levels, I will have to consider them true as well. It is not often the War Council will not speak openly about something.

Little one, if what I believe about you is true, then you will not die, even if you are defeated, but you may have to run a little early. For this, I am sorry. For this, I will give up all Honors and run with you if need be.

But for now, let's see what your made of.

She let out a sigh. It was time to test this one's skill level, not admire what they accomplished. If she killed this one, then they could make another. They still had the second one anyway.

And if I die? I have been wondering that for long enough. Today isn't a bad day to find my answer. But if they are who and what I think they are, then should I . . ..

CHAPTER 36

DARK WATERS

Nite and Ultimate Munitions started a standoff much like he and Mike. The eternity of time elapsed seemed to have drifted to the back of his mind. There was only one thought there now.

How do I destroy the Dire Wolf?

His outer ring was empty, but he had expended them wisely enough. It would look like he was firing the last of his ammo, lightening his Abas. Likely to be faster against the last Red Wolf. They were fast even when weighted down.

Nite had all his lasers, which gave him a high destructive power on their own. His Gauss rifle would get one clean shot before they realized he still had it, and he didn't have too many rounds left with it anyway.

The Dire Wolf is carrying four gravity cannons able to reach out eight kilometers before the antimatter collapsed on itself. She has to be very accurate with them as well.

She hit my missiles at max distance and only those that hadn't turned toward Demagogue.

Her ten APLs would be able to rip down any missile fire I tried to unleash on her. I doubt they would even get close enough to trigger them unless I got closer than I wanted to the Dire Wolf before firing them.

If the four gravity cannons weren't enough, she also has twin PBCs placed into her left arm. A rotating tri-barrel coil gun was fixed to her right. The tri-barrel was cut down to four-kilometer fire range to keep from the coil flux from interfering with each other. But it could continue to put rounds down range at a firing rate of sixty rounds per minute.

If that wasn't enough, each arm also has two sets of DWBLs hard mounted like little axes on either side of the squared muzzles. Did I mention enough armor to walk through a city without moving for buildings? How do you fight this?

Nite would have to hit her hard and quick while drawing her into his own ranges and keeping her from tracking him while he dropped out of hers. She knew this as well. She could counter by staying in the open fire lanes and making him cross to trade fire.

If I got close enough to not be hit by the coil gun, and successfully countered the rest of her fire, I might be able to use the last of my missiles to clear shots to put her down. That would be difficult for even me. Am I willing to bet my life on being that much better than her?

No. I need another option. Next bet, figure out if she knows the terrain as well as I do.

Nite was running out options other than killing her in one shot. Something he didn't think was possible with the heavy amount of armor she was capable of carrying.

He finally decided he would pick her apart as fast as he could, if the opportunity presented itself, but he would have to kill her. If she was able to even get one shot on him, he might as well be happy with the life he had lived so far.

He made the first move, dropping deeper into the woods and went silent. He didn't need his Fire Control Radars Systems for what he was planning. He was going to use her radar signatures to track her down and fire on the center of the location.

Hope she doesn't shift her radars to confuse her location.

******

Ultimate Munitions saw the student disappear from her screen as she circled a thick patch of woods.

He went deeper into woods to get me closer. Very good. It was your best move, but you don't know, I helped design this battlefield.

She would have used the same tactic if the roles were reversed. She saw it used several times against her on other planets with this type of terrain. It was why she had added it into the design all the APLs. They would help to fight at extremely close range.

It was, however, the first time someone secured all their radars. For them to get that close and see her meant he had his center armor opened and his blast shields raised.

Or he's going to use his local visual and hearing to track me. He might try to read my radar. That isn't a skill most at his age would be able to do successfully. And he has been going for a while. He might be dropping back, hoping to have me wait for him while he rests.

She couldn't say it was because his life wasn't truly on the line. People tried this kind of stupidity on her before as well. Not in this combination of terrain. Only when in a simulator as well. It made sense for him to lure her closer, but not too close. With his radar off, she would have to be almost right on top of him for him to get accurate enough fire on her Abas.

She could have made a move for the high grounds and forced him out, but it was on her to hunt him, not the other way around. She was the Elite. She needed to come to his game to win. By backing away, she was admitting he was better than her on his grounds. Something an Elite didn't like to do with anything other than another Elite.

A small smile creased her face.

This will be fun! There is no way for you to track me either, my little friend. We will play the darkness game together.

She laughed to herself as she secured her own radars to prevent him from using them to tracking back on her. Visual and hearing was the only way either of them would see each other now.

******

Nite saw her blink offline. She realized his plan of attack within seconds of his first move. It didn't matter. With both their radars secured and neither of them carrying EMS detectors, it would be impossible for them to track each other outside of signs, visual and hearing. This was a hunter versus hunter game now. Who was the better stalker?

She might give him his one-shot kill if she opened her blast shields to see with her own eyes. He didn't want to take the easy way out with her. She deserved to live. Nite wondered if he though she deserved to live more than him?

The disadvantage was still to Nite, but Nite had been at greater disadvantages before. He dropped back a little more to a deep pond that was barely large enough to hide his Abas squatting. He had the home field advantage, and in this game of cat and smaller, friskier cat, it was the greatest one.

******

The students were still glued to their seats. This battle seemed as good, if not better than, the ones with the brothers against themselves. And this one had a Dire Wolf. It wasn't common to see them in the schools even as instructors. If she was playing in the games, she had to be coming here as an instructor.

Most Elites, especially Dire Wolves, were

rewarded to students after the End Games by the War Council. Once you were in an elite, you had to have private lessons. It was not like school, where you were being graded. You were being molded into something that was not . . . normal. It was said you were becoming the next thing to a god!

You wouldn't be able to receive the training in school because all you did was Elite Training. All the Pack's Elite's trained together, or at least that was what the rumor said. It was because Elite's should know each other since they are their only equals.

Learning to pilot an Elite Abas was like learning to pilot a Zhayedan from a Scout. It was honorable negotiations to have at least two to three Heavy Zhayedan's fielded for one Elite on the other side. Now one of their own was stepping on the field one-on-one after a grueling battle. An undefeated, recently proven best one. The one that destroyed instructors and . . . well, was their elite pilot.

They knew this was a lifetime memory in the making. One they would always be able to reflect on. One that would mark their life and this battle seemed to be its collimation. The perfect focal point at which all things would be seen and measured.

The fight moved into the Black Woods. The trees grew tall enough for any two Abas to stand atop each other and walk under their lowest branches untouched, as well as wide enough for any six Abas to pass without any touching. Yet no light penetrated into this area. It was the most dangerous area in the Arena.

The cameras in this area were designed for the darkness. It was still hard to find an Abas if you didn't see them moving or catch a close sight of their armor. Using radar was normally reduced to short range due to the random planting of the trees causing too much feedback, but no one went in there without some type of sensor on.

Normally command could track them with their radar signatures or other EMF. But both had secured these. Even with the special equipment, finding them seemed impossible.

No one saw where Nite went. They could find the Dire Wolf easy enough. It was blasting its lights to search for Nite every few seconds. Then it would vanish into the darkness before it lit it up again in a new area.

The lights were bright and sent in every direction. It would have been a beacon to where the Abas was if the lights didn't blind the students for the same seconds it was meant to blind Nite. By the time which was plenty of time for the pilot to attack.

******

Nite saw the fifth flash light closer to his area. The swamp pond was covered in leaves and looked like it was solid ground, especially in the dark, and it was shallow enough and small enough no one would have noticed it walking by, or even through, if they didn't slip. They would have thought it no more than a gorge.

Nite marked its location near Lake Cherish a long time ago but had never had the need to use it. There was always something like this on the field. Sometimes several, but not all of them could support a heavy Zhayedan.

Nite waited for the sixth flash of light to give him an idea of where to raise and fire. As soon as the light dissipated, Nite raised with a quick slowness just high enough to fire from his hiding place. He didn't wait to see what had happened or if he hit. He dropped back down into the pond and hoped the water had settled over before she looked in this direction.

******

A flash of red lights zipped through the darkness in a tight bunch. The operators' auto cameras followed them right into the left arm of the Dire Wolf. The impact rocked the Abas toward its right side, but Ultimate Munitions' ability to pilot her Abas stabilized and turned to fire on the target but saw nothing.

She looked into the trees, wondering if Nite might have had some Tutevibians working with him in secret. It was unlikely since they were not in these schools. The shots seemed to come from nowhere. The damage she suffered hadn't come from nowhere.

******

"What is the battle damage?" the man yelled at the operator.

Her face swelled around her right eye. She could not see out of it. Instead, she direct connected to the council, showing she was not human. But she refused to allow this cyborg to abuse another. She refused to allow him to get to the last brother. The blood finally stopped and dried. The streaks still marked her once-beautiful face.

Her speech was slurred a little from the dizziness the impact with the wall caused, but she shook her head and answered a little more smoothly.

"Left arm weapons are destroyed. Left Arm severed and dropped by the pilot. No other damage has occurred from the attack. All lighting systems are still functioning."

"FIND HIM! Report his position to him. YOU ARE NOW HER BATTLE COMMAND!" he yelled at the operator, gripping the handles of his seat.

She flinched back a little. Falstar's hand was on her shoulder before she saw him approach. She turned from the screen and started to check the areas to find Nite. As long as she didn't have an obvious location on where he was, she refused to report him.

******

Ultimate Munitions heard the call come across

that battle command had been shifted to the General Brazen's control. She shook her head. She knew General Brazen must have been in the command center the entire time.

He had been furious to let his only Dire Wolf go from real battle to retire to the schools and decided to come and see her settled in. They had not been close. He was supposed to have left the school by now.

She personally wanted to see the cyborg cut into pieces. Having to deal with by him always laughing and praising her work, as if she were some kind of sled dog, didn't make her fond. He was only functioning because the opportunity had not presented itself.

Maybe after this, I will just take a small vacation and he will vanish. I might need a break after the way this fight started.

Her lips curled at the memories, but she quickly brought the thoughts back to finding Nite. She lost her advantage over the Gauss Rifle and would have to keep the fight closer for her own purpose now. Nite was smart to take her left arm first as he did.

He had wanted her to think he was out of missiles, which meant he could still fire them from a great distance. He probably hadn't honestly counted on them because of the way she had taken out the others that she thought were coming for her.

It was a good move at the time. Good wasn't Elite. It gave the other tactician too much information about her too early. She should have waited. Her APLs could have handled it.

At least Ultimate Munitions felt the guess was accurate about his plan. She had been lighting up in the same area and he could have gone for her right where there was more armor.

He wouldn't have seen that in the design, yet he realized her left arm was the first target for equalization. That was all of his plan she knew. He was going to try to reduce her weapons in here. His movements were as silent as standing still, yet she had been over the area where the shots came from, and there was nothing there.

If she went back in that direction, she might have been feeding into a trap. But if she didn't, then she would have no hope of finding him again until he fired on her. Patience was one of his virtues, and he seemed to have it in spades.

******

Nite felt the sudden weight pushing down on his head. It was only mental effect of hearing something pressing down on his Abas. His teeth gritted at the pain from hearing the metal on metal clashing together. As soon as it had started, it had ended, but Nite could still feel the pressure in his head as if it really had been stepped on by an Abas and survived.

******

Ultimate Munitions could feel the unsteady step

of the terrain she had stepped on and quickly shifted forward before her foot could be caught in the sludge. She looked back, but the area had returned to a steady flat sheet.

He must have hoped the weight of my Abas and the short legs would have gotten sucked in there, and then he could attack me while I was trapped. A smart move, but now I know he is close to here. I will play the patience game with him and wait now.

Come out! Come Out! Wherever you are, I am ready to play! She flashed her lights a few times to make sure he saw it before she settled down to wait.

******

Nite saw the several flashes of light just in front of him. She was not moving but signaling where she would stand to meet him. He had no choice but to come out of the water. His cockpit was already flooded to his knees, and his feet were almost ice now. He brought his systems back online and stood quickly from the pond.

Nite had come up at her rear in the dark. He fired off his right arm into the connecting joint of hers. The lasers severed it as if in a surgical procedure, coming up at the exposed joint from point blank. His left made a cut across the top with the DWBL to damage the gravity cannons. Again, Nite didn't wait to find out what kind of damage he was able to inflict. He dashed at full speed back into the darkness.

The Dire Wolf turned quicker than he had seen any Abas move, even faster than him or his brother, and fired all the gravity cannons for his front armor.

Nite already put several trees between him. If he hadn't been running the moment he came up while firing, he would have been severely damaged if not destroyed. The darkness hid the charging.

The balls were absorbed into tree bark. They still split the bark bad enough one of the trees started to tremble, and finally fell, leaving a beam of radiance coming through the roof of the canopy. The brilliant light was at his back, but still blinded him for a few moments. The Dire Wolf could be seen smoking, but it was moving steadily after him.

He was sure he had reduced her weapons a great deal with the two attacks. She still had plenty left to destroy him. Nite felt it was best if he didn't wait to find out exactly what else she could do with that beast.

******

Ultimate Munitions knew it was a risk to wait for him in one spot. To realize it was a puddle he was hiding in. And she stepped on him. It made her furious. No pilot should have been able to better her in such a way. No pilot should have gotten that close to her.

It was time to stop the playing and kill this warrior hidden in a child's body. Whatever his record held his rank at, he was not a student. He was a full-fledged warrior and deserved to be treated as such.

How many times have I scolded people for looking down on lesser ranked warriors or armors? How many times I have said the day you underestimate your enemy is the day you give them the win. It seems I have not learned the lesson in all my long years, no matter how much I have preached it.

******

General Brazen stood this time with a fury that made even Falstar lean his head back but kept the hand on his operator's shoulder relaxed for comfort.

"How could you have not known he was in that water hole?"

"I didn't know that water whole existed, and I have been all through that terrain. Until the tree went down, we would not have had the proper lighting and situation to find it," Falstar started with a strong voice, now taking the question of truth on his plate instead of hers.

He might have been talking to a senior officer as far as the Pack Military ranks went, but this was his school, and his command. General Brazen had nothing more on Falstar than Falstar had on him.

"This boy found it," the general snarled this time with the accusation and display of his anger at having his command questioned.

"Those boys find a lot of things, including

weaknesses in your Dire Wolf piloting. That is why they have gone so long without being named," Falstar fired back, calmly this time.

"They train harder than any other student I have ever had. They have met every challenge with explicit regard. To lose to them is no loss of renown. I believe with this fight, I will be able to reinstate an old rule of No Loss in facing them. Your pilot will, of course, fall under this as well. This entire battle will be considered the Trial of Proof."

General Brazen settled back down. There was nothing he could say.

"I will also have the spot marked and the tree repaired so it provides its normal cover as soon as the battle is over, as always. We do not let our preserved life suffer." Falstar finished with this.

It was a command for the operators' staff to pass on to the simulator's technicians. It was not something he had to command, normally. Yet this battle was taking a toll on a lot of people, and he wanted the tree preserved.

Falstar knew as soon as the battle was over, he would be required to leave with General Brazen. Not that he would ever let this cyborg wander his halls alone. In fact, if he had anything to say, this cyborg would never be in his halls again. He would just have to say it nicely.

Or discretely . . . and deadly!

CHAPTER 37
FINELY DEFEATED

The students cried out with the second set of red flashes, never seeing where they came from. It was as if a monster from their younger years came to life, attacking their greatest defender, the Elite. One that hid under the bed or attacked from the darkness of the lockers and closets. Before their hearts could settle all, the cameras were blinded by the sudden light and switched into color view.

A few caught the glimpse of Nite's Abas as he ducked behind another tree and vanished from that camera's sight. But the armless Dire Wolf was following as quickly as it could. The students waited with bated breath, hoping that their brother was going to win, no matter the odds.

"He has disarmed a Dire Wolf," Subterfuge spoke in awe as the rest realized what had happened.

It was as if everyone realized it with her words.

Nite had taken both the arms of the Dire Wolf and had so far suffered no damage from her.

"Where had he been?" Subterfuge wondered out loud as she made mental notes of all that had been raging during the battle.

She would have to file a new report on the abilities of the twins. She had seen more from this one battle than she ever thought she could record for her reports on them. It was these reports that she had been studying to create her own battle style in private. One she was sure would one day be able to match the twins with the right set of pilots.

******

Ultimate Munitions lost track of Nite as the darkness settled back in. The trees were lowing and the light started to penetrate a little more. She left what remained of her lights on, not caring if Nite tried to attack her full out. It was better than playing hide-and-seek with an Abas warrior beyond her skill within the present terrain.

Admitting as much in her own head raked her across the coals. Yet, she felt no dishonor in the thought. She may have helped to design this terrain, but like any great pilot, he took what she built and made it his own.

She circled a little wider to her right side since it was the most injured with the internal shoulder damage going into the torso. Whether he meant to or not, he turned perfectly while fleeing to unleash damage into her weakened area. The strafe across the back was also an excellent move. Ones she would not have expected from a student.

But he is not just a student. M. was right. He is much more than just a student. He is much more than just . . . that isn't going to help me defeat him. I need to stay focused.

If Nite was going to attack a side against the Dire Wolf, it would be logical for him to go for the right this time. She needed to get to the open spaces, where terrain advantage would be equal among them. Even in the light trees, Nite had the faster Abas, and could use them as cover from her only remaining effective weapons.

And without arms, I am limited on a firing arch. Okay. How would I beat me?

Ultimate Munitions could see the plains about to open in front of her, but she had not seen hide or hair of the student or his Abas since the last of the close-quarter attacks. This was an equal battle, and he had been fighting much longer than she. He might have slipped somewhere to get some rest, but she doubted it. This was a war, and he was waiting for her somewhere.

Pride kept her from asking if the ranges were cleared from satellite view. It was one thing to do it when you were in a real fight, which this test had quickly become. She also knew he would not get the same support if he asked for it.

General Brazen took command of the support center. This might have been a battle, but it was a battle against someone that had never seen real war. He earned every right to know what was outside these walls, including the parts that had nothing to do with battle. She would not dishonor that by letting General Brazen have any part of her victory.

Besides, she was a Dire Wolf Pilot. What Dire Wolf Pilot needed to request help against a student that was not getting any assistance?

One that didn't deserve to be in this Abas. Well, I haven't shown what got me in this Abas, but if I had to go that far to win this, then it isn't worth it. Fifty percent should have been enough to take any nineteen-year-old. And I want to have something to push him with when no one is watching.

She would never be able to show her face, much less feel the prestige needed to enter her Abas if she called for help. This was a battle of honor, not one won by who had the best backing. If she was to beat the student, she was going to beat him on her own, even if she had to hold back on some of her most important of talents. If she died, she would die with her morals in tack.

And risking death is more important than others learning the truth too early on what we can really do. Oh, but if I could truly test you . . . you would not be so . . . well, that wouldn't be honorable either. And we set the Packs based on an honor we all follow, even if it means our death. Which one day, for some, it will.

******

Nite was stalking the injured elite. He gained only a slight advantage over her, but she still had the ability to fire faster and a lot more than he did at a great range. Closing on her before she got into the plains would only have him jumping between trees and hoping to hassle her into submission before she brought the forest down on him.

Besides, she could possibly calculate where he would go next. It was only a matter of time before she got the shot she needed to end everything. Time was not on his side.

He waited silently where the trees would reveal him to her just as she reached the plains. Then it would be down to his one shot to end the battle. If it didn't work, he had little hope of winning. Even with speed on his side, she would sooner or later hunt him into exhaustion. He waited patiently for Dire Wolf.

Soon, so soon, it would finally be over.

******

Ultimate Munitions saw Nite just as she was stepping out onto the plains. He had been waiting for her where she had the greatest advantage. And she played right into him. The picture of him running was to set her up to move out here.

Before she could react, her Abas went to the ground. Her head bounced around off the back wall from the impact of the cockpit. The warm liquid streaked down the left side of her face.

She could feel the swelling coming around her eye. Her belts were holding tightly to her chest, but her body was lying limp otherwise. Her face shield was cracked in several places from the impact with the protective bars.

Where do you attack an enemy? The place they feel the strongest, because you can break them easier. Am I broken? Or am I just getting started?

******

The students watched as Nite fired off his lasers and the Gauss Rifle at the footing of the Abas just as it came into the clearing. He squatted his Abas down to almost prone, but every weapon was pointed at one spot. He had not moved in minutes. From what they could see, he may have finally given into exhaustion. Weariness finally overtook him.

Some were crying as they saw the Dire Wolf approaching out of the woods. They didn't understand how it could not detect or see him. They couldn't figure out how he had hidden so well. He ghillie suit was caked in mud and limbs and dead trees. He looked like a pile of leaves next to the tree. If only he was awake to take the shot or run.

Then, the weapons buckled the leg. It split from the body as the weight of the Abas came down on it. Nite moved with such quickness, shoving his weapons directly into the workings of the hip of the downed Abas. He unleashed everything he had left other than his missiles. The massive Abas rolled across the ground as if running from the flash of light.

It was so quick. The students didn't even see the Dire Wolf really move. It was in one location, then it was tumbling meters away before settling on the ground. One leg still stood next to the Timber Wolf.

That Abas kneeled on the ground as if it had expended everything it had in that one last move. It either ended the battle or bowed to death. It wasn't moving.

Subterfuge was scribbling away while never taking her eyes from the screen. Nite never got so close to an opponent that was fully capable of fighting before. Even with the instructor scorpions he and his brother tore apart. Nite stayed high, guarding, and covering. Mike went in close to them to cut off most of their weapons. Then they gathered and tore them apart like chickens fighting over the most scrumptious pieces.

It was not that he was scared of close combat in or out of the Abas. Nite just liked his space when fighting. Hitting someone from a distance with a perfect shot was his style. The target would think they were safe. They would think they couldn't be touched. Then they were dead.

The students could see the pilot laying limp in the cockpit, part of her helmet's protective visor shattered from the impact of the weapons explosion and the banging around in the combat harness. With a slight shake of her head, life from the pilot had been detected.

The students held their breath as the screens finally went blank. The last of the battle was complete. No one moved from where they were this time. It was one thing to see the great Abas fall, but it was another to watch the death of the second-best pilot they had ever seen by a mere student. Second best only to the student that had just beaten them, like he beat everyone else in this school.

Was there anyone in the Pack that could defeat this one? The one Subterfuge knew was Nite, although no one in the school would have been able to guess until he had come back into the Abas bays. The other had just been dug out of the mountain and was in fairly good condition by the view screen.

******

General Brazen stormed out of the control room. Falstar grabbed the door before it could slam shut. He gave a quick nod to a dark corner before he slammed the door on his way out. All the operators turned to look at each other, wondering whether they should be celebrating.

Dracon appeared out of nowhere behind the injured operator. He turned her chair around slowly, but she shielded her now-tear-stained face from him. He gently pulled her hands back and cooed to her as he lifted her up and put her in his lap in the main council chair.

She tried to bury her face in his shoulder. He pulled her where he could look at the cuts and bruises she sustained. She must have known about him. She must have read the signs his body language said as well as Dracon. And she faced the danger with more honor and dignity than he could have.

Dracon pulled out a cloth and bottle from his breast pocket. She had flinched at his quick movement. He let out a small smile.

"I will not hurt you. This is going to help with the cuts. I have some pills you can take for the swelling as well. But don't tell anyone I gave it to you. This is all part of a quick med kit a couple of friends helped design for Androids.

"It works on Humans as well, so I find it is useful in my area of education. But it is not approved yet, so issuing it to someone out of . . .," he paused. "Approved conditions are not typically allowed. And you know how much the school nurse loves those two. I don't want to cross her any more than necessary. She's got a mean streak."

The operator laughed. They all knew about the school nurse. Mean streak was putting it nicely if you crossed her. It was a wrath even the brothers didn't chance.

He talked while he gently patted the cloth across her face. The wounds numbed slowly, but she didn't dare reach for them.

Dracon softly washed all the android's blood from her face after he finished with the first run, then put on a second solution for the cuts themselves.

"What is your name?" he asked as he put the second bottle away and pulled out a squeeze tube of some smelly ointment.

"Venzela, Honorable One," she barely whispered while choking back the tears as best she could.

Being an android, she could have turned off the pain receptors, but the pain was human, and she wanted to honor the reason she was feeling it. It seemed to make the connection to the ones she had watched since them coming to the school greater.

She looked instead, for just a flash, at her friend Sophie. Sophie almost killed the General when he reacted. Falstar stopped her. They could not kill him without reason, and his abuse of her was not reason enough. It wasn't even enough for her to turn off her human side.

Falstar made sure all the androids either had or were skin jobs. He wanted the students to see them as human as possible. He wanted them to connect to the part human circuits. For the most part, most androids were treated very well in the schools. Even those that were used for the rougher side of training.

Dracon put the cream into the deepest of the cuts, pinched Venzela's skin together and counted to ten. Then let go. The skin remained closed and smooth. The irritation around the outside of the slice was still red, but there was no longer a visible break. The pain had completely disappeared, and some of the tender swelling was reduced.

"This is going to hold your skin closed and help it heal at the same time. You might have a light scar, but this is the best I can do. The rest of them don't look like they will do too much to your exceptional beauty."

Dracon liked to add compliments to his patients to help them smile. Smiling and laughter always helped a patient heal better. He moved down to the strap injuries on her legs next. They would require her to pull her pants off, but most of the damage was superficial. She would be able to heal it herself without having a complete skin graft redone.

"Thank you. I have a wedding in a few days."

Her voice caught short when she realized she had spoken to an Abas warrior on personal matter without being spoken to first.

"I'm sorry for addressing you, Sire. Please forgive me. No disrespect was intended. I am not sure if it is the medicine that is affecting me so or if my circuits aren't working properly."

"Not all Abas pilots believe they are over the kind words of a beautiful woman," Dracon reminded her that she was more than a pile of circuits. "Please enjoy your wedding. If you would allow me to send a Gift of Honor, I would be very appreciative."

Dracon smoothed back her hair from her young face. He was inspecting for more cuts and damage that would need further treatment. He also wanted to check her head for damage or signs of distress. The only thing he could do was give her another set of pills for the swelling and an assignment for rest.

"Sir, we are not of high-enough rank for an honorable warrior such as you to send us a gift. Please, allow me to get back to my watch," she said as she peeled herself out of Dracon's lap.

She staggered a little, putting her hand to her head. Dracon had caught her up in his arms before she hit the ground. Heavier than the average human, she was still light enough for him to handle holding her.

"It is I who owe you. You saved my boys out there," Dracon laughed as he held her, and she began to ball into his chest again. She weighed less than a hundred kilograms (220 lbs) at best. Dracon could carry her as easily as empty air. The weight to size always gave away an Android to a real Human. Other than that, there was very little difference in physical appearance and even some abilities depending on the upgrades. A few had been upgraded with an actual digestive system, although cleaner than a human's.

"The pills are going to be in your pocket. Take them when you wake up the first time, and then lie back down. The medicine is going to put you to sleep. Do not worry. Your friends here will make sure you are safe to your bed.

"But sir . . ." Venzela had tried to cover her lies, but her mind couldn't form the words.

She felt warmth cover her body when she realized she had been laid down on one of the folding stretchers that would carry her to medical. She could still hear Dracon's voice close to her ear, but she could not get her body to respond.

"I know how they work. I know you could have secured one by transferring the other to a different council. It would be as if they were in different battles on the same field.

"You don't have to worry. Your secret is safe with me. Now you must sleep and remember to take the pills the first time you wake, and then go back to sleep. And don't tell the nurse. I can't get graphed as easily as you."

Dracon looked to one of the control supervisors, who nodded silently to him. She knew the works of those magical little pills as well as any. It was due to her that they had been developed in the first place.

"Yes, sire," Venzela thought she might have said, but it seemed only to echo in her mind.

She remembered trying to change it back to sir. After he had offered a gift of honor status, he might find it offensive if she continued with such a formal title for the extremely higher ranking official.

Most expected to be addressed with either the title or the higher commanding general form if you did not know what they were beyond Abas Pilot. Them being Abas Pilot was enough. Especially to an operator when they were no longer behind their council, ensuring their safety and life while in the simulations and live battlefields. Even in the fleet, simulations were used to protect assets when the Packs were fighting in areas that may require them to be ready to respond.

The rambling thoughts were the last of her memories until the morning the day before her wedding. She could not have put a face to Dracon's memory, but her wedding day gave her more surprises than she could have ever hoped for. More than she even knew was possible.

Not only did she have the honor of gifts from five different Abas Warriors, but three were there dressed in full formals at the closest row after her family. The Honor gained from the relation of the guest list alone would be so high she would never have to return to the schools.

It was something she might consider once her Abas heroes left. She might even request to be allowed on their operating team. But she knew that was a different story. For now, she would continue to watch over them.

CHAPTER 38

AFTERMATH

Falstar grabbed the older gentleman as they walked into his private office. "Don't you ever," his hands shifted to both sides of the general's collar once he was facing him, "Abuse one of my," he lifted a little higher, with little effect with the man's height advantage over him, "staff members again. I know they are lower ranks, but—"

The man smacked Falstar to the ground in one clean short motion. He then straightened out his outer attire and looked over himself in Falstar's half mirror.

While looking at Falstar on the ground through the mirror, he spoke.

"The next time you are addressing a superior officer, use a little more respect. And don't ever question my motives again, or I will have you killed."

"I am not sure you could get an assassin into the school that could kill me." Falstar spat a line of blood onto his polished floor. "You have yet to get one past their objective now."

"I will not bother to ask how you figured it out. You know to keep your kuso mouth shut, or I will open mine."

"You would be signing your own death warrant from the Cyborg Council if you did that."

"I have little time left anyway. Death being close does not bother me."

"Those twins should have stayed out of it the first night. It is harder to kill with assassins when the target knows they are coming, or at least the ones defending them do. There are other plans in motion now. But I can't risk a higher-ranking assassin for such a little job. Numbers don't seem to matter either. No, they will stop for now, and I will be patient.

"My question for you is what you are going to do about the unnamed one?" General Brazen asked, finally finishing fixing himself and turning from the mirror.

"I've had a plan in motion for a couple of years now. It still needs time to finish working itself out. It will be effective, nonetheless. That is, if you will sign these." Falstar passed him a disk as he lifted himself off the floor.

"Are you sure?" General Brazen asked as he raised his eyebrows. "This is an unanswerable advantage to your rival."

"If my theory is wrong, then I will resign from the school, and you can put someone else here. I believe it will be in line with my present mission." Falstar smiled faintly.

Both of them.

"You will not resign. I like you where you are. No, if that one fails, then we will send him to your father's school and separate the twins. That might weaken them enough to name him. Let the Abas pilots work against each other.

"Besides, you do not need all three of them here, even if the prestige stays with her. No, there is no Honor Loss with them, remember.

"Once instated, I am sure you will have your hands full with fights for him inside and outside the schools. There is no loss and so much to gain in defeating him. What more could you have asked for? This will keep him busy while you are preparing your weapons. I hope they are better than this one," he signaled toward nothing.

Outside that area was solid planet crust.

"Aye, sir." Falstar answered.

He was thinking his student just destroyed General Brazen's best weapon.

And I hope to ensure you find a much messier end.

******

Ultimate Munitions limped off the transport to a barrage of cheering and clapping. Her uniform and helmet were in disarray at best. The students were cheering her as if she was a heroic war hero just coming back from the victory of the last century. Most of that was right, but they had to be confused on the manner of her return.

She held up a hand to silence them. "Why are you all so happy to see me?"

"You are still alive!" a girl in the front row blurted as if it was the most obvious thing in the world.

She had blond hair just beyond her shoulders and shiny light pink lips as if she was moistening them all the time with her makeup. Her nose was narrow and awkward between her jade green eyes. Even from the stage Ultimate Munitions could see she made up for it with her posterior.

"I see. Do you know . . .," she stopped as the crowd parted for someone in a full school uniform.

The male android with short-cropped hair looked highly agitated approached her. He held his voice to a tight, controlled level while he handed her the letter. As soon as she accepted it, he started back through the crowd, but stopped with the approach of another member splitting the crowd. There was no doubt of who this was.

The one in the operator uniform came to a halt in front of Nite without the respects of an operator to an Abas warrior.

He finally forced his hand up in salute, but as soon as it dropped, he said, "How many people will be hurt to protect you? How long will you allow those under you to sacrifice their selves without your notice? Will you ever answer for your own actions?"

The man couldn't hold back the tears, but Nite had no idea what the operator could be talking about. He barely caught the man's last words under his breath.

"Sent to the hospital trying to keep him safe during this battle. He has nothing to say. He is probably too high to notice the help someone of our stature would give."

His mumbles grew to beyond even that of Nite's suit's enhancements to hear. He would have to find out the rest of the story to ensure that was not the case. He had never shorted the Operators their due respect.

He even sent them things in the control center after a battle to show his thanks for them being there. Of course, it was sent anonymous. That was only to prevent them from giving him an edge he didn't deserve.

Asyl will talk to me about it. She can explain what happened to them in there. And the rest of his story as well.

Nite turned back to why he had come here. There were fewer students here than had greeted him. He was happy for that. It made this easier to get to her. They did not try to slow him down as he approached the platform. Something else he was happy for.

I thought we were over this idiocy. We don't need people greeting us back like we came from some epic battle. It was just the next step in training. Not like we haven't all been through something like this.

The pilot of the Dire Wolf was still in her battle uniform without a cover. It fit to her much older body. Even in her advanced years, she kept her body trim and fit. Nite found another reason to be impressed. Her grey-silver hair had been braided in several strands and hung just below her shoulders.

The helmet was being held to the side, which was unusual. It's glass was missing a large piece. It helped to explain the dried blood staining her collar. A few wrinkles on some smooth skin showed the rest of her age. Even with all this, she was still the greatest warrior Nite had ever faced outside his brother.

When he stepped on the stage, she flung her hair back over her shoulder and pulled it back into an awkward-looking ponytail. Nite could see small white lines of old scars, but they had long healed before the battle and only appeared now because of her aged skin.

"I wanted to apologize for the damage I caused to your Dire Wolf. I did not mean to hurt you so badly," Nite spoke as he saluted her.

She reached out and pulled him into a tight embrace that surprised him. Her strength was great. He was not sure if he could pull out if he wanted. He wasn't sure he wanted to. He had never felt something like this before.

Screams erupted from the surrounding crowd. It got louder as Nite reached around her, and for the first time, gave someone he faced in battle a loving embrace. It was strange.

They finally let each other go as the screams died down. She investigated his face with tears going down hers. Nite had not realized that he was slightly taller than her.

"I had come to this school to help you become the best you could be. I have been given other orders now that I am here. The Council has other plans for me since you won. I guess they believe I have taught you all I can, but maybe we can find a way to still work out," she added with a ruffling of his hair and holding him close again.

Nite didn't know what to say. There was nothing he could say. He only had two options on the table for winning, and he couldn't change either of them to get her to stay at the school.

"What school will you be going to?" Nite asked in hopes of her going to Canine Prime with Selina. It was his best chance.

"Canis Lupus Training Facility under an old friend of mine, Headmaster Nox. Don't worry, I'll keep in touch. You have not lost me, even if I am not here physically. Let me ask you one thing," she started as she leaned in close to his ear.

She cupped it so that no listening devices would hear what she had to say.

"Do you know who your parents are?"

Nite shook his head no. Holding back the tears became even harder. She stood up away from him and looked deep into his eyes.

"Well, you now have a sergeant grandmother if you will have me."

Nite couldn't answer with anything more than a nod.

"Remember, I am always with you," she added to comfort him. "You boys are not alone."

What Nite hadn't known, was that he had just been accepted into a Wolf Pack family. Once Ultimate Munitions put down his name into the books, the unnamed student would be known as Student 1321456 Fenrir.

"I don't like calling you by student. I will just refer to you by Fenrir until you are otherwise named, if that is okay with you," she told him into his ear as she led him away. "Do you think Student 6541231 would be interested in joining our family as well?"

"I am sure he will once he gets out of the cave he blew himself into," Nite laughed.

******

The move from the school was not immediate, even though Ultimate Munitions hadn't unpacked her bags. She didn't want to travel with General Brazel, who waited a few hours before going on a transport. She decided to book her own travel a few weeks later.

Mike and Nite didn't leave her side until she had stepped onto the platform for the trip away. Mike had no problem with accepting her in the family. She referred to them both as Fenrir, but the way she said it made them understand which one she was addressing or calling forward.

Their instructors didn't bother to send any students in search of them, as they would have with any other student that had missed classes. They didn't like the twins being in their classes, often showing them up and they knew they were with the Dire Wolf Pilot. If that level pilot wanted something, you didn't ask why, you just rodgerred up and moved on smartly.

Ultimate Munitions gave them more than anyone ever could have in her personal Abas training data. Most of the information was taken from her battles, but there were a handful with some of the greatest warriors she served with while deployed. The actions within them were amazing and didn't match up with anything shown over Wolf Net.

She explained how trading battle information was just above sharing your true names with another warrior. It was a sign of great honor and respect. She must have been respected across the Packs because she had different recordings with several other Packs. Some were almost two-hundred years old.

She also spent several hours reliving the great battle and told about the two that had won it in the end. The twins took a special interest in them and continued to ask her about the two until their short time came to an end. They found it especially exciting to have a large quantity of their battles.

In return for the gift, they gave her all the information they collected. It was a dangerous move, but since she had shared her real name with them, and they with her, there was little more they could do to prove each other's loyalties. The hidden videos she had taken the most interest in, but it was the under-breath comment that had gotten both twins wondering after she had left.

"I didn't know you had progressed so far already. I should have come earlier," she said, almost to herself, but she didn't seem to hide the thought from them either.

An Agreement of Tribute was the only step left between them, but they agreed that it would be best to not enter into such an agreement before the twins left school. It would not be fulfilled while they were in school. They would have to reenter it once they had left the school, anyway, just to ensure they were of the right mind. No one was considered an adult until the age of twenty-five standard years in the Pack, unless special permissions were granted by the planetary council.

Ultimate Munitions was enormously proud of the two who won the great battle since she was their original Headmaster. Nox served under Ultimate Munitions while Nox was stationed in the schools. Ultimate Munitions returned to battle to later be selected as their platoon leader when they were selected for the special teams. She was the one who taught the female to pilot her Dire Wolf.

Ultimate Munitions collected a great deal of students from those years, and they all served under her during the Crusader Olympia. If it hadn't been for Her platoon, they would have lost it all. The two she told them the most of were the ones who secured the win.

It was their old school battle disk the twins secretly treasured the most. With these, she empowered them to reach beyond anything they would ever receive in the schools even with her leaving. Many of their post battles were on the disk as well.

The chapter with Ultimate Munitions was the shortest of their lives, lasting only three weeks. On 685.11.25, she departed to join back with Nox on a special project in the schools. It was likely Nox's daughter. She was special enough to have a Dire Wolf Pilot called in to train her and she had the genetic history for it as well.

For the twins, those three weeks turned out to be one of the most important and the most treasured. For the first time in their lives, they had battle footage of people fully capable of beating them. They knew the use of these in their secret training would push them beyond what they had accomplished so far. Beyond what they ever thought possible.

After fighting each other and reviewing the data on the fights, they felt they were just getting ready for Echelon Two to begin again. It wasn't just a handful of excellent fighters on there. Hundreds of them, if they fought at full potential, would be able to annihilate the two of them. Ultimate Munitions, alone, took a pretty good chunk out of the two of them on a secret mission with a two on one battle scenario, although the twins did defeat her in the end.

If she had fought like that against Nite, he would be named right now. Instead she took a more bull approach to the battle, hassling him, not playing strategy. But she said that was not a proper naming battle and she had to give him a good chance to show what he was made of.

She figured at best he was at twenty-five-percent capacity when she entered. She claimed she kept her efforts less than fifty-percent weapons and twenty-percent piloting. After the two on one battle, they believed she used way less than that of her fully capable actions.

Fighting her now was like working with Master Raven. It was truly teaching, not fighting. She would stop them as they were overcoming an engagement and show them mistakes that started twenty moves before it accumulated into disaster. Or what they could have done differently to avoid the dog-mess-dinner they allowed themselves to get in.

It was amazing, picking up different perspectives. Breaking outside their own boxes, like they broke outside the box of the Pack. She gave them a new way to train. She gave them the tools that would make them more.

Then she left.

******

Falstar called Nox just before Ultimate Munitions

left on the transport. He simply asked her, "Will he be ready in two years? We're running out of time."

She gave a cold glare into the monitor.

"There is over six and a half years left in their training. Why do you ask?"

"I just want to ensure he will be ready in one and a half. The last five years will be especially important for my student."

"Only if he wins. I do not believe it will happen if the rumor is true. Are you really sending me Ultimate Munitions to train my . . . student? I just got the orders of her acceptance today."

"She is getting on the transport as we speak."

"Then he will be ready. *She* would have been better for the job. He has never been able to beat her. Her receiving training from Ultimate Munitions would be icing to the cake to prepare her.

"They will stop fighting when Ultimate Munitions comes. She will not be happy about this, but I think it will be for the best. Besides, she still has the younger one to fight with. He'll provide a better sparring partner. And she needs to break away from her obsession with *them*."

"No. I agree with the Wolf Council. We cannot have them face each other, especially now that you will have Ultimate Munitions. The battle would become public record when they graduate. It would give too much away.

"Besides, I do not want another one of those battles. Just make sure he is ready."

Falstar killed the coms and looked deep into his small mirror at the end of his bedroom desk.

"I hope it is worth all the trouble," he added as the cone of silence fell.

"It is necessary," a woman's voice answered from behind Falstar. "Have I ever steered you wrong?"

He always enjoyed his mother's voice. She was helping to hold a one-sided conversation that the security program would continue while he was within the cone. She was to pick up on his signal of it dropping. The simple phrase.

Falstar turned his eyes to the floor, noticing a small spider-like creature carrying something on its back. At first, he thought it was a bug, which only bothered him because it meant the protections against these things weren't working properly.

It happened. Some arthropods didn't respond to the signals that kept them away or ignored the pheromones. But his eye focused on it just as it seemed to notice him noticing it. It scurried into a fitting and vanished.

It wasn't carrying a bug. It was carrying a bug*! Why would it carry someone's spy equipment off? That was built by Intruz. Did Intruz create a retrieval device? Was that what those bugs were all those years ago? Amazing.*

The hidden Master name was well earned. I'll ensure the promotion to Medium Zhayedan is awarded through the hidden work Intruz was doing. Simply amazing! Better than the graded work of TTG. Still, I think she'll be a Heavy.

Too bad Quick Hit can't know the truth. Might make her life easier. Too many cooks in the kitchen as they say. And who wants an easy life as an Abas Pilot.

Well, me.

THE END OF
PART 1 SECTION 1:
FOR LIEF OR LOVE

www.ingramcontent.com/pod-product-compliance
Lightning Source LLC
Chambersburg PA
CBHW030905300726
48970CB00001B/17